Did she have everything figured out?

No. But it didn't matter. She wasn't alone anymore.

"I know you didn't come here for a sermon," she said. "We need to get back anyway. I'm a little hungry and I could use a slice of Mom's pumpkin pie."

William grinned. "I'm so glad it agreed with the baby. I could barely gag down a couple bites of mine, let alone eat both pieces."

"I just have to figure out how to convince Mom to make more without telling her my reason why."

William touched her arm gently. "I know your mom is a bit much with the way she hovers. But maybe she would surprise you with her reaction about the baby. One more person for her to love and care for."

She liked the warmth radiating from him. In truth, some of her restored faith came from the love and support William had given her. But she also knew that it wasn't so simple. Yes, she could count on William now, before he knew the truth about her baby's parentage.

Danica Favorite loves the adventure of living a creative life. She loves to explore the depths of human nature and follow people on the journey to happily-ever-after. Though the road is often bumpy, those bumps refine imperfect characters as they live the life God created them for. Oops, that just spoiled the ending of Danica's stories. Then again, getting there is all the fun. Find her at danicafavorite.com.

Books by Danica Favorite

Love Inspired

Double R Legacy

The Cowboy's Sacrifice
His True Purpose
A True Cowboy

Three Sisters Ranch

Her Cowboy Inheritance
The Cowboy's Faith
His Christmas Redemption

Love Inspired Historical

For the Sake of the Children
An Unlikely Mother
Mistletoe Mommy
Honor-Bound Lawman

Visit the Author Profile page at Harlequin.com for more titles.

A True Cowboy

Danica Favorite

LOVE INSPIRED
INSPIRATIONAL ROMANCE

LOVE INSPIRED®

INSPIRATIONAL ROMANCE

Recycling programs
for this product may
not exist in your area.

ISBN-13: 978-1-335-48880-0

A True Cowboy

Copyright © 2021 by Danica Favorite

This edition published by arrangement with Harlequin Books S.A.

For questions and comments about the quality of this book,
please contact us at CustomerService@Harlequin.com.

Love Inspired
22 Adelaide St. West, 40th Floor
Toronto, Ontario M5H 4E3, Canada
www.Harlequin.com

Printed in U.S.A.

And now abideth faith, hope, charity, these three;
but the greatest of these is charity.
—*1 Corinthians* 13:13

For the Badgers, who put up with my craziness
while writing this book. I'm richly blessed
to have you as friends, and I love that
you accept me for who I am.
Thanks for all you've given me.

Chapter One

William Bennett hadn't had such a bad week in all his life. As he looked around the large dining hall at the Double R Ranch, where everyone else was celebrating all the things they were thankful for this Thanksgiving, he felt out of place.

He and his parents had been invited for the holiday, but William wondered if coming to Columbine Springs, and the Double R Ranch, had been the right decision. People were lined up at the buffet, filling their plates, and even though everything looked delicious, William hadn't been able to bring himself to eat.

His twin brother, Alexander, was on the other side of the room celebrating his engagement. Everyone else seemed happy about that fact, and William guessed that he was happy for his brother, too. No, he was happy. After spending a few months in Columbine Springs, Alexander had recently returned to Denver only briefly to get his things to move back here permanently, having been offered a cabin on the ranch. Alexander had been completely twitterpated over this woman, Janie, and her son, Sam. William just hadn't expected an engagement to come so soon, considering Alexander wasn't one for long-term relationships. He'd been too focused on his career to date.

Not William.

He'd always planned his life around having a family, and look where it had gotten him. Alone on Thanksgiving.

As if he knew exactly what William was thinking about, his dad came over to put his arm around him.

"Great celebration, isn't it, son? I'm glad we managed to convince you to come. Pity Hailey couldn't make it."

Right. Because he still hadn't told anyone that Hailey had dumped him for some rodeo cowboy because he was so masculine, and William was just a boring guy in a suit. Oh, and Hailey was expecting the guy's baby.

William might be a boring guy in a suit, but at least he didn't spend most of his time living out of the back of his horse trailer, like Hailey's cowboy boyfriend.

Making the situation even worse was that Hailey was William's boss's daughter. And suddenly, William's position was made redundant. Which meant he hadn't just lost his fiancée, but his job, as well. It was a good thing William had plenty of savings.

Talk about awkward conversations that didn't need to overshadow his brother's happiness. William didn't answer his father, and instead drained the remainder of his coffee.

"I need a refill—be back in a second."

He wandered off, not wanting to rain on anyone's parade.

What was it with cowboys anyway? He didn't see the appeal.

But apparently, a lot of women did. The Double R Ranch, a place William had never imagined he'd set foot on, seemed to be swarming with cowboys. Almost every guy here today wore a cowboy hat.

Weren't cowboys supposed to take their hats off when indoors?

Though the criticism made him feel mildly better, it didn't ease the discomfort in his spirit. William had done everything right in his life, but somehow, it hadn't helped him keep the woman he loved, or his job.

William reached for the coffee carafe.

Hadn't his life been in enough turmoil already? He'd recently found out that his father wasn't his biological father; that honor went to some rodeo cowboy his mom had had an affair with. That was the whole point of being here. While the rodeo cowboy was dead, the man's father, Ricardo Ruiz IV—or Ricky, who owned the Double R—was alive, and wanted to get to know William and his brother. Actually, Ricky wanted to get to know all of his son's misbegotten offspring. Why, William didn't know. So far, it seemed to be creating a whole lot of chaos in everyone's lives.

Funny how a few days ago, that had been the biggest of William's problems.

"Hey, watch it!"

He looked over at the woman he'd just bumped into, pouring coffee all over her.

"I'm sorry. I've got a lot on my mind, and I wasn't paying attention," he said. "Again, I'm really sorry."

But instead of looking like she accepted his apology, the woman turned a strange shade of green, and ran for the door.

Wow. It was bad enough that he'd been so cruelly rejected by his fiancée, but now he was scaring women off so bad, they literally ran from him.

But he had just dumped a pot of coffee on her. The least he could do was make sure she was okay and hadn't suffered any serious burns as a result of his carelessness.

The cold drinks were in a trough filled with ice, so he used his empty cup to get some and grabbed a bottle of water.

When he got outside, he didn't see her, or anyone, for that matter. They'd gone out a side door that appeared to be more of a service entrance than anything else. But she couldn't have gone too far.

A gust of wind blew through, and William was glad he'd kept his suit jacket on. Yes, it had meant he was overdressed for the occasion, since everyone else was in Western wear, but he hadn't known the dress code. Not that it would have made a difference. William didn't own any Western wear. A fact that probably added to his boringness.

What was it Hailey had said? He was the safe choice for a woman who needed stability, which was fine until she'd realized she was going to die of boredom. Something like that.

And what was wrong with safety and stability anyway?

A noise by the bushes drew William's attention to a figure, hunched over, mostly hidden by the evergreen foliage.

The woman he'd dumped coffee on.

He walked toward the bushes. "Miss? Are you okay? I'm sorry about the coffee. I brought some ice and water if you think that might help."

The woman crawled out of the bushes and lay on the rocks. "I'm fine. Please, just go. Forget this ever happened."

He took a good look at her. She'd been getting sick behind those bushes. Her now pale skin was evidence of someone who was truly ill. William might be responsible for a lot of things in this world, but even he wasn't capable of causing this level of illness in someone.

"Are you okay? Can I get someone for you?"

She shook her head. "No."

The sound of laughter came through the windows. "Surely someone in there…"

She shook her head. "Please, no. I meant to come as a surprise, and now I don't think I can do it."

He didn't want to be here, either, but he also hadn't known what other option he had. He could hear his dad in his mind, telling him he always had a choice.

But sometimes your choices didn't really feel like choices at all.

"What's your name? Is there anything I can do to help?" he asked. She looked a mess, and talking to her, it was obvious she wasn't well.

"It's Grace. I'll be okay. Just go."

The look on her face told him she wasn't okay.

"I'm William," he said, giving her a smile that would hopefully make her feel more comfortable. "I don't feel right just leaving you here."

A thought occurred to him. "Do you think it's something you ate? Should I warn people?" Suddenly, he was glad he hadn't eaten anything at the Thanksgiving dinner. His stomach had been too tied up in knots, and even now, he wasn't sure he could choke down anything.

"No," she said. "It's not the food, and it's nothing contagious. That's why I don't want you to go in there and tell anyone. I don't want anyone to be worried."

He held out the bottle of water to her. "Will this help? Or make it worse?"

This time, instead of her usual refusals, she burst into tears.

Clearly, William had no idea what he was doing when it came to women. He gingerly reached forward and touched her arm, hoping that it would be somewhat comforting to her. What were you supposed to do when your only obligation to someone was that you just dumped coffee on them, but clearly their problems were way bigger than that?

"I don't know what's wrong, but I'm sure everything will be okay," he said, trying to sound encouraging, knowing he probably didn't.

"I'm pregnant," she said. "Okay? I'm pregnant."

She accepted the water and took a small sip. At least it was progress.

And her pronouncement did explain the vomiting, and probably the tears. The guys he played basketball with all said that when their wives were pregnant, all they did was cry. William didn't know. He'd never been in the situation before, and while he'd hoped that he and Hailey might someday have a child, obviously that wasn't in his future, either.

"So I guess you're not happy about being pregnant?" he asked, not sure if he was helping or hurting the situation, though that seemed to be how his entire encounter with this poor woman had been.

For a moment, she stopped crying. Looked up at him. Her face was such a mix of emotions, that even if he'd known her, he wasn't sure he'd have been able to tell what was going on in her head.

"This was definitely not part of the plan," she said. Then she squared her shoulders. "But I'm keeping my baby."

The words came out with such force that he imagined someone else must have suggested not doing so to her. And probably not in a nice way.

"I'm not here to judge. But I do want to help. Should I call the baby's father?"

Obviously the wrong question, because she burst into tears again. Now that he thought about it, her response to his question about being happy about the baby should have clued him in that maybe this wasn't the ideal situation.

"Okay, I get it. No father. But you've got to let me do something."

She looked up at him, tears streaming down her face. "What? What could you possibly do for me? I'm alone and pregnant, and I can't bear the thought of telling my mother how much I've let her down."

In a way, it made sense. Everything made sense. She'd probably come home for Thanksgiving, hoping to find a way to tell her mother, and everything here was overwhelming. Just like William felt. Thinking he could do this, being a mature adult about meeting a family he hadn't known he had and didn't want. He thought he would find a way to tell his family that his fiancée had broken up with him. But how was he supposed to do that when his brother had just announced his own engagement and was so happy?

William took a deep breath. "I know it's not the same, but I'm afraid to tell my family something, too."

That at least got the tears to stop.

"Oh yeah? What?"

William took a deep breath. Funny thing was, he hadn't ever actually admitted it out loud. But there was safety in this young, vulnerable woman who had just confessed her own secret to him.

"My fiancée dumped me for some cowboy she's been having an affair with."

He sighed, feeling the weight lift from his shoulders at having said the words. "She's pregnant with his baby. She said she needed a real man."

He hadn't thought he was going to share that last piece. Still wasn't sure why it slipped out. But ever since Hailey had said it, those words haunted him.

Grace looked up at him. "Sounds like you're better off. At least you weren't already married."

He'd thought about that one, and yes, he did take some comfort in it. He'd seen enough of his friends go through rough divorces. But it didn't mean his heart wasn't broken.

"I guess that's the silver lining," he said. "What about you? I know you're going to keep the baby, but have you thought about what else you're going to do?"

It would be good to have an answer to the question, not just about long-term plans, but he was kind of hoping she might clue him in to what she might be doing in the next few minutes, so he could get her to a safe place.

She shook her head. "The baby's father was my boss. Getting one of his employees pregnant doesn't exactly look good on the company plan. I know I could technically get him in trouble for firing me, but it wasn't that great of a job to begin with, and I certainly don't want to work for him anymore. Still, my finances are a mess, and I don't know how I'm going to support a baby."

Basically the same situation he was in. "I understand. My ex's father was my boss. I'm also out of a job."

"Funny how easily your life gets ruined by someone you thought you loved," Grace said, looking forlorn. "But you're right. It is comforting to know I'm not the only one."

As she took another sip of water, some of the color returned to her face. "I can't go back in there."

He scooted closer and put his hand on her arm. "Sure you can. I'll go with you. Maybe, since we know we're not alone anymore, it won't be so bad."

The thought strengthened him more than he could have imagined. He wasn't the only person to fall in love with someone who wasn't as committed to the relationship. What kind of guy would leave his pregnant girlfriend alone, anyway?

Probably the same kind who'd get someone else's fiancée pregnant.

However, instead of looking encouraged, Grace shook her head again. "You don't understand. My mom is a strong Christian. She raised me better than this. She's going to be so disappointed in me."

"I'm sure she loves you. She might be shocked initially, but she'll get over it. You should let her help."

As he spoke, he thought of how telling her mom applied to his own situation. His family had always been supportive of him, and he couldn't see that changing now.

"To be honest," he continued, "part of why I don't want to tell my family is that my brother just proposed today at the dinner. I hate overshadowing his happy news with my depressing circumstances."

Grace looked up at him. "You're Ricky's long-lost grandson! Whenever I talk to Mom on the phone, she's always going on about Ricky's search for his family. My mom is Wanda, Ricky's live-in house-keeper. I grew up here on the ranch. We're practically family."

The excitement in her voice brought a sinking feeling to his stomach. "I guess. This didn't come as welcome news to me. It's weird, learning that the man you always thought of as your father isn't, and that your mom cheated on your dad. I know it's not Ricky's fault, but it doesn't feel right, being here."

"I'm sorry," she said. "I understand it came as quite the shock. If it helps, I grew up here on the ranch, and Ricky is one of the best people I know."

Another Ricky fan. Alexander couldn't stop singing his praises, and William supposed it wasn't Ricky's fault that his son fathered a bunch of kids people were just finding out about. But it didn't make things easier.

"I'm sure you're right," he said. "Ricky might be okay, but I'm not sure I want to know anything about his son. I have zero respect for people who cheat, or would be with someone who was with someone else. How could my mom do that to my dad? And Hailey? If I was so boring, why not break up with me, then go chasing after some cowboy? And that cowboy? Why would he even think about going for someone who was engaged? That just tells me what low-class people they are."

Thankfully, the door opened before he could continue spilling his guts to this virtual stranger who thought they were practically family. She'd flinched at his words about cheaters, so he'd probably come on too strong. He needed to tone it down, especially in front of his mom, but he didn't know how to let go of his anger.

An older woman came out, looking around like she was searching for someone. And judging by the expression on the woman's face when she saw them, this was Grace's mom.

"Please," Grace said in a rushed whisper. "Don't tell her anything about what I said."

Grace Duncan had no idea what had possessed her to confess her situation to a complete stranger. Other than telling Jack, and talking to her doctor, she hadn't found it in her to tell anyone she was pregnant. Maybe she could call this a test run. She had to admit that this guy seemed rather sweet.

Awkward, and clearly uncomfortable with the situation, but he hadn't backed down and run away. Though she wasn't sure what he'd do when he realized that in this instance, Grace was the other woman.

Not that Grace had known. Jack had told her that he and his wife were in the process of getting divorced. She was in California with the kids, and he was here in Colorado, starting over. Since he'd just transferred here, and no one knew much about him, she'd had no reason to doubt his story.

Until she'd told him she was pregnant.

Funny how a guy who promises forever can so easily run when things didn't go as he'd planned.

Grace had thrown up a couple of times when she'd been with Jack, before she knew she was pregnant, and it had disgusted him so much that she'd been so careful lately. If she thought she was going to be around people, she'd avoid eating or drinking on purpose, but that tactic hadn't worked today.

And now her mom was here, looking like she'd been searching for Grace for a while. Since Grace had raced straight for the drink table instead of greeting her mom, word must have gotten around that Grace was back.

"Grace!"

Grace moved to stand, but she could feel the nausea building up again. Ugh. She could smell the coffee on her, and the scent did not agree with the baby. Movement made it worse.

William seemed to sense her hesitation.

He stood and held his hand out to her mom. "You must be Wanda. I've heard so much about you. I'm William, Alexander's brother."

Her mom ignored his outstretched hand. "What are you doing out here with Grace?"

She peered past him and over at Grace. "And why didn't you come say hi?"

"That's my fault, I'm afraid," William said. "I was clumsy and dumped coffee all over her. She just came out here to cool down, and I wanted to make sure she didn't suffer any serious burns."

He'd been sweet to bring her some water and ice, and thankfully, the only damage had been to her pride.

"Grace!" Her mom pushed past him. "Are you

okay? Should I get a first-aid kit? Doctor Bob is inside—I can get him."

This was one of the other reasons why she didn't want to tell her mom about the baby. Most people loved how her mom cared for everyone. But with Grace, it ended up being almost smothering.

"I'm fine." Grace took a deep breath and stood. This time, she felt a little less wobbly, and if she could get rid of the coffee smell, she'd be able to handle things. "Which is what I've been explaining to William here, who's been so sweet and helpful."

She shot him another pleading glance.

"I just feel terrible," William said. "I hate that I ruined your reunion with your mom."

He gave her mom the kind of smile that usually would appease her.

"Well get over here and give me a hug. It's been months since my baby came home."

Grace tried not to groan. Always with the guilt trip. So far, she'd only seen a million reasons why she shouldn't tell her mom.

"I'm all wet and smell like coffee," Grace said. "I'm going to go to my car and change. You don't need to get this all over you."

She gestured at her stained blouse. William had done a nice job of covering her with the stuff. And maybe if she didn't smell the coffee on her anymore, she would stop feeling so bad.

"Well, I…"

Grace could see the wheels spinning in her mom's

head. William must have noticed, too, because he gave her mom another smile.

"You know, I haven't eaten yet. I'm told you're the best cook in town. Why don't you take me inside and tell me what you made, Grace can go change, and when she's done, she can join us?"

Grace closed her eyes and said a silent prayer of thanks for William. She'd fallen so far from her faith, and yet, in her time of need, she couldn't help thinking that God had brought him to her for a reason.

"We should have Doctor Bob take a look at those burns," her mom said.

"I'm fine," Grace said. "The only sign I had a cup of coffee dumped on me is my stained clothes. Go make sure William gets a slice of your pumpkin pie. You know how fast it goes, and there's nothing like it in the world."

This time, her mom smiled. "It would be a shame if he accidentally got a piece of that slop Bessie Rogers makes. You hurry up, and I'll be sure to save you a slice, as well."

Food of any kind sounded absolutely disgusting about now.

But Grace smiled. "Sounds like a plan."

Hopefully, William wouldn't spill the beans while she was gone. But he'd been so earnest in his attempts to help her thus far, she couldn't imagine him sharing her news.

The bigger question, and thing she was going to have to figure out in the next ten minutes or so, was how she was going to manage to get through the community Thanksgiving dinner when anything food related made her sick. Her mom would know if she didn't eat, and worse, would keep giving her more food if she didn't think Grace had eaten enough. Wanda Duncan's main mission in life was to fatten Grace up, and given that Grace had already lost five pounds being as sick as she'd been, her mom was sure to comment on it.

So many things she hadn't thought of when she'd agreed to come home for Thanksgiving. And now, jobless and pregnant, she wasn't sure if she had any alternative but to extend her stay.

God, please. I know I don't deserve it with all the mistakes I've made lately, but help me find a way to make all this work.

Chapter Two

When William walked back inside with Wanda, Alexander was waiting for him.

"Where have you been?" he asked.

William shrugged. "I accidentally spilled coffee on Wanda's daughter, and I was trying to make up for my clumsiness."

"Grace is here?" Alexander asked, looking around, then smiled at Wanda. "You've told me so much about her, and I'm eager to meet her."

"Hold your horses," Wanda said. "I haven't even gotten to hug her, thanks to your oaf of a brother."

Alexander took a long look at him. William knew that look. And he knew the next thing out of Alexander's mouth would be a question William wouldn't want to answer.

"That's not like you. You're usually so careful. What's going on with you, anyway? It seems like you're avoiding everyone."

"I have a lot on my mind, and I didn't want to spoil anyone's fun."

It was the truth, and saying it out loud to his brother made him feel a little better. He and Alexander had never had secrets from each other. The fact that Alexander had so willingly welcomed their new family with open arms had created a gulf between them that William hadn't liked.

"I'm going to go fix some plates," Wanda said. "I know who made what, and I'll make sure you get some of the good stuff."

William opened his mouth to tell her that she didn't know what he liked, but Alexander shook his head.

It wouldn't have mattered anyway, since Wanda was already walking off.

"Just let her do her thing," Alexander said. "You'd have a better chance arguing with a rock."

His brother's laugh gave William some comfort. In the past, when William was dumped by some girl who thought he was too nice, he and Alexander would go do something, like hiking or fishing, and even without talking about it, William would come home feeling better.

"It means a lot to me that you're here," Alexander said, then gave him a hug. The family wasn't much into hugging, and it felt strange, yet right, to have his brother's arms around him.

One more thing that had changed about his twin.

He wanted to be here for Alexander. It was the whole reason he'd put aside his feelings of anger at his mother to come. The whole reason he'd been stuffing down his heartbreak. But when Alexander stepped away, the happiness in his eyes made William realize that he couldn't be what Alexander needed him to be.

Yes, he was happy for his brother, but the man in front of him didn't seem like his sibling anymore. Was it possible for twins to grow apart?

"You want to go fishing tomorrow?" Alexander asked. "There's a great lake on the property that's pretty well stocked. We could go just the two of us, or we could invite Dad."

As he spoke, Alexander led him through the crowded room to a table, where their family was gathered. It was weird to think of them all as their family. He was used to the sight of his mom and dad, but his mom was talking animatedly to a dark-haired woman who had to be William's half-sister, Rachel. And the little girl animatedly talking to William's father, William's niece. The new family William hadn't known he had.

Even more strange was the fact that for the first time at a family gathering, the people actually looked like William and Alexander. Their parents were light haired and fair skinned, as was the rest of their extended family. The dark coloring of William and Alexander had always seemed out of place at large family gatherings.

Until now, he hadn't realized just how much so.

For years, their mother had told William and Alexander that they didn't look like anyone else in the family because of a recessive gene as a throwback to some Italian ancestors. But the genealogy tests

proved that theory wrong. And let loose a chain reaction of truths that exposed years and years of lies.
Namely that they had a different father from the man
who had raised them.

Ricky got up from the chair he'd been sitting in.

"William. I'm sorry I didn't get much of a chance
to talk to you when you first arrived, but I'm glad
you're here now."

The warmth on the older man's face made it hard
for William to continue thinking about rejecting him.
Everyone else here seemed happy about the situation,
and it felt wrong to be in such a miserable state. But
how was William supposed to pretend to be happy
when everything in his life was falling apart?

For the sake of his brother, who just walked over
to Janie and put his arm around her, William would
do just that.

Pasting a smile on his face, William said, "Thank
you for the warm welcome."

"I can't tell you how much it means to me, to all
of us, that you're here," Ricky said.

Alexander had warned him that Ricky's charm
and welcoming attitude would be hard to resist. At
first, William had thought Alexander a traitor for so
easily warming up to this new family. But seeing everyone together made it hard for William to hold a
grudge. Especially as he looked at the other end of
the table, seeing his parents smiling at each other as
if it was the most natural thing in the world to discover a new family.

"I'm glad to be here," William said. "Alexander

has told me a lot of great things about everyone. I'm eager to spend some time relaxing and enjoying myself."

Funny, he'd thought he was only saying it to be polite. But as the words came out of his mouth, he realized he meant them. Maybe this time away was exactly what he needed to gain some perspective.

Alexander groaned. "Tom hasn't been working you too hard, has he? I know he's going to be your father-in-law, but you can say no to him. What's he going to do when you and Hailey are married and you're spending the holiday with him? Surely he wouldn't take you away from family activities then."

How was he supposed to keep up the farce now?

"Hailey and I broke up. Tom let me go. I didn't want to say anything and ruin your big celebration, but I don't want to lie to you, either. You know how I feel about lies."

He looked at his mom as he said the part about lies, but he immediately felt bad when he saw the look on her face. She was still his mom, and even though he was still mad at her, part of him also loved her. Funny, now that he made that connection, as he thought about Hailey, he could honestly say that he couldn't manage to find any love in his heart for Hailey.

Alexander pulled free from Janie and walked over to William. "I'm sorry. I didn't mean to—"

"Don't," William said. "I'm happy for you. You deserve to have someone special in your life. I just didn't want to ruin anyone else's celebration with my own depressing news."

At least it was out. Having ripped the bandage off and come clean to everyone, some of the uneasiness William had been feeling disappeared.

Maybe Grace would feel better, too, if her secret was out of the bag.

He saw her exiting the restroom out of the corner of his eye. Though he hadn't been consciously watching for her, he recognized that they shared a strange bond that made him protective of her.

Alexander put his arm around William. "You're not ruining anything. I want to be here for you. Support you. I can't believe Tom let you go because you and Hailey broke up."

It felt awkward, having everyone staring at him, especially since he hadn't gotten to know many of the people in the room. But, he supposed if they were his family, they might as well know what kind of person he was.

"Technically, it was a reduction in force, because my position was no longer needed. That's what it was recorded as, and I got a decent severance package. I could fight it, but why? Tom was upset about the way things went down, and he blames me for not keeping Hailey happy. I don't think I could go into the office every day and deal with him."

Alexander nodded sympathetically. "I can understand that. What happened between you two? You guys seemed like the perfect couple."

"I don't want to talk about it," William said. "We're here to have Thanksgiving, enjoy each other's company and be grateful for what we have. I may have lost a lot lately, but I still have many blessings to be grateful for."

Alexander gave William a pat on the back. "I know it's still hard. We're here to support you in any way we can."

"I'll be fine," William said. "Financially I'm okay enough that I can be picky about finding another job. As for my romantic life, I can put that on hold indefinitely. I need to figure out why I can't make a relationship work."

Ricky stepped forward. "It takes two to make a relationship work. You can do all the right things, but if the other person isn't putting in the same effort, it will never work. That's the one thing my sweet Rosie taught me, and why I haven't been able to remarry after her death. But regarding your other problem, I might have a solution."

Ricky turned to the man who'd been sitting on the chair opposite him. Ty Warner, the ranch's attorney who'd first contacted Alexander and his brother about getting to know Ricky, who was now married to their half sister, Rachel.

"The youth equestrian organization, The Comets, lost their barn in the recent wildfire," Ricky said. "We told them they could use the facilities at the ranch for now, but the insurance company is giving them a hard time, and there isn't enough money for them to rebuild. I don't want to kick the kids out of my ranch, but once we reopen to guests, I don't know how we can accommodate everyone. I was just telling Ty that we should do a rodeo fundraiser for the kids so they can get their facility back, and I can have mine."

Though Ty nodded like he could see where Ricky was going with this, William had no idea what it had to do with him.

"I don't have time for a fundraiser," Ricky said. "And my staff is already spread too thin. What if I put you in charge of raising money for the kids' horse facilities? Alexander says you're a financial whiz, and I know he has consulted with you on some of the other fundraising projects for the town. I could hire you to handle this for me."

William took a step back. "With all due respect, I'm not here for your money. That, and Alexander may have misrepresented my skills. I'm a financial advisor, and while I've helped my clients make a lot of money, that doesn't necessarily qualify me for a fundraising job."

"Stop," Alexander said. "You don't give yourself enough credit. One email to some of your business contacts got us the last of what we needed for the community Thanksgiving dinner. Every time I talk with someone who you've helped with their finances, they sing your praises."

"Okay, so I'm good with numbers," William admitted. "But that's exactly why I don't need a handout."

Ricky chuckled. "I didn't say I was giving you a handout. I'm offering you a job."

A job. One that felt like his last one, where he'd thought he'd been doing everything on his own merit, but now he wondered if it had been all based on his relationship with Hailey. Would Ricky have offered this to him if they hadn't been related?

Alexander nudged him. "You should take it. With me staying here now, it would be nice to have you around for a while, and even though you say you have money put aside, this will keep you from having to dip into your savings. Once the fundraiser is over, you can go back to Denver or somewhere else to follow your passion. Think of this as breathing room."

Breathing room. Now that was a funny joke. How could you call this breathing room, when being here reminded him of everything uncomfortable in his life?

"You don't have to give me an answer now," Ricky said. "At least sleep on it."

Before Alexander could respond, a little boy ran to their table, pulling at the hand of an older man. The boy wrapped his arms around Alexander.

"Dad, Poppa said that I can start calling you dad whenever I want. So I decided I'm calling you dad right now, Dad."

This must be Sam, Janie's son, soon to be Alexander's.

The wide grin on the little boy's face brought a smile to William that reached all the way down into his heart. Especially when Alexander scooped Sam into his arms and hugged him tight.

"I'd like that, son."

Once again, it made William aware of how love transcended biology, and how what William had felt for Hailey wasn't the kind of love either of them deserved. And maybe it explained why, even knowing their father wasn't their biological father, he still felt 100 percent like he was their dad.

Alexander set Sam down and gestured at William. "Remember how I told you I had a brother who looked just like me? This is William."

Sam looked him up and down. "You don't look just like my dad. My dad doesn't have such a frowny face."

Not much was going to get past this kid. William grinned. "Now do I look like him?"

Sam shook his head. "Nope. You still seem too frowny. I've always wanted an uncle. Can I call you Uncle William, even though my mom and dad aren't married yet?"

William couldn't help the laugh that escaped. He barely knew Sam, but he was already grateful to have the little boy in his life.

"I've always wanted to have a nephew. So if you're ready to be my nephew, I'm ready to be your uncle William."

Sam threw his arms around him, and just as soon as William returned the hug, the little girl he'd guessed to be Rachel's daughter came up to them.

"And I'm Katie, your niece. Have you always wanted a niece? Sam is my best friend, but now he gets to be my cousin. I never thought I'd have a family besides my mom, but now I have two uncles and a cousin."

Then she turned to Ty. "But best of all, I finally have a dad."

"And now I get a dad," Sam said. "We all get dads!"

The kids squealed excitedly and hugged each other, jumping up and down. Funny how, to children, the prospect of finding new family was the best thing ever. They didn't have to deal with the complicated emotions of lies and betrayal, and somehow finding a way to forgive.

Could it be that simple?

"Hey," William said. "Do I get a hug from the niece I've always wanted?"

Katie let go of Sam and wrapped her arms around William. It had already felt good to be hugged by the little boy, but at the genuine affection from his niece, a child whose dark hair and dark eyes were so much like his own, the sense of belonging that filled William's heart shook him to the core.

When he released Katie and looked around the room, he realized that his acceptance of the little girl had also given him acceptance of this group of people he hadn't realized he'd needed to be accepted by.

The man Sam had dragged into the room stepped forward. "I'm John Roberts, Janie's father."

"He's my poppa!" Sam said, grinning.

"He's also the pastor of our church," Alexander added. "He helped me a lot as I navigated the emotions I was feeling around…everything."

William stared at his brother for a second. Alexander? Into church? They only went at major holidays because their mom had always insisted. But it wasn't like any of them were big churchgoers.

Was anything in his life sacred?

As Grace returned from putting her dirty clothes in the car, she took a deep breath, steeling herself for the discomfort of sharing a meal with her mother. Her stomach already felt terrible. The smell of Thanksgiving dinner, usually one of her favorite things, was making her even more queasy.

But when her mother greeted her, carrying two very full plates, Grace knew she was going to have to make the effort. Otherwise, her mother would know something was off.

"I hope those both aren't for me," Grace said, trying to laugh. "I'm really not that hungry. I'm not sure I can even do the one plate justice."

"You need to get some good food in you. I made a plate for William, too. He and Alexander might be twins, but I can tell them apart already. William is nothing but skin and bones. I'm going to fatten him up."

At least that took some of the pressure off Grace. Usually her mother said the same thing about her.

When they got to the table, her mom set a plate in front of William. He cast Grace a pleading eye, like he didn't want to be abandoned. She didn't blame him. Right now, he was the only safe person for her in this room.

Grace sat next to William, and her mother didn't comment as she put Grace's plate in front of her.

"Wanda!" one of the ladies called out, and her mom went to see what she needed.

"I don't know how I'm going to eat all of this," Grace whispered to William.

"Leave it to me," he said. "Alexander and I came up with a system as kids. We might be twins but we have opposite tastes in food. Mom was a believer in the Clean Plate Club, so we know how to eat each other's food without being caught. You'll be fine."

He took a bite of the turkey, then leaned in and said, "Just push what you don't want to the side closest to me."

Then louder, he said, "This turkey is delicious. I've never had it so moist and tender."

"That's the deep-fried one," her mom said, returning to the table. "I know some people say it's dangerous, but we take all the precautions, and in the end, you won't find a tastier bird."

"Really?" Alexander asked. "I didn't know that. I think I just had the regular turkey."

Grace watched as William speared a large piece with his fork and handed it to his brother.

"That's good," Alexander said, chewing thoughtfully. "I've had dessert, but I might need more turkey."

William gestured at his plate. "Have some of mine. You know I won't be able to finish it all."

"Don't mind if I do."

Alexander plopped into the seat on the other side of William, and as the brothers joked back and forth, Grace could see exactly how William's plan would play out. He was sharing with his brother so he could eat some of Grace's.

The way William was trying to protect her brought a warm feeling to Grace's heart. It had been a long time since she'd felt so cared for, and just this slight gesture made her realize that she'd never had this feeling with Jack.

Maybe she didn't know what love was, after all.

But then she thought of the baby growing inside her. Yes, she did know about love. She'd do anything for her baby.

Including scarf down as much of this food as possible without getting sick.

Grace took a bite of the potatoes. Actually, they tasted pretty good.

And when they hit her stomach, it didn't protest.

Maybe she could do this.

A round of introductions were made, leaving Grace's head spinning. True, her mom had told her about all these people and how they came to the Double R, but having to put faces to names was going to be interesting.

At least it gave her something to think about other than the baby, and the fact that the only thing on her plate that seemed remotely appetizing was the potatoes.

William looked over at Wanda. "I'm usually not a big fan of stuffing, but this is really good. Do you do anything special?"

William's mom, Kara, laughed. "It's true. I've

never seen you eat much in the way of stuffing. But you sure are putting it away."

It had been the right thing to say. Grace's mom had been staring at Grace's plate, almost like she was judging the amount Grace had been eating. The question took her mom's eyes off Grace's plate, and onto William's.

"I usually just tell people that my extra ingredient is love." Then she straightened. "But since you're family, I'll tell you the real secret." Grace stifled a giggle, because she'd heard it before, and Wanda shot her a glare before continuing. "So here's my secret— love."

Then she laughed, like the joke she must've told a hundred times was something she'd just thought up.

"My mom never shares her recipes," Grace said. "She pretends to, but she always leaves an ingredient or two out, or gives one of the measurements wrong. I'm still trying to figure out what I do wrong with chicken enchilada casserole."

Wanda snickered. "Well I'm making turkey enchilada casserole with the leftovers tomorrow, so maybe you can help me and find out."

Given that she almost couldn't handle the smell of food in here, Grace wasn't sure how that was going to work, but she nodded slowly. "You know how much I love helping you in the kitchen."

"If you don't mind, I'd love to help, too," Kara said. "I'm always looking for creative ways to use turkey leftovers. My boys hate leftovers, so if I can repurpose them, that's a big win for everyone."

"I usually don't let strangers in my kitchen," Wanda said. "But since you're practically family, I can make an exception."

"They *are* family," Ricky said. "I know that no one wants my money, and the ranch is in a trust anyway, but I'm putting you all in my will."

Ty set his coffee down, shaking his head. "How many times are you going to make me redo that will of yours?" Then Ty shrugged. "But at least you're not making good on your threat to donate it all to some cat preservation society. You don't even like cats."

Ricky squared his shoulders. "I like my barn cats just fine and I feed all those feral beasts running around. I just don't want them in my house. If I give them some of my money, then all those cats will be taken care of and I don't have to feed them anymore."

"You'll be dead," Ty said. "You won't be feeding them."

"Exactly my point," Ricky said. "That's why I've got to leave them money. Who else is going to feed them?"

"You can give my share to the cats," William said. "I don't need your money."

William's denial made Grace like him even more. Over the years, a lot of charlatans had come to the Double R, claiming to be long-lost relatives, hoping for a cut of Ricky's riches. But William was different. He seemed hesitant about even being here.

Ricky glared at him. "It's my money and I can do with it what I want."

William looked like he was going to argue, so she shot him a glare.

"Seriously," Grace said. "Don't get him started. For everyone's sanity."

Ty looked over at Grace. "Thank you. It's been a while since you've been home. How are things going for you? How's the new job of yours?"

"Not so new," Grace said. "I was there for almost a year."

"Was?" Ty asked. "You don't work there anymore?"

Grace shrugged. "My position was just eliminated. I'm not sure what I'm going to do, but I thought I'd take a break over the holidays to figure it out and find something after the first of the year."

"What's this about losing your job?" her mom asked, her voice raising to a high pitch.

Confirmation that Grace was right in easing her mom into the news of all her life changes. How was she going to react when she learned that Grace wasn't just unemployed, but pregnant?

"Simmer down, Wanda," Ricky said. "You haven't even heard the girl out."

"There's not much to tell," Grace said. "They did a reorganization in my department, and they weren't able to keep me. I got a small severance package, and when that runs out, if I don't have a job, I'll be eligible for unemployment. I'll be fine."

Ricky pounded on the table. "Yes, you will. And that settles that. Ty and I were just trying to talk William into coming to work for the ranch for a while, to help us put on a fundraiser for the youth riding organization. They need new riding facilities, and everyone here is tapped out because of the fire. William knows how to raise money. You know how to run a rodeo. You've helped with ours countless times. As of today, you both have jobs. This summer the Double R Ranch is hosting a charity benefit rodeo to give the youth of our community a new place to ride."

The look on William's face told her he wasn't too sure about taking it. But for Grace, it was a guaranteed job, and if she was careful with her severance package, and depending on when in the summer they had the rodeo, she'd be done with the rodeo right about the time the baby was born. Which meant she'd have some money to pay her bills and could then take a little time off after the baby was born before looking for another job.

She looked over at William, and he gave a small nod before turning his attention back on Ricky.

"Does this job come with health insurance?" William asked.

The glance William gave her told Grace exactly why he was asking. He wanted to make sure she and the baby were going to be okay. A sweet gesture, considering they barely knew each other. For whatever reason, William had set himself up to be her champion.

She hoped it wasn't for a romantic reason. Just as immediately as the thought hit, she pushed it aside. Of course William didn't have romantic thoughts. He'd just been dumped by his fiancée. Likely, he was just trying to be nice to a fellow dump-ee in an even worse situation than him.

Ricky looked thoughtful for a moment, then turned to Ty. "Do we pay health insurance?"

Ty shrugged. "For full-time employees, we do. I don't see why we couldn't offer them health insurance."

Then Ricky looked over at William. "Why do you care about health insurance? You're not sick, are you? You are not like Rachel, looking for a kidney or some other vital organ?"

Grace's mom had told her that Rachel had come looking for Ricky, hoping to find a kidney donor. Ricky, of course, had not been able to donate a kidney, but God had worked in His way to make sure Rachel had gotten what she needed.

Would God be willing to work in Grace's life when Grace had messed up so badly?

"No, nothing like that," William assured him. "Healthcare is important these days, and while I do have COBRA benefits, it'd be nice to know I had something else, just in case. You never know what's going to happen."

Ty nodded approvingly, like that was exactly what everyone needed to hear. Truthfully, Grace was relieved, because while she could sign up for coverage under her termination agreement, it was more expensive than what she'd been paying. Having employer-sponsored insurance would save her money.

"It's settled, then," Ricky said. "As of today, you two are officially employees of the Double R Ranch.

Ty can take care of the paperwork. Come summer, we'll have a rodeo to help the kids. If we get good enough sponsors, we can attract some real big names. If we get big names, big crowds will follow."

Excitement filled the old man's face, and the rest of the table seemed to catch that same air of excitement.

"Yes, siree!" Ricky pounded the table again. "This is going to be the best rodeo anyone has seen in a long time."

Ricky's enthusiasm made William smile. The fundraising part would be easy, because he knew a lot of people with a lot of money, and all of them were looking for tax write-offs. A feel-good project like a rodeo charity event for kids fit the bill nicely. And, if Grace knew how to put on a rodeo, all the better.

He glanced over at Grace, who looked like some of the weight had come off her shoulders.

"I'm in," Grace said. "But I'm going to be honest with you. The reason our last rodeo series didn't do so well is because you wouldn't let us have bull riding. I know you hold the bull-riding event responsible for Cinco's death, but with all the safety measures that have been put in place over the years, it's pretty rare to die in a bull-riding accident. The draw of most rodeos is the bull riding."

Hushed silence filled the table, and Wanda looked at her daughter as if she was a preschooler who'd spoken out of turn.

But Ricky nodded slowly. "I suppose you're right. The truth is, I blamed the bulls for killing my son, because sometimes it was easier than blaming myself. I always felt like I'd done a poor job as a father. I drove my son away. It's only because of God's grace that my son's children have seen fit to forgive the mistakes of the past and move forward. If they can do it, then so will I. You tell people there will be bull riding at this event."

Ricky stood on his chair. "I'd like everyone's attention."

The room stilled at the sound of the old man's booming voice.

"The Double R Ranch is hosting a rodeo this summer to benefit The Comets. My grandson William Bennett and Wanda's daughter, Grace, will be in charge."

A murmur went through the crowd. It had been a while since the Double R had hosted rodeo events, which used to be a cornerstone of the community. Grace could remember, even before she'd started helping with them, being a little girl, sitting in the stands and watching the cowboys.

"And," Ricky continued, "there will be a bull-riding event. I will personally sponsor the grand prize, which will be named the Cinco award."

This time, a hush came over everyone gathered for the community Thanksgiving dinner. Everyone in these parts knew about Cinco's tragic death, and Ricky's resulting bitterness.

Tears streamed down Ricky's face, and Grace had to believe that if God could bring that much healing to Ricky's heart, surely He could forgive Grace's mistakes.

Someone started clapping, which led to the rest of the room joining in. Ricky got down from his chair.

"I guess I just made a right fool of myself. But these kids need a place to ride, and this town needs something else good to look forward to. I'm going to get me some pie."

Grace grinned. Now that was the Ricky she knew and loved.

Her mom looked over at her. "For someone who said she wasn't that hungry, you did a fair enough job clearing your plate. You want me to get you some pie? I set aside some slices of mine just for you."

Grace looked down at her plate. Nearly empty. Enough that her mom would be satisfied with what she ate.

She glanced over at William, whose plate was also clear. As if he knew what she was thinking, he winked at her.

"I'm a big fan of pumpkin pie," William said.

"What do you mean?" Kara asked. "Alexander is the one who likes pumpkin. You've always preferred apple."

The poor guy was trying to help, and he'd just gotten busted by his mom. Grace grinned.

"I'd love some pie, Mom."

"Me, too," William added. "Can I have a slice of pumpkin and apple?"

Her mom's smile warmed Grace's heart. She'd do her best to eat the pie, which actually did sound kind of good now that her stomach had settled.

"Of course you can. I'll get you some of both. You want whipped cream on that?"

Before he answered, he looked over at Grace, like he was making sure of her tastes.

"Only if it's your homemade." She smiled at William. "You've got to try it."

Her mom's grin made the struggle through the meal worth it. Having William here had really helped.

As her mom left to get the pie, she gave a little squeal. "My baby girl is home from Denver. It looks like she'll be staying a while."

Everyone else got up and started mingling with the crowd, who seemed to be energized by the rodeo announcement.

William turned to Grace. "So you know about rodeos, huh?"

She shrugged. "I competed in them, and I helped put them on when Ricky was doing them at the ranch. We weren't making as much money with it, given Ricky's refusal to have the bull riding, but I know what I'm doing. Now that we can have bull riding, it will be a successful event."

William nodded, like her words were reassuring. He'd probably been nervous about taking the job if he didn't know much about rodeos. "And you know a lot about cowboys?"

Grace shrugged. "Probably more than I want to. You forget, that's all I grew up around, and maybe that's where I went wrong. I don't really understand city men like Jack."

Maybe that had been her problem. Thinking she

could forget her roots. That's what her mom had always accused her of—abandoning her roots for the city. It wasn't like she'd even had that great a job. Just doing admin work, thinking it was giving her a better life than staying on the ranch.

"And like me," William said. "That's what I want your help with. I don't want to be some boring city guy. All these women seem to be into cowboys. I want you to teach me what you know about being one. What I need to do to be exciting enough to finally keep a relationship."

Was he serious? The expression on his face was just as earnest as it had been when he'd offered to help her earlier.

When she'd said she'd gone wrong with city men, she hadn't thought about how it would make William feel. There was nothing wrong with him, except maybe that he'd proposed to the wrong woman.

Grace shook her head. "But that's just it. We need nice guys like you. Most of the cowboys I know are all jerks. Why do you think I went to the city? I was tired of chauvinistic pigs pushing me around. That's not you. Frankly, I think what woman need are men exactly like you."

William groaned.

"Tell that to every woman I've ever dated. According to them, I'm a nice guy, but too nice."

Grace placed a hand on his arm. "Maybe you've just been looking at the wrong women." Sighing, she shrugged. "But what do I know about relationships?

Look where believing I was in love got me. Sure, I'll help you learn about being a cowboy."

William smiled. "And I'll help you. You said you were worried about finances and supporting your baby. Since I'm a financial planner, I'll help you get things sorted out."

Grace had always wanted to sit down and talk to a financial planner, but she'd worried they were too expensive. But with the baby coming, it would be reassuring to know that she had everything in order.

"That sounds perfect," she said. Then she stuck out her hand. "Partners?"

"Partners."

Chapter Three

William had never been on the inside of an arena before. He'd always just been in the stands, viewing from above. Something about standing in the dirt took away some of the mystery of it. The dirt was just regular dirt. He kicked at it.

"You're going to need some better shoes if you're going to be running a rodeo." Grace pointed at William's shoes.

He lifted a foot. "What? These are good shoes. High quality. Good arch support."

Grace groaned. "No offense, but the ladies don't care whether or not your shoes have good arch support."

She looked him up and down, then added, "As a matter of fact, you're dressed completely wrong for being on a ranch. That getup is screaming, *I don't fit in here*. You look like you're on your way to a board meeting."

William looked down at his clothes. "What? I wear

suits to board meetings. These are just khakis and a casual button-down. It's our first official day of work, so I wanted to look professional. I asked Ty if it was too informal, and he just laughed."

They'd taken the weekend after Thanksgiving to relax, but here it was a new week, and they were getting down to business, figuring out what needed to be done for the rodeo.

"Did you notice what Ty was wearing?" Grace asked.

William thought for a second. "He was pretty casual, in jeans and a Western button-down."

Grace looked at him like he was missing the point. "That's what the chief legal counsel for the Double R Ranch wears every day. Everyone wears jeans and a Western shirt. Do you even own a pair of jeans?"

The mirth in her eyes made him smile. "I guess I see your point. Everyone is dressed like a cowboy, down to the hat. I have jeans, but not the style everyone else wears."

"Do you have money to go shopping?"

This time, William couldn't help grinning. "I have money. I meant what I said when I told you I had some saved up. I only took this job to figure my life out."

She gave him a funny look. "That was the only reason?"

William looked around the arena. Tried picturing it full of people, realizing that even when he'd gone to rodeos, he'd always stuck out. No wonder women said he was boring.

"And I want to learn about being a cowboy. I guess

dressing the part will help. I'm just tired of women looking past me because I'm so dependable and re-liable."

Grace stepped forward and put her hand on his arm. "You act like that's a bad thing. Most women would kill to have a reliable and dependable guy. You've been such a big help to me."

"Exactly my point. I've helped you. Would you like me otherwise?"

William turned to survey the rest of the arena. He didn't want to see the pity on her face as she gave him some placating comment. That's what they all did. At least things weren't romantic between him and Grace so he wouldn't get the "it's not you, it's me" speech.

"You're a nice guy, of course I'd like you," Grace said.

And the nice-guy talk. The whole cowboy plan was definitely looking better and better.

William turned back to look at her. "So where do we get the appropriate footwear and other attire?"

"We used to have a store here in town, but it burned down in the fire. There's a town about an hour away with a good selection. I'd like to talk to them anyway to get their help in spreading the word. They used to be one of the sponsors for our old rodeos."

It didn't take long for them to get on the road and to the Western wear store. Grace had fallen asleep shortly after they'd gotten started on the drive, so it had been William alone with his thoughts.

He didn't feel much better about his situation as they entered the store. Inside was everything he needed to transform into a woman's dream. And while he had no personal objection to wearing those clothes, it felt a little like selling out.

But who knew? Maybe he'd meet someone at the benefit rodeo and she could appreciate not just the cowboy image, but the man inside.

William picked up a hat from a display and set it on his head. "What do you think?" he asked, turning toward Grace.

Instead of being impressed, Grace giggled. "For one, it's a little too big."

She picked the hat off his head. "But also, you have it on backward."

Clearly, he still had a lot to learn about being a cowboy.

Grace set the hat back on the display and picked up a different one. "Try this."

"I liked the other style better," William said, pointing at the one she'd set down.

"Straw hats are for summer. You'll need one then, but for winter, you need a felt hat."

"I didn't realize cowboy hats had rules," he said.

Grace shrugged. "It depends on the region and tradition the people there follow. I've heard that you're supposed to always take your hat off when indoors, for example, but most of the guys I know only do so to be respectful at certain times, like during a prayer or the pledge of allegiance. But if you follow the lead of the other guys around you, you should be just fine."

She pointed to the hat she'd given him. "In terms of felt versus straw, it's a warmth thing. In the winter, you'll freeze with the cold air and breeze coming through a straw hat, but you'll sweat to death in the summer with a felt hat."

William put the hat on.

Grace giggled. "It's still on backward. Let me help."

As she reached for the hat, she came in close enough to him that he could smell her perfume. Nothing overpowering, just the soft, sweet scent of lavender. Simple. Beautiful. Just like her.

William took a step back. What was he thinking? He didn't need to be having thoughts like this about Grace. Not only was it terrible timing for them both, but she'd already told him that she liked him for how helpful he was. Exactly what he didn't want in a woman. Besides, she had way more to worry about than some dumb cowboy wannabe being attracted to her.

"I've got it," he said.

He flipped the hat around and set it back on his head. "Better?"

The smile that lit up Grace's face made him happier than he should admit to. He liked it when she smiled, especially when it wasn't because he was being a doofus.

"Very nice," she said. "Now we just have to get it shaped for you."

One of the sales staff approached. "Are you finding what you're looking for?"

Then the woman stopped and stared at Grace. "Grace Duncan, is that you?"

Grace nodded. "Nice to see you again, Stacy. How are Dave and the kids? I think my mom told me you had another baby not too long ago."

"Two years, more like," Stacy said. "And Dave is a pig who went chasing after some buckle bunny. I should have known better than to fall for a cowboy."

Grace gave him a pointed look, as if to say not all cowboys were great. And William got it. After all, Hailey's cowboy had known she was engaged and went for her anyway. That didn't exactly say "class act."

"Is this your man?" Stacy asked, stepping between Grace and William.

"No," Grace said. "This is William Bennett. He's Ricky's long-lost grandson. We're helping Ricky put on a benefit rodeo to raise money for the youth riding organization. I was hoping to talk to Steve to see if you guys can help spread the word. He still owns the place, right?"

William could feel Stacy's gaze drift to his ring finger. "I heard Ricky had relatives coming out of the woodwork. Are you single?"

Wow, and he thought the ring check was obvious. "Unavailable, I'm afraid. But someone like you shouldn't have any trouble finding a guy."

Stacy groaned. "Not in these parts. They're all a bunch of worthless cowboys. Or married. Or otherwise unavailable. Is it so much to ask to find a decent, hardworking man?"

He didn't like the "I told you so" expression on Grace's face.

"Well, don't lose hope," William said, unsure of what else to say. "Is Steve around?"

A weird sort of giggle snort came out of Grace's mouth.

"Oh, him. Yeah." Stacy shrugged. "He's in the back. I'll let him know you're looking for him."

Grace took the hat off William's head and handed it to Stacy. "Can we go back with you so we can get this shaped for him?"

Stacy nodded and took the hat.

They followed, and on the way, Grace pointed out a few shirts. "Those would look good on you. Perfect for work wear."

Her selections weren't half bad. He'd have chosen something similar on his own. And at least she wasn't ribbing him about Stacy's cowboy comments. Maybe the ones Stacy had met were jerks, but William had seen so many women sighing over cowboys that he knew they found them appealing. He'd never seen anyone sigh over a guy in khakis and a button-up.

When Stacy went into the back to get Steve, Grace turned to him. "Just ignore Stacy. She's always been a big flirt, especially if she thinks the guy has money. I probably shouldn't have told her you're Ricky's grandson. Most people don't realize that all of Ricky's money is in a trust to preserve the ranch for future generations. Saying you're unavailable is good, because people like Stacy are going to glom on to you, hoping to get their hands on Ricky's money through you."

Great. One more reason to wonder if a woman

liked him for who he was. He wasn't interested in Stacy anyway. She was too obvious of a flirt.

Once Stacy came back with Steve, she got to work shaping William's hat. He had to admit, there seemed to be an art to it, and when she was done, it fit him a lot more comfortably.

"That should be perfect for you," Stacy said.

"Thanks," William said, looking over to where Grace and Steve were talking. "I should probably join them. I appreciate your help."

Stacy must have gotten the hint, because she nodded and turned away.

On his way over to talk to Steve and Grace, William spied a table with baby clothes and baby cowboy boots. Something about the display tugged at his heart. He'd never been into babies, but he also hadn't been close to anyone who was pregnant before.

Maybe later, he'd get something for Grace's baby.

He also spotted some toys for older kids on the display. It wouldn't hurt to pick up something for his new niece and nephew. They were cute kids, and he counted them as part of the blessings he'd received with all the changes in his family.

When he joined Grace and Steve, they were deep in conversation about the rodeo.

"I think it's great that Ricky is bringing the rodeo back," Steve said. "You know we need more for folks to do other than cause trouble. And for the kids? I've already given a lot to support the rebuilding effort in Columbine Springs. But you can count on me to be on your sponsorship list."

William hadn't realized it would be that easy. Steve's enthusiasm made him feel almost bad for having this as a job. He'd expected to work for his money.

"Thanks, Steve," Grace said. "We've got some shopping to do, but I'll be in touch with details. I didn't get the chance earlier, since they were busy with his hat, but I wanted to introduce you to Ricky's grandson William."

Steve looked William up and down. "I would have known, even without the introduction. You're the spitting image of your father, did you know that?"

William wasn't prepared for the emotion that welled up inside him. No one had ever told him that growing up. Usually, people commented on how odd it was that neither boy looked like their parents. Alexander had told him they looked like Cinco, but William had done his best not to stare at the picture of their biological father to work it out for himself.

"So I've been told," William said, trying not to let his feelings show.

"You've probably heard some stories about Cinco that weren't too good," Steve continued. "I used to pal around with him back in the day, so I know all those stories. But you should also know that your father wasn't all bad. He had a good heart. He'd be the first guy to buy everyone in the bar a round of drinks. Of course, that was also his problem. Drinking too much, then getting in trouble as a result. But when he wasn't drinking, he was the kind of guy who'd give you the shirt off his back. Much to his detriment at times. He was a lot like Ricky, though I suppose people are too busy remembering the bad to think it."

William tried to remain calm as he processed the information. It was weird to think of the villain in his life as a human being. But without Cinco, William wouldn't be alive, so he had that to consider, as well.

"Thank you for telling me about him," William said. "I don't know if you and Ricky ever talk about him, but I think Ricky would like to hear your good stories about his son."

Steve nodded. "He never wanted to talk about Cinco much. But maybe you're right. Next time I'm out that way, I'll be sure to stop in."

Someone came into the store, and Steve turned. "That's one of my suppliers I need to talk to. Keep me posted about the rodeo, and we'll stay in touch."

As Steve left, William felt Grace's hand on his arm. "Are you okay?" she asked.

William took a deep breath. "I think so. I just wasn't expecting…"

"It's a small town," Grace said. "They may be an hour away, but given how spread out everything is, our communities know each other well. I hadn't realized Steve had known Cinco, though. Most of us spent a lot of time avoiding the topic, for Ricky's sake. It hasn't been until recently that Ricky's been talking about him."

He turned to face her. "Why the change?"

Grace shrugged. "Mom says that with Ricky getting older, he's been thinking a lot about his regrets in life. Cinco's death, and never meeting Cinco's child, or, as we know now, children, has weighed on him. I think he just wants to make things right."

His brother had said something similar.

Even though William hadn't wanted to know this side of his family, there was no denying it was part of him. Especially since he could walk into a place he'd never been, and be recognized.

"Now, let's find you some clothes," Grace said.

On their way back to the men's clothing, William paused at the baby display. "I was thinking…"

Grace looked down at it. "Wow. I haven't gotten anything for the baby yet. It's so early, since I'm only in my first trimester. But it also makes it real."

William picked up a pair of baby boots. "Would you mind if I got these for the baby? Since you don't know what it is yet, an outfit probably isn't a good idea. But these would work for a boy or a girl."

For a moment, she didn't speak, but then she nodded. "That's really sweet, thank you. We'll have to keep them hidden for a while, but it feels good to have something for my baby."

As they continued shopping, William sensed a strange distance between him and Grace. But why? Part of him wanted to ask her, but the other part of him said it was none of his business. She still talked to him like normal, and he didn't want to question her based on some weird feeling he had. They didn't need to go digging and prying into deeper emotions.

They were just here to do a job together, nothing more, nothing less. But when William paid for his purchases, he couldn't help adding a baby blanket with a horse pattern and a matching stuffed horse to the pile.

Why did William have to go and be so sweet? Grace couldn't help noticing the way he'd stealthily added baby items to his purchases. She hadn't even thought about baby clothes yet. She'd been too busy freaking out and trying to come up with a plan. But seeing the tender way he'd stroked the stuffed horse before purchasing it somehow made the baby more real to her.

Grace hugged herself around the middle, hoping the baby could feel her love. She didn't know what she was doing here, but it seemed like God had been answering her prayers so far. She might have abandoned Him, but He certainly hadn't abandoned her.

In just a few short days, she'd gone from having no idea what she was going to do, or how she'd support herself and the baby, to having a good job with benefits, and people around her who cared for her. True, William was the only person who knew about the baby, but she still felt a great deal of love from everyone at the Double R.

Things had changed since she'd last been home. With the expansion of Ricky's family, Grace felt her own had expanded, as well. The ranch house was full of children's laughter, and she couldn't help thinking that's how she wanted her baby to grow up. Just one more way she felt God telling her everything was going to be okay.

A True Cowboy

William stepped out of the store, carrying several bags.

"You look like you bought out the whole place," Grace said.

William laughed. "Not hardly. But if I'm going to be a cowboy, I need to look the part. Plus, now that I have a new niece and nephew, I couldn't help buying them a couple of little things."

The impish grin on his face made Grace smile. "You're going to spoil them."

"Isn't that what a bachelor uncle is for? But who knows, maybe this cowboy thing will work for me, and I'll give them some cousins to play with."

Something about his tone brought an uneasy feeling to Grace's stomach. And for once, it wasn't the baby.

"You know you're just fine as you are, right? It seems like an awful lot of pressure, trying to be someone you're not to win someone over. Does this mean you're trying to get your ex-fiancée back?"

William carried the bags to the car and unlocked it. "I know what you're saying. First of all, no, I'm not thinking of getting Hailey back. I could never trust her again, and that doesn't seem like a good basis for a relationship."

He put the bags in the backseat, then turned to look at her. "And yes, I know. The irony of trying to be a cowboy to get women to like me when I just want people to like me for me isn't lost on me. But they say the definition of insanity is doing the same thing over and over, expecting different results. Is it so wrong to try something different?"

Considering that Grace's idea of trying something different left her pregnant and alone, she wasn't a big proponent of the idea. She also wasn't sure when, if ever, she'd be willing to get back in the dating game. Especially now that she had a baby to think of.

William kicked at the ground. "I don't know. I'm not ready for another relationship right now anyway. If Ms. Right came knocking on my door tomorrow, I'd probably ask her to leave. I just wish I knew what was wrong with me that I keep getting into the same situations."

"What if there's nothing wrong with you?" Grace asked. "I get it. I felt that way before dating Jack. Then I met him and made a lot of decisions that weren't like me. And look where that got me."

She put her hand over her still-flat stomach. "My baby will never be a regret. It's probably the one blessing God has given me after all of my mistakes. But I have learned that I will never turn my back on the things I believe in for the sake of impressing a man. I hope, regardless of whatever changes you make in your life, that you never lose sight of your values."

Instead of looking encouraged by her words, William looked only more ill at ease.

"And what if you don't believe in God?" William hesitated. "I mean, I guess there's a God or something up there. We go to church on holidays to make our mom happy. Though lately, Alexander has talked about his faith. I don't know. It just makes me uncomfortable. If God is so great, then why does all this crazy stuff happen? I'm a reasonably good person. I live a reasonably good life. Why do I need God?"

Grace had never strayed so far from her faith as to believe those things. She'd made mistakes, yes, but now, more than ever, she knew how much she needed God. William likely didn't know what it meant to have a real relationship with the Lord. To him, faith was meaningless because he'd never really experienced it.

"But that's not what God is about," Grace told him, not sure how to explain what faith meant to someone who didn't understand. She quickly asked God to give her the right words.

"This may be oversimplifying it, but having faith in God is like having a friend to walk through life with. It doesn't automatically make everything better, but it sure makes things easier having someone to be there to share your load."

William sighed. "It does get pretty lonely sometimes. It used to be that I had Alexander, and we always had each other's backs. But we grew up, led our own lives, and now I don't feel as close to my brother anymore."

"God never grows apart from you," Grace said. "Sometimes you move away from Him, like I did, but the good thing is, if you choose to move toward Him again, He's still there."

Suddenly, she realized that her words weren't just for William, but were a truth she needed to hear. When she'd moved to Denver, she'd broken completely from the life she'd always known, thinking it was the change she needed to take charge of things. She'd thought she was leading a good life, but she hadn't been following the faith she'd been taught from an early age. Unfortunately, doing it on her own, without God, was exactly how she'd messed up everything so badly.

Finding herself alone and pregnant had been the jolt she'd needed to realize just how far she'd fallen. And how God had never left her.

The realization gave her a strength in facing her future that had been missing. Did she have everything figured out? No. But it didn't matter. She wasn't alone anymore. Never had been.

"I know you didn't come here for a sermon," she said. "We need to get back anyway. I'm a little hungry and I could use a slice of Mom's pumpkin pie."

William grinned. "I'm so glad it agreed with the baby. I could barely gag down a couple bites of mine, let alone eat both pieces. It was nice to give you my food for a change."

"There seems to be a limited amount of food I can keep down, so if the baby wants pumpkin pie, I'm going to make sure he or she gets it. I just have to figure out how to convince Mom to make more without telling her my reason why."

William touched her arm gently. "I know your mom is a bit much with the way she hovers. But maybe she would surprise you with her reaction about the baby. One more person for her to love and care for."

She liked the warmth radiating from him. In truth, some of her restored faith came from the love and support William had given her. But she also knew that it wasn't as simple. Yes, she could count on William now, before he knew the truth about her baby's parentage. But what would happen when he found out that she was the other woman? He had such a disregard for cheaters. Rightfully so. Except that sometimes it wasn't as cut-and-dried as William made things out to be.

Would her mom accept the baby? Eventually. But in the immediacy of her situation, Grace wasn't sure how she'd handle her mom's disappointment.

Which meant she'd have to cling to her faith even more. And pray that when the truth came out, God would give her the strength to handle whatever fallout there was—including losing William's friendship.

Chapter Four

The cold January air made William pull his scarf tighter around his neck. Funny how easily they'd made the ranch their home, save for a quick trip to Denver so William could get some more things from his place, and Grace could move out of her apartment completely. The condo William had purchased, intending to make home, had felt less like home than the cabin Ricky was letting him stay in did.

After the wildfire, the Double R had temporarily ceased operations as a guest ranch, letting community members stay in the cabins until they could find more permanent solutions. Many of those people were gone now, leaving cabins available for people like William and Grace to have places of their own to stay. William had a cabin near Alexander's, and while Grace had been invited to stay in her mom's quarters, she'd opted for a more private cabin on her own. She'd told Wanda she didn't want to be in her way, but William suspected it was more because she didn't want her mom to realize she wasn't feeling well.

If only Grace would tell her mother about the baby.

Until then, he'd continue supporting her as a friend. The fact that most of the ranch family and staff took their meals together in the main ranch house meant he would have plenty of opportunity to do so.

Initially, William had intended on just staying long enough to get the rodeo going. But as he stood at the entrance to the barn at the Double R, he couldn't imagine being anyplace else. Today was to be his first riding lesson. Snow blanketed the ground, but given that the Double R was in Colorado's high country, they had an indoor arena for such an occasion.

This was one of the things they'd hoped to give the kids. He walked over to the Double R foreman, Hunter Hawkins.

"Grace says you've got a horse for me," William said. "I just hope she explained that I have never been on a horse, except for maybe one of those pony rides when I was a kid."

Hunter chuckled, a broad smile filling his face. "I know. But if we can get Alexander on a horse, there's no reason you can't learn to ride, as well."

That only gave him a little more hope. While both brothers liked sports, of the two, Alexander had always had more athletic ability. William had heard that Alexander had struggled learning to ride, and it made him nervous.

Hunter led William to a stall. "This is Floofy, my daughter's horse."

William had seen the little girl running around the ranch. "She can't be more than three. And she has a horse?"

The foreman grinned. "She's been in the saddle practically since the day she was born. First thing I did when we brought her home from the hospital was to go for a ride, holding her in my arms. Ranching is in our blood, and I wanted her to know from day one that she was always safe with the horses."

What would it be like, guiding a child in the principles of ranching? Grace still hadn't told anyone about her baby, but William couldn't help thinking that it was a mistake for her to keep the news to herself for so long. Everyone here seemed to love children and included them in all areas of the ranch.

Sometimes he wondered about what it would have been like if he and Alexander had gotten to grow up here. But they had also had a very good life, a childhood with no complaints. Their parents had done everything they could to support the boys in their dreams.

Hunter handed William the halter and the rope. "Has anyone shown you how to catch a horse?"

Grace came around the corner and joined them. "I have. I told him he had to get comfortable with the tack and how to do everything on his own before he could ride."

She looked more pale than usual, and the dark circles under her eyes told him that she hadn't slept well. From the articles he'd read online about pregnancy, women were supposed to sleep better in the second trimester, but Grace confessed she wasn't sleeping well at all. Partially because of her upset stomach, but William also suspected it was because of the secret she was keeping from her family. He just wished she would come clean about it instead of being up all night worrying. It wasn't good for her, or the baby. But how was he supposed to convince her of that?

"Well," Hunter said. "Go get your horse."

It was unnerving, knowing that Grace and Hunter were watching him. He knew it was for his safety, but as he fumbled to tie the knot on the lead rope, it only made him more nervous he was doing something wrong.

Neither said anything as he led the horse out of its stall into the area where they saddled the horses. Hunter reached over and tugged at the knot. "That's some fine knot there," he said. "I haven't seen anyone go about it the way you do, though."

Grace grinned. "When Ricky saw him do it, he said it was just like the way Cinco did, on account of being left-handed."

William hadn't ever told anyone, but he used to be left-handed. Except his mom had thought there was something wrong with a left-handed child, or something like that, because she'd painstakingly taught him how to do everything with his right. Yet, when instinct took over, he always naturally switched to his left, like when playing baseball or other sports. Funny how as much as his mom had tried, she couldn't train the biology out of him. The thought both angered him and made him feel a strange sense of connection. It seemed that everything here did that. He felt an exquisite moment of belonging in realizing that doing things with his left hand was who he was, yet it also felt like it was somehow a betrayal of how he had been raised.

William saddled the horse, surprised at how much he remembered, noting that everyone's eyes weren't on him as intensely as they had been before. Grace had gone to get her horse, and Hunter had wandered off to talk to one of the other hands. Not having an audience made him relax slightly, and he finished saddling by the time Grace returned with her own horse.

She tied up her animal, then walked around to check William's work. "Really great job. You're a good student. But it's no surprise, considering—"

"Don't tell me. Because I'm Cinco's son."

He hadn't meant to sound as bitter as he had, but when the words came out, the expression on Grace's face told him he'd gone too far.

"That's not what I meant at all," she said. "What I was going to say, before you so rudely interrupted me, was that you have been picking up on everything rather quickly. You're a fast learner, and I was going to say it speaks to how much you care about everything around you, but you're so wrapped up in your resentment of Cinco that you don't always see clearly."

She turned and went back to her horse. From the way she busied herself with saddling it, it was clear she'd said all she wanted to say, and had no desire to further the conversation.

It was probably a good thing. Every time they tried to talk about his family and his feelings, especially how he felt so mixed about his mother's cheating, she grew quiet and distant.

Though he enjoyed the friendship they were developing, William often found himself frustrated because Grace didn't seem to understand where he was coming from on so many things. Yes, she had her share of romantic troubles, but did she know the pain of being cheated on? She'd never said so. And based on her reactions when he mentioned it in his own life, she didn't seem to have a clue as to how devastating infidelity could be. Not just because he'd been cheated on, but finding out the truth about his birth father, while it had explained so much in his life, had also created so many doubts.

When Grace finished saddling, they led the horses into the nearby indoor arena. The kids from the local riding organization were just arriving, getting ready for their own lesson.

William turned to Grace. "Are you putting me in the riding lesson with the kids?"

She shrugged. "Darby Dixon, who specializes in teaching equitation, is their guest teacher today. It'll be good for you to get a basic foundation of good equitation skills to begin with. It's easier to start out right than fix bad habits."

They led the horses into the arena, and Darby approached. He was everything William thought of when he thought about what the perfect cowboy would be like.

"Good to see you again, Grace," Darby said, giving her the kind of look that William imagined melted most women's hearts. He studied the man, trying to remember so that he could do the same.

"Nice to see you again. This is William, the one I was telling you about."

Darby gave him the kind of appraising look William was used to from all the cowboys. It was like they knew he didn't fit in, and that he was only playing at being someone he wasn't. At what point could he honestly say he was a cowboy?

Darby held his hand out to William. "Nice to meet you. My dad used to rodeo with Cinco, so it's funny how we're both carrying on the family tradition."

Family tradition? Was he kidding?

"This is the first I've ever been on a horse," William said.

Darby looked at him like he was crazy, but then inclined his head toward the horse. "All right, then. Get on up there."

As William put his foot in the stirrup to hoist himself into the saddle, he wasn't prepared for all of the emotions to hit him. What was he doing, thinking he could ride a horse like a real cowboy? But as he swung his leg up and over, then firmly planted himself in the saddle, all doubt and fear left him.

He'd never thought about how high up you were when sitting on top of a horse. The whole arena spread out before him, and he could see everything from a new angle. But it was about more than what he could see—this feeling of power and knowledge and strength came over him.

Something about this, just sitting on a horse, felt more right than anything else he had experienced here on the ranch.

"Look at you," Darby said. "Already looking like you were born to sit in the saddle. Now give Floofy here a little squeeze with your legs to go forward and join the rest of the class."

"Floofy?" William asked. "I thought Hunter was joking."

Darby chuckled. "That's what Hunter's little girl named the mare. I trained the horse and while it's not my first choice for a horse's name, it's what she's called."

They walked the horses to the middle of the arena, and William, Grace and all the kids formed a circle around Darby, who stood in the center.

As Darby explained what they were going to do, William felt more and more confident. The instructions sounded simple, and when they were directed to ride along the outside edge of the arena, William wondered why Alexander had had such a hard time learning to ride.

The hour-long lesson came to an end more quickly than William would have guessed. The easy rhythm of the horse felt natural to him, almost as if, to borrow an expression from the other cowboys, he was born in the saddle.

When they returned to the barn, Darby came with

them. As William was unsaddling, Darby asked, "Are you sure this was your first time on a horse?"

William shrugged. "My mom has some pictures of me and my brother on a pony ride at a fair, but other than that, yes."

He pulled the saddle off the horse and carried it to the tack room, where he placed it on a saddle stand. Darby followed.

"Me and some of the boys are getting together over at Joey Carter's place to do some practicing for the rodeo. Why don't you come on over? Try a few things. You probably wouldn't win anything at the rodeo, but I'm sure it would make Ricky happy to see one of his kin competing."

William hadn't expected such easy acceptance. An invitation? To learn how to be a real cowboy? He grinned.

"That would be great," he said. "If I'm going to be running a rodeo, it would be good for me to learn more about it. Even though Grace is the brains behind that part of the operation, it wouldn't hurt for me to have some knowledge, as well."

Darby slapped him on the back. "That's the spirit. Let me get your number and I'll text you the details."

The simple transaction made William want to laugh. He didn't know how he expected cowboys to communicate with one another, but it was funny that they, just like everyone else, texted each other the details.

After he and Darby made arrangements, Grace walked into the tack room, looking angry.

"What are you doing, lollygagging? You've got a horse to put up."

Feeling like a scolded child, William nodded. "I just need to get a towel to rub her down."

Grace didn't look impressed. She gestured at a cabinet on the other end of the room. "Towels are in there."

Her tone of annoyance bothered him. What had he done wrong? He'd done a great job at the lesson and was making friends with the riding instructor. Weren't those all good things?

He walked over to the cabinet and got the towel as indicated.

When he turned to go back out to his horse, both Darby and Grace were gone.

Probably for the best. He didn't want to be distracted by further conversation with Darby, which would have apparently annoyed Grace even more, and he really didn't want her to be mad at him.

He rubbed Floofy down with the towel, even though she really wasn't that sweaty. He felt her chest just like he'd been shown, but it didn't feel that warm. At least he didn't think so. What was too warm?

As Grace passed with her own horse, he said, "Wait. You told me not to put the horse back until she was cooled off properly. I rubbed her down with the towel, even though she wasn't that sweaty, and I felt her chest, but I don't know if it's too warm or not."

Grace's shoulders relaxed. "Sorry. I should have taken the time to explain more about it. We really didn't work the horses hard enough to make them break a sweat. I just wanted you to get in the habit of making sure they were properly cooled down before putting them away. Floofy is fine to go back."

She started to turn around, but he said, "Wait."

An exhausted look crossed her face. "What?"

"What's wrong with you all of a sudden? I'm trying to learn here, and you're acting like I've done something wrong. So if I messed up, tell me, don't just act like you're mad."

Grace tried not to sigh as she thought about William's words. She owed him an apology, but how was she supposed to explain why she was so mad?

"I'm sorry. You didn't do anything wrong," she said.

Her words didn't erase the confusion on his face. "Then why are you so snippy with me?"

She supposed she owed him an explanation, but it wasn't one he was going to like. Darby had just dangled one of William's dreams in front of him, but what was he going to do when he realized that it wasn't all it was cracked up to be?

"It's not you. It's Darby. He's a great instructor, don't get me wrong. But the crowd he hangs out with, the ones you just got invited to spend time with, they're bad news."

As expected, William just looked puzzled. "But they're rodeo people. Shouldn't I be spending time with them so I can learn about the rodeo?"

Grace shrugged. "I suppose. But you'd learn far more from Ricky or some of the other hands here.

Those guys are a bunch of jerks, and they're not the best examples."

She wanted to tell him that they were the reason she'd left Columbine Springs. Darby wasn't so bad, but she'd dated a couple of the other guys, and they were the reason she wished William would give up on his idea of being a cowboy and realize that a nice guy like him was exactly what the women around here needed.

"What do you mean by bad news?"

Grace shrugged. "Everyone has this romanticized view of what a cowboy is. The charming good manners, the skills, but there's also a dark side to a lot of these guys in the rodeo. So many of them are womanizers and drunks, including many of Darby's friends. I know you think you want to be a cowboy, but you don't want to be like them. If you really want an example, you should just spend more time with Ricky."

William nodded slowly. "I do spend time with Ricky. But he always says that I shouldn't waste all my time with an old codger like him. He keeps encouraging me to hang out with people my own age. And now you're telling me not to?"

The horses whinnied, as if to remind them that they still needed to be cared for.

"We need to get them put away," Grace said. "I know I don't have any right telling you what to do, but you wanted my help in learning how to be a cowboy. If you want to be the kind of cowboy like Stacy was bitterly complaining about at the Western wear store, then go ahead. Hang out with them. But if you want to know the truth, you'll only be worse off for doing so."

She turned to take her horse out to the corral where many of the other horses spent time, which was in the opposite direction of Floofy's stall. Grace was glad for the space between them, because she didn't want to keep arguing with William. His idealized vision of what women wanted was so messed up.

Sure, Darby was nice enough to look at, and had all the right words to charm a woman. The same with his friends. But they lacked the constancy of character that most of the women in her acquaintance so desperately needed. She didn't know how to explain that to William, to make him understand that he was enough. He'd just chosen the wrong woman to fall in love with.

As Grace let her horse out to pasture, she took a moment to draw the cold air into her lungs. Maybe she was wrong for warning William off. It wasn't like she was an expert on men or cowboys. All she knew was who to avoid.

Hunter walked up and stood next to her, watching the horses.

"I hear he did real good," he said.

"Darby thinks he's a natural," she said.

"You disagree?" he asked, turning to face her.

Grace shrugged. "I don't. He didn't even have to be told how to position his body, and yet he had a perfect seat. It was like he belongs there."

Hunter nodded. "That's what Darby said. So why do you sound so disappointed?"

Grace blew out a breath. "Did Darby also tell you that he invited William to join them for one of their rodeo practices?"

He kicked at the ground. "Yeah, I heard. He invited me, too."

Hunter used to hang out in that same crowd.

"I have a kid to think about," Hunter said. "You make different choices with your life once you become a parent. I used to get into some scrapes with those boys. But after I met Felicia, tried to settle down, that life didn't hold any appeal to me anymore. I thought being the family man was the answer, but who knew that what Felicia wanted was the wild cowboy?"

He shrugged, then continued. "I found the Lord, became a father, and none of that stuff mattered to me anymore. Sure, I'd love to go throw a rope with them. But I know the things that go with it, and that's not anything I can do, not when I'm raising a child on my own. Not when I'm held accountable to a higher power."

If only William could understand that.

"William thinks that his failure with women is because he is not like those guys. I've been trying to convince him otherwise. I know it's not my place, but he did ask me to help him be a cowboy. Do you think maybe you could offer to teach him some things so he isn't tempted to hang out with that crowd?"

Hunter nodded slowly. "I can try. But I don't know any more about keeping a woman than the next guy. I'm sure you've heard what happened with Felicia."

Grace put her hand on his arm. "I'd heard about her death, and I'm sorry. I should have reached out to you, but I was caught up in my own life."

He gave her a sad smile. "You did right by getting out. This place is so good, the land so rich in all the things I love. And while there are a lot of good people here, the old crowd wasn't healthy for either of us."

Grace nodded slowly. "I know. So how do we get William to see it?"

"Get William to see what?" William asked.

She hadn't seen him walking toward them. Hopefully he hadn't heard too much.

"That there is a lot more to being a cowboy than sitting pretty on a horse," Hunter said. "Grace and I were just reminiscing. We used to run with Darby and his crowd, and we were talking about how life takes us in different directions."

William looked confused, but Grace appreciated how Hunter had taken the heat off her.

"Anyway," Hunter continued. "I was just thinking it's been a while since I've swung a rope, since my priority has always been my family. Raising a little girl on my own, I haven't had a chance to do much roping. I'm too rusty to compete with the big boys, but I could teach you. We won't be winning any awards, but we could try it together."

His offer was an answer to a prayer Grace hadn't even known she'd uttered. Hunter used to be as wild as the wildest in that group, but becoming a husband and father had changed him. This was the kind of man William needed to emulate.

"Really?" William asked. "You have time for that? You always seem so busy—I don't want to bother you."

His statement proved to Grace exactly why he didn't belong with that other crowd. Not one of them would worry about being an imposition on anyone else's time or taking away from someone's job.

Hunter shrugged. "It's the excuse I keep making," he said. "But I'd be lying if I said I didn't miss roping and everything else about the rodeo. There's something about that adrenaline rush in those few seconds of chasing after a calf that you can't duplicate. It's not as exciting as bull riding, but that's never been my thing, and I suspect you're not willing to go that far, either."

William looked surprised at the idea, but then he laughed. "No, thank you. I've seen bull riding, and I'm not that stupid."

"Let's get you a rope and see what you can do."

To Grace's relief, William nodded. "That would be great, thanks."

No one mentioned anything about Darby or his offer, but Grace didn't want to bring it up. Maybe it was selfish of her, but she just couldn't bear the thought of seeing William turn into everything she didn't want. It was silly of her to even think about it, considering she had no interest in him.

Even if she was interested in William, she didn't have the luxury of being able to have that kind of feeling for someone. Not when she had a baby to think about. Being a mother had to be her first priority, and the last thing she needed was to be focused on anything else, especially on someone like William, whose quest to be a cowboy was moving him further and further away from what she needed in her life.

Chapter Five

William hadn't been at the rodeo practice for more than ten minutes before he knew he'd made a mistake. He should have listened to Grace when she'd told him they were a bad crowd. Darby was nowhere to be seen, and while there were a number of cowboys riding in the indoor arena, it seemed like the majority of the people were standing around a makeshift bar and chattering. He might be dressed like all of them, but he still didn't seem to fit in.

Stacy from the Western-wear store approached. "I wasn't expecting to see you here," she said.

He looked around the arena. "Darby said people were getting together to practice for the rodeo. I thought I'd see if I could pick up a few tips."

Stacy laughed. "It's the excuse everyone gives, but really, we just like to get together for a good party. Is Grace with you?"

William shook his head. "No. She advised me against coming, and I guess now I can see why."

"She always acted like she was too good for us." Stacy laughed again. "Then when Ralph broke her heart, she up and moved to the city."

Ralph? That was the first he'd ever heard of this guy. The woman must've sensed his confusion, because she gestured at a loudmouthed cowboy swinging a rope around.

"That's him. He's a real piece of work. He's broken just about every heart in the county. Including mine."

Then she laughed ruefully. "It wasn't her fault she fell for such a jerk. Pickings are slim around here, so I don't blame her for leaving town."

She waved at a lanky cowboy coming toward them. "That's Javier. He's new to the area, so I'm hoping to get to know him before any of the other gals sink their claws in him."

She made introductions, and before they were able to start a conversation, Hunter joined them.

"What are you doing here?" William asked. "I didn't think you were interested in coming."

Hunter shrugged. "I sometimes like to make an appearance to make sure none of our guys are misbehaving."

Then he looked over at Javier. "Javier Valdes? Is that you?"

Javier grinned. "Sure is. Do I know you?"

Hunter returned the wide smile. "No, but I know you. I watched you on TV at the PBR finals. That was an amazing ride on Little Annie."

Javier beamed. "Best ride of my life."

As Javier regaled them with the story of that ride,

William looked around again. The ladies here, while they seemed to be having a good time, weren't the sort William would want to spend time with. Maybe he was boring, but to him, a night out with friends involved having a good meal, maybe seeing a movie, and this crew seemed like they'd never left the college party scene.

Grace joined them.

"What are you doing here?" he asked.

"I thought I'd check things out and see what was going on."

The tension in her body told a different story. After her warning, and the expression on her face, it was clear she'd rather be anywhere but here.

"They don't have anything I can drink," Grace said, looking even more grumpy.

"It's okay," Hunter said. "I have some sodas in my truck."

"I can get it," William offered. "Why don't I get us all something?"

Hunter nodded. "There's a variety in there, so take what you want and bring me a root beer."

"I'll go with you," Grace said.

This would give them a chance to talk. And from the look on her face, she clearly wanted to. She didn't say anything until they got out by the truck.

"I can't believe you came," she said.

"You're here."

She glared at him. "Only to keep you out of trouble."

He stared at her for a minute. "What makes you think I need your help?"

"You don't know these guys like I do. Is the drinking and carousing in there what you want? You asked for my help in becoming a cowboy. I'm just trying to steer you in the right direction."

William shook his head. "No. I'll admit I was a bit taken aback by it. People talk about the good morals of cowboys, but—"

Grace sighed. "It all depends on the cowboy. Cowboys are just like everyone else. There are good ones and bad ones. This group happens to be full of the bad ones. Do you really want to be like the guy who stole your fiancée? He probably hangs out with a crowd just like this one. Just because a guy wears a cowboy hat doesn't make him any better or worse than anyone else. What matters is what's in his heart. If you want to learn about being the kind of man a woman wants, then get back to the ranch. You're not going to find what you're looking for here."

He opened the cooler in the back and noticed the ginger ale, which had become a staple in Grace's diet.

"It was nice of Hunter to bring some ginger ale for you. I guess people are noticing your drink choices," he said.

He grabbed the drinks for everyone and handed her the ginger ale. "I don't know why you haven't told your mom yet. She cares about you. Hasn't anyone questioned why you're drinking so much ginger ale?"

Grace shook her head. "I've always liked ginger

ale. I've tried to make sure nothing appears to be out of the ordinary."

She took a sip of her drink, and it brought back some of the color to her face.

"It has to be exhausting, being pregnant, but also having to lie to everyone."

She shrugged. "I haven't lied to anyone. I just haven't told them about the baby."

"It's kind of the same thing, don't you think? You're keeping the truth from the people who care about you. People who want to help you."

"That's some talk, coming from you. You want me to let people help me with my pregnancy. But here we are, trying to help you stay out of trouble, and you're walking in all bullheaded about it. You don't take advice any better than I do."

He held up his soda. "Does this look like I am walking into trouble? It's true, I didn't realize what was going to be happening here. But I can take care of myself."

They walked back toward the arena, and William could feel a new distance between them. They were just so different in what they wanted, and how they approached life. Clearly, Grace didn't understand the pain of having something important kept from her for so long.

He paused at the entrance to the barn. "Look," he said. "I know you're trying to look out for me, and I appreciate it. I hope you know I'm trying to look out for you, too. I missed out on so much of my life with family. I know you'll tell your mom about the baby before he or she is born. But think about all the moments in between she's going to miss out on experiencing with you. I don't mind helping you, like taking you to the baby doctor, but I feel bad because it's a special moment for you and your mom, and it would probably make her feel good to be part of it."

Grace sighed. "She'll spend her time fussing at me. If you don't want to come, just say so."

"I didn't say that at all," he said. "I'm honored that you asked me to be there for you. I don't mind making the drive to Denver."

He took off his hat and ran his fingers through his hair. "I wasn't trying to make you feel bad. Just like you're doing with me, I only want to help."

Her expression softened, and she sighed. "I know you're probably right, just like I think that deep down, you know I'm right. So maybe we give each other a little space to make the mistakes we need to make? Do you think we can do that and still be friends?"

Funny, he hadn't seen it that way before. "I've stuck by you this long, haven't I? I promised I wouldn't tell, and I've kept that promise. You can't blame a guy for attempting to help."

Grace laughed, and it struck him how pretty she was when she was smiling. He'd always thought her attractive, but laughing put a brightness into her eyes that made him wish things could be different between them.

But it was just a silly wish. He still didn't know how to be whatever it was women wanted, which meant even if he attempted to have a relationship with her, he couldn't guarantee that it would be successful. And he wasn't going to do that to her or her baby. Besides, Grace had way more to consider when trying to figure anything out in a relationship. Her focus, and rightly so, was on her coming baby.

As they entered the barn, Darby strolled toward them, a wide grin on his face. "You made it. And I see you managed to drag Hunter and Grace out with you, as well. Looks like everyone got the party started a little early, but some of the guys over there are setting up. Have you thought about what event you're going to do?"

William looked at Hunter. "Hunter was telling me about roping. I've seen it before, and if I could get the hang of the rope thing, I could probably give it a try."

Darby laughed and patted him on the back. "That's not a bad idea. Have you ever swung a rope?"

William shook his head. "No. Now that I say it out loud, it sounds like a stupid idea. I won't be as good as any of you guys."

As he watched the different cowboys practicing roping, like they'd been doing it their whole lives, William felt even more inadequate.

Who did he think he was kidding? He wasn't a cowboy.

Maybe Grace was right. Maybe he just didn't know where to find the kind of woman to fall in love with a nerdy financial planner.

But that was the thing no one seemed to understand. Women didn't want good guys like William. Even the lady from the shop had said she wanted a good dependable man but was carousing with cowboys who were anything but.

Truth be told, he didn't want that kind of woman, either. So where did that leave him? Not good enough for the kind of woman he wanted, and not wanting the kind of woman who seemed to be easy to get.

Darby handed him a rope. "I'll show you how it's done."

All thoughts of his romantic conundrum disappeared as Darby demonstrated how to hold the rope and how to use it. At first, it felt awkward in his hands, but after a few tries, it felt natural, like it was something he was supposed to be doing.

"Are you sure you've never done this before? You keep saying you're a beginner, but everything you do looks like you're a natural." Darby looked from him to Hunter. "You gave him lessons before he came here, didn't you?"

Hunter shook his head. "No. I told him we'd toss a few ropes around this week, but we had a problem with the herd, so I didn't have the chance."

Darby whistled. "That's some natural talent you've got there."

A sick feeling rose up in William's throat. Everyone was looking at him, and he knew what they were all thinking. He'd gained his talent from his dad.

"It was just a fluke," William said, turning away to look at Grace.

That was a mistake. She had stars in her eyes like she thought that he was rising up to claim his birthright. The thing was, he did kind of like playing with the rope. And as much as he was fighting the idea of being connected to the stranger who had given him life, there was a part of him that craved it.

What did this mean? Was he disloyal for feeling this way? And who was he being disloyal to? Even though he thought that these questions of loyalty were about his biological father and the man who raised him, the crazy thing was, what he really wanted was for Grace to keep looking at him like that.

Maybe that was the most bizarre thought of all. After all, he and Grace were just friends. Two people helping each other out in a time of mutual need. No, they were more than that. They were friends, people who had come to count on each other to navigate unfamiliar waters.

"I hate to do this to you," Hunter said. "But I just got a text from the ranch, and there's a situation I need to deal with. You don't mind taking Grace home, do you?"

William looked over at Grace, who wore the same look of fatigue that she did at the end of a long day. She should be home resting, not babysitting him on an ill-conceived outing.

"You go on ahead," William said. "We won't be too far behind."

Hunter nodded, then turned away. "Thanks. This is why I don't usually get out. It seems I'm not gone very long when a crisis happens."

He turned away before anyone could answer.

"We don't have to leave early on my account," Grace said.

William glanced at the makeshift bar area. The laughter that rang out told him that whatever antics the rest of the crew were getting into weren't anything he wanted to be part of.

"No, it's fine. I was just thinking we should leave before things got too crazy."

Darby took his hat off and scratched his head. "Crazy? Things are just getting started."

As much as he hated to admit it, Darby's words kind of proved William's point.

William held a hand out to Darby. "Thank you all the same. But it's not really my kind of scene. I guess I was expecting a little more rodeoing and a lot less partying. It doesn't seem very safe to me for all this to be going on."

Darby shrugged. "We look out for each other," he said. "But I can see why you spend so much time with Gracie. She used to be fun."

"We just have different definitions of fun, that's all," she said.

"Whatever floats your boat," Darby said as he walked away.

Grace sighed. "We used to all be friends. But a lot of them stopped going to church and started making bad choices."

They started walking toward his car, and a group of giggling cowgirls walked by, but not before checking him out. They were pretty enough, but he didn't need to have a conversation with them to know they weren't his type.

"I went to school with them," Grace said. "I could introduce you."

William shook his head. "I was just thinking that they're not my type."

"What is your type?" Grace asked.

Good question. He liked Grace. She was pretty, but not the sort of pretty that made a woman spend hours in the bathroom. He should know. He'd spent enough time with her lately. Half the time, when he was picking her up to start their day working on the rodeo, she looked like she'd just barely dragged herself out of bed. As far as he was concerned, women didn't need all that makeup and junk. When he and Hailey were dating, he'd always thought she looked prettier without. But when he told her that, she'd said that he didn't know what he was talking about. Maybe he didn't.

But it wasn't just looks he was interested in. Sure, he wanted to find someone he found attractive, but to him, the more attractive parts of a woman were things like her smile, her eyes when they lit up and a good laugh.

"Someone who's easy to be with," he said. "In the beginning, that was Hailey and me. We did a lot of fun stuff together, and she said I was a good listener. That's what a lot of people I've dated have said about me. I like listening. But that seems to put me more in the friend zone."

They got into the car, and Grace didn't say anything until they'd hit the road, but then she said, "I wish Jack had been a good listener. The more I think about it, the more I realize he never really listened to me at all. I'm finding it harder and harder to remember what I saw in him in the first place."

"As you've figured out, I'm not exactly an expert," he said. "But it seems to me that if you care about someone, you would want to hear what they had to say. Maybe I cared too much. I always listened, but like you, I'm realizing that no one ever listened to me."

Grace was quiet for a moment, then she said, "Funny, that's exactly how my relationships have been. You talk and you talk, but then you realize that maybe you don't see things the same. One of you is more invested in the relationship than the other, but I honestly don't know how to tell when that is happening."

Then she sighed. "I guess that's the good thing about being pregnant. Rather than jumping into another relationship, I have the time and space to figure out what's really important to me. And I won't be choosing the next person I date based on just my own ideas, but also on what's best for my baby."

Her logic made sense. Maybe that's what he needed to look at before he thought about having another relationship. Except that was kind of what he was doing. Trying to be the kind of man a woman wanted. Still, if he'd learned anything this evening, it was the kind of woman he didn't want and the kind of man he didn't want to be.

So where were the people he wanted in his life?

"You seem to get uncomfortable when I talk about

church, but I'll be honest. My bad choices started when I stopped focusing on my faith. What I need, and what my baby needs, are the kind of people I find there."

She gave him a sad smile. "You said you wanted to be a cowboy because you wanted to be the kind of man a woman wanted. I don't know any better cowboys than the ones at Columbine Springs community church. Maybe, instead of spending your time with these yahoos, you should think about coming to church with us on Sunday."

Both Alexander and Ricky had invited him to attend multiple times since William's arrival. But William didn't see the appeal.

Then again, Alexander had started going to church, and he had to admit that while there had been some changes in his brother, they had all been changes for the good. Would it be so bad for William to give it a try?

"All right," he said. "I'll come."

Grace looked around the church, seeing the families with babies and the joy they all had. It brought tears to her eyes as she realized that in just a few months, she would be here with her baby. Though she knew in her heart that William was right and everyone would be too happy at having someone to love to worry much about Grace's circumstances, she also wasn't naive enough to think that getting to that point would be easy.

But they were just at the beginning of January,

and the New Year made her feel more hopeful about the future. She just had to find a way to tell everyone about that future.

William sat in the pew next to her. "I tried to dress like I see Ricky and Alexander on Sundays, but I feel out of place. Like everyone is staring at me."

Grace laughed. "They kind of are. Most people know by now that Alexander has a twin brother, but they haven't seen you in church before. They're curious and want to get to know you."

"And probably figure out why I'm not a church-goer and try to convert me," he said.

The bitterness in his voice made her wonder if they'd been pushing too hard, trying to get him to go to church.

"I hope you don't feel too pressured," she said. "I don't think that's anyone's intention. But we do care about you, and our faith is very important to us. As for everyone here speculating about whether or not you are a churchgoer, since you're here with us, they're going to assume that we've already been talking to you about God. So don't be nervous in getting to know anyone. Most of them just want to know more about you and to be your friend."

He relaxed slightly, and as she thought about her words to him, she wondered if maybe she needed to give herself a break, as well. Every single one of the people in this room considered children a gift. She glanced over at Janie, Alexander's fiancée, sitting in the next pew. As the pastor's daughter, she'd received a few sidelong glances at her unexpected pregnancy years ago, but now, her son, Sam, was a valued member of the community. Could Grace be overthinking the whole thing?

That seemed to be the message God was giving her, since Pastor Roberts's sermon was all about grace, and how God freely forgave everyone of their sins. She'd already spoken to God about her sin, already asked for His forgiveness. And if God so freely gave it as they learned in the Bible, perhaps it was time for Grace to accept that the members of her community would do the same for her.

Funny how her mother had given her the name specifically because she wanted her daughter to always remember that God's grace was free.

By the time the sermon ended, William looked a lot less ready to bolt and more comfortable. As everyone else was filing out of the pews, William remained seated.

"Everything all right?" she asked.

"Yeah," he said. "I guess I never heard God being talked about like that. I always thought you had to live by a bunch of rules and if you broke them, God would be mad at you."

Grace nodded slowly. "He is, in a way. He's disappointed that you made a bad choice, but it never keeps Him from loving you or makes Him love you any less."

"So why be good then?"

She could tell his question wasn't so much about challenging her as it was trying to understand.

"Why do you obey your parents? Even as an adult,

why do you care what they think, or try to please them?"

"That's simple," he said. "I love them. I respect them. I want to make them happy."

"That's what God wants from us, and why we obey Him."

He looked thoughtful for a moment. "If that's what you believe, then why do you refuse to tell your mother about the baby?"

It was like he'd been in her head the entire service, wrestling with the realities of her life and her faith.

"Because I don't want to see the look of disappointment on her face," she said.

"I get that," he said. "I guess it's easier with God, because you can't see the look on His face. You just know in your heart that you haven't been living the right way."

Grace shrugged. "Probably. How do you know about that knowing in your heart?"

"Partially because of what the pastor said today, but also because I've connected the dots about what he said and times in my life when I've done the wrong thing. The truth is, I knew there were things in my relationship with Hailey that weren't right. Times when I compromised what I thought was the right thing because I thought it would make her happy. But it seemed dumb, so I ignored that feeling. Now I'm wondering if it was God."

He could have been talking about her and all the times she'd compromised her faith with Jack. "I know exactly how that feels. It's how I ended up pregnant and alone."

"Do you think God would have been talking to me, even though I didn't have a relationship with Him?"

Grace nodded. "Of course. We are all God's people, and He loves us all, whether we love Him back or not. He wants us to love Him, but He's not going to make us do so. Maybe that was my mistake. I thought if I did all the things Jack wanted me to, I could make him love me the way I loved him."

"We all do it," he said. "Your words made me realize that's exactly what I did with Hailey. Have done in all my relationships. I thought if I could do all the right things, be the right man, then I would be worthy of the love of a good woman."

William looked up at the side area where Pastor Roberts often counseled people after the service. "I think I'm going to go talk to the pastor about that whole accepting Christ thing. I don't know if I'm ready to commit to being a Christian or not, but I'd be interested to read the literature he says he's got."

"Do you want me to come with you?" she asked.

He shook his head. "I appreciate your friendship and the wise counsel you've given me. But I think I need my relationship with God to be about me and God, and I have to do this on my own."

She patted his arm gently. "I understand completely. Just know that if you ever need someone to talk to, I'm here."

The smile he gave her did a funny thing to her insides. "I know. You've become a valuable part of my life. But I also know that you have more important things to think about. I don't want to be a distraction from you doing what you need for your future."

He nodded in the direction of her stomach, so she knew what he meant without saying it and risking being overheard. It was sweet the way he brought things back to the baby, and were she looking for a relationship, a man like William was exactly what she'd be looking for. She needed someone who could put her values first, put the baby first.

But as he got up and walked over to the pastor, she knew that it was for the best that William was choosing to take his spiritual journey without her.

And yet, the thought of not being part of this place in his life made her heart ache in a funny way she hadn't expected.

What was wrong with her?

Maybe this whole emotional connection, especially with a man, was a side effect of the pregnancy. That internal longing to have a father for her baby.

When she got up, Janie greeted her warmly. "How are you doing? It looked like you and William were having a pretty intense conversation."

She looked over at where William was now talking to Janie's father. "I think William is starting to be more open to the idea of faith. I don't want to say much more, because I don't know how much of that he intended to be confidential, but I'm sure your father will be able to point him in the right direction."

Janie grinned. "He definitely did for Alexander. But don't discount the influence you have. The only reason my father was able to get through to Alexander and help him understand God's love was because of my relationship with him. The opening was created in William's heart because he sees God's love in you."

Grace tried not to groan, but she apparently failed, because the look on Janie's face told her that she caught it.

"My dad doesn't have any special powers for making people believe in Jesus. We all have the obligation to live a Christlike life, and through us, people understand God's love."

Unfortunately, that was the last thing Grace needed to hear. "Trust me, I have been anything but Christlike to William. In the time we've spent together, he has seen all my flaws."

Janie examined her face, like she was trying to figure some things out. "Are you involved with William in more than a friendship?"

The way she stumbled over the words, Grace knew exactly what Janie was getting at. And it was definitely not the impression she wanted to give. "No, nothing like that," she said quickly. "We're just friends, that's all. I'm just saying that he knows I'm not perfect, and I know I don't have to be, but I feel like I'm a terrible example of a good Christian."

Janie shrugged. "None of us are a perfect example. That's kind of the point. People need to know that we aren't perfect, and that God loves us anyway, because that's what we all need to know. Trust me, I've needed that reminder often enough."

Grace looked over at the church entrance, where

Alexander was walking in, holding hands with Sam. "I guess you did make your share of mistakes."

"And I don't regret it for a minute," Janie said. "Look, I know that I sinned along the way. But I consider Sam a sign from God that though I make mistakes, He chooses to bless me anyway."

Peace washed over Grace at Janie's words. Part of her had felt guilty for the deep love she felt for this baby knowing the mistakes she'd made in getting here. But when Sam leaped into Janie's arms, Grace had absolutely no doubt that her baby was a precious gift indeed.

"Mom! Look what I made," Sam said, thrusting a paper into Janie's face.

"We're having an adult conversation here," she said, laughing.

"It's okay," Grace said. "We were just finishing up."

Alexander gestured at William still talking to Pastor Roberts. "Everything okay there?"

Grace nodded. "He had some questions about God. I don't want to overstep or violate any implied confidence, so you can ask him about it later."

Alexander nodded slowly. "I will. Thanks. You've been good for him. Before coming here, William was so angry and bitter about the situation with our parents. I wasn't happy about it, but the more time I've been at the Double R, the more I've come to understand that what we all thought of as a terrible tragedy has actually been an incredible blessing."

How many times did she need to hear something

to that effect? It was like God kept pounding that answer home.

"We should get out of here," Janie said. "Other than William talking to my dad, everyone else is cleared out. I understand your mom is making fried chicken for dinner tonight."

Grace's stomach automatically twisted at the thought. Fried foods hadn't been sitting well with her lately, but at least there would be mashed potatoes. She always sat next to William so he could help her out. Their system had been working out beautifully, and so far, no one, not even her mother, had questioned what Grace did or didn't eat.

As they walked out of church, Grace's mom met them in the parking lot. "Good," she said. "You're still here. I didn't mean to take so long, but I was talking to Jennifer Evans, whose daughter is pregnant again. You'd think she would have learned her lesson the first time she got pregnant by that no-account boyfriend of hers. Whatever happened to waiting until you got married?"

Then Wanda stopped. "I'm sorry, Janie. That wasn't a slight against you. You've done very well for yourself on your own, but I worry about girls these days."

All the hope Grace had been feeling disappeared. No, she wasn't ready to tell her mother about the baby.

"She's doing the best she can," Janie said. "It's easy to look at Cindy and think you know what's best. But having been down that road, I can honestly say that what Cindy needs more than anything right now is for all of us to come around her and love her."

Grace liked that Janie knew Jennifer's daughter's name, but more important, that Janie spoke of supporting her. It wasn't going to be pretty, but it was good to remember Grace would still have an ally in this fight.

Chapter Six

William left the church, feeling more hopeful than he had in a long time.

His heart felt a little lighter as he spied Alexander and Janie talking with Grace and Wanda. Funny how in such a short period of time his life had become so completely different. When he'd first come to Columbine Springs, he hadn't understood the change in Alexander, but now he did.

However, as he approached the group, his heart sank.

"I'm just saying that a child needs a father to be around. Grace's dad died when she was so young, and I know the difficulty of trying to do it on your own. I'm incredibly grateful for the fact that I had all the people at the Double R and their help. I wouldn't have been able to do it without them."

"And for someone like Cindy, don't you think the importance of having a community helping her with her unplanned pregnancy is exactly what she needs?"

Oh no. Based on the conversation, and the expression on Grace's face, all the hope William had had of Grace finally coming clean to her mother was now gone.

Wanda sighed. "I understand what you're saying, but it's been a while since you've been home. Still, I shouldn't have been gossiping. Why don't we head on home, and we can have a light lunch to hold us over until dinner?"

William knew the look on Grace's face. Not only was she annoyed with her mother, but food wasn't sounding good to her right now.

"Do we have to eat right away?" William asked. "Grace said we could go riding again today after church, and with the way the clouds are looking, I'm not sure we'll get a better chance later."

He gestured at the mountains, where a storm was obviously rolling in. Wanda scowled. "If it moves in too fast, you'll get caught out there and catch your death."

Grace groaned. "We have time for a quick ride. The wind isn't blowing that hard, in fact, there's barely a breeze. There's enough time to do a loop around the lake."

"Ricky says it's the prettiest place on the ranch," William said. "We've been too busy to go that route, so if there's time, I'd sure appreciate getting the chance to see where Ricky proposed to my grandmother."

The relief on Grace's face was evident. William didn't understand why, if her mother cared about her so much, she couldn't read her daughter this well. Maybe she just accepted it as fact that Grace would go along with whatever she wanted. He knew Wanda loved her daughter, but she seemed clueless when it came to deciphering Grace's emotions.

"That sounds like an excellent idea," Ricky said, joining them. "I can't tell you how much it means to me that my grandkids are taking such an interest in the place. It almost makes me regret putting it into a trust that will keep it from ever being theirs."

William hated it when Ricky reminded them of the inheritance or lack thereof. "That's not what I care about, and you know it," he said. "I wish you'd stop bringing it up."

Ricky scowled. "That land is in your blood. It's a part of us. You can't deny your heritage."

William felt Grace's hand on his arm, like she was asking him to go easy on Ricky. He had no intention of hurting the older man. But Ricky didn't seem to understand that William was still coming to grips with all this. On one hand, he did like knowing where he came from. Yet he thought of his dad, who was probably sitting at home, watching whatever game was on TV, and William wished that all this family connection didn't feel so disloyal to the man who had raised him. Everyone kept saying that it didn't change the fact that Bill Bennett was his dad, and William didn't disagree. After all, William had just accepted Christ, and the person he most wanted to talk to was his dad.

Did that make everything else here okay?

He didn't know. But it didn't make the sick feeling in his stomach, like when he was a kid and had done something wrong, go away.

"The longer we stand here talking, the less time we have for riding," Grace said. "Anyone want to join us?"

"With the storm coming in, I have to check with Hunter to make sure our stock are taken care of," Ricky said. "But I sure would like to spend some time in the saddle with my grandson one of these days."

The wistful tone in Ricky's voice only made William feel more guilty. He was making an old man's dream come true, so why didn't it feel good to him?

"I know you came to church with Ricky," Grace said. "But why don't you ride home with me so we can go straight to the barn?"

"Good idea," William said. Then he turned and smiled at Wanda. "I hope you have some extra mashed potatoes to go with the chicken you're making."

Wanda beamed. "And some pumpkin pie, too. Your mom said you don't like it much, but don't think I haven't noticed the way you eat it up."

William's stomach churned. He hadn't liked the pumpkin pie any of the other million times Wanda had served it to him with a smile. But it sure did ease Grace's upset stomach. People said pregnancy was supposed to agree with people, but Grace only seemed to look thinner and more tired. He'd been watching her stomach for signs of the baby bump, even though it was probably rude to do so. At some point her pregnancy was going to start showing, and then how she was she going to explain it?

He examined her for signs of fatigue as they got in her car. He'd been trying to encourage her to take care of herself, but he didn't want to sound too much like her mother. And yet, he wondered how the baby was doing. He supposed they'd find out later in the week when he took her to the doctor.

Grace slumped against the back of her seat when they got into the car.

"I can drive if you want to rest," William said. "And we don't have to go on a ride if you don't want to."

Grace turned her head and smiled at him softly. "I have been looking forward to going for a ride all week. Just being out in the fresh air on a horse, enjoying nature. Do not take that away from me."

"I wouldn't dream of it," he said. "But I'm happy to drive back if you need some rest."

"I've noticed that I don't feel as sick if I'm driving as opposed to being the passenger. My stomach has been really off today, so even though I appreciate the offer, I'd prefer to drive."

William gave her a smile. "I'm trying not to be too overbearing, because I know you don't like to be coddled. But I'm not just looking out for you, I'm also looking out for the baby."

The sweet smile she gave him made his heart melt. "I know, and I appreciate it. It's nice to know that me and the baby have someone looking out for us."

"Despite what your mom said out there," he observed, "I think you'll find that everyone is going to be just as supportive and loving to your baby. I just can't wait till it's out in the open so I can stop pretending to like pumpkin pie."

Grace giggled. "You have no idea how much that means to me. It seems like that's one of the few things I can keep down that actually tastes good. I wouldn't be surprised if instead of a baby, a pumpkin came out."

She laughed and William laughed with her. "Maybe that's what we should call the baby. Pumpkin," he said.

"I kind of like the sound of that," she said. "After all, Pumpkin is a term of endearment. And I do love this baby."

She cradled her stomach as she often did when she thought no one was looking, but William had to admit that even though it wasn't his, he loved the baby, too.

"Pumpkin it is," he said. Then he paused for a moment, trying to think through his words. "I hope you don't mind that I'm so involved. I know it's not my baby, but with everything we've been through together, I feel like I'm a part of his or her life. And you did ask for my help. Which reminds me, I went through your finances, to keep up my end of the bargain, and I think there are a few places where you could do better with your money. I know you said your retirement plan wasn't that big, but there is a decent chunk of money in it, and it's not invested in the best funds. I have a few ideas for you to maximize it if you're interested."

She nodded slowly, and he knew her next question was going to be about a college fund for the baby.

"I know you wanted me to move some of the money into an account for Pumpkin's college fund," William said. "But I think that's a mistake a lot of people make, sacrificing their retirement for their children's college. There is a way you can do both, but I think right now, it's best that you leave the money you have in a retirement account, and we can find alternative ways to fund Pumpkin's college. In fact, I'm opening college accounts for Sam and Katie. Partially because it's a good tax break for me, but also because it seems like a good uncle thing to do."

"I asked you for help with my finances, not a handout," Grace said.

"I know," William said. "I thought about doing it as a surprise after the baby was born, but since I knew you might not like the idea, I thought I would let you know up front. Secrets are more harmful than helpful, and I don't want to hide anything from you. The thing I love the most about our relationship is how open and honest we are with each other. You're a good friend, and it feels right to me to do this."

They pulled up to a parking spot in front of the barn, and Grace rested a moment, her eyes closed, like she was thinking about his words.

"It's like with me and the ranch," William said. "I didn't come here asking for any of this. I didn't need another grandfather. Don't need connection—"

He caught himself in the lie before it came out. "I guess that's not true. I didn't think I needed the connection. It just leaves so much unresolved in my heart. I always thought my mom was Christian, and if you ask her, she says she is. But how could she have had a relationship with a married man while still being married, and then hide the fact that my brother and I were the result of it? Everything she always taught us about morality, she said one thing, but she did another."

Grace turned to look at him. "Do you think maybe you're being too hard on her? Her affair was a long time ago. I can't say for sure what the state of her faith is. That's personal between her and God. But the Bible says that if you repent of your sins and ask for forgiveness, then you are forgiven. And if that's the case, then none of us has any right to hold those sins against her."

The passion in her voice almost made him feel bad for bringing it up. "But what if those sins hurt someone else? At what point do you get a pass for causing harm to someone else?"

She gave him a hard look. "And just how have you been harmed? Sure, you found out that something you always believed to be true wasn't. But it's not like you had a bad life. It's not like Ricky is a bad person. So many good things have come out of this bad thing coming to light, so maybe instead of thinking of that one bad thing, you should take the time to stop and count the many blessings that have come from it. Right now, I consider you a great blessing in my life, which would have never happened had you not come to the ranch. Has anyone told you the story of Joseph being sold into slavery by his brothers?"

The intensity in her voice made him realize he'd touched a nerve. He hadn't meant to upset her.

"Yes," he said. "Alexander told me that it was one of the first stories Janie told him when they met, and that he considers it a metaphor for their relationship, that things meant for harm were brought about to bring good. I guess maybe you're right. I have been thinking more about the harm than the good. So how do I change that?"

She reached over and gave his arm a gentle squeeze. "You can start by counting your blessings. Think about all the good things that have happened in your life since coming here and thank God for them."

Grace was definitely one of the blessings. He couldn't imagine life without her. When Hailey had broken up with him, he didn't know how to move forward. And now, everything about that situation seemed like a bad dream from so long ago he couldn't even remember why it had upset him. Factually, he knew, but it had been weeks since he'd felt any pain in his heart.

Maybe Grace was right. Maybe it was time for him to let go of his resentment and instead see the blessings. After all, today the pastor had told him he was a new creation in Christ. And starting today, he was going to embrace that newness and enjoy the many blessings he had received.

Getting out on the horses was exactly what Grace had needed. As much as she had dreamed of moving to the city growing up, all this proved that Grace was a country girl at heart and here on the ranch was where she felt most at home. She eased JJ to a stop at the overlook above the lake.

"This is where Ricky proposed to Rosie, your grandmother. She died when I was too little to remember her, but both Ricky and my mother speak highly of her. Ricky loved her so much that he never remarried."

William stopped his horse next to her. You would have never known that he hadn't been riding very long. True, Floofy was a gentle enough horse that even a child could ride her, but even the best horse could be unpredictable and difficult to manage, especially if they knew their rider was new.

"How do you find a love like that?" William asked. "His face still lights up when he talks about her, almost as if she's still with him."

"You're asking the wrong person," she said. "I thought that's what I had with Jack. The trouble is, I think sometimes we want so badly to be in love that we miss the signs of what it actually means. To be honest, I'm afraid to date again, but the thought of spending the rest of my life alone like my mom did after my dad died, and Ricky after losing Rosie… I never had a strong enough love that could sustain me like that."

She gently caressed her stomach. "I suppose my baby will be that for me. My mom used to say that she never remarried because she didn't want anything to take away from the love she had to give to me. But sometimes I wish she did have someone else to love. It's an awful lot of pressure to be all she has."

"She'll have Pumpkin now, too," he said. "I know it was hard to hear what she said after church today, but I have to believe that once it's your baby, she'll see things differently. And who knows, maybe she'll even be more sympathetic to that other woman."

Grace tried not to sigh with discouragement. "Maybe," she said. "But I've always felt like she held the bar so high for me and I could never measure up."

"But the longer you keep it a secret from her, the more she's going to be upset that you didn't trust her enough. I know you think you're protecting her, and yourself, by not telling her the truth, but trust me, the longer you keep it a secret, the longer you eat away at the trust in your relationship."

He patted his horse gently. "One of the first things you told me about riding was that you had to earn the horse's trust, and that it takes time. If you do something to violate the trust with the horse, it's something the horse will never forget. I think human relationships are a lot like that."

Though she knew he was talking about her relationship with her mom, and his with his mom, she couldn't help thinking of the secret she kept from him about the fact that Jack was married. William was so bitter about cheating and cheaters and she couldn't bear the thought of his disappointment in her. They had such a good relationship, and she couldn't stomach the idea of him looking at her the way she sometimes looked at his mother. At least this was one secret he would never have to know. Jack had made it abundantly clear that he never wanted her to contact him again. He also made it clear he didn't want anything to do with her baby.

But as she looked at the deep expression on William's face as he stared out over the ranch, she couldn't imagine that explaining any of this to him would be so simple. She still hadn't found a way to come to terms with it in her own heart, let alone explain it to someone who was already predisposed to thinking the worst of her for it.

Why she cared so much about what William thought of her, she didn't know, except that he knew most of her shortcomings, and didn't think less of her for it. Was it so wrong to not want that to change?

"I'll tell her when the time is right," Grace said. "Maybe after my doctor's appointment so I can reassure her that everything is okay with the baby."

He gave a quick jerk of his head as he always did when she told him that, like he didn't like her answer but would accept it anyway.

The wind picked up a little bit, and a few stray flakes hit her face.

"We better head back," she said. The second my mom sees these snowflakes she's going to get worried."

"She worries because she loves you," he said.

She turned JJ and squeezed her legs against the horse's middle, and with the click of her tongue, brought her into a trot. Maybe it was a bit of a cop-out to ride too fast for conversation, but she couldn't give William the answers he wanted, and the more they talked, the more her secrets weighed on her. They said the truth would set you free, but no one had told her just how hard it would be to share that truth.

As they came around the bend of the lake, the snow picked up, and what had been just a few flakes were now furiously flying flurries.

She turned to William. "I know a shortcut," she said. "Follow me."

She turned her horse toward the old cow trail, which used to be the main route the Double R used to get the cattle from the winter pasture to the summer pasture. Now, with the land used differently, they took a different route, and the old trail was seldom traveled except for a few brave riders and the occasional summer hiker. It wasn't as pretty of a trail as the rest on the ranch, but it was efficient, and that's what mattered right now.

Even though she picked up her pace slightly, she could see that William was still keeping up, and didn't appear to be struggling. Another sign of six generations of horsemanship in his genes.

She wished he wasn't so bitter about the situation. Especially because she was painfully aware that at some point, Pumpkin would want to know about his or her father. And what was Grace supposed to do then? Would Pumpkin and his or her siblings harbor the same resentment? Grace hadn't been the one to lie, but it didn't make her life any easier. Even though she hadn't spent much time talking to William's mom, Grace felt a kinship with the woman who'd likely had to make some difficult choices and had done the best she could in a bad situation.

Why couldn't William see that? If he was so unsympathetic to his mom, Grace couldn't imagine he'd be very kind to her. Maybe in time, she'd figure out the best way to reveal the truth about Pumpkin's father.

Another strong gust of wind hit, sending a chill down Grace's spine.

"Are you okay to pick up the pace?" she asked. "If the snow starts sticking, the trail will be slick, so I'd like to make up as much time as we can."

William nodded. "I've loped on her before. I've been hoping to do so on this ride, but I wanted to take it easy on you."

"Well, you got your wish." She made a kissing noise to urge her horse on faster, and with a gentle squeeze of her legs, they were off. She glanced over at William, whose wide grin reminded her that this was exactly where he belonged. Maybe someday he would realize what a beautiful gift being part of the Double R was.

Halfway down the trail, a fallen tree blocked their path. Grace urged her horse to jump as naturally as she always had, but as soon as the horse landed, she realized William had likely never done this before. But when she looked over at him, he, too, had just finished the jump, and was grinning broadly.

"What a rush," he said. "Wow. I know that was an accident, but you've gotta teach me how to do that again."

The joy on his face was evident, and she hoped that at the end of the day, he would count this as one of his many new blessings.

As much as she hadn't wanted to come home, and in some ways had seen it as a sign of her failure, being back in the land she loved, she knew now without a doubt that this was where she belonged. The ranch was the perfect place for Pumpkin to grow up.

Pumpkin. Funny that William had been the one to come up with her baby's name. Okay, so she wasn't going to literally name him or her Pumpkin. But she was pretty sure that was the nickname her baby would grow up with.

When they got to the clearing, Grace realized the flaw in her plan. While they no longer used the trail to get the cows to this pasture, this was still their winter home.

Though the horses were trained to be around cattle, in this weather, under these conditions and with an inexperienced rider like William, anything could happen. Grace slowed her horse to a walk, then stopped to open the gate. "Stay close," she said. "And keep an eye on your horse. It's amazing the weird things that will spook them."

William nodded. "Hunter has told me the same thing many times. But I appreciate the reminder."

She kept them to the outer edge, away from the cows. And even though cows usually stayed away from the horse and rider, they also weren't known to be the smartest of creatures.

In the distance, she could see Ricky and his crew

on their ATVs, spreading the hay. Unfortunately, her horse must've noticed it, too, because she pricked her ears and started in that direction.

Grace tugged on the reins and, with a kick, directed her back in the right direction. Only the stupid mare, with her eyes and nose on food, didn't comply. She started to take off, and Grace had to fight with her to keep her in check. As much as she hated to admit it, she wished she'd asked for an easier mount. But that would have made people suspicious about why she wanted one, and...

William had no idea how hard it was to keep all this a secret. All the things she couldn't say or do. But she also wasn't ready to deal with their disappointment.

She turned to William. "Keep as close to the fence line as you can. My horse is trying to take off on me, and if she does, don't follow. You stick to the fence. It will get you back home. I'll be fine."

William stared at her. "If she takes off with you, I'm going to follow to make sure you're okay."

Now was not the time for him to argue. "If she takes off, only an expert rider can stay with me. Please. Do as I ask."

William looked like he was going to disagree, but it was taking all of her energy to fight the horse, not the man. Later, she'd talk to him about safety and following instructions. For now, she had to get her horse under control.

It was as if JJ knew Grace was momentarily distracted with her thoughts about William and his safety, because she took full advantage. She broke into a full-out run, and none of Grace's usual tricks were getting her to obey. Though Grace was trying to focus on her horse, she could hear William keeping pace behind.

At that same moment, Grace's horse hit a small dip in the paddock, and before she even knew what was happening, Grace hit the ground with a thud.

"Are you okay?" William asked, jumping off his horse.

She tried to take a couple of breaths to calm herself, but it was hard. She'd definitely had the wind knocked out of her. As she mentally scanned her body, it didn't feel like anything was injured. But she knew better than to rely on that initial instinct.

Pumpkin fluttered inside her, and the gentle kick was like all the normal ones she'd been feeling. The baby articles she read online all said that if the baby was moving normally, the baby was fine.

Thank You, Lord, that my baby is okay.

She'd lie here a minute to catch her breath. But at least this gave her the perfect opportunity to talk to William.

"You just couldn't listen, could you?" Grace asked. "I'll be fine. Make sure the horses don't run off."

"Too late," William said, kneeling beside her. He paused, looked over to where the horses must've gone, then said, "but it's okay. Some of the guys on the ATVs must've seen what happened, because a couple of them are going after the horses, and a couple more are headed our way."

Great. Just what she needed. Of course she'd have to fall with a bunch of cowboy witnesses. They would never let her live it down.

"Tell them I'm fine. I just need to lie here a minute and get my bearings. Even though you see them do it all the time at the rodeo, in real life when you fall, as long as you are safe, you need to be still for a few minutes to make sure the adrenaline wears off. Oftentimes, when you're hurt, you don't notice because the adrenaline is so strong. Now, if you were in a rodeo, you'd want to get up and get out of there as fast as you can."

She was rambling, but she had to keep her wits about her to keep from crying. This wasn't how she planned this ride to go. And she sure wasn't going to cry in front of any of Ricky's hands.

"I should check for injuries," William said. "Except I don't know anything about first aid. I wish I had cell service, because I would look it up on the internet."

"I told you, I'm fine," she said. "I just need a minute."

But so that everyone else coming to her rescue would realize she was okay, Grace turned to roll onto her side so she could sit up, and felt a twinge of pain on her side. Pumpkin? Grace took a deep breath. She looked where she'd been lying and saw the rock she'd landed on. She'd be black-and-blue for sure, but it wasn't anywhere that would impact the baby.

At least she hoped.

Please, God. I want Pumpkin to be okay.

She was pretty sure everything was fine. But some extra prayers wouldn't hurt. She groaned as she scooted away from the rock so she wouldn't sit on it.

William said, "You're not okay. You're hurt."

Grace finished sitting up, gritting her teeth at the pain. "Just bruised. I'll be fine."

The roar of an ATV approaching told her she'd now have even more people bugging her. Thankfully, when she opened her eyes, Hunter was standing above her.

"I'm fine," she said. "Just got the wind knocked out of me."

He nodded, then said, "That was a tough fall. I saw it myself. What happened?"

Grace sighed. "Just a stupid horse with a one-track mind who noticed you guys feeding the cattle. She hit a dip and tripped, and here I am."

Hunter laughed. "It happens to the best of us. Are you sure you're okay?"

Grace nodded. "Yes."

"If you're okay, then why are you still sitting there?" William asked. He turned to Hunter. "I think she's more hurt than she's saying. Why can't she get up?"

"I tried explaining to him about the adrenaline. I just need a minute," Grace said.

"Still, it wouldn't hurt for me to check you over for injuries," Hunter said. He looked at William. "There's a first-aid kit on the back of my ATV. I don't think we'll need it, but grab it just in case."

As Hunter inspected her for injuries, more ATVs arrived. Just what she needed. A bigger audience.

"What happened?" Ricky's voice boomed over her, which meant that any hope she had of keeping this from her mom was gone.

"I'm fine," Grace said. "Nothing you haven't seen before."

William returned with the first-aid kit. "I don't know how to use any of this stuff, but you tell me, and I'm here."

Grace couldn't help smiling at his eagerness. For all his faults, he had the best heart of anyone she knew. Yes, he held grudges a little too tightly, but they were the result of deep hurt, and that was because of how deeply he cared. Were circumstances in her life different, she could see herself liking him as more than a friend.

The fact that she could have such coherent thoughts reassured her that she wasn't injured. Now, to convince everyone else of the fact.

"I think it's just as she says," Hunter pronounced. "Just some bumps and bruises. She's even talking rationally, and it didn't look like she hit her head, so I'm not worried about a concussion."

"I'm sure Wanda has heard about this and is worried sick," Ricky said. "I'll go let her know that you're fine, but you get on to the house as quickly as possible to reassure her."

The old man got back on his ATV and headed in the direction of the house.

"Are you sure you feel okay?" William asked.

The worried look on William's face made her feel bad. He genuinely cared. Obviously, as part of his horse-and-rodeo training, he was going to need to learn about first aid and what injuries may or may not be serious.

"What about internal injuries?" he asked, looking at her intently, more specifically, her stomach. She appreciated that he was trying to casually ask about the baby, and if they could speak more openly, she would tell him that was fine, too.

Hunter shook his head. "On a little spill like that? Not likely. I trust Grace. If she says she's not hurt, then I believe her."

But the concern on William's face made her realize that more than her pride was at stake. This wasn't just about taking a spill in front of a bunch of cowboys, or even keeping her pregnancy a secret. In all the baby books she'd read, they hadn't covered what to do if you got thrown from a horse.

What if she'd hurt Pumpkin without even knowing it?

Grace sighed. "Just to be safe, I probably should go see the doctor," she said. "I'm pregnant."

The stunned silence across the pasture was palpable. Grace was pretty sure that none of them had ever expected that to come out of her mouth. She closed her eyes, unable to look at any of them. Her secret was out.

Chapter Seven

William paced the lobby of the town clinic, hating that they wouldn't let him inside the exam room with Grace. He just hoped Pumpkin would be okay.

Pumpkin. He already thought of that tiny little baby as a person. And, truth be told, he kind of thought she was a girl. Granted, he'd be thrilled if it was a boy, he just wanted Pumpkin to be healthy. It was hard to believe how much he cared about a baby that wasn't even his.

Please, God, make sure Pumpkin is okay.

Wanda raced into the clinic. They'd taken Grace directly from the pasture to the doctor, which meant Wanda was just now getting here.

"Where's my baby?" Wanda asked, her voice a screech.

William turned to her. "Still in the exam room," he said. "They're not letting anyone back to see her until she's ready."

"How could you?" Wanda asked, marching right

up to him and getting in his face. "I trust you, and this is how you pay me back?"

William took a deep breath. "She's the better rider. How was I supposed to know the dangers?"

"Not that," Wanda said. "You took advantage of my daughter and got her pregnant."

It hadn't occurred to William that anyone would make that assumption. But he supposed, in a way, it made sense.

"It's not my baby," he said. "But I care about both Grace and the baby, and I want to make sure they're both okay."

"If it's not your baby, then why would she tell you about it before she told her family?" Wanda asked. "From what one of the ranch hands told Ricky, based on how you acted while they waited for the ambulance, you already knew."

It was a good question, and even though he felt bad for already saying more than he should have, he felt guilty for his part in the hurt and confusion on Wanda's face. So much damage had been done because of Grace's need to keep this all a secret. And he couldn't do it anymore.

"Because she was afraid of how you would judge her, like you judged that woman you were talking about at church. And how you automatically jumped on my case when you arrived here, not even asking how she was."

Before she could answer, Alexander and Janie entered, looking worried. Alexander immediately rushed over and gave him a big hug.

"It's going to be okay, bro. No matter what happens, we're here for you, Grace and the baby."

Another person worried thinking that it was his baby.

"It's not mine," he said. "But I promised Grace I'd be here for them."

Alexander gave him a big pat on the back and stepped away. "That doesn't change the fact that we're all here for you."

Janie nodded. "She must be scared to death, pregnant and alone."

"She's not alone," William said. "I've been here for her."

"We would have been there for her, too, if we'd been given a chance," Wanda said.

William turned to her. "That's what I've been trying to tell her. But she was so scared of how everyone would judge her that she couldn't bring herself to tell anyone. The only reason I know is because I caught her getting sick and she confessed everything."

He took a deep breath, then continued. "And while we're on the subject of telling the truth, you need to know that I actually hate pumpkin pie. But it's one of the few things that Grace can keep down right now, so I pretended to like it so I could give mine to her. But now that you know the truth, maybe we can be honest about the things she can and can't eat because of the baby and we don't have to go around hiding anymore."

Alexander nodded slowly. "That's why you've been using the old fool-mom food trick. You weren't making me eat your food to spare Wanda's feelings. You were eating Grace's, and spreading some of it out to me so no one got stuck eating two dinners."

William laughed. "Yeah, sorry. I remembered our old childhood trick, and since Grace was so desperate to hide her pregnancy, I decided to try it. I'm sorry for using you and not explaining why."

Instead of looking disappointed, Alexander laughed again. "Are you kidding? That was awesome. It was like we had the good old days back."

He reached out to do the special handshake they'd created as kids, and in that moment, as William went through the strange motions they'd done for years, it was like everything that had felt wrong in his relationship with his brother was suddenly right again.

After the grand ending, Alexander brought him into a big hug. "That felt good. Lately I've felt like I was losing my brother, and being up to our old tricks seemed like maybe you weren't lost to me, after all."

So it hadn't just been him. "I was feeling the same way. You'd gone through so many changes, and I'd been left out of all of them. But being with Grace has helped, and today, when I talked to the pastor about accepting Christ, I felt like I understood better."

Though it was gratifying to have this moment with his brother, it also seemed strange doing it in front of everyone else. Before they could say more, the door to the back office opened, and Grace walked out with the doctor.

"Both Grace and the baby are fine," the doctor

said. "She wanted me to be the one to tell you so that you would believe there is nothing to worry about."

Then he looked over at Grace. "That's not to say that you can continue racing about the countryside on a horse. You've got to take care of yourself, which also means letting these fine people in this room help you."

Grace nodded, looking sheepish. "I know. And I'm sorry for causing anyone any worry. I'll do better."

She walked over to William. "I'm sorry for making you keep my secret. I should have told everyone about the baby sooner, which the doctor also reminded me of. It's not just about what I want for me, but making sure that everybody knows so we can keep our little Pumpkin safe."

Our little Pumpkin. Was it over-the-top to feel so much joy, knowing that not only was Pumpkin okay, but that somehow, Grace still saw this as something they were in on together, and that she recognized how much he already loved the baby?

He held his arms out to her. "Can we seal this deal with a hug?"

When Grace came into his arms, suddenly it felt like everything really was going to be all right. The weight of having so many secrets fell off his shoulders, and it was like he could finally breathe again. When Grace released him from the hug, she pressed something into his hand.

"We've always said that we're in this together, so I wanted you to be the first one to see. They usually don't do them this early in an otherwise healthy pregnancy, but with my fall from the horse, the doctor wanted to make extra sure."

He looked down at the tiny blob on the paper that barely looked like a baby, but as he examined it, he could see some of the features.

"Could they tell if it was a boy or girl?" he asked.

Grace shook her head as she took the picture from him. "I'm a week shy of being able to tell. But I just want a healthy baby, so I don't care."

He grinned. "I just want Pumpkin to be healthy, too. But now that the secret's out, and I'm having so much fun getting gifts for my niece and nephew, it'd be nice to know what kind of stuff I should get for Pumpkin."

Grace laughed as she shook her head. "You need to hurry up and get married and have kids of your own, so you don't spoil everyone else's."

Alexander laughed with them. "You're telling me. If Sam is with him in any store and asks for something, you can guarantee that William will buy it."

"That's not fair," William said. "I've said no every time he's asked me to buy him candy."

Alexander shook his head. "Small mercies."

For the first time since exiting the exam room, Grace turned to her mother. "I know you're disappointed in me, and I'm sorry. But I can't be who you want me to be, because I'm just me. I make mistakes. But you need to know that I love my baby very much, and I hope you will, too."

Tears had filled Grace's eyes, and her voice was shaking. William knew how she'd struggled with this, and now that the moment of truth was here, he wished he could hold her and take the pain away. But he also knew that like him coming to terms with God, this was something Grace had to do on her own.

Wanda stepped forward. "I guess I can be pretty judgmental at times," she said. "I never imagined that it would make my daughter so afraid to share something so important in her life."

Wanda was openly crying now, and part of William felt guilty for calling her out about her behavior. But maybe it was what had been necessary to get her to give Grace the love she needed.

"Can I see a picture of my grandbaby? You call it Pumpkin?"

Grace nodded and handed her the picture. "William gave the baby that name since all I seem to be able to keep down is pumpkin pie. But as you can see from the picture, there really is a baby in there, not a pumpkin."

As Grace laughed, Wanda threw her arms around her and held her tight. "I'm so sorry for making you feel like you couldn't share something so important with me. I promise you, I love you and Pumpkin with all my heart."

As mother and daughter embraced, a deep peace settled over William's heart. It made him happy to be part of such a deep family healing, and he prayed that he could find that same healing for himself. He just didn't know how to get there. But he would give Grace's suggestion of counting his blessings a try.

The clinic door opened again, then Ricky stormed in.

"Where is that scoundrel?"

He whirled around and stared right at William. "I took you into my family, and this is how you repay me? I hope you're willing to make an honest woman of her."

He should be used to the accusation by now, but before he could defend himself, everyone in the room started laughing.

"Relax," Grace said. "William did nothing wrong, except help a friend in need. There is no need for a shotgun wedding."

The doctor laughed. "And thank you for not bringing your shotgun."

Ricky glanced around the room. "Were you all playing a joke on me?"

Grace stepped forward. "No joke. I'm having a baby. I did some things I'm not proud of, but that's in the past, and God's mercies are new each day. And now we have a tiny blessing on the way."

Ricky glanced over at William, and for the first time, William could understand why people were afraid of Ricky's hard side. "And you had nothing to do with this?"

William shook his head. "She was already pregnant when I met her. But she's a good friend, and I care about both her and the baby. I've already promised that I'll be here for her no matter what."

Grace came to stand beside him and gave him a warm smile. "William has been nothing but a perfect gentleman. You'd be proud of the way he has taken care of me over the past few weeks."

Ricky rubbed his chin as he nodded. "Seems to me, by the way you two are carrying on together, it might be reasonable for folks to assume you're involved."

William stepped forward. "If you are implying that there has ever been anything inappropriate between me and Grace—"

"Hold your horses. I'm just saying that it's obvious to anyone with eyes that there's something between the two of you. You like her, and she likes you. That baby of hers is going to need a father. Might as well be you."

William glanced over at Grace, whose look of horror made him want to laugh. But this was no laughing matter.

Before he could answer, Wanda said, "He did already give the baby a name. He calls it Pumpkin. Isn't that sweet?"

"I've just done what anyone would do," William said. "That doesn't mean I'm ready to be a father."

Alexander started laughing.

"How is that funny?" William asked.

Alexander grinned. "I said the same thing when I was spending time with Janie. Everyone kept telling me how special it was, all the things I was doing for her, and I told them all that it was what anyone would do. But the thing is, it wasn't. I didn't realize it at the time, but I did all that stuff because I loved her. Ricky is right. There is something special between you and Grace."

"Now, that's just ridiculous," Grace said. "The something special you all think you see was just two friends, helping each other out. And William being so kind as to keep my very extraordinary secret. I know he felt bad about it, so I'm very grateful that he did."

Instead of looking convinced, everyone else seemed to look only like they thought William and Grace were protesting too much. But maybe, maybe there was something to that absurd idea.

William turned to Grace. "You know how we've talked about our failures at relationships and how we don't understand why we keep making such bad decisions?"

Grace nodded. "You'll find the right woman, and I'm sure I'll find the right man."

He looked around the room at all the smug expressions of people who were so sure that he and Grace were right for each other.

"What if it's not about falling in love and looking for that giddy feeling?" William asked. "What if it's just about two people who need each other and care about each other and have a strong friendship?"

Alexander held his arm out to William. "Don't do it. Just stop right there. Don't say another word. Let's just all move along and pretend like this conversation is ending right now."

William stared at his brother. "I have no idea what you're talking about. And you don't know the conversations I've had with Grace about relationships. She told me I was wrong for trying to be someone I'm not. I've resented being the means to an end for the other women I've dated. But I don't resent helping Grace. I like her. I want to help her and the baby."

Grace's warm smile further convinced him that this was the right thing to do.

"You have no idea how much I appreciate having you here," Grace said.

William turned to her and took her hands. "Then why not make it official? Everyone else seems to think it's what we should do. We get along well enough, and Pumpkin is going to need a father. Why don't we get married?"

Grace dropped his hands. "You have got to be kidding me. Was that your idea of a proposal?"

"I told you not to do it, bro," Alexander said.

"What's wrong with that?" Ricky asked. "He is trying to do an honorable thing."

Suddenly everyone in the room started talking, and William couldn't make heads or tails of it, but what he did see was the hurt in Grace's eyes. It wasn't like they were in love with each other, was it? Had he misinterpreted Grace's feelings for him?

He held his hand out to Grace again. "I'm sorry. I was trying to do the right thing, only I seem to have botched it. Why don't I take you home and we can talk about it without everyone interfering?"

Grace nodded slowly. "Okay. But you have to promise not to propose to me again."

William took a deep breath. "I can do that," he said.

But as he spoke, he almost choked on the words, because they felt like a lie. That, however, was preposterous. After all, they were just friends.

Chapter Eight

The kindness everyone showed Grace since she announced her pregnancy made her wonder why she'd been so afraid of telling anyone. She'd underestimated her mother, underestimated everyone. And now, a month later, with her little belly poking out, the reality that Pumpkin was on the way was starting to hit.

She glanced into the backseat at the box of baby things that they'd picked up from one of her mom's church friends. Everyone was offering her their hand-me-downs to reduce the expense of having a baby.

She and William were on their way to the Merrick Ranch, where they were going to talk to the staff about becoming the stock contractor for the rodeo. Finding a stock contractor had been the hitch in organizing the event. In the past, the Double R had used their own stock to put on rodeos, but because it had been so long, they'd sold all of those animals, and it was important to have stock meant for rodeo, not just any animals pulled off a ranch. Rodeo stock had a better sense of what needed to be done and why, as opposed to some random bull thrown in a chute. Those creatures could be dangerous in an already risky sport.

Plus, when you worked with a respectable rodeo contractor, you knew the stock was being treated ethically and humanely in accordance with all the rodeo rules.

The problem was, the July date they'd chosen for the rodeo was a popular one and it seemed like all the contractors' cattle were already spoken for.

But if they had the rodeo any earlier, it would be too close to the birth of the baby. Everyone had agreed that putting on a rodeo at nine months pregnant was not going to be a lot of fun, so they moved the date later to give Grace time to give birth and recuperate.

When they arrived at the Merrick Ranch and got out of the truck, Grace smoothed the maternity top over her stomach. She was finally starting to show now, and while it was nice that she didn't have to hide her pregnancy any longer, she still felt self-conscious about her baby bump.

As they walked to the barn, a familiar face came out to greet them.

"Gracie."

Grace smiled at Darby. "What are you doing here?"

Darby grinned. "I just took a job here. Mr. Merrick asked me to show you around. He's interested in creating a name for himself in the rodeo community. There are so many bigger outfits these days, that it's getting harder for the little guys to compete. So much of who we are as cowboys is built on being small, family-oriented outfits. It's a shame to see so many of the bigger outfits taking over. I don't want the cowboy way to die out."

"Do you think you can provide stock for our rodeo?" William asked.

Darby nodded. "Yes. And I think you'll agree that having the rodeo with local stock will get some good attention on Columbine Springs. Not only is this going to be a boost for our local economy, but maybe it will help businesses like us in the long run because other rodeos will want to use us, as well."

"I agree," Grace said. "It fits well within Ricky's vision. Yes, he wants to help the youth organization, but his commitment has always been to the community at large. Small towns in general are struggling, but ours in particular has been having a tough time since the wildfire."

"Agreed," Darby said. "Why don't I show you some of our stock? I think you'll appreciate all the hard work everyone has put into our animals."

Though such a personal visit wasn't necessary, Grace was grateful for Darby's enthusiasm and his desire to do some good.

"You'll find that Mr. Merrick has updated a lot of things here. I don't know if you were ever here when his father was alive and running things, but a lot has changed."

That was what Ricky had told them, and while he'd had some choice words for the older Merrick, he seemed to be hopeful that the son had some good things planned.

As Darby walked them to the barn, the sense of pride he seemed to have about the place made her smile. But what she especially appreciated was the way William appeared to be interested in everything.

But that was William. And one of the things she really liked about him. As they walked into another section of the barn, Darby paused. "You want to see some babies?"

He opened the door, leading them into an area where several calves were penned up.

"We have to bottle-feed these ones," he said. "They're almost due for a feeding. I thought maybe the city slicker here might like to give it a go."

The grin on William's face warmed her heart. He had such a nice smile. And it was genuine, the kind that made you feel at ease whenever he shone it your way.

Darby took them into a utility room, where he showed them how to prepare the calves' food. Though Grace had fixed bottles for many an animal before, it felt different now, as she wondered what it would be like to make one for her own baby. She'd been reading up on baby care, and while she hoped she'd be able to nurse Pumpkin, she also knew that it wasn't possible in every situation, so she was trying to be open to all options.

Once the bottles were made, they went out to the calves. The animals immediately knew what was coming, and they mewled with glee at the sight of the bottles. At least that's how she was going to interpret their reaction. Maybe calves didn't have emotions like that, but they sure looked happy to see her.

Was it weird to have maternal feelings at the sight of baby cows? Though it wasn't just the young ones, but the way William sweet-talked the calf he was approaching.

"Hey there, little guy," William said. "Or girl. Are you hungry?"

Most cowboys Grace knew wouldn't have taken the time to be so tender. And that was one of the things she truly was glad for about him. He kept saying how badly he wanted to be a cowboy, but the thing he didn't understand was that most cowboys didn't have his tender heart. And Grace would take a man's tender heart over any other characteristic.

William was such a good man. He was so compassionate and loving, and the way he always cared for Grace with consideration made her feel safe and, dare she say it, loved. No, this wasn't the giddy feeling she'd had with Jack. This was something warm and comforting, like the fuzzy blanket she curled up with at night sitting on the couch, watching television with William and the rest of the family.

And yet, moments like this, where she saw his tenderness toward others, her heart skipped a beat.

Nonsensical, since there was nothing romantic about a smelly, slobbery calf sucking down a bottle.

"Look at this little guy," William said. "I had no idea that a cow could be so cute."

As the calf drank its bottle, William reached forward and patted its head. You didn't usually pet calves when you fed them, but William didn't know that, and with the grin on his face, she wasn't going to tell him any differently.

She came alongside him to give another calf his bottle and as William smiled at her, it warmed her heart. There was a constancy to William that Grace couldn't help but like. There was a lot to like about him, but it felt weird thinking about William in this way, considering she was still recovering from her mistake.

She'd thought that what she had with Jack was special, but obviously, she'd been wrong. Whatever the elated feeling inside her was when she was with William, it was better to push it aside and ignore it for now. What if this wasn't real? Pregnancy hormones did a lot to a woman's emotions, and the last thing she needed was to have her wild emotions mess up her friendship with the nicest guy she'd ever met.

Yes, she liked him, but she had a baby to think about, which meant focusing on the fluttering in her stomach from the baby, not the flutters from William.

Who knew that feeding a baby calf could be so fun? William glanced over at Grace, wondering if any of this was bringing out maternal feelings in her. The tender way she cared for the calf told him that she was going to be a great mother to little Pumpkin. Not that he had any doubt of that fact. Grace was a warm and loving woman. Naturally, she would be a good mother. It was just sweet to see her attending to this baby calf with such love.

"You guys know these calves are going to be dinner eventually, right?" Darby asked, coming over with more bottles.

Grace looked up and smiled. "I have no illusions about that, thank you very much. But it doesn't mean I shouldn't enjoy them while I can. Soon, they will be slobbery stinky beasts out in the field. But for now, who can deny the cuteness?"

Darby laughed. "You always were a softy."

Grace looked a little hurt by the comments, so William turned to her and smiled. "There's nothing wrong with that. Your tender heart is what makes you—"

He paused for a moment. What he wanted to say was that her tender heart was what made him like her so much. But it didn't seem right to say something like that when it might put pressure on her or make her think he was interested in something more.

Wait a second. Did he want something more? He hadn't really thought about it that way, because he'd been so focused on being her friend and helping with the baby. But as she laughed at something Darby said, William had to admit that maybe there was more to his feelings than that.

Grace caught his eye. "You didn't find the joke funny?"

William shook his head. "Sorry, I must've been wool gathering." Then he laughed. "Except cows don't have wool."

They all laughed then, and William couldn't help thinking how nice it was just being with her. Grace was a good woman, and maybe his real problem in searching for the right woman was that he hadn't found one who had that same level of character as Grace.

When he'd proposed to Grace, it was with the idea of a marriage of convenience. A family for Pumpkin, and he and Grace got along well enough that they could have a happy life together without all the romantic entanglements. No more heartbreak for either of them. But maybe he was selling himself, and Grace, short. They both deserved to have love.

The question was, was it possible with each other? He liked Grace a lot, and the more he thought about how much he liked her, the more he wondered if maybe there could be something in addition to friendship between them.

The cow sucked the last of the bottle dry, and as William tugged it out of the calf's mouth, he pulled a little too hard, hitting Grace in the arm.

"I'm so sorry," he said. "I wasn't expecting that."

Grace laughed. "It's fine. Everyone treats me like I'm fragile and going to break. It was just my arm."

She reached down and stroked her belly. "The baby is fine. Pumpkin is a lot stronger than everyone thinks. Remember, the doctor said after my riding accident that you don't need to treat me with kid gloves."

"Riding accident?" Darby asked. "What happened? Are you okay?"

In such a small town, it was surprising he hadn't already heard. But it had been over a month, so probably dozens of other stories in town had been told, and this had just been a blip on everyone else's radar. At least those not connected closely to Grace. But to William, keeping her and Pumpkin safe was his top priority.

"I'm fine," Grace said, looking pointedly at William. "My horse tripped and threw me when we were riding last month, and while I did get checked out as a precaution, the doctor said everything was fine. I'm not supposed to go riding anymore, but everything else I do is perfectly safe. Which means William doesn't have to worry about accidentally smacking me in the arm."

Her voice held laughter as she spoke, and Darby laughed with them.

"I don't know," Darby said. "If it was my woman and baby, I'd be a little protective, too."

"We're just friends," Grace said quickly. "It's not William's baby."

Her words stung more than they should have. She'd only told the truth. They were friends, and Pumpkin wasn't his baby. But he cared about Grace, as much as he was struggling to admit it, as more than a friend. Pumpkin might not be his baby, but he couldn't deny the love he already felt for the unborn child.

So where did that leave him? Wanting more, but knowing this was not the right time to be pursuing Grace romantically. She had so much on her plate, trying to grow a baby and figure out what things would look like for them once the baby was born.

Why did he have to go and have silly romantic notions now?

They brought the bottles back into the workroom and William felt himself aware of Grace in a way he hadn't been before. He'd always thought her attractive, always thought her sweet. But now, realizing that his feelings for her might be a little deeper than friendship, he felt like a schoolboy around her. Awkward, like he wasn't sure what he was supposed to say or do.

"Are you going to wash those bottles, or just stare at them?" Grace asked.

He was a fool.

"Sorry," he said. "I guess my mind was elsewhere."

Grace rested her hand on his arm. "Is everything okay? You seem a little distant."

It wasn't like he could just say that he'd suddenly realized that he might like her as more than friends. Especially since she'd just made it clear to Darby that that was all they were.

"Everything's fine," he said. "Let's get these bottles washed and then we can take a look at the rest of the stock and talk to Darby about what we need."

Getting back down to business seemed to free him from the weird thoughts he'd been having about Grace. At least temporarily.

But as Darby showed them around and explained about the stock they had and how they would be used for the rodeo, it only made Grace more attractive to him.

Like now.

Darby gestured at a pen filled with sheep. "I'm assuming you're planning on having mutton bustin'."

Grace grinned. "Honestly, it's my favorite part of the rodeo."

She rubbed her belly, then said, "I'm already looking forward to Pumpkin being able to do it when he or she is old enough."

Then she turned to William. "It's just so fun watching the kids hang on to the sheep for dear life. Have you ever seen it?"

She'd been doing this the whole time they'd worked on planning the rodeo. Making sure he understood what was happening, but not in a way that made him feel stupid.

William laughed. "Yes, but I'll admit I'm not as keen on the idea as you are. What if Pumpkin gets hurt?"

Darby patted him on the back. "You're worried about Pumpkin getting hurt? We do this all the time, and I haven't seen too many injuries, and certainly nothing serious. The kids wear helmets and vests for safety, and there's plenty of supervision. I've spent my whole life around rodeos, and I'm passionate about safety."

Then Darby turned to Grace. "It's not William's baby, huh?"

Grace turned red, and William wished he hadn't said anything.

"Just because it's not mine doesn't mean I don't care," he said quickly. "I'm starting to see Grace's baby just like my niece or nephew. I probably do overstep, though, so I'm sorry if that gives you the wrong idea."

He hoped his words would smooth things over, but Grace's furrowed brow made him wonder if he'd said the wrong thing. Was he going to start questioning everything they talked about? He'd expressed concerns for Pumpkin's safety many times before, but this time, knowing that it came from a place of maybe caring about Grace in a deeper way, it felt strange to him.

He had to do something about these growing feelings. The last thing he wanted was to make things awkward with Grace, but it seemed like even the most well-intentioned things coming out of his mouth today were all wrong.

"It's okay, I understand," Darby said. "We're all a little protective of her. We might not run in the same crowd anymore, but when we were kids, Grace was one of my best friends."

Grace stepped away for a moment, and Darby leaned in to him. "For what it's worth, it's obvious to anyone who looks at the two of you that there's something there. I can understand why you'd want to take it slow, because of the baby and everything, but don't let her slip through your fingers. A good woman is hard to find these days."

William looked at him for second, trying to see what was going on with this little talk, but Darby laughed.

"There has never been anything between the two of us," he said. "But I did love someone once, and Grace probably would have liked her. But I was a bonehead, and I didn't tell her until it was too late, and now she's married to someone else, and I missed my chance. All I'm saying is don't let Grace slip away."

He definitely didn't want to do that, because Darby was right. But he also knew all the stress on Grace's mind, and he didn't want to add to it.

"I'm not planning on it," William said.

As Grace walked back toward them, a smile on her face, William promised himself that he'd find a way to let Grace know he cared for her without making her feel pressured. He just wasn't sure how he was going to keep from making a complete fool of himself in the meantime.

Chapter Nine

Things were rolling along nicely with the rodeo. They'd gotten an agreement with the Merrick Ranch to provide stock, and sponsorships were increasing. It was only March, but everything appeared to be in place, and it felt nice to not have to stress over details.

After yet another satisfying meal consisting mostly of mashed potatoes and gravy, Grace was resting on the couch in the main ranch house, reading through one of the new sponsorship contracts that had just come in. Once everything looked okay to her, she'd pass it on to Ty to make sure all their legal bases were covered.

William walked in, carrying two plates.

"I hope you're not working," he said. "We got a lot done today, and I'm happy with where we're at. There's no reason work can't wait until tomorrow."

She set the folder aside, not so much because William had told her to, but because one of those plates had a generous slice of pumpkin pie.

"If that's a bribe, I'll gladly take it. But you're right. I was just thinking about how nicely everything is falling into place. I wanted to read over this new contract that came in, but your idea is way more tempting."

Especially since she'd been spending most evenings on the couch with William. She liked that there was no pressure to do anything other than just sit and hang out. Although when he gave her that smile, she still wondered if there could be something more.

William grinned. "Your mom still feels bad for making me eat all that pumpkin pie, so I'm going to milk it for all the dessert I can get. Her apple pie is amazing."

Happiness bubbled up in Grace at the reminder of how everyone had been coming together to support her. "I thought I smelled something good."

He sat down next to her on the couch and handed her the plate.

As she took a bite of her pie, she felt the small flutter of the baby moving, as if little Pumpkin was happy to be getting some more of the much-loved pumpkin pie.

"What's that smile about?" William asked.

Was she smiling? It didn't feel like it, however, Grace felt so much lighter, having the burden of her secret taken off her. Even two months later, she still couldn't get over how good it felt to have everyone supporting her.

William hadn't seemed as bitter lately, so maybe it was time to tell him the truth, as well. She hated feeling like she was keeping things from him by not sharing about Pumpkin's biological father. But things were going so well between them, she didn't want to spoil it.

"Pumpkin seems to be very happy to be getting some of his or her namesake," she said instead. Then she looked over at him. "Is it strange that I already feel like I'm starting to get to know the baby's personality? I haven't even met him or her yet, and I'm already talking about traits and preferences."

William gave her an indulgent smile. "Not at all. You have a person living inside you, so of course you would know what he or she was like."

"The baby books don't tell you that," she said.

"I don't think you need a book to tell you what's true in your heart."

This time, when he smiled at her, the flutter in her stomach wasn't the baby. Actually, she'd been feeling those flutters a lot, too, and the more she tried denying it, the worse they got. Things were mostly normal between them, except for the moments where she felt a little awkward, because she thought she might feel something more than friendship. And they had both made it clear that the feelings they had for each other were just friendship.

Which was why she was doing her best to ignore these strange, random moments. Obviously it was just her pregnancy hormones getting to her. It couldn't be anything else.

William turned on the TV. "There's a rodeo special on tonight, and I thought we could check it out together."

He sounded like a little boy, and she loved getting to experience these new things with him. They were both on this journey of discovery, and being included by him never failed to touch her heart.

"It would be good research for the rodeo, don't you think?" he asked.

Was she wrong for having a sinking feeling in her stomach that he brought it back to business, after he'd just told her to take a break? It was silly to even think this way, considering they talked about business all day, and they often mixed personal things in with it. It wasn't like their relationship had to be either/or.

"Good idea," she said, taking a bite of her pie.

"Also, I put together a few investment options for you to roll over your 401(k). You don't have to make any decisions now, but I had some time this afternoon, so I looked at the account info you'd given me."

Grace had forgotten that she'd given him the information to see how best to handle her accounts now that she was no longer with her old company. So much had been going on that it had fallen off her radar.

"Thanks," she said. "I appreciate your help with it. I'm clueless about stuff like that, so it feels good to have someone looking out for me."

William gave her a grin that melted her insides. His smiles had been doing that a lot lately, and she didn't know what to make of it.

"Of course," he said. "You said you'd teach me about cowboys, which you've done an amazing job of, and I said I'd help with the financial stuff. A deal's a deal."

Grace sighed. She'd hoped they were past all that nonsense. This was why she had to ignore the weird feelings she had for him. He was still trying to prove he was man enough, and she liked him just the way he was.

Even though she'd only eaten about half of it, she set her slice of pie aside. It was good, but with all the mixed emotions inside her, she didn't feel much like eating anymore.

They hadn't been watching the rodeo for more than a few minutes when she felt a strange tap against her hand. No, not a tap, but when she felt it again, she realized that for the first time, she didn't feel the baby just kicking inside her, but her hand could feel it on the outside, as well.

"Wow," she said.

William turned to her, a startled expression on his face. "What? Is everything okay? Is Pumpkin okay?"

Grace smiled as she nodded, then grabbed his hand and placed it in the spot where Pumpkin had been kicking.

"Feel. This is the first time I've been able to feel her kicking with my hand."

The look of wonder on his face told her she hadn't been imagining it.

"It's real," he said. "I mean, I knew it was real, but to feel her…"

She placed her hand over his, and they sat in silence for a moment as Pumpkin kicked. Then the kicking stopped, but the air around them still seemed precious and special. He didn't move his hand from her stomach.

"That was amazing," he said. "Does it hurt?"

Grace shook her head. "No. It's like a little tickle, only a bit more. It's a different enough sensation that I know it's her."

Grace closed her eyes, thinking about the blessing of this moment and having William here with her. Then another thought struck as she opened her eyes and turned to look at him again. "Now you've got me doing it. We don't know that it's a girl, yet you already have me calling Pumpkin *her*."

"I just have a feeling, that's all."

He started to move his hand away, but the gesture felt reluctant.

"You don't have to stop if you don't want to. It's kind of nice, having someone else feeling my belly, confirming that there is a baby in there. I mean, I wouldn't want just anyone touching my belly, but it feels right for you to do so."

He was so close to her, his touch so comforting, and that not-baby feeling in her stomach welled up inside her so strongly that she couldn't help herself.

"I hope you know how special you are to me," she said. "We talked about being friends, but the feelings I have—"

Before she could finish what she had to say, William leaned in and kissed her tenderly.

Grace had been kissed more times than she wanted to admit, but in this moment, she couldn't think of any that had been more perfect. He pulled her closer to him and deepened the kiss as she put her arms around him.

She was a fool to think that her life was complete without him. That's why she'd wanted him to feel Pumpkin kicking. Maybe he wasn't her baby's biological father, but he was already an important part of her life.

When William ended the kiss, he pulled away and brushed the hair from her cheek. "I hope that was okay," he said. "I care about you, too, and this is something deeper than I've ever experienced."

Grace took a long breath. "I feel the same way. I trust you more deeply than I have trusted anyone. You care for me and Pumpkin in such a special way. I'm so grateful for you that I find myself thanking God for you multiple times a day."

She thought her words would have brought them closer together, but William stiffened.

Was he thinking this was going to be another friend conversation?

Taking William's hand, Grace said, "I should have accepted when you asked me to marry you. You're a good man, and I don't need you to be a cowboy to see that. I like you just as you are. As you've always been. You take good care of me, and make sure that all of our needs are provided for. You treat me with respect. You listen to me, really listen to me, and even when you disagree with me, you make me feel heard. Like how you kept Pumpkin a secret even though you didn't like it."

He was quiet, like he was taking in her words and didn't know what to make of them. "We talked about relationships, and me not knowing what I wanted in a man and needing to figure it out. I don't have to figure it out anymore. I know what kind of man is best for me and Pumpkin. It's you."

William leaned in to kiss her again. He brushed her lips with his then said, "It's a little hard for me to process, because I thought I was the only one feeling this way."

Though it was only a quick kiss, she could feel the emotion behind it. "I thought so, too."

He nodded slowly. "I don't want you to feel like I'm rushing you. I know you have a lot on your plate with the rodeo and Pumpkin. I know I proposed before, but I'm willing to take it slow now. I want you to be sure this is the right thing for all three of us."

All three of us. Once again, proving that William had her best interests at heart. Could he make himself any more dear to her? Another vast change from what had gone on with her and Jack, who had pushed her to move faster than she would have liked, but she'd thought it had been because he loved her. Now she knew that love also meant taking things slow and keeping the other person's concerns in mind.

"I like the idea of taking things slow," she said, giving him another soft kiss. "I jumped into things way too soon with Pumpkin's father, and I appreciate the chance for us to make sure that this is right for all of us."

She gave her belly another gentle caress. "Thank you for understanding."

William tenderly kissed her on the forehead, then put his arm around her, making her feel safe, secure and confident in their future.

William hadn't slept well the previous night, because all he could think about was the kisses he'd shared with Grace, and as he walked to the main ranch house to start work, he was looking forward to seeing her.

He just wasn't sure how he was supposed to greet her. Obviously, they were more than friends, but they hadn't fully established what this relationship was, other than they were taking it slow.

Did he greet her as usual? With a hug? With a kiss?

He wanted to take her into his arms and give her a big hug and kiss, and, as cheesy as it sounded, place a small kiss on Grace's belly, so he wasn't leaving Pumpkin out.

A strange car had pulled up in front of the main ranch house, and a woman he didn't recognize was getting out.

The ranch hadn't yet reopened to guests after the town fire, and it was odd that a stranger would be coming to the main house instead of the lodge.

"Can I help you?" he asked, walking briskly toward the woman.

"Where is that seductress?"

Seductress? What was this, the turn of the century?

"I think you're at the wrong place, ma'am. We're a guest ranch, but we're closed for the time being."

"Her mother works here. I'm told she came here to lick her wounds after she tried to seduce my husband and he fired her."

The only person whose mother worked here was Grace. But she couldn't be talking about Grace, could she?

"I'm sorry, who are you looking for?"

The front door opened, and Grace poked her head out. "Who's here?"

"There you are! How could you try to break up a family like that?"

Grace turned, and her belly was obvious.

"You're even worse than I thought," the woman said. "It's Jack's, isn't it?"

William looked over at Grace, whose face had turned pale. "I don't know what Jack told you, but it's not what you think."

The woman marched past William and onto the front porch. "Do you deny that you had an affair with my husband?"

William waited to hear Grace tell her no, that she got the wrong person, but his heart sank when Grace shook her head.

"No. I dated Jack for over six months. But you have to understand—"

"How could you?" Tears were streaming down the woman's face, and William's heart broke for her. He'd been in her shoes. No, he hadn't confronted the person responsible, but he'd asked those very questions.

Worse, he'd confessed his deep pain at having been in that situation to Grace, and she'd said nothing. Why wouldn't Grace have told him about this? He knew what this poor woman who'd arrived was going through, and in this moment, he felt a kinship with her. Yet this woman was upset with Grace.

Part of him thought he should step in somehow, but his feet were rooted to the ground. What was he supposed to do when the woman he wanted to protect was being confronted by the woman whose predicament he'd recently been in?

Before Grace could answer, another car pulled up.

"Jack!" both women said, almost in unison.

By the time the man got out of the car, other ranch staff had gathered. They all knew the new arrivals didn't belong here, so of course they'd be curious. Good. At least one of them could handle the situation, considering William's heart felt too torn to know what to do.

It was as if the pain of being cheated on had hit him all over again, seeing the unhappiness on the woman's face. And other than her feeble attempts at defending herself, Grace had said and done nothing.

"Allison, what is the meaning of this?" Jack asked. "I told you things were over between me and Grace."

Allison turned to face her husband. "You didn't tell me she was pregnant. You said our family was complete and you wouldn't let me have another baby. But you go and get this troll pregnant?"

So it was bigger than what William had originally thought. This poor woman. He remembered what Grace had said when he told her that Hailey had cheated on him. *At least you weren't already married.* Now her words took on a deeper meaning as they came back to him.

How was this family going to deal with the fact that the father's carelessness had resulted in a sibling? A new pain hit William—that of discovering he had siblings he didn't know about. What was it going to be like for Pumpkin? For Pumpkin's brothers or sisters?

"I don't even know that it's mine," Jack said. "You can't trust a woman like her."

William wanted to tell Jack that he knew Grace could be trusted, but maybe he was wrong. After all, William would have never believed that Grace would do something like this. Or that, knowing how much William had been hurt by being the product of an affair, she would keep this from him.

Grace stormed over to Jack. "You know it's yours. I can't believe you told her that I seduced you. It seems to me things were the other way around. You lied to me about having a wife. You said you were in the process of getting a divorce."

Instead of responding to Grace, Jack turned to his wife. "She's lying. I don't know why you had to come here to confront her, but I told you that it's over between us. My focus is on you and the kids."

Grace also looked over at Allison. "I'm truly sorry. I would have never gotten involved with Jack had he not told me you were in the process of getting divorced. He said that's why you were in California and he was in Colorado. You were just waiting for the allotted time to pass before signing the papers."

William heard the unshed tears in Grace's voice, and while part of him wanted to go to her and comfort her, hearing her defense only made him angrier. If the situation had been as innocent as all that, then why couldn't she confide in him? Did she think so little of him that he wouldn't have understood?

His heart was breaking, and he didn't have the right to say a word, not when a more serious issue was being dealt with.

Jack and his wife continued arguing, but somewhere in the middle of it, William shut out all the words and could only stare at Grace. All this time, he'd been telling her how painful it had been to be cheated on, but also to be the result of an affair. He told her how much he hated keeping secrets. Even when he'd been helping her keep hers, he'd urged her to come clean, because the truth was so much easier than a secret. But she'd kept so much from him.

William had thought he'd known her. He thought they'd been completely open with each other. But it had all been one-sided.

Yes, he knew she had the ability to keep secrets, considering she'd kept so much from her mother. But he thought he was different. He'd thought they'd had something special.

This just confirmed to William that Grace was the same as every other woman he'd known. She'd used him. William was still that good friend who was always willing to help. He'd kept Grace's secret and helped her hide her pregnancy from everyone else. It was a good thing she hadn't accepted his proposal.

In that sense, Grace had helped him, telling him not to settle for someone who wanted him to be someone other than who he was, that he deserved more. He did deserve more. He deserved a woman who understood his need for openness and honesty, and gave him such. What a fool he'd been to think that last night had changed that.

Jack and his wife were still arguing with Grace, and this time, William wasn't going to step in to save her. She'd gotten herself into this mess, and it was time she figured things out on her own. He'd spent so much time covering for her, helping her, being there for her.

William was done being used.

But this just proved that as much as he'd hoped he was making better decisions about women, he clearly hadn't learned his lesson.

As William turned to walk away, he almost ran right into Ricky and Alexander.

"What's going on?" Alexander asked.

"The wife of Grace's baby daddy decided to confront Grace for being a home wrecker," William said. "I'm sorry, but I just can't do this. Grace knew how much our mother's secrets and lies hurt us, and how devastated I was by Hailey's infidelity. She also knows how much I hate secrets. I've been here for her for everything, and she couldn't be honest with me."

The look on Alexander's face told William that his brother wasn't on his side. "You should at least talk to her," Alexander said. "Maybe there's more to it than that. I hurt Janie with the secrets I kept, and though I was wrong to do so, at the time I thought I had the right reasons. I'm sure that's the situation with Grace. Give her a chance to explain."

Logically, William could see Alexander's point. However, his brother's situation had been different. Unlike Alexander, William had a history of trusting in the wrong person and being used.

Why couldn't a woman just see him as a man and appreciate him for who he was? If Grace had really seen him and understood his heart, she would have realized how important it was to him to be told the truth. Would he have liked it? No. But had she been the one to come to him and tell him the truth, he liked to think that he would have been willing to give her a chance. He liked to think that he could have helped Pumpkin understand the situation, so that if some strange siblings popped up, it wouldn't be as devastating to Pumpkin as it had been to him.

"It doesn't matter what her explanation is," William said. "She didn't trust me, and she knows how important that is to me."

That was the bottom line for him.

Despite being told countless times by William that it was better to be honest, even when the truth was difficult, and then having it proven, she had still chosen to hide the truth from William. Even when she'd learned that there were no bad consequences for telling her mother the facts.

"Don't be so stubborn that it ruins your chance at love," Alexander said.

Him stubborn? Maybe Alexander should have given that lecture to Grace.

William kept walking.

"William!"

This time, it was Grace's voice calling after him. He stopped, though he didn't know why. What was the point? She'd tell him how afraid she was of how he'd respond when he learned the truth, which was why she'd hidden it from him. He knew all that. But that wasn't why he was angry. At least not fully. It was that she didn't believe in love and him and them enough to work it out together.

He turned to look at her. "I don't have anything to say to you. You didn't trust me. And in doing so, you've made it clear that you don't love me. We'll still finish the rodeo project together, but we're co-workers, nothing more. I'm tired of being dependable William, who is good enough for everything but a woman's heart."

Tears streamed down her face. "But I do love you," she said. "What we shared last night was special. Please. Talk to me."

He gestured at the couple arguing by their cars. "I have been talking to you. All this time, I've shared my heart openly. But that hasn't meant anything to you. If it did, you would have given me the same thing. I don't think you know what love is. Or maybe I don't. But whatever was between us, it's not love."

This time, when he started walking, he didn't look

back. He hadn't meant to say what he'd said about love, but as each footfall hit the ground, the words echoed in his heart. Maybe the deeper truth was that neither of them understood love, which meant that neither of them belonged in a romantic relationship.

All this time, he'd been trying to become a cowboy, to learn how to be the kind of man a woman could love. But as each shattered piece of his heart fell away the further he got from Grace, the more he realized that perhaps he'd been asking the wrong question to begin with.

What was love?

He didn't know, other than this mess he and Grace were in wasn't it.

Chapter Ten

So far, every plan Grace had made over the past few months had fallen apart completely. But it wasn't just her plans, it was things she'd thought to be true. Her mother hadn't reacted as she'd expected to the news of her pregnancy. And while William had rejected her when he'd found out the truth about Jack, his words about trusting him and not keeping secrets kept coming back to her.

It had been almost a month since their blowup, and still they hadn't reconnected. They were just as William had said, coworkers, and barely that.

Would things be different if she'd told him the truth about Pumpkin's parentage? That Jack had lied to her, lied to his wife, and Grace was just trying to do the right thing?

Jack and his wife had finally left after Ty stepped in, threatening legal action, as well as a paternity test and child support. Grace didn't want any of those things from Jack, but knowing the pain William and

Alexander had gone through finding out about their father as adults made her realize that this was about more than just her preference or Jack's, but what was best for Pumpkin.

She'd have liked to have gotten William's opinion on it, but he wasn't speaking to her. Until her confrontation with Jack, she hadn't made the connection that in some ways, Pumpkin was William. How was she going to raise Pumpkin so they didn't have the same shock at learning about other siblings?

After the confrontation, Grace had experienced some strange contractions and had gone to the doctor. William hadn't come. He hadn't answered any of her calls or texts, for hours. He'd finally texted to ask if she and Pumpkin were okay, and when she'd said yes, he'd said good, and that was it.

The doctor had told her to reduce her stress and had put her on a modified form of bed rest, just in case. Pumpkin was fine, but apparently, the stress Grace was under was causing issues with her pregnancy.

Which meant, for Pumpkin's sake, Grace would lie on the couch, reading over documents and making notes, but feeling utterly useless on the rodeo project.

William entered the family room that had become her base of operations.

"I talked to Javier Valdes, the bull rider we met at that party a few months ago, about using his name as a competitor in the rodeo publicity," William said, not bothering with a greeting. "He needs to talk it over with his sponsors, but he likes the cause, and is going to do what he can to participate. He's also putting word out to his buddies on the rodeo circuit to encourage them to compete, as well."

"That's good news," Grace said. "These contracts are almost ready to go to Ty for review. I'm feeling really good about where we're at with the rodeo, but I'm concerned that we still don't have any big-name sponsors. I was starting to work on that before I got put on bed rest, but I hadn't gotten any meetings set up yet."

"Email me the list, and I'll talk to them."

All business. And a coldness she'd never seen in him before. In the past, he'd have come in with a smile, asked her how she was feeling, then asked about Pumpkin.

"That's just it," she said. "Other than the Western wear store, most of my contacts are tapped out. The fire put a strain on everyone's resources. We need to look further afield, and I was only starting to do the research."

He looked at her, almost like he was looking past her or through her, but not seeing her. "Send me what you have. I've been talking to some of my contacts. Many of them are looking for a feel-good project to put their name behind. It's how I helped Alexander with the Thanksgiving dinner fundraiser."

"I could do some more research," she said, trying to find a way to break through the barrier he'd erected.

"It's okay," he said. "You're on bed rest. I might not know rodeos as well as you do, but I know people with deep pockets and the desire to support a good cause for a tax write-off. Ricky asked me to take over so you could focus on the baby. That's why I'm here. Just send me the files on what you have, and I'll do the rest."

Could he turn off his emotions that easily? Forget about Pumpkin?

He said he cared about the baby, but he hadn't even used her name. The name he'd given her. Yes, he was mad at her, she understood that. But it felt wrong for him to also turn that anger on her baby.

Maybe he'd been right. Maybe they'd both been mistaking their feelings for one another. She'd thought she loved him and if the heaviness in her heart as she clicked open her email and sent him the files was any indication, part of her still did.

But if you loved someone, wouldn't you be willing to talk it out to understand where the other person was coming from?

William hadn't even tried.

As Grace waited for the files to send, she said, "I'm sorry for not trusting you with the truth. You were right. I should have believed in you enough to know that when I shared the truth, you would have found a way to understand."

William shrugged. "I'm just glad I found out who you were before you risked any of my heart. But that's all I'm going to say on the matter. I was asked not to upset you and put the baby in any danger, and for the baby's sake, I'm willing to do that."

That was the trouble with having such a large extended family. They all wanted to look out for you and protect you, even if it wasn't what you needed.

"But this is what I want. I want us to talk this through. I don't like how things are between us."

He looked at her coldly. "And maybe what you want isn't what's best for the baby. I may not know much about love, but I do know that it means putting others' needs ahead of your own. I won't risk upsetting you and causing more trouble for your pregnancy. While you might have some things to say to me, it's not worth the potential harm you could cause to the baby by getting upset. So just drop it."

At least he still cared about Pumpkin.

And maybe he was right. No, she knew he was right. Love was about putting others' needs before your own. And it felt good to know that as angry as he was at her, he still loved her baby.

"Okay," she said. "I get it. What about those financial documents you gave me? You said something about wanting to move my retirement fund into a different account, but I'm not sure I understand the different options."

William shrugged. "I promised to help you, and I won't break my promise. But I'm also not comfortable working so closely with you. I've got a friend I can call who will take care of it for you for free."

He really was closing every door.

"And your cowboy lessons?"

"I think it goes without saying I'm no longer interested. You said something that night we were out at that barn party that's stuck with me. About the kind of man I want to be. I know I don't want to be like the guys we saw, but I'm also not sure you can give me the best advice, either. So I've been reading my Bible and looking at the kind of man God wants me to be."

The only reason she wasn't insulted was the fact that he was seeking the truth from a far better source than she could be.

"I'm glad you're reading the Bible," she said.

William shrugged. "I'm not doing it for your approval. This is about me and God, nothing more."

Then he looked at his watch impatiently. "Do I need to be here for you to send me the files? I'm supposed to meet up with Hunter for some roping lessons."

She would have liked him to stay if he'd been the old William. But she didn't want to have anything to do with the angry man before her. She'd always been bothered by the unforgiveness he harbored toward his mother for her sins and his bitter resentment over having been cheated on. Grace might not be perfect, and she'd made mistakes in her relationship with William; she didn't deny that. But he wasn't free from sin, either.

At least, though, he was turning in the right direction. Hunter had been through a lot in life and had every reason to harbor unforgiveness in his heart. But he'd built a good life for himself and was a godly man. It would be good for William to spend time with him. And, if William was studying the Bible, looking for answers, all the better.

So maybe, when he was spending time in the

Bible, William would understand that the pain he held on to wasn't worth the damage it did.

As much as Grace wanted to fix what was broken between them, until William learned a little bit about forgiveness and giving grace when people made mistakes, she wasn't sure their relationship could be repaired.

If only her heart didn't hurt so much at the thought.

When William left, her mom came into the room. "I just thought I'd come and check on you. Is everything okay?"

She knew that protective look. But her mom didn't have to protect her. Grace had gotten herself into this mess all on her own.

"It's fine. William still barely talks to me and treats me like a pariah. But it's what I deserve."

Her mom handed her a glass of lemon water. Lately, it had been doing a great job of settling her stomach. People said morning sickness only lasted a couple of months, but so far, Grace had experienced it her entire pregnancy. While her doctor had reassured her that Pumpkin was perfectly healthy, it still worried Grace. One more area where she knew William would have encouraged her, if he'd still been talking to her.

"You don't deserve anything of the sort. He hasn't even let you explain. And to not come to the hospital when you called?"

Grace sighed. "I know you're trying to be helpful. But I'm supposed to be reducing my stress, and talking about this only makes me more so."

"You're also supposed to be drinking more water, since part of your problem was dehydration. I know it's hard to keep things down sometimes, but you have to do better."

Grace took a sip of the water. "This helps, thank you. I'm trying. And I need you to try to be nicer to William. Stop serving peas at every meal, just because you know he hates them. And stop trying to get me to hate him more. I don't hate him. I'm hurt, but I hurt him, too. Just because I don't see a way back for us doesn't give you the right to treat him like a monster."

"So you still love him."

Grace sighed. "I wish the answer was as simple as that. I care about him. But I can't see a way for us to be together unless he deals with his unforgiveness issues. And then we have a lot to work through. I won't be waiting around, hoping for him to change. That's what's always gotten me in trouble in the past. I'm building a life for me and Pumpkin."

Letting go of her feelings for William brought a new lightness to her heart. This wasn't a battle that was up to her. As her mom left, Grace closed her eyes and prayed for God to work in everyone's hearts. Clearly, they all had a lot to deal with, but Grace was thankful that none of it was too big for God to handle.

Once again, William was in the barn practicing with his rope as he found himself doing most evenings after finishing up work over the past couple weeks since his falling out with Grace. He'd done his best to spend as little time as possible around her, given that he couldn't avoid her at family meals or for work. But he had to keep it professional, because if he caught a glimpse of her in an unguarded moment, he found himself remembering things.

Like the way little Pumpkin had kicked against his hand. How Grace had felt in his arms. And how, at least until her betrayal, William had thought he'd found a partner in life.

But it was just an illusion, and maybe it was something he wanted too bad, because sometimes he still wondered if he could find a way to make things with Grace work. But that was silly. She didn't love him, nor did she trust him enough in the deepest places of her heart. He swung the rope around the roping dummy, pleased that once again he'd hit his mark. Hunter had warned him that they likely wouldn't win anything, but having William participating in the benefit rodeo would be a nice gesture of goodwill to the community and remind them of the power of family connections.

"That's some fine roping there," Ricky said, stepping into the barn. "You remind me a lot of—"

"I know, Cinco."

William sighed. He wished he didn't feel like everything he did was a comparison to his biological father, and he wished it didn't hurt so much.

Ricky walked over and picked up one of the spare ropes on the side. "Actually, I was going to say myself when I was younger. I used to wish he'd follow in my footsteps and rope, but he was always more interested in the bulls."

William watched as Ricky made a loop, then tossed it perfectly over the dummy's head. "Yep. I still got it. Been a long time since I've done that."

"Why did you quit?"

Ricky shrugged. "I was getting too old, and wanted to give some of the young bucks a chance."

"You should rope at our rodeo."

"Like I said, that's for the young bucks." Ricky held the rope in his hands like he was considering it.

"I know I won't win, but I'm going to give it a try with Hunter." William didn't know why he was attempting to convince the older man to participate, but something about it felt right. "You should do the same. I'm sure people would love to see you out there."

"You know what they'd love?" Ricky asked, a twinkle in his eye.

As William shook his head, Ricky went into the tack room, then came out with some other ropes.

After a few deft movements, Ricky was swinging the rope and jumping through it. "They call this the Texas skip," he said, grinning. "Wasn't sure I could still do it, but it's just like riding a horse. Your body remembers."

He jumped through the rope a couple more times, then stopped to look at William. "My father used to travel with a Wild West show, and his specialty was rope tricks. He taught me everything I know."

He did a few more moves, demonstrating a variety

of tricks. William watched with interest, appreciating the passion on the older man's face.

After a few minutes, Ricky paused, and William said, "Maybe you can teach me sometime."

It was the right thing to say, because the grin on Ricky's face brightened the room more than any of the floodlights they'd ever put on.

"Really? Everyone thinks it's interesting, but no one seems to have much of an interest in learning."

The vulnerability on the older man's face touched a part of William's heart he hadn't expected. As he reached for the rope his grandfather held out, William felt a new peace about being here. He'd done many things with his other grandparents as a child, and they were gone now. But he had enjoyed every moment of them. And now, here he was, with a new grandfather, who was just looking for someone to connect with and love. William possessed a rich family life, always had, and had never found it lacking, which was why he hadn't realized he'd needed this connection.

But as he went through the motions Ricky was showing him with the trick rope, William wondered if maybe this wasn't about what William needed in a family relationship, but giving it to a lonely old man. Yes, Ricky had many friends who loved him but the longing in Ricky's heart was to be connected to his blood.

"You're picking it right up," Ricky said, beaming with pride. "You're a natural."

Those words didn't sting as much as they once had. Ricky had needed to know that something of him that was good was being passed down, and William was proof of it.

"I know I said I was going to do the team roping with Hunter in the rodeo, and I'd still like to do that, but do you think maybe we could also have a Ruiz family trick-roping demonstration? You could show some of your tricks, teach me a few, and we could do a little performance. I haven't seen it at the regular rodeo, but one time I went to this Mexican rodeo, and they had some amazing trick ropers."

Ricky grinned. "I've seen those. I can do all those tricks. Some, even better."

If the old man puffed out his chest any farther, it was likely to cause him injury. But it was neat to see the pride and the joy on Ricky's face to have someone appreciate him for who he was. William understood that longing. It was all he ever wanted from someone. And while he understood that love was more about what you gave than what you received, what was the point at which you should also receive?

William had always done more than his share of giving in his romantic relationships, and it wasn't that he minded doing it. He hadn't minded doing all those things for Grace, but she hadn't given to him the things he needed.

And it wasn't like he'd been asking for a lot. Respect. Trust. See him and love him.

The sound of laughter from the other part of the barn made him pause.

Grace.

"What's she doing in the barn? She's supposed to be resting."

Ricky laughed. "For a man who is doing his best to act like Grace doesn't exist, you're sure worried about her."

William rolled up the rope into a loop the way Ricky had and shrugged. "I care about the baby's safety. And I'd be a monster if I didn't care about hers."

"Why aren't you telling her that, then?"

He did his best not to glare at Ricky, but by the hard stare he received back, he probably hadn't done well in succeeding.

"I can't put myself in the position to be hurt again. I'm not going to deny that I care about Grace. But I also can't keep investing in relationships where I'm always getting the short end of the stick. It needs to be more of a partnership, like fifty-fifty."

He expected Ricky would've agreed with him, but Ricky laughed.

"Is that what you think relationships are? Ha! You've been watching too much of those girly shows on TV. Let me tell you what a relationship is. It is about giving one hundred percent all the time. Now, sometimes that one hundred percent looks to other people like fifty, or twenty-five, or when you're having a really bad day, five. Maybe it looks like nothing, but you give what you can, and the other person needs to realize that and accept it with grace."

It sounded all right in principle, because a partnership where both people gave one hundred percent seemed really good. "But what if the other person doesn't ever give their one hundred percent? What if you're the only one doing the giving?"

"Then maybe you're asking too much. When my Rosie got sick with cancer, could she give me everything? No. It was all she could do to say thank you when I helped her with basic things. Sometimes I didn't even get that. Sometimes she would just turn away from me and weep. But I loved her. I knew she didn't have anything to give, so I made sure to give her enough that she knew I loved her anyway."

Tears filled the old man's eyes, and once again, William wished he could have found someone like that to love.

"She had cancer. Of course you would help her without expecting anything in return."

Ricky glared at him. "And Grace is just pregnant. But you can't even man up and be there for her. You have some fool notion about wanting to be a cowboy. But let me tell you. A cowboy isn't all whiny about his feelings getting hurt when his woman has something bigger to deal with. You think it's easy being pregnant? To have to worry about the safety of her baby? I've never had a baby, but I sure know that if it was my woman, I wouldn't be letting some sorry excuse like my feelings being hurt keep me from her."

He wished it was as simple as Ricky was painting it to be.

"But she deliberately hid the truth from me, and she knows how I feel about secrets. It's the major thing that hurt me in life."

Ricky snorted. "Hurt you? Seems to me you found a pretty good life in spite of it. Maybe the folks keeping secrets from you have good reason to do so. And maybe instead of throwing a tantrum about it, you should go talk to them and figure out what's really going on. If it was the right thing to do in this day and age, I'd put you over my knee and tan your hide for being so stupid."

He grabbed a couple more ropes and tossed them at William. "You practice the tricks I taught you. I'm going to go do what a man does and see if Grace needs anything."

William caught the ropes, but he didn't feel much like working with them anymore.

"He's right, you know," Alexander said, entering the barn. "Didn't mean to eavesdrop, but it was an important conversation and I also didn't want to interrupt."

William stared at his brother. "So much for having my back."

Alexander shrugged. "I don't know the details about what happened between you and Grace. I've purposely stayed out of it. You're my brother, but I can't deny that I care about Grace. But I've known you forever, and I know that your biggest problem is your inability to forgive people for what they've done wrong. The past few months, my whole life has been built around forgiveness, both giving and receiving. I haven't seen you do either."

Harsh words, but he also knew that his brother's focus on forgiveness was because of the journey he'd been on in his own life. Although William hadn't messed up as badly as Alexander had in his relationships.

"Look," Alexander continued. "I know you're hurting. But it wouldn't hurt so bad if you could let go and forgive. I know you keep reading the Bible, looking for answers about love, but I think what you really need are answers about forgiveness. See what God says about that."

Since becoming a Christian, William had been focused a lot on learning what the Bible said about things. Alexander was right. He had been focused on love, and had merely skimmed the parts about forgiveness, because he hadn't thought that was an issue in his life.

"Okay," William said. "You have a point. At least in that I haven't spent much time studying forgiveness. So maybe I'll do that tonight in my reading."

Alexander nodded. "Sounds good. Which brings me to why I was looking for you in the first place. Mom came up from Denver to spend the weekend here so she could help Janie with wedding details. Thought you might like to come by and say hi. But maybe you could also start practicing that forgiveness thing with her."

William closed his eyes. Tried to ask God for guidance on the situation. But he wasn't even sure what to ask for.

He looked back at Alexander.

"I get it. Everyone wants me to forgive her for what

she did. But no one understands how much it hurts. Not even you, and I don't understand why."

Alexander shook his head slowly. "You think I wasn't hurt? I was so mad I could spit bees. But for the sake of my heart, I had to let go. The hurt isn't going to go away until you forgive. Talk to Mom. Honestly, at this point, she'd feel a whole lot better if you just yelled at her as opposed to the coldness you keep giving her."

He hadn't wanted to talk to his mom because he didn't want to hurt her by letting her know the depth of his anger. But maybe, not wanting to hurt her was exactly why he needed to work this out. He did still love his mom. And possibly, figuring things out with his mom would help him see what to do about Grace.

As he thought back over Alexander's words, he started laughing. "Did you just say you could spit bees? I don't think I've ever heard that expression."

Alexander laughed. "I guess the ranch life is starting to wear off on me a little. It's a good phrase, though, isn't it?"

William nodded. "I kind of like it here, too. The longer I'm here, the more I don't want to go back to Denver."

"You know I'm not going back, right?" Alexander asked. "Janie and I talked about it, but her life is here. And, I kind of feel the same way you do. I love it here."

"Yeah," William said. "I just don't know how it's going to work out with Grace, though. Being in the same town and all. I've been thinking about this a lot, even before our falling out. I didn't want to not watch Pumpkin grow up."

Alexander gestured toward the entrance to the barn. "I think, deep down, you know the answer. But it's gonna be up to you to learn how to forgive. You want me to come with you to talk to Mom, or do you want to do this on your own?"

His brother had always been there for him. But this time, Alexander knew he had to do it himself.

"I'll talk to her. As for Grace, I'm going to need some more time."

On the way to Alexander's cabin, William caught sight of Grace, sitting on a bench, laughing at some story Ricky was telling her. He wanted to laugh with her.

Was this longing in his heart love? He didn't know.

When he got to Alexander's, his mom was carrying things in from the car.

"Let me help you," William said, grabbing a basket out of her hands.

It was full of baby clothes.

"Is Janie expecting?"

His mom laughed. "They aren't even married yet. No, these are for Grace."

A small dagger hit his heart as he realized that his mom was buying things for Pumpkin. In the short time they'd known Grace, she'd touched the hearts of everyone in the family.

"I didn't realize you cared."

His mom shrugged. "It's scary, being pregnant and alone. I know Ricky and everyone at the ranch are taking good care of her, but I remember those days. Even though you have enough for now, you're always worried about tomorrow, or whatever happens in the future."

"But you had Dad," William said.

She gestured at the coffee table. "You can set that there." Then she pointed at one of the chairs. "Sit. I didn't always have Dad. When I met Cinco, your dad and I were separated. We'd been fighting nonstop, and here was this charming, handsome cowboy, who as much as you hate being told, you look exactly like, and he told me all the things I hadn't heard from Bill in years. At first, Cinco had told me he and his wife were separated, and we bonded over that. I found out it was a lie, but it was too late. My heart was broken, and I'd done a lot of things I regretted."

In all this time, William hadn't asked what had gone on. Didn't want to know. But the sadness on his mom's face made William want to call Cinco out or something, except he was dead, and without him, William wouldn't be here.

"Where did Dad come in?" William asked.

"I met with Bill to go over separation things, and one thing led to another. For a month or so, it looked like we might be able to work things out, but then I found out I was pregnant, and I didn't know whose baby I was carrying. I was honest with Bill, and he was deeply hurt. He left in a fit of anger, and said he needed space. I wasn't sure we were going to be able to work it out. At first, he said he would stay with me until he knew whose babies I was carrying, because if they were his sons, he'd want to be involved in their lives."

His parents hadn't told him that part of the story. Just that the situation had brought them closer.

"At what point did you find out that we weren't his?"

His mom laughed. "The second you came out. I can't believe people bought the Italian throwback story."

Then her face softened and tears filled her eyes. "But when they handed you to him, he cradled you close and said that you were his boy. And he told you how much he loved you and how he was going to raise you to be a good man and that you had the best mother in the whole world. He did the same thing with Alexander."

As absurd as it sounded, William understood. He got up and held his mom close to him. "Is that why you named me after him?"

"It's what he wanted. We decided to wait to name you guys until we met you, and from the very start, he wanted to call you William. He said he'd always wanted a son named after him. Since he was Bill, you got to be the long version. We thought it would be fun to keep Alexander as Alexander so you both had long names. I guess that was our weird 'make twins be alike' thing."

She gave him another hug. "I'm sorry that you felt slighted by any of this. I was ashamed of what happened between me and Cinco. He died while I was still pregnant, so I don't know what would've happened if he had lived. Bill always told me that if Cinco was the father and wanted to be a father to you guys, he would gladly step aside. But I'm so grateful he didn't."

William nodded slowly. "I'm glad he's my dad. And I'm glad you told me, because sometimes I feel guilty, wanting to be part of Ricky's family."

His mom gave him a tender smile. "It was never our plan to deny you that. But with Cinco dead, and knowing I was the other woman, it just didn't seem right to stir things up and hurt people. If my family had known what I'd done with Cinco, they would have been ashamed of me. I was already so ashamed of myself that I didn't need any more piled on top of it."

Though he knew she wasn't trying to, her words hit a very painful part of his heart. Grace had been keeping her pregnancy a secret because of her shame, and given that she had also been the other woman, he could see where that would have been a very deep shame for her, as well.

"Don't feel bad about being here," his mom said. "I'm so glad to be part of Ricky's family, too. He and I have talked a few times, and my only regret is that I didn't figure out a way to reach out to his family. But I couldn't break the heart of a heavily pregnant grieving woman, and I didn't know that she and Ricky were estranged."

All this time, William had been making the situation about him and how it had hurt him, and he thought his mother the bad guy. But having talked to her, he could see where it wasn't as cut-and-dried as he'd made it. And suddenly, it was his turn to feel ashamed. Alexander had been right. William was the one who needed to be forgiven.

"I'm sorry for judging you," William said. "And I'm sorry how I've treated you lately. Can you forgive me?"

His mom brought him into her arms. "Of course. I have been forgiving you constantly this whole time. I know you were hurt and confused. I'm sorry for keeping the truth from you."

She gave him a final squeeze, then released him. "Since we're being honest, when you guys got us that DNA test kit last Christmas, your dad and I were hesitant. We knew what those test results would be, and we weren't sure what can of worms it would open up. He threw his in the trash, but I pulled it out and mailed it anyway, because I'd wanted to tell you so many times. Not because Bill isn't a great father, but because you hear the stories about people with diseases and things, where they needed blood relatives. I didn't want you to be in a position where you had some kind of thing wrong and we couldn't help you because we kept the truth from you."

Then she shook her head and chuckled softly. "I understand that's how Rachel found Ricky. I'm glad she got the kidney she needed, and I'm glad to be getting to know her. We couldn't give you any other siblings, but God found a way to make it happen anyway."

His mom gestured at the basket on the table. "Now

come, help me sort through these so I can get them over to Grace."

She pulled out one of those things Grace said was called a onesie, and it had a similar pattern to the horse blanket he'd bought her. The sight put a deep longing in his heart.

In some ways, his parents' story was similar to his own. Grace wasn't carrying his baby, but he'd be lying if he said he didn't love Pumpkin. And, understanding his mom's shame helped him understand more about Grace's.

She was ashamed, and he'd rejected her. True, it was mostly about the secrets she kept, but they hadn't talked it through. Who knew what Grace thought, and how much more ashamed he'd made her feel.

William didn't, but that was because when he was mad at someone, instead of working through it, he shut them out and wallowed in it. How much better would things have been between him and his mother had he just talked to her in the first place? How much less guilt would he have felt at being here had he understood her desires for him?

Everyone was right. While he couldn't go so far as to say that he and Grace belonged together, or that what they had was love, he owed it to them both to at least find out.

Chapter Eleven

Grace sat on one of the rocking chairs on the front porch, petting Ty's dog. The nice thing about working on a ranch was it was always bring-your-dog-to-work day, and it gave Grace the chance to enjoy other people's dogs. She was trying to have a baby on her own, so a pet was the last thing she needed.

"Good morning, Grace," William said, walking up onto the porch.

She ignored him. Two could play at this game, and even though it felt childish, she was tired of the way he was always so brusque with her.

But instead of doing his usual and walking right past her into the main ranch house, he came over and petted the dog.

"She's such a good dog. Makes me want one of my own, except that I'm not at a place in my life where I could give it the attention it deserves."

Grace looked up at him. "Are you talking to me, or the dog?"

He took a step back. "I'm not one to talk to dogs, so, you?"

"Hard to tell, since you barely say a word to me anymore these days. I figure you'd be friendlier to the dog."

Maybe it was immature to think in terms of scoring points, but she liked that he looked visibly wounded at her words. He'd done enough of that to her lately, so why not get in some digs of her own? Did he really think he could just walk up to her like nothing had happened between them?

"I'm sorry," he said. "That's why I'm here. I owe you an apology."

She hated that those simple words were enough to make her want to automatically forgive him. And if it had just been about their little fight, then maybe it would be easier. But he'd been so cold to her lately, and each icy response had chipped away at another piece of her heart.

"More like several, but I stopped counting," she said.

Pumpkin kicked, and Grace rubbed the spot. But it was a good reminder of where her priorities had to be.

"So do it, then. Apologize. But I think you are right to keep our relationship business only. My sole focus is on Pumpkin, and I don't need you distracting me from it."

The expression on his face told her that he didn't like her answer, and she was disgusted that she cared. Hadn't she been hurt enough? Hadn't this whole relationship been enough of a roller coaster? Given his grudge against his mom, and how easily he'd turned on Grace, she couldn't risk him hurting her again. Not when she had a baby to keep safe.

"I guess I really hurt you," he said. "I'm sorry. I should have talked to you that day at the ranch when you were trying. Instead, I was a jerk. I didn't hear you out. And I've treated you abominably since."

The trouble with him owning his wrongdoing was that it made it harder for her to stay mad. "You really have," she said. "I didn't deserve that."

William nodded. "I know. I was protecting myself, and I didn't think about how it would impact you or the baby."

He came closer, almost close enough that if she stood, she could hug him. But she wouldn't.

"How is Pumpkin doing?" he asked. "You seem to be feeling okay, and at meals you seem to be eating a wider variety of foods. I acted like I didn't care, but I pray for you both every day, multiple times."

She wrapped her hands around her stomach, cradling Pumpkin. Why did he have to bring it back to this? The worst part about their estrangement was not having him to share her pregnancy with. Yes, she had the support of all her friends and family, but there was something special about what William gave her that had been missing in her life.

Grace had to learn to do without. "We're fine. The doctor says everything has been looking good, and I'm allowed to get up and do more things, provided I don't overdo it. But he still thinks it's important for me to reduce my stress."

"I'm sorry if I've caused you stress," he said. "Please, tell me what I need to do, because I will do anything I can to make sure you and Pumpkin stay healthy through this pregnancy."

And that was the trouble. She didn't know what she needed from him. The coldness was hurtful, yes, but she also wasn't sure she could handle any more of the emotional turmoil from William.

"I don't know if I have an answer for that," she said. "You hurt me, and you weren't there for me when I needed you the most. That day with Jack and his wife was horrible. What I really needed from you was for you to hug me and tell me it was going to be okay. But you didn't. You reacted exactly as I thought you would when you found out."

The expression on William's face made her regret her words. "You're saying I'm the reason that you were having problems with your pregnancy and had to go on bed rest."

She hadn't thought he'd blame himself. "No, I didn't say that at all. Yes, stress contributed to the situation, but you weren't the only stressful thing in that moment. I never imagined that Jack's wife would confront me. Or that he would tell so many lies about me. But also, I was dehydrated, and I hadn't been eating enough protein or taking my vitamins."

Instead of looking relieved, William looked only more upset. "I'm making it about me again. I'm sorry. I just want to do right by you and Pumpkin, but no matter what I say, I seem to keep messing it up."

He gestured at the rocking chair next to her. "Is it okay if I sit down?"

"Yes," she said.

She wished she was strong enough to say no, because it was clear he wanted to talk, and if they talked, she might do something ridiculous like giving him another shot. When she wasn't actively angry at him, she could still close her eyes and feel his lips against hers, could still remember what it was like to be in his arms, and she missed it.

"I talked to my mom," he said. "You were right. I should have done it a long time ago. We've forgiven each other. Talking to her and hearing how ashamed she was made me realize the shame you probably felt in your situation. I'm sorry for adding to that."

She blinked back tears, despising how easily he'd said exactly the right thing. How was she supposed to respond? Yes, she should forgive him, but what then?

"Thank you," she said. "I forgive you, but this doesn't change our relationship. We can't have one."

Pumpkin kicked again, but it hit her funny in the ribs, causing her to wince.

"You okay?" William asked. "Should I get the doctor?"

He had jumped up before she could even answer, and it was like the old William had returned.

"No, I'm fine. But telling you about my dehydration has reminded me that I haven't been drinking my water and I should."

He nodded slowly. "You stay there. I'll get it for

you. I noticed your mom has been putting little lemon slices in it. Do you want me to do that?"

Tears stung the backs of her eyes. Even when he was shutting her out, he was still noticing. And just that small gesture...

A car pulled up in front of the house, and William stilled. "What is he doing here?"

"You know them?" Grace asked.

"It's my old boss, Tom."

The passenger door opened, and a pregnant woman got out. "And his daughter," William said.

Hailey walked up the steps like she owned the place. "William, baby!"

She acted like she was going to give him a hug and kiss or something, but he stepped back.

"I'm not your baby," he said. "We broke up, re-member? You wanted to be with the father of your child."

Hailey rubbed her belly and made a pouty face. Grace hoped she didn't look like that.

"Colt said he wasn't ready for the responsibilities of being a father. I made a terrible mistake. Being a parent is all about responsibility, and I was stupid to ruin the life we built because I thought I wanted excitement. You and I talked about having children together, and I know you're going to make a great father."

Grace looked at William to see if he was buying this, but she couldn't read the expression on his face.

"You're right," he said. "I am going to be a great father. But it won't be to your baby. I'm sorry you wasted a trip out here, but you killed any love I had for you when you cheated on me."

He looked over at Grace when he said the part about not being a father to Hailey's baby. Was it implausible that Grace still wanted him to be Pumpkin's father? She didn't need this right now. She had a baby to grow, not these emotions to deal with.

Tom joined Hailey on the steps. "Now I know you're probably bitter about what happened," he said. "But I am prepared to make things right. You'll be a full partner in my firm, and I heard that you're trying to find sponsors for this rodeo that you're running. You can count on the firm for any dollar amount sponsorship you want. You just take my little girl back."

Was he kidding? Grace looked from the man over to William, then at Hailey. It was like being in the middle of some weird bride-selling scheme.

"I do think that what you did was wrong," William said. "But all this isn't going to make it right. I don't love Hailey, and she doesn't love me. That's a bad reason for marriage."

William glanced at Grace. "When I get married, I want it to be because both of us love each other and are committed to making a relationship work."

That's kind of what he'd said to her the day he'd suggested they get married, only neither of them had been communicating to each other well enough to understand that it was what they both wanted. But the question still remained whether or not they loved each other to actually make it work.

Still, it put a flutter in her heart to have him look at her like that.

Her stomach felt worse, and she'd have liked to get up and go inside, but she didn't want to draw attention to herself.

"You are the only good guy Hailey has ever dated," his ex-boss said. "You gave her the stability she needs. I can't have her living in some trailer with the rodeo cowboy."

Hailey sighed. "There wasn't enough room for all my shoes. How was I going to fit a baby in there?"

Once again, Grace had to wonder if this woman was for real, but the sympathetic way her father patted her on the back made her realize this wasn't a joke.

No wonder William was tired of women using him. If this was the sort of woman he was attracted to, there was no way he could have made a relationship with any of them work. She hoped he'd be able to see that. It was what Grace had been telling him all along. The problem wasn't with William, but with his choices in women.

Well, okay, there were some problems with William. Grace smiled slightly, rubbing her stomach in hopes that the strange pain she was feeling would settle down.

Then Hailey smiled at William. "But look at you, dressed all handsome like a cowboy, with your hat and boots. I underestimated you. I think we need to give us another try."

He'd definitely become what he'd thought he needed to be to win over a woman. And it had worked.

But, as Grace had often thought, it wasn't going to get him what he wanted.

William shook his head. "I don't. I wear these clothes because they're practical for working on a ranch. You might think you want to date a cowboy, but for a real cowboy, it's not all about the trappings. It's what's inside that counts. I'm not a good cowboy, not in the way I'd like to be. But I'm learning things from my grandfather, Ricky, and I hope someday I can be half the cowboy that he is."

Grace's heart welled up with joy as she heard his words. This was what she had been trying to get him to understand from the beginning. In spite of their estrangement, William had figured it out.

As much as she wished she could have helped him through it, she was grateful he'd been seeking God, as well as the advice from godly men.

If only it didn't make her heart hurt just a little bit, knowing that he was just what she wanted in a man. Even though it was frustrating to have Hailey interrupt their conversation, it proved to Grace all the ways William had been growing.

But was it enough for them to make things work?

"I hear Ricky has a nice portfolio. This ranch is probably worth a bundle," Hailey's dad said.

William shrugged. "I honestly know nothing about Ricky's finances, and I don't want to. I'm not here for his money, but for our relationship. Like I said, I'm sorry that you two wasted all this time driving out, but I am not interested in your offer."

The man looked a bit stunned, then said, "But I

understand you're desperate for sponsors for some rodeo fundraiser thing."

"Not that desperate," William said. "Now if you'll excuse me, I think it's time you two went on your way. It's a long drive back to Denver, and I have things to do."

He looked over at Grace. "You never did tell me whether or not you wanted lemon in your water."

Grace closed her eyes and leaned back against the chair. She was feeling a bit lightheaded all of a sudden, and her stomach felt weird.

"It doesn't matter," she said. "I can wait."

"You have got to be kidding me," Hailey said. "You keep looking at her like she means something to you. Are you with her? No wonder you weren't interested in getting back together. You've already got some tramp knocked up."

Grace wanted to argue, to say something, but the pain in her stomach was making it impossible to put words together.

"Grace isn't a tramp," William said. "She's a good woman. While I don't deserve her, she's taught me that you don't deserve me."

"I cannot believe I was ready to put my trust in you," Hailey's dad said. "You had to have been carrying on with her while dating my daughter."

It was almost laughable how many people automatically assumed that William was her baby's father.

"How dare you be mad at me for cheating on you when you clearly had to be cheating on me," Hailey said, her voice a screech. "She's bigger than I am! That cow is huge."

That woman did not just call Grace a cow. Grace pulled herself out of the chair. Except when she did, the pain tore through her side.

"Grace! Are you okay?"

The next thing she knew, Grace was in William's arms. Part of her wanted to tell him that she was fine and she didn't need his help. But the truth was, she was scared, more scared than she'd been the first time she'd gone to the hospital. Everything had been okay with the baby then, but what if it wasn't this time?

The doctor had warned her to avoid stress. She was supposed to be drinking lots of water, and she'd been bad at it lately. Sometimes she got so busy that she forgot. She just hoped that her forgetfulness hadn't harmed her baby.

But this pain was different. It was worse than anything she'd ever experienced.

Tears rolled down her face, and William held her tighter.

"It's going to be okay. Pumpkin is going to be okay."

William shouted for help.

Grace was trying to take deep breaths, using the stress-relieving technique the doctor had taught her.

Please, God, let Pumpkin be okay.

Chapter Twelve

The drive to the hospital had been the longest William had ever remembered. Ricky had insisted on taking Grace and her mother to the hospital while William remained behind to deal with Hailey and her father. Fortunately, they were under the impression that Grace was carrying his baby, and William wasn't about to dissuade them of the notion. They'd left almost right after Grace, so William wasn't too far behind everyone.

Besides, as he drove a bit faster than he should have to get there, all William could think about was that it was the woman he loved, his baby, and he needed to be there. He still kicked himself for having not been there the last time, but after he'd stormed off, he'd gone for a hike where there wasn't cell reception and didn't see the missed call until it was too late. He wasn't going to miss being there for his baby this time.

No, not just his baby. The woman he loved.

Though he'd been fumbling over an apology about having not listened to Grace, he owed her an apology for a lot of other reasons.

Ricky had been right. Yes, William had given Grace a lot of love. But he'd failed to give her understanding and compassion over a difficult situation. He should've listened to her. Should have given her the chance to explain. But more important, he should have trusted her anyway, and believed that even if she had been with a married man, there would've been a good explanation for it. He should have been more understanding that she'd had her reasons for keeping it a secret.

He thought about his mother's words, about the shame she'd felt, and understanding Grace's shame. William knew Grace had issues with feeling shame. He should have put his need for the truth below Grace's need for acceptance and reassurance.

Today on the porch, Grace had made it clear that he'd hurt her deeply with his actions. But seeing Hailey and hearing her father's offer for him to become her baby's father had made something very clear. William loved Grace.

He hadn't offered to become Pumpkin's father simply to help out a single mom. If that's all he'd wanted to do, he could have married Hailey. But it was a resounding no in his heart before the words even came out of his mouth.

Which left William knowing that he loved Grace.

He'd already known he loved her. That was clear the second his lips touched hers, maybe before. But now he knew that he loved Grace enough that nothing mattered to him, other than being there for her.

All his nonsense about it being fifty-fifty or getting back a certain percentage had been way off the mark. Ricky was right; you gave one hundred percent, trusting that whatever the other person gave you was enough.

So what did it mean to love Grace, moving forward?

He spent the entire drive trying to think of how he could show her. Especially when she'd made it clear how badly he'd messed up.

When he got to the hospital, he raced to the room Ricky had texted him. But as he started down the hall, the nurse stopped him.

"You can't go in there. Friends and family have to wait in the waiting room. I'm tired of telling you people that."

"Who's in there with her?"

"No one," the nurse said.

Grace shouldn't have to go through this alone. William didn't need to have the feelings talk with her to sit beside her, hold her hand and pray that everything would be all right.

"I'm the baby's father," he said.

The nurse looked doubtful.

"Please," he said. "Pumpkin's life might be in danger, and maybe Grace's. I don't know. But I need to be with them. They need to know that they are loved through this difficult time."

The nurse nodded. "Okay. As long as she's okay with you being in there."

She opened the door, and William went inside, where Grace was lying in a bed, hooked up to some monitors.

"Grace, how are you? How is Pumpkin?"

"William! I'm glad you're here." She pointed to one of the screens. "That's Pumpkin's heartbeat. They did an ultrasound to make sure she's okay. I know I said I wanted to be surprised, but I had to ask. You were right. She's a girl."

"I hope he's not intruding," the nurse said. "But he insisted that he is the baby's father. I can make him leave if you want."

"I just want to be here for you and Pumpkin," William said. "You shouldn't have to go through this alone. We're in this together. However you want me."

"He is the baby's father," Grace told the nurse. "He can stay."

Her words put a new hope in his heart. Could God have answered his prayers?

When the nurse left, William reached for Grace's hand. "I'm sorry. For so many things. And I don't want to talk about any of it, if it's going to upset you or stress you out. I want to do what's best for Pumpkin. I was wrong to take my frustrations out on you and make it all about me. That's not what's important here. I'm willing to put aside my desires so that you and Pumpkin can have what you need. Whatever you need me to do, I'm here."

William was rambling, but he had to get it all out,

so Grace understood how sorry he was, and that he was there for her, and willing to be what she needed during this time.

He squeezed her hand. "I mean that. I don't want you dealing with this alone. I'm willing to let our relationship be what you're comfortable with. You're the boss here. Thank you for letting me stay."

Grace looked up at him and smiled. "You're welcome. The last time I went through this, all I could think about was how much I wanted you to be there. I was hurt and angry, but I still thought it would be easier with you."

"I'm sorry I wasn't. I know we have a long way to go, but can you forgive me?"

She gave him another smile as she squeezed his hand. "As much as I didn't want to admit it at the time, I forgave you the second you walked up the stairs and said you were sorry. I don't want to fight. And I don't want to pretend that I don't care when I do. Hiding things and pretending is what got me in this position. I was under so much stress, keeping my pregnancy from everyone, and then feeling guilty about my secret over the circumstances and being afraid to tell you. I have to recognize that some of my problems, I brought on myself."

The door opened, and the doctor came in. "None of this is your fault. Everything with the baby is fine. That pain you're feeling is appendicitis. But we'll get that taken care of, and both you and the baby are going to be fine."

As the doctor explained about the surgery, and the

risks to Grace and the baby as well as what they were doing to minimize those risks, William alternated between listening and praying. He prayed for the safety of Grace and Pumpkin, as well as for the doctors who would be treating them. But he also thanked God, for giving them the blessing, and hopefully for the chance to make their relationship right. Whatever it looked like.

He'd meant it when he said that he was willing to let Grace take the lead on this one.

When the doctor left, Grace sighed deeply as she leaned back against the pillows. "I'm scared," she whispered. "I know the doctor said that they do this all the time, but it doesn't make it any less scary to need surgery so close to where little Pumpkin is."

"I'm here for you," he said. "I'm glad the doctor reassured you that nothing you did hurt Pumpkin. I know you wouldn't hurt her for the world."

"What if I'm not a good mom?" Grace said, her voice shaking slightly. "Pumpkin isn't even born yet, and I've messed so many things up."

William reached forward and brushed the stray hair that had fallen down her cheek. "None of that. We just settled that you didn't cause this. And as for all the ways we've messed things up, the important thing is how we put things back together. We're human. We're going to make mistakes. I made so many with you. But you're choosing to forgive me anyway."

He left his hand resting on her cheek, and he couldn't bear to take it away, but she didn't seem to mind. "I think you're going to be a great mother. You're choosing to put Pumpkin's needs first, and that's what any parent would do. It seems to me that you have it figured out even before she's born."

Grace took his hand from her cheek and rested it on her belly. "She's kicking again."

William closed his eyes and breathed a prayer of thanks to God as he felt his daughter moving underneath his hand. The first time Grace had let him feel her kick, he'd thought it was the most amazing thing ever. But this moment was even more so. His daughter was saying hi to him, or at least that's what he was going to let himself believe, and Grace was encouraging it.

"No matter what happens with us, I'll always be there for her," William said.

"I—" Grace said. "Even though you told me you didn't want to talk about it, I do. Are you making a commitment to both of us, or just her?"

His eyes met hers; he could see the fear in there, just as strongly as she feared having surgery.

"I'm making that commitment to you both. I love you, and I stupidly didn't ever express that properly to you. But I'm going to keep loving you, no matter what."

He thought about Ricky's words, but he also thought about his parents, and how they had worked through so many of their relationship issues during his mother's pregnancy.

"I've had to think a lot about what love meant, because I've mistaken it for so many things when it wasn't. But here's what I think love is. Love is watching your wife die of cancer and doing whatever you can to be there for her. Love is working through a relationship with the woman who may or may not be carrying your babies and immediately accepting them as your own when they're born because in your heart, they are. You don't have cancer, but I'm still not leaving your side. I know that Pumpkin isn't biologically mine, but she's mine in every way that counts. So the only thing that's left for me to learn about love is how to be a little less worried about what I'm getting, and more concerned with what else I can give. So what can I give you to make you feel loved?"

Grace smiled at him. "Another one of those amazing kisses."

William bent and kissed her gently, tenderly. If she hadn't been hooked up to all the machines, he would've taken her in his arms and done it properly. But just the lightest touch of his lips on hers was all they could manage for now.

"I love you, too," she said. "And I want to work on us. I want to talk about the things we've been running from, and I want to be open with you. I want to explain everything about Jack, and how I found myself in such a terrible situation. I didn't—"

William put his finger over her lips. "I don't need to know. Someday, when we aren't trying to sort through our relationship, and it feels right, then you can tell me. But for now, I need you to know that I trust you. When everyone was arguing that day, you said you didn't know he was married, and I believe you. I believe that you would have never intentionally gotten involved with a married man. I believe that you wouldn't have tried to hurt a family. I can't imagine the burden you must feel over the entire situation. That's a heavy load for you to carry, and I'm sorry I heaped more onto it. You don't owe me anything in terms of an explanation."

Grace took his hand and moved it back to her belly. "She's kicking again. I was so ashamed, and I thought you would think badly of me. I should have trusted you to work through it, rather than have it blow up in all of our faces."

Funny how he'd already figured that out. But it felt good to have her trust him enough to tell him that.

"My reaction when I found out didn't help," William said. "I hated that you kept it from me, knowing how strongly I felt. But I can also see why I would have made you afraid to tell me. The real question is, can we work through things like this together in the future?"

Grace nodded. "I want that with all my heart. You said you didn't know what love was, but I didn't know, either. I think we've both taught each other what it means to love and be loved. I did a terrible job of explaining to you why I loved you before. That's what I was trying to say."

She gave him a tender look that melted his heart. "Yes, I love you for all the things you've done for me, not because of what you've done for me, but because it reveals your heart. I always hated the idea of you needing to become a cowboy so that women would want you, because I always thought you were enough just as you were."

It was all he had ever wanted. Looking back at all the things they'd talked about when she was trying to teach him how to be a cowboy, he could hear her telling him over and over that he needed to be content in who he was.

"I appreciate that," he said. "But I also kind of like being a cowboy. And I like that I'm getting in touch with my roots, being part of this ranch and learning Ricky's family traditions. Just as you told me, I've been counting my blessings, and I'm so grateful for being here, especially because it brought me to you."

"You're one of my greatest blessings, too," she said. "You're going to be a wonderful father to Pumpkin."

As if the baby agreed, Pumpkin gave his hand a tiny kick.

"So what does being Pumpkin's father mean? Am I the guy who sees her on weekends or do I live with her and her mom? And what about Jack?"

Grace sighed. "He still insists he's not the father, and he wants nothing to do with Pumpkin even if he is. Ty put together an agreement for Jack to sign away his parental rights. It has a clause that will allow me to tell Pumpkin the truth when the time is right. I don't know what that timing looks like, because I know how much it hurt you to find out the way you did. But I'm hoping that we will come up with a good plan together."

She paused for a moment, then continued. "As for

our living situation, I'm pretty sure that Ricky would bring out the shotgun if we were living together and not married. But I sure would like to have you in our lives all the time. I don't want you just to be a father to Pumpkin. I need a husband who will love me and cherish me just like you do."

It was everything he wanted. More, actually, because he hadn't known how the parental rights thing would work, since he wasn't Pumpkin's biological father. He loved that Grace wanted to make him a part of whatever process needed to happen so that everyone could feel good about Pumpkin learning about her biological father.

"In that case," he said. "Will you marry me? I feel weird asking because it seems this conversation never goes well for the both of us, but I also don't want to beat around the bush. It sounds like that's the kind of commitment you want from me, and it's what I want from you."

Grace leaned forward. "I thought you'd never ask. Yes, I'll marry you. Now let's get this nurse in here to get me ready for surgery so we can all get healthy, and we can plan the rest of our lives together."

They had just enough time for another tender kiss before the nurse came in. William went and got their friends and family to see Grace before she went into surgery, and other than that, he remained by her side until the doctors wheeled her away.

When she woke up, William was still by her side.

"Good morning, soon-to-be Mrs. Bennett," he said.

"Then it wasn't just a weird dream," she said.

"Not a dream, and nothing weird about it."

He pointed at the heart monitors. "That says Pumpkin is doing just fine," he said. "The nurses tell me she's going to be a feisty one, and I told them that's a good thing, because her parents will need her to keep them in line."

Grace smiled weakly. "Not me. Just her father."

"Seriously, though," he said. "The doctor told me everything went perfectly. You'll be back to your old self in no time, and Pumpkin is going to grow into a healthy, happy baby."

"The doctor didn't say Pumpkin was going to be happy," Grace said. "How could he know?"

William leaned forward and kissed Grace's forehead. "Because he could tell that Pumpkin's parents love each other very much. Now get some rest, and I'm going to tell our families that you and Pumpkin are doing well. Later, we can tell them about the wedding they're going to plan, which I hope is before Pumpkin is born, because I don't want anyone questioning whether or not I can be in the room with you."

"Deal," Grace said. "Because I definitely don't want to do that alone."

He gave her a gentle kiss on the lips, then left to go reassure everyone that the two people he loved the most in the world were going to be okay.

No, more than okay. They were on their way to a beautiful life together.

Epilogue

Grace adjusted the baby in her arms for a better view of the rodeo arena. "Look, Pumpkin, that's your daddy and your great granddaddy doing those rope tricks."

They hadn't literally named her Pumpkin, because that would be just silly. Her name on the birth certificate was Rosie, after the great love Ricky had for his wife that had inspired William and Grace's marriage. Still, everyone called her Pumpkin, and maybe someday, they'd figure out how to get her to answer to a name that wouldn't get her teased in school.

And yes, Grace also knew that at a month old, Pumpkin couldn't actually see the two men doing their trick rope routine in the arena. But it didn't matter. History was being made, and they were both here to see it.

Judging from the oohs and ahhs of the crowd, William and Ricky's act was a hit, and it warmed Grace's heart to know that the family tradition wouldn't end with Ricky.

Because it was easy enough to work remotely as a financial planner, William had set up his own financial planning business, working out of their cabin at the ranch, though he was looking at renting space in Columbine Springs. He wouldn't be a rancher in the traditional sense, but the Double R legacy would live on in William.

"They look good, don't they?" her mom said, leaning in to Grace.

"They do. I love how happy they both look."

"Ricky's Rosie would have been proud," her mom said. "She loved watching Ricky do his rope tricks. He used to get so frustrated that Cinco didn't want to learn. She used to tell Ricky to be patient. Funny how it took a whole new generation for that dream to come true."

Grace kissed Pumpkin on top of her head. "I wish she knew just how many dreams she's made come true. If it wasn't for her example, I don't think any of our lives would be as good. I don't remember her, but I thank God for her."

Even though Grace had been watching them practice for months, there was something special about seeing them do it in front of a crowd who appreciated the artistry. When the performance was over, Grace carried Pumpkin to the arena entrance and gave William a big hug.

"You did amazing. I knew you would, but I'm glad I get to say it now."

Ricky trotted over to them. "That was fantastic. We've got to do that more."

Then he took Pumpkin out of Grace's arms and swung her around. "And you, our sweet little Pumpkin girl, you are eventually going to be the star of our show."

Ricky cradled the baby close to him, then wandered off chattering to her about the rodeo.

"Did he just kidnap our baby again?" William asked, sounding indignant, but his eyes twinkled.

"That does seem to happen with a great regularity," Grace said. "He never got to have this time with his grandchildren as babies, so I think he's going to make up for it with his great-grandchildren."

They watched him for a minute, then laughed as he said something to William's siblings, then walked away with Alexander's son, Sam, and Rachel's daughter, Katie, as well.

"I think you're right," William said. "So there's only one solution."

"What's that?" Grace asked.

William pulled her into his arms. "We're going to have to give Pumpkin a brother or sister so that when Ricky steals Pumpkin, we have another one we can love."

When he was finished kissing her, Grace pulled away and smiled. "There's only one problem with that plan."

"What's that?" William asked.

She gestured over to where Ricky was showing

the kids off to a group of old cowboys. "He'll just steal that one, too."

The look of contentment on William's face made Grace's heart melt. "I guess there are worse things in life than having an old cowboy love your kids. If Ricky takes them all, that just gives me a little more alone time with you."

William grinned, then bent to kiss her again. She would have liked for the kiss to never end, but they were standing at the entrance to the arena in the middle of the rodeo.

"Stop. You're going to get us in trouble," she said.

William gave her one more quick kiss and she laughed. "I don't mind getting in trouble, as long as it's with you. That's how I feel about life in general."

Before she could answer, the announcer called Ricky out into the middle of the arena, and Ricky looked like he was expecting it. Grace looked over to see that Rachel and Janie had the kids at the edge of the arena. Then Ricky got a hold of the mic.

"Some of you know that I've always said there would never be bull riding in my arena, on account of me losing my son to a bull. But that was a grieving foolish old man. My heart is healed, thanks to the love of my family. Rachel, Alexander, William, will you come out here? When I went searching for Cinco's child, I never expected to be so richly blessed in spite of my bitterness. I didn't find the child I was looking for, but I did find three grandchildren I didn't know about, as well as a deep healing I never expected. That's not me bragging on me, but bragging on God, for being able to do a great work in all of us. That's the only reason we're doing this event here."

Ricky gestured at the stands. "And all of you fine people are part of it. I wouldn't be who I am without this community, and I'm proud to say that based on feedback from our competitors and sponsors, we'll be hosting this rodeo as an annual event, and each year, the proceeds will go to a different community organization."

Applause thundered through the crowd.

Grace pushed William to go out to the arena, but William took her by the hand. "Not without you. You're part of me, and part of this healing that this family has received."

As they walked out, Grace noticed that Rachel and Alexander had brought their spouses, as well. As the stands thundered with applause, her heart welled up with joy and gratitude, knowing Ricky was right. They were all richly blessed, not because of anything special they had done, but because God loved them, and she was excited to see where the rest of this adventure would take them.

* * * * *

*If you enjoyed this story, be sure to pick up
the previous books in
Danica Favorite's Double R Legacy miniseries:*

**The Cowboy's Sacrifice
His True Purpose**

Available now from Love Inspired!

Dear Reader,

When I started this book, I had a different idea of what the world would look like, and what the process of writing this book would look like. But things changed, and so many things that I thought were constant had changed. Thankfully, the love of God is always constant, and as I wrote this book, I was always drawn back to the constancy of God's love. That constancy is what allowed my characters to share the love they did. I pray, in a world where we never really know what's going to happen, that we cling to the reminder of that truth.

I love hearing from my readers, so if you want to keep in touch, please contact me at DanicaFavorite.com.

May you and your family continue to abide in God's love,
Danica Favorite

**WE HOPE YOU ENJOYED
THIS BOOK FROM**

LOVE INSPIRED
INSPIRATIONAL ROMANCE

Uplifting stories of faith, forgiveness and hope.

Fall in love with stories where faith helps
guide you through life's challenges, and discover
the promise of a new beginning.

6 NEW BOOKS AVAILABLE EVERY MONTH!

LIHALO2021

Arleta had tossed and turned all night ruminating over Sovilla's
and Noah's remarks. And in the wee hours of the morning, she'd
come to the decision that—as disappointing as it would be—if
they wanted her to leave, she'd make her departure as easy and
amicable for them as she could.

"Your *groossmammi* is tiring of me—that's why she wanted
me to go to the frolic," she said to Noah. "She said she wanted to
be alone. And if I'm not at the *haus*, I can't be of any help to her,
which means you're wasting your money paying me. Besides, her
health is improving now and you probably don't need someone
here full-time."

"Whoa!" Noah commanded the horse to stop on the shoulder
of the road. He pushed his hat back and peered intently at Arleta.
"I'm sorry that what I said last night didn't reflect the depth of my
appreciation for all that you've done. But I consider your presence
in our home to be a gift from *Gott*. It's invaluable. Please don't
leave because of something *dumm* I said that I didn't mean. I was
overly tired and irritated at—at one of my coworkers and… Well,
there's no excuse. Please just forgive me—and don't leave."

Hearing Noah's compliment made Arleta feel as if she'd just
swallowed a cupful of sunshine; it filled her with warmth from

her cheeks to her toes. But as much as she treasured his words, she doubted Sovilla felt the same way. "I've enjoyed being at your *haus*, too. But your *groossmammi*—"

"She said something she didn't mean, too. Or she didn't mean it the way you took it. If I know my *groossmammi* as well as I think I do, she felt like you should go out and socialize once in a while instead of staying with her all the time. But she knew you'd resist it if she said that, so she turned the tables and claimed she wanted the *haus* to herself for a while."

That thought had occurred to Arleta, too. "*Jah*, perhaps."

"I'm sure of it. I can talk to her about it when—"

"*Neh*, please don't. I don't want to turn a molehill into a mountain." Arleta realized she should have spoken with Noah before jumping to the conclusion that neither he nor Sovilla wanted her to stay. But she'd been so homesick yesterday, and she'd felt even more alone after she'd listened to the other women implying how disgraceful it was for a young woman to work out. Hannah's lukewarm invitation to the frolic contributed to her loneliness, too. So by the time Sovilla and Noah made their remarks, Arleta already felt as if no one truly wanted her around and she jumped to the conclusion they would have preferred to employ someone else. She felt too silly to explain all of that to Noah now, so she simply said, "I shouldn't have been so sensitive."

"*Neh*. My *groossmammi* and I shouldn't have been so insensitive." Noah's chocolate-colored eyes conveyed the sincerity of his words. "It can't be easy trying to please both of us at the same time."

Arleta laughed. Since she couldn't deny it, she said, "It might not always be easy, but it's always interesting."

"Interesting enough to stay for the rest of the summer?"

Don't miss
Hiding Her Amish Secret *by Carrie Lighte,*
available May 2021 wherever
Love Inspired books and ebooks are sold.

LoveInspired.com

LIEXP0421

From the corner of my eye, I saw the little pistol flash up in the girl's hand. Immediately recognized the weapon as a New Line .32-caliber pocket pistol.

For reasons I could not have explained to God, or anyone else, afterward, the fact that Clementine Webb had the barrel of a loaded weapon pressed to the end of the dying Roscoe Pickett's nose just didn't register with me for about half a second. When it finally dawned on me what was about to occur, I made an awkward, squatting lunge at the miniature shooter just as the gun went off. Burning powder singed my fingers when they wrapped around the weapon's tiny cylinder.

The little gal's well-aimed bullet hit Roscoe right in the mouth. A searing chunk of peanut-sized lead knocked all his front teeth out, carved a tunnel through the soft tissue at the back of his throat, and blasted its way through a spot in his neck just below the skull bone . . .

"Damnation, girl," I yelped, then flicked a glance at Roscoe Pickett's shattered teeth, blasted skull, and sagging corpse. I shook my head in total disbelief, then locked Clementine in a narrow, steely gaze and added, "You've grown a mighty thick layer of hard bark around your heart since this morning, darlin'."

Praise for
J. LEE BUTTS

"J. Lee Butts keeps his readers on the edge of their seats."
—*True West*

"A writer who can tell a great adventure story with authority and wit." —John S. McCord, author of the Baynes Clan novels

"One of the top writers of Westerns working in the genre today." —Peter Brandvold, author of *Helldorado*

"Lawdog has it all. I couldn't put it down."
—Jack Ballas, author of *A Town Afraid*

"J. Lee Butts is one fine Western writer whose stories have a patina of humor; nonstop action . . . and a strong sense of place."
—*Roundup Magazine*

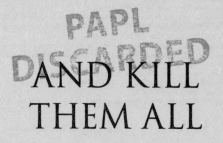

AND KILL
THEM ALL

TAKEN FROM THE ADVENTURES OF
TEXAS RANGER LUCIUS DODGE

J. LEE BUTTS

BERKLEY BOOKS, NEW YORK

THE BERKLEY PUBLISHING GROUP
Published by the Penguin Group
Penguin Group (USA) Inc.
375 Hudson Street, New York, New York 10014, USA

Penguin Group (Canada), 90 Eglinton Avenue East, Suite 700, Toronto, Ontario M4P 2Y3, Canada
(a division of Pearson Penguin Canada Inc.)
Penguin Books Ltd., 80 Strand, London WC2R 0RL, England
Penguin Group Ireland, 25 St. Stephen's Green, Dublin 2, Ireland (a division of Penguin Books Ltd.)
Penguin Group (Australia), 250 Camberwell Road, Camberwell, Victoria 3124, Australia
(a division of Pearson Australia Group Pty. Ltd.)
Penguin Books India Pvt. Ltd., 11 Community Centre, Panchsheel Park, New Delhi—110 017, India
Penguin Group (NZ), 67 Apollo Drive, Rosedale, North Shore 0632, New Zealand
(a division of Pearson New Zealand Ltd.)
Penguin Books (South Africa) (Pty.) Ltd., 24 Sturdee Avenue, Rosebank, Johannesburg 2196,
South Africa

Penguin Books Ltd., Registered Offices: 80 Strand, London WC2R 0RL, England

This is a work of fiction. Names, characters, places, and incidents either are the product of the author's imagination or are used fictitiously, and any resemblance to actual persons, living or dead, business establishments, events, or locales is entirely coincidental. The publisher does not have any control over and does not assume any responsibility for author or third-party websites or their content.

AND KILL THEM ALL

A Berkley Books Book / published by arrangement with the author

PRINTING HISTORY
Berkley edition / November 2010

Copyright © 2010 by J. Lee Butts.
Cover illustration by Bill Angresano.

ISBN: 978-0-425-23777-9

BERKLEY®
Berkley Books are published by The Berkley Publishing Group,
a division of Penguin Group (USA) Inc.,
375 Hudson Street, New York, New York 10014.
BERKLEY® is a registered trademark of Penguin Group (USA) Inc.
The "B" design is a trademark of Penguin Group (USA) Inc.

PRINTED IN THE UNITED STATES OF AMERICA

10 9 8 7 6 5 4 3 2 1

For My Wife, Carol
*I am daily inspired by her strength, tenacity,
determination, and will to survive.*

and

For My Good Friend Linda McKinley
*Perhaps my most enthusiastic cheerleader,
collaborator, and critic. She made me a better writer.
This is one of the few efforts I've produced
that doesn't have Linda's fingerprints on it,
along with her cat's tracks.
I will miss her more than mere words can tell.*

O! My offense is rank, it smells to heaven;
It hath the primal eldest curse upon't,
a brother's murder.

—*Hamlet,* Act 3, Scene 3

The path of the just is as the shining light,
that shineth more and more unto the perfect day.

—Proverbs 4:18

What charm can soothe her melancholy?
What art can wash her guilt away?

—*The Vicar of Wakefield*

ACKNOWLEDGMENTS

Special tip of the sombrero and bow at the waist for Sandy Harding. Perhaps the most personable and amiable editor I've had the pleasure to work with. And many thanks to Faith Black for her stellar help with this particular piece of work. Muchas gracias to Roxanne Blackwell Bosserman. She helped start me down this rugged trail years ago and still shouts encouragement from the sidelines when I appear ready to falter. And, as mentioned on the previous page, especially to my friend Linda McKinley. Not sure what I'm going to do without her editorial skills, advice, and willingness to spend hours discussing my writing. We made a good team. She's gone on ahead to scout the great unknown. I miss her every time I sit down at the computer.

PROLOGUE

AUTHOR'S NOTE TO THE READER

ATOP THE CREST of a tidal wave of unprec-
edented death and destruction, they poured into Texas—
desperate, hard as nails, the men of blood. Men who were
forged in the crucible of America's bloody Civil War and
tempered to the consistency of weapons-grade steel. Their
conflict-acquired skills, stock, and trade often included
brutality, murder, and a penchant for vicious mayhem.
The unfortunate citizens who crossed the gore-drenched
paths of those war-hardened gents referred to them as gun-
men, shootists, gunfighters, or pistoleers—a grouping of
benignly euphemistic terms that every man, woman, and
child who lived between 1865 and 1900 understood to really mean *man killers*.

The frontier West's slayers of men came from every
sort of background imaginable. Prior to the great war of
Yankee aggression on the South, many worked the land as
hardscrabble farmers. At one time or another, some pur-
sued employment as storekeepers, dentists, barbers, and
butchers. Others worked as actors, doctors, lawyers, clerks,

miners, buffalo hunters, Pony Express riders, or school-teachers. More than a few had once borne the badge of law enforcement officers.

Regardless of their previous backgrounds, upon arrival in the great Lone Star State, they plied whatever trade necessary to survive. In the process, a goodly number became double-dealing, card-marking, itinerant gamblers, swindlers, thugs, pimps, stock and property thieves, footpads, train and stagecoach robbers, con men, pickpockets, tricksters, rapists, murderers, and assassins of every stripe, variety, and type imaginable.

Life for such dangerous gentlemen (for the brotherhood of audacious hired gun hands, bandits, and charlatans proved almost entirely male) could generally be described as wicked, violent, and in most cases, extremely short. Death usually came for the men of blood by way of a gun or knife. And while a miniscule number of the most infamous slaughterers managed to die in their beds as the result of natural causes, or at the end of a legally applied length of oiled Kentucky hemp, most went to the judgment of their Maker surrounded by a roiling cloud of acrid-smelling, freshly spent gunpowder accompanied by the bitter, coppery taste of spilled blood.

A short listing of some of their names literally defines the *real* West in that period between the Civil War and the dawn of the twentieth century. Their grisly ranks included the likes of Luke Short, Longhair Jim Courtright, Clay Allison, Henry Newton Brown, Ben Thompson, and John King Fisher. Such man killers were the ill-famed contemporaries of Dallas Stoudenmire, Henry McCarty, the James boys, the Younger brothers, Jim Reed, Harry "The Sundance Kid" Longabaugh, Tom Starr, John Sellman, Harvey "Kid Curry" Logan, Sam Bass, and John Wesley Hardin. The worst of them all was the dignified, churchgoing assassin for hire, Deacon Jim Miller—also know as Killin' Jim, a shotgun-carrying back shooter of the first water.

Perched on the razor-thin precipice between living to a ripe old age and an early death stood the guardians of law, life, liberty, and civility. Men charged with the protection of the weak and easily intimidated from those who would, without compunction, rob or murder any luckless citizens unable to defend themselves. Unfortunately, cold-eyed killers would commit such dastardly deeds for little more than the change an undertaker could find in a dead man's pockets.

These stalwart defenders of law-abiding citizens, the edicts of God, and the rules of men included heroic figures like Texas Ranger Captains Lee H. McNelly and John B. Armstrong. Men of grit and backbone such as John R. Hughes, Jim Gillett, Heck Thomas, and Texas John Slaughter. And while these redoubtable gentlemen diligently served the state and their fellows as rangers, marshals, deputy marshals, police officers, and sheriffs, they often found that even their extensive experience and talent could accomplish little against the baddest of the bad men.

At such critical junctures, local, city, and state law enforcement officers often found themselves compelled to call upon a special breed of men who could bring the worst malefactors to book. Dedicated men gifted with nerves of iron. Men who would, without remorse, ride the practitioners of evil to ground like the brutish animals they really were, drag them back to justice, or kill them one and all.

What follows is a tale of viciousness and ugly death taken from the heroic adventures of one such man. A man who would, when circumstances required, do whatever he deemed necessary to bring evil to heel. In guarded whispers his numerous enemies called him Lucius "By God" Dodge.

1

"Blew His Three Biggest Toes Clean Off."

DON'T KNOW ABOUT anybody else, but until recently I've always been partial to hot weather—the steamier the better. Scorching sunshine coming down hot enough to bake blisters on a bayou-dwelling turtle's hard-shelled back used to be just my cup of tea.

But, you know, for unfathomable reasons, if it gets too hot or too cold these days, I swear 'fore Jesus, seems like each and every one of my ancient hurts and past injuries start to aching something fierce. And usually, all of them at the exact same instance. Seems the rigors of advanced old age can sure enough border on a downright hellish torture at times.

Especially problematic are the numerous bullet holes in my antiquated, wrinkled ole hide. Last I counted there were eight of them. 'Course I might've missed a couple here and there. Way I figure it, if I'd a got shot about two more times, back when my teeth were still new and not worn down so much, my whole body just might've fell apart like a newspaper suit in a rainstorm.

Woke up around midnight. Horse killer of a heat wave must have blown through Domino and the Sulphur River country whilst I was asleep. I was hurting like hell from the blue whistler that motherless brigand Irby Teal put in the meaty part of my right side. Ragged vent's just above the spot where my pistol belt used to hang.

As bullet wounds go, ole Irby's unwanted outlet never really amounted to much—leastways not till here of late. Now she throbs like the pure dickens when excessive heat, or numbing cold, hits me just right. Damn that sorry-assed weasel for being a pretty good shot with a pistol, by God.

Anyhow, ole Irby's antique pain got me up and prowling around the house in the middle of the night. That achy, scarred-over hole set me to thinking about how I came to have the ugly blemish on my hoary hide. As I remember the events surrounding the shooting and its later consequences, me'n Boz Tatum had been running buddies and man hunters for about three or four years back in '82 or '83—no longer certain of the exact year to tell the truth. Captain Horatio Waggoner Culpepper, commander of Ranger Company B, sent us down to Rio Seco 'long about then.

At the time, our loose-knit bunch of hard-eyed lawdogs was headquartered out on the banks of the Trinity River a bit north of Fort Worth. Before we left town and headed south, Cap'n Culpepper had me and Boz up to his pavilion. Personally gave us strict instructions as to the disposition of a stack of boot-wearing manure named Boston Teal, younger brother of the aforementioned Irby.

Remember as how Boz didn't care much for the assignment from the outset. Wagged his leonine head back and forth, then mumbled, "'S a long damned way to Rio Seco, Cap'n. 'Bout as far south as a body can go in Tejas and not have to speak Messican like a native."

Culpepper nodded. "That's right, Boz," he said. "Near sixty miles north of San Felipe Del Rio. Out on the Dry

Devils River. Hotter'n hell under a Dutch oven down that way 'bout now."

From the corner of my mouth I said, "'S okay with me, compadre. Like it hot myself."

Boz ran a finger across a dripping forehead, flicked a gob of sweat onto the sleeve of my shirt, then grinned.

Cap'n Culpepper, a smoldering see-gar clenched between his horsey teeth, stared off into space like a politician about to make promises he couldn't keep. "Hell, I'll own as how it is indeed a far piece, Tatum. Ass buster of a trip for a man on a horse. But Boston Teal is a murderous brigand. Man has personally delivered the souls of near a dozen innocents into the heavenly presence of a benevolent Jesus."

"I done heard tell of even more'n that, Cap'n," Boz said.

"True enough," Culpepper continued. Hands clasped behind his back, he puffed away and paced to and fro, as though agitated. "Sad to say, you're right as rain, Boz. I harbor not a single doubt that the evil-doin' bastard has snuffed the candles of any number of folks we know little or nothing about."

Me and Boz nodded our mutual agreement.

Culpepper kept his rant going. Didn't even slow down. "Want the widow-making slug back here so's I can hang 'im. Now, I wouldn't force an extended horseback trip like this on any man without good reason. Bein' as how the Southern Pacific pushed through there not long ago, I'm more than willing to foot the freight for whatever you might require by way of tickets for yourselves, and transportation of your animals, all the way down to Del Rio."

I knifed a glance over at my partner and said, "Well, that ain't a'tall bad, Boz. Hear tell as how the area around Del Rio's something of a garden spot, what with San Felipe Springs supplying water for that whole vicinity."

Culpepper grinned. "Town's a growin' all right, Lucius.

Somethin' close to five hundred souls livin' there these days, maybe more."

"Most of 'em weevil-brained railroad workers. And every one of them boys dumber'n a bag of busted hammers, I'd wager," Boz grumped.

As though pleased by the ease of his sales job on me, Culpepper added, "Figure as how it's a fairly easy horseback jaunt up to Rio Seco from Del Rio. Want you fellers to make damned sure Teal gets back to Fort Worth as quickly as possible. If he tries to escape though, you have my permission to kill the hell out of 'im."

Boz and I sat at attention in a pair of rickety canvas chairs. Cap'n Culpepper's massive, treelike bulk loomed over us from behind his battered, Civil War cavalry officer's field table. Swear that mountainous man could fill up all outdoors like he was wearing it.

A booted foot crossed over one knee, Boz thumped the musical, solid silver rowel of a Mexican spur. He glanced up at the cap'n and said, "So, Teal's corralled in whatever goes for a jail in Rio Seco, Cap'n? That the whole, complete, and entire deal?"

The open, tentlike structure Culpepper used as his official office flapped overhead in the scorching Texas breezes. Filtered sunlight seeped through the thin, frayed material. A moving, crosshatched, shadowy pattern played back and forth across Culpepper's square-jawed, rugged countenance.

Our fearless leader snatched the well-chewed, rootlike panatela from between chapped lips. "Indeed, Boz. My old friend Jacob Cobb, one of the finest rangers I ever rode with, acts as city marshal down that way these days. Appears Jacob scooped Boston Teal up during that belly slinker's slack-jawed attempt to rob Rio Seco's pissant-sized branch of the Texas State Bank."

"Thought them Teal boys usually worked those kinda

jobs together. Bein' as how they're such a tight-knit, God-fearin', lovin' family and all," I offered.

Culpepper dismissed my clumsy effort at humor and waved the stubby piece of his stogie around as though he might be about to make a long-eared jackrabbit appear out of the upturned Stetson hat that rested on his rude desk. "Could very well have been the case in the past, Lucius," he said, "but not this time."

"How so, Cap'n?" Boz said.

Culpepper raked stubby, dirty-nailed fingers through sweat-drenched hair. "Oddly, in this particular instance, appears the youngest of the Teal boys acted alone. Telegraph message I got from ole Cobb indicates as how Boston Teal is something of a blanket-headed idiot."

Boz flashed a toothy grin. "I've heard as much."

Company B's commander nodded. "Friend Cobb allows as how given the slightest opportunity he felt certain Irby Teal's baby brother could single-handedly screw up a one-hearse funeral. Get the distinct feeling that the poor, broke-brained bastard could mess up a ball bearing with a soiled dove's favorite powder puff."

"He botched the robbery?" I asked.

Culpepper took a lung-filling drag off his smoldering stogie. Blew a tub-sized smoke ring that circled over our heads, then gathered into an ominous, hovering, steel-colored cloud.

The cap'n flashed a sly grin then said, "Damned fine assessment of the circumstances there, Lucius. Seems the squirrel-headed son of a bitch had the money in hand. He was heelin' a hot path to the street and the prospect of imminent, glorious escape, by Godfrey. Bet my entire poke the man had unrestrained visions of Messican senoritas, tequila with lime and salt, and a plate of fire-breathin' enchiladas as he headed for his horse."

"Cobb caught him?" I said, then grinned.

Culpepper waved away my comment with his cee-gar again. "No, Lucius, no. See, Teal hit the boardwalk out front of the bank at a run. Clumsy jackass stubbed his toe on something."

"Aw, geez," Boz mumbled, then rolled his eyes.

The cap'n almost laughed out loud. "Yep. Uh-huh. You see it a-comin', don't you, Boz? 'Pears as how the rusted head of an errant nail must've been pro-trudin' from a loose piece of rough-cut pine. Or, hell, maybe the clumsy idiot just got tangled up in his own spurs. No way to tell, really."

"Could be he's just born dumber'n a baby bird, Cap'n," I said. "You know, all mouth and no brains."

Culpepper let out a short, snorting chuckle. "Doesn't matter," he went on, " 'cause Teal tripped. Went down like an anvil in a well. Fell on top of his very own, fully cocked Colt's pistol."

Boz threw his head back, let out an extended, hacking snigger. "Don't tell me."

The cap'n showed a set of choppers fully capable of biting through an arm-sized cottonwood limb. "Yep. You guessed it, Boz. Landed on that big ole .45-caliber popper of his like a load of bricks. Shot his more'n stupid self in the foot."

Boz grimaced. "Damnation, Cap'n."

"Uh-huh. Blew his three biggest toes clean off. Made one helluva mess, according to Marshal Cobb's wire. My friend said the boardwalk out front of the bank was covered with all manner of bones, toenails, rendered flesh, blood, and such."

I squirmed in my chair and stamped a foot then mumbled, "Makes my own kicker hurt just thinkin' 'bout it."

The cap'n knuckled a stubble-covered chin with the back of a hand the size of a camp skillet. "Yeah, well, sorry skunk injured himself so bad he managed to get back up, but couldn't run for spit on that blood-gushin' two-toed stump of his."

"That's when Cobb got him?" I said.

Cap'n's grin widened even more. "Nope, Lucius. Seems a group of wild-eyed, angry Rio Seco citizens jumped on his toeless, would-be bank-robbin' ass. Came nigh on to kicking him slap to death before friend Cobb could arrive on the scene and stop 'em."

Boz giggled like a little girl. "Too bad those good people didn't save us a trip and just go on ahead and kill 'im."

Another satisfied grin etched its way onto Culpepper's face. "Cobb's telegram mentions as how the youngest of the Teal boys had so many knots on his thick noggin when them town folk got finished with him, the man bore a striking resemblance to a west Texas horned toad."

Well, the three of us got a rib tickler of a hoot out of that one. The pleasant thought of Boston Teal getting the crap kicked out of him by a bunch of angry hoople heads had the mystic power to satisfy the souls of all us badge toters and man hunters.

A sudden thought struck me. "Bein' as how they ain't all that far away, why don't we just have some of them boys from Company A waltz over and take Teal in hand? Escort him on up our direction. Be a site easier than makin' the trip all the way down to Rio Seco ourselves."

Culpepper sliced a squinty, corner-of-the-eye look my direction. "Because I want him back here so I can be absolutely certain he's dead once his neck's been legally stretched. Let them boys from Company A get their hands on the walking stack of hammered manure, and there's more'n a good chance we'll never see hide or hair of the iniquitous polecat. Besides, I want the unqualified opportunity to piss on that bastard's grave soon as he's under a thick layer of legally sanctified Texas dirt."

Boz squirmed in his chair. Picked at lint on one of his pants legs. "Now, that sounds right personal, Cap'n."

Culpepper flopped into the chair behind his desk for the first time since we'd entered the pavilion. He stared off into space, as though distracted. "Boston Teal murdered my brother's son during the course of one of his more heinous crimes over in Mesquite, boys. Nephew was only sixteen. Had his whole life ahead of him. Smart young feller. Think he would've made a fine man."

That's all me and Boz needed to hear and, from every indication, as much as the cap'n cared to say on the matter at the time. So we stuffed our hats on. Heeled it for our camp digs—a tent-and-log affair Boz had named the Viper's Nest long before the pair of us had even met.

We set to getting ourselves ready for the trip. But you know the prospects for that particular excursion just didn't sit well on my gizzard for some reason. Couldn't put a definitive finger on the why of it, but like Boz, I began to feel uneasy about the whole situation from the minute we stepped out of the capn's pavilion that blazing hot afternoon.

2

"... BLOW YOUR DUMB ASSES BACK INTO THE STREET ..."

NOW, BACK IN them long-ago days weren't no real easy method for getting yourself from Fort Worth to an out-of-the-way, one-dog burg like Rio Seco. So, with the captain's emotional admonition to drag Boston Teal back up to Fort Worth quick as we could, or kill him, still a-ringin' in our ears, Boz and I lodged our animals on a cattle car of the M.K. & T. flyer and rumbled south.

Feller just never knew what might happen on one of those raids, and we both hated like sulfurous Hell trying to make do with rented animals. Besides, I'd grown used to my blue roan, Grizz, and didn't care for the experience of having to deal with the peculiarities of some bang-tailed rental nag that might well break down a few miles from the stable. Like the wise feller said, a man without a horse is riding the boot leather express. And you for damned sure didn't want to be afoot out in the briars and brambles between Del Rio and Rio Seco. Stretch of sandy dirt, rock, and cactus is so desolate in places even rattlesnakes won't pitch a tent.

Anyhow, we took the Katy line down to Waco. Loafed around in the depot there for nigh on two hours waiting on the Missouri Pacific passenger train that carried us on south to San Antone.

God, but I hated sitting around twiddling my thumbs. 'Course Boz proved the exact opposite. I am convinced the man was the most creative porch sitter and all-around loafer I've ever run across.

We wasted another four hours rubbing blisters on our rumps in San Antone's fancy, palatial station house. Ole Boz was happier than a gopher in soft dirt. He pulled his hat down over his eyes, and I don't think he moved a muscle the whole time. I still harbor the belief that the man had a bit of Messican blood in him.

We rode the Southern Pacific line's day coach on west to Del Rio. Not much of a town, but it was nice and green. Greenest spot in that part of Tejas. Still and all, train didn't even stop there 'less a passenger forced the issue. While growing at a pretty fair clip, the isolated berg could just barely boast of anything like a real depot. Nothing more than a sap-oozing, one-man shack constructed of warped, rough-cut boards, midways of an even rougher loading platform.

Once called San Felipe Del Rio, because of its proximity to San Felipe Springs, most of the town's permanent population made its living as sheep herders and ranchers. If memory still serves, good many of those as didn't ranch plied the trade as railroaders for the Galveston, Harrisburg and San Antonio line, as it continued on west to link up with the Southern Pacific again.

Constructed of adobe bricks and topped with tin or wooden roofs, most of the visible buildings were scattered hither and yon in the most haphazard of manners. The village appeared to have grown up like a crop of overnight mushrooms after a rain. A single central thoroughfare, labeled Main Street by signs all along the way, bustled with people, animals, and a constant parade of wagons that rattled back and forth along the rude street's entire expanse.

The meandering main street moseyed its leisurely way from south of the tracks and headed north. We rode past the remains of an old stockade, once used in the Indian fights, and the typical businesses you'd expect in a slow growing, barely civilized town. There were several nice-sized cantinas here and there—three as I recall, one of 'em pretty good-sized. Couple of recently erected hotels, a gun shop, meat market, liquor store, and one thriving mercantile. Even had a spanking new post office that couldn't have been more than a year old, along with a number of other commonplace businesses scattered about.

Must admit I was tickled slap to death to get off that train's day-coach seat and onto the back of a horse. Tell the God's truth, I ain't never cared a hoot in hell for trains. Mechanical monsters stink of hot grease and burning coal no matter where you picked to sit. And, Lord God, every one of those iron beasts rattled like a bucketful of loose gravel in a metal barrel.

Besides, ain't nothing to do on any kind of a train car except stare out the window till your eyes feel like they're about to drop onto your chest. Hell, anyone who's seen a mile's worth of south or west Texas has seen just about all there is to see. So, mostly, only thing left for a body to do on a train is sleep.

But even that weren't easy. Those passenger benches were covered with a worn piece of padding about as thick as a single page from a family Bible. Damned uncomfortable seats could just by God beat a man to a mumbling, whimpering pulp in a matter of hours.

Entire trip, including that horseback jaunt from the fairly pleasant climes of Del Rio then north on up to Rio Seco, took the better part of two and a half days. By the time we finally reined up outside Rio Seco, situated along the east bank of the Dry Devils River, the pair of us were tired to the bone.

Boz stood in his stirrups and swept the town with a narrow-eyed gaze. "Don't know 'bout you, Lucius, but I'm damn near wore to a fuzzy-assed frazzle."

Rio Seco's dust-blown main thoroughfare kind of started on the west side of the near nonexistent waterway. The rutted, dirt road oozed up out of the sandy stream's waterless bottom like a lazy snake. It wandered in a more-or-less southeast-to-northwest direction. Buildings on either side of the street appeared to have grown out of the ground in much the same fashion as those we'd observed in Del Rio earlier that day. It was almost as though nothing by way of serious thought had gone into the rapidly dilapidating town's initial planning.

We crossed the dust-choked watercourse's exposed bed and didn't get a drop of liquid on either of us, or the horses. Rode past a wagon yard, a run-down liquor store, a Chinese laundry, a boot and shoe shop, and an abandoned saddle-making operation. Hard to make definitive comparisons, but the graveyard-quiet town actually appeared a bit larger than Del Rio, leastways on the surface of it.

The street out front of the town marshal's office was as empty of people as a Baptist church and sing-along on Saturday night. At first, we didn't see a living soul. Hell, as I remember it, weren't even any skillet lickers, or free rovin' pigs, in evidence to greet the weary traveler.

"Town's got a serious ghostly look 'bout 'er, don't she?" Boz muttered.

I nodded, then ran an appraising gaze from one end of the street to the other. "Appears as how Rio Seco, Texas, is sure 'nuff locked in a losing battle with the sun and wind to me, Boz."

A runtified branch of the Texas State Bank stood kind of catty-cornered and across the street from the jail. It was cheek by jowl to the Barnette Brothers' Hardware and

Mercantile operation on one side and a saloon on the other. The boardwalk out front of the shabby, well-worn emporium was littered with piles of galvanized washtubs, racks of ready-made clothing, and wooden barrels decorated with hand-printed signboards. Whole shebang appeared designed to draw the prospective customer into partaking of pickles, crackers, and blocks of hook cheese, as could be easily purchased within.

We stepped off our animals out front of Marshal Jacob Cobb's sturdy blockhouse of a jail. Building appeared to have been constructed from a pile of discarded crossties. Couldn't have blown up that jailhouse with a Concord coach loaded to the roof with dynamite. We both went to hobbling around like all the gears in our hips and backs were out of mesh soon as our feet hit the ground.

Rubbed my aching rump. "Tell you what, Boz, don't know 'bout you, but my dauber's sure 'nuff dragging in the dirt. 'Bout another hour on that damned train, or ole Grizz here, think I'd be needin' a cane right now. Swear 'fore Jesus, seems like the older I get, the tougher these raids of ours get."

Tatum swayed in the street beside his hammerhead like a weeping willow in a wind storm. A thin cloud of powdery grit swirled around his feet. He stooped over at the waist and massaged his back. "Right there with you, pard. You know, way I'm going, be willing to bet that I'll be a hobblin' cripple by the time I turn forty."

I straightened up, stretched, and grinned. "Yeah, ole buddy, can see that 'un comin' myself. Worse, you'll still be uglier'n a hatful of horned toads, on top of it, by God."

Boz threw his head back and guffawed. I glanced around just in time to notice a pair of indolent-looking, heavily armed gun hands push through the batwings of the Saratoga Saloon, across the alley from the bank. They slouched their way up to the nearest porch pillar. Slumped against either side of the veranda's wooden prop, then cast sneering, self-important glares our direction and passed a smoking, hand-rolled ciga-reet back and forth. Looked, for all the world, like they wanted to amble on over and slap us nekkid just for the belligerent, hellacious fun of it.

Don't think Boz noticed the gunnies. He sliced a smirking look back at me. "Should be hereby noted that I take umbrage at the snide remark you just made about my personal handsomosity, Dodge. Want you to know they's many a beautiful woman in Tejas as will gladly testify that I'm a damned good-lookin' man, and will likely be so till the day I die."

Pitched my reins over the hitch rack's cross bar. Kept a corner of the eye check on the men watching us from across Rio Seco's empty main thoroughfare. As I eased up beside my friend, I slapped his shoulder. "Yeah," I said, "but all that proves is that there must be troops of females in Tejas that're blinder'n a row of fence posts long enough to circle the entirety of Val Verde County."

Still yammering at each other, when we stepped up to the jailhouse door and tried the knob. Turned it, but the heavy entry wouldn't give way.

Heard a less-than-friendly voice from inside the sturdy building call out, "Who'n the hell are ya? Best speak on up and be damned quick about it, lest I cut loose with this here coach gun of mine. Got 'er loaded with heavy-gauge buckshot. Blast'll take down the door, most of the frame, and probably blow your dumb asses back into the street with 'em, by God."

Crazy-sounding son of a bitch sure as hell got my attention.

3

"MIGHT JUST SEND YOU TO JESUS MYSELF."

TO SAY OUR reception, in one of south Texas's more secluded villages, wasn't exactly what we'd expected can only be described as a blue-eyed understatement. Course we'd considered an encyclopedic list of deadly possibilities for the trip, but having a local lawdog draw a bead on us with a shotgun wasn't one of 'em.

In an effort to get away from a potential flesh-rending gob of buckshot, Boz took a higgy-jiggy step to one side of the jail's iron-hinged door. I hopped the opposite direction. Boz knifed several quick, darting glances at the shuttered and barred windows of the fortresslike poky.

Then, appearing convinced he was fairly safe, my partner leaned back against the wall and hooked both thumbs over his double-row cartridge belt. Twisting his head toward the disembodied voice inside, he yelled, "Now don't shoot us, friend. We're rangers. Have official business with Marshal Jacob Cobb. Come on and open up."

A long pause followed. Then sounds of shuffling and scraping went on behind the door. We heard a couple of loud bumps and an odd thumping noise. Finally, a grinding racket like something big being dragged aside.

Slotted peephole in the thick slab of wood popped open. Hands raised, we moved out onto the boardwalk so the guy inside had a reasonably good view of his visitors. Set of disembodied, bloodshot eyes floated up in the slit and flicked nervous glances from one of us to the other.

"You bastards prove that?" feller behind the door yelled.

Look of tired disgust, and fleeting resignation, etched a path across Boz's face. "Tell Marshal Cobb that Ranger Randall Bozworth Tatum is out here in the street waitin' to see him at his personal request. And be damned quick about it."

Second later the peephole slammed shut. Action left us standing there with our faces hanging out. We stared at our feet for what seemed near a minute. Then we heard one heavy bolt snap aside, then another. Door swung open on a set of hammered iron hinges in sore need of some attention from an oilcan.

We eased over the threshold and into an office so small a feller couldn't cuss a cat in there lest he ended up with a mouth full of fur. Thick-walled, dirt-floored, poorly ventilated room couldn't have measured more than twenty feet across and maybe half again that deep.

Much-abused banker's desk sat on our right, just inside the door. Ragged, dog-eared map of Tejas, tacked to the wall behind the desk, looked as though it just might end up on the floor with passage of the slightest breeze. A half-empty rack for weapons covered most of the entire wall next to the map. Total armament stored there didn't amount to anything but a couple of old Henry rifles and one of them ancient black-powder Walker Colts with what looked to be a busted cylinder.

Pair of four-by-eight cells made from two-inch-wide, basket-woven straps of hammered metal that matched the front door's hinges stood against the back wall. Farthest of that pair of chicken coops appeared the only one of the closet-sized spaces occupied. Looked as though the entire building had been erected around that brace of tiny, metal enclosures. No air circulated in the room at all. Place was sure enough ripe. Smelled like an open chamber pot.

Sounded like a cannon shot when the door slammed behind us. Both bolts clattered into place with loud metallic clanks. Badge-wearing feller armed with a short-barreled scattergun crab-walked around us to his station of authority. He pushed a banker's chair, located behind the desk, aside with one foot.

Jaw clenched and red-faced, the local lawdog flopped into the raggedy seat with that big popper laid atop across one arm. Had it aimed at a spot about level with our bellies. Haggard-looking gent eyeballed the pair of us as though he just might cut loose with that intimidating blaster at the least provocation. Figured if the twitchy feller got heavy fingered, he wouldn't leave enough of me and Boz to scrape up in a saloon swamper's best dustpan.

Boz took plenty of time as he peeled his leather riding gloves off. He tossed an amiable, toothy grin at the red-faced feller. Sure he tried his level best to sound sociable when he said, "You Marshal Cobb, friend?"

Gent behind the desk didn't look old enough to be Jacob Cobb to me. Not a wrinkle on his face, as I could detect. And his droopy moustaches appeared a fairly recent cultivation. He confirmed my suspicions when, with a sneering insolent look, the local star toter leaned back in his squeaky seat.

Chapped lips peeled away from tobacco-stained teeth. He fiddled with the hammers on that massive smoke pole. "Nope. Marshal Cobb ain't here right at this exact moment. Name's Rufus Cosner. Deputy City Marshal Rufus Cosner. What can I do for you boys?"

Boz chucked our thick sheaf of bona fides onto the dep-

uty's desk. "Well, ugly sucker wearin' three pistols and lea-
nin' against the doorframe yonder's none other than famed
Texas Ranger Lucius 'By God' Dodge. I'm just the poor
son of a bitch who has to put up with his unending verbal
abuse—Senior Corporal Randall Bozworth Tatum."

"That a fact?" the impudent deputy snapped.

"Is indeed," Boz went on. "Based on a telegraph message from your Marshal Cobb, we've been sent down here
from Company B, up in Fort Worth, to relieve the good
citizens of Rio Seco of a murderous brigand named Boston
Teal. Figure on taking his more'n worthless ass back north
and stretching his neck."

Cosner's truculent attitude changed quicker than a min-
now can swim the inside of a tin water cup. He hopped out
of his squeaking seat. Dropped that double-barreled blaster
onto the battered desk's scarred top. Grabbed up our wad
of papers. Slapped them back into one of Boz's hands and
then grabbed the other and shook it like he was the happi-
est man in south Texas.

A toothy grin now plastered on his face, the deputy said,
"Sweet Lord Almighty, but I'm serious glad to see you
rangers, and that's the God's truth. Teal's just about to rub
my last nerve as raw as a slab of fresh butchered beef."

From the corner cell I heard, "You bastards won't get
me past the town limits of this one-dog, jerkwater hellhole.
Probably won't get me off the boardwalk outside. So much
as try to leave this stink hole of a jail with me in tow and
you'll all end up deader'n a trio of rotten cottonwoods."

I turned to see a scruffy, bearded joker leaned against
his cage's chained and padlocked door. A set of nasty
moustaches hung down past the prisoner's chin and swept
the upper part of a thick chest. Smart-mouthed jackass had
one foot wrapped in a wad of blood-encrusted bandages.
Big ole dressing made the end of his leg look about the size
of a sixty-pound, yellow-meat watermelon.

"Brother Irby'll kill the hell out of both you ranger sons

a bitches 'fore he lets you take me anywhere, much less Fort Worth for a hangin'," the foot-shot idget growled. "Ain't neither one a you bastards got grit 'nuff to string up any us Teal boys."

Cosner rolled his eyes and looked like he wanted to puke his socks up. "He might be right. This jackass's brothers and several other gunnies are holed up over yonder at the Saratoga Saloon. They've been hanging around ever since the day after Marshal Cobb had to leave town."

"When was that?" I said.

Cosner scratched a tobacco-stained chin. "Well, he struck out four days ago. This walking pile of dung's friends and family showed up next morning 'bout ten o'clock. Done kept me holed up in here the entire time. Haven't even been able to visit the outhouse. Got four chamber pots and they're all overflowing. Wasn't for a Messican friend of mine guess I'd've already starved."

"They threaten you?" Boz said.

"Hell, yes, they threatened me. Threatened everybody in town. 'S why ain't nobody out in the streets. I 'uz about to give up and let 'em have this no-account, low-life stack of skunk shit."

"His friends been pressin' you?" Boz said.

"Damn right. Several of them boys stood outside the door earlier this mornin'. Said if'n I didn't give the smelly bastard up, they'd set fire to the jail. Wait in the street and kill me when I come out. Don't 'specially wanna die over a shit heel like this 'un, tell you for certain sure, fellers."

Boston Teal's unshaven face went scarlet. "Come on. Lemme outta this here cage. I'll kick the dog crap outta yer smart-mouthed ass, star toter. Callin' any of us Teal boys skunk shit and such is an act that can sure 'nuff get yer narrow ass put in a coffin."

Cosner didn't bother to so much as glance his prisoner's direction when he shot back, "Aw, shut up, you stupid son of a bitch. One more syllable from you's gonna be just about all I can stand. Might just send you to Jesus myself. Save these fellers the hellish task of havin' to escort you all the way back to Fort Worth. A fate I personally consider worse than gettin' my family jewels caught in the clothes wringer on my wife's new washtub."

Sure all he wanted was to diffuse the tension a bit when Boz offered, "Why'd Marshal Cobb leave town in the first place, Deputy?"

Cosner resumed his seat behind the desk. He appeared to soften a bit. "Man's wife passed away. 'Fore she went and sprouted wings, he'd promised that good lady he'd take her back to Columbus, Mississippi, for proper burial. 'S where her family's all planted."

"Got any idea how long he figured on being gone?" I said.

Cosner scratched an ear, then slapped at the side of his head like a dog that might've come across a flea. "As much as three weeks, I 'magine," he mumbled, then gazed at his fingers, as though he'd squished something on one of them. "Maybe longer. Didn't leave me with any definite date of return, tell the God's truth."

Boston Teal let out a derisive snort. "Gutless pile of runny dung heard brother Irby was on the way. Just used his ole lady's passin' as a coward's excuse to blow out of town. Man's yeller as mustard, by God. Got henhouse ways and smells of feathers."

Cosner grabbed a half-filled tin cup from the top of his desk then threw it across the room at Teal's cell door. The battered utensil bounced off the rough-textured iron straps right in front of the mouthy prisoner's face. Coffee flew all over the grinning, foot-shot bank robber. The unexpected bath really set him off and the water-headed jackass jumped up on the cell door and hung there like some kind of bug-eyed tree squirrel. Gritted his teeth and went to growling and slobbering in the manner of a hydrophobic dog.

Cosner whacked the desktop with an open palm. Flat-handed lick sounded like an angry kid whacked an empty barrel with a long stick. He eyeballed the jailbird and yelped, "Stop that goddamned racket, you gallin' son of a bitch. Fine woman's gone to her heavenly re-ward, and you got nothing to offer on the matter."

Red-faced, purple-necked, and crazy-looking as hell, Teal screwed his head sidewise. Eyes a bulging, he glared through one of the openings between the iron straps in front of his face. "Well, I can sure as hell say this. You boys don't let me outta this here animal cage, and damned quick, bet none of you'll live much longer. Figure the only reason brother Irby ain't stormed this sorry excuse for a hoosegow and freed me already's a 'cause he thought an idiot like you might well go and shoot me for sure 'fore he could get in here and get me out."

The deputy jumped to his feet again and shook an angry finger Teal's direction. "Well, if that's what your brother thinks, he's right. If'n he'd a put one booted foot over my threshold, I'd a blasted the bejabberous hell out you first, then him, by God. Same fate applies for any fires he might attempt to set."

Teal spit a glob of snotty phlegm onto the dirty floor just outside his cramped enclosure. Shook the door of the cell by rocking back and forth from his hanging position. Yelled, "You ain't gonna live long enough to shoot any-body, you stump-jumpin' hick. Bet all three a you badge-wearin' bastards'll be deader'n a trio of them boys what fell at the Alamo 'fore it gets good dark."

Boz turned and, very politely, I thought, said, "Shut the hell up, Teal. I'm already tired of the sound of your voice. Every time you open your mouth, it sounds like a crosscut saw going through petrified oak knots. And, hell's bells, I just walked in the door."

Teal dropped to the floor with a heavy, one-footed thump. Twisted around on his good kicker like a crippled terpsichorean at a hoedown. Took aim and spit again.

"Well, screw you and the horse you rode in on, you law-bringin' son of a bitch."

On a personal level, I thought Teal's jail-cell bravado grossly misplaced. Man just didn't seem to realize the gravity of his arrogant mistake. Not even when Boz strode over to the cell's chained-and-padlocked door. My amigo's spurs clinked and jingled when he came to a grinning stop and motioned for the prisoner to come closer.

All I can say on the matter, now, is that Boston Teal had to have possessed just about as much intelligence as a south Louisiana cantaloupe, when he dragged his damaged foot back over to the tiny cubicle's door and leaned forward. I couldn't help but grin as I had no doubt as to what was about to happen. Tell the honest to God truth, I felt a sense of real joy at the prospect of the entertainment in the works.

Teal turned his scruffy noggin sidewise. Sneered when he got right up against some of those iron straps. "Yeah, you badge-wearin', ass-ugly bastard. Whaddaya want?"

Boz's hand darted forward like a fanged diamondback's poison-filled head. Somehow, and don't ask me how he managed it, my friend got his fingers laced into that surprised outlaw's scraggly moustaches and beard. He latched on and jerked the man's face up against that metal cage with a resounding clunk and held on like a Mississippi snapping turtle. Bounced Teal's empty-sounding noggin off that cell door three or four times before he finally spoke.

I barely heard him when Boz leaned up next to Teal's bloody ear and hissed, "Sit down on your cot, and shut your irritating mouth."

Got to give Teal the credit where it's due, he didn't back off much. With blood-oozing lips pressed against the cell's door, man could barely speak when he muttered, "An' if'n I doan, whachu figger on doin', you goober-headed turd knocker?"

A twisted, nigh gleeful smile crept across Boz's face.

"I'll have Deputy Cosner open this door for me. Then, I'll come in there and kick your lardy backside till your nose bleeds."

Teal matched Boz's sneer with a mocking grin of his own and said, "The hell you say."

Boz broke into a pleased smile. "The hell I do say, Boston ole friend. Get started and I just might keep on bootin' your blubbery rump till you'll have to unbutton your shirt when you're once again able to hobble your way to an outhouse. Then I could just go on and stomp on that damaged foot of yours till it thunders. Hell, have to admit I'm right on the irritated edge of believing as how I might be willing to work like a Georgia field hand kicking the crap out of you."

Then, damned if he didn't jerk one whole lip's worth of Boston Teal's whiskers right out of the man's face. Toeless outlaw grabbed his mouth and went to bellering like a red-eyed cow. Hooted and hopped around the tiny enclosure on his only usable foot. Squirrelly bastard cussed everyone ever born from Adam to the most recent president. Ranted, raved, and acted like a mistreated lunatic.

'Course Boz thought that was the funniest thing he'd seen in about ten years. Man laughed like something crazed as he strolled back toward the marshal's rickety desk. Still in mid-chuckle when he flicked a wad of Teal's lip hair onto the floor. Stuff hadn't come to rest when several loud thumps and breaking glass against the jail's front façade jerked our attention to the shuttered windows and barred door.

I already had a pistol in each hand when I heard someone out in the street yell, "You mother-humpin' lawmen get your sorry selves on out here, and right by-God now. Come on out, Deppidy Cosner. Bring your idiot friends with you. Gonna cut you boys down pocket high."

4

"Meaner'n a Bucket of Teased Rattlers."

WITH ONE BULGED eye pressed against the hoosegow's partially opened peep slot, Boz crooked a finger my direction. "Take a gander at this, Lucius," he said, then stepped out of the way as I strode up to the viewing port.

I took my friend's place and peeked outside. Four men swayed in Rio Seco's central thoroughfare like a stand of drunken cottonwood saplings in a light, blistering hot breeze. The quartet couldn't have been more than twenty feet from the boardwalk that ran along the calaboose's front entrance.

Unshaven, red-faced, and grubby as hell, all those boys bristled with pistols and knives. One feller carried an amputated shotgun that appeared to have been sawed down from both the barrel and stock ends. A tall, disheveled joker, who bore a striking resemblance to Deputy Cosner's prisoner, occupied a spot about a step ahead of the other three. While I watched, he threw his scruffy head back and tried to suck the bottom out of a whiskey bottle.

"Feller pullin' at the jug's Irby Teal. Young Master Boston's eldest brother," Boz hissed into my ear.

Idiot locked in Rio Seco's *juzgado* just couldn't keep his mouth shut. "Yeah, by God. And ole Irby's meaner'n ten acres of south Texas tarantullers. He's gonna jerk a knot in you boys' asses and that's fer damned sure. The three of you'd best get yourselves ready to shake hands with Jesus." Loony son of a bitch went to slapping his good leg and laughing like a thing insane.

Didn't see him when he did it, but Boz must've turned toward the racket. Still up close to my ear, though, when he snarled, "You ain't outta here yet, Teal. Best keep your stupid mouth shut, or I'll come in there and rip out the rest of that scraggly mess hangin' off your butt-ugly face. Swear 'fore Jesus I will. Get finished, you'll have a mug what looks like the badly shaved ass of a broke-legged dog."

I backed away from the door about the time another whiskey bottle slammed against the wall and exploded in a shower of splintered glass and misted spray of cheap hooch. Marshal Jacob Cobb's jail house began to reek of backwater panther piss like a Dodge City saloon's outhouse after a trail herd's arrival.

"You recognize any of those others out there, Boz?" I said. "Might be helpful if I had some idea of what we've got confronting us."

"Repulsive bugger on Teal's right, one with the gigantic bone-handled bowie shoved behind his pistol belt, is Pogue Keller. Man's always been partial to a cutter the size of a meat cleaver. Hear tell he's right skillful in the use of 'em, too. Don't let that fool you, though. He's a fair hand with a pistol from all I've ever heard as well."

"How 'bout the other two?"

My friend snuck another quick peek outside, stepped back, and shook his head. "Think that 'un on Teal's left is Hector Manion. Hard to tell given the layer of trail dirt on 'im. Dangerous son of a bitch if it is ole Hector. Man'll kill you faster'n spit can sizzle to nothin' on a Montana train depot's stove lid."

"And the weaselly-lookin' squirt toting the sawed-off shotgun? One weighed down with the brace of Schofield pistols."

Boz toed the dirt floor, squinted at me, as though deep in thought. "Not absolutely certain, Lucius, but that 'un just might be China Bob Tyler. Been strong rumors flyin' around of late as how he'd taken up with Teal. Heard tell more'n once that man's deadlier than chained lightning. Meaner'n a bucket of teased rattlers."

Shoved my cross-draw gun into its holster and set to checking the loads in my hip pistol. Flipped the loading gate open. Rolled the cylinder across my arm. Inspected the primer of each cartridge as it passed. Snapped the gate shut, then gazed over at my friend. "Well, what we gonna do, Boz?"

He flashed a toothy grin my way. "Sure as hell ain't gonna stand around in here and wait for them knee-walkin' drunks to set this place on fire, that's for damned certain. One thing I ain't got no use for is goin' to my Maker like a piece of flamebroiled beefsteak. Rather go down shooting. How 'bout you, Dodge?"

Swapped pistols as I said, "They're not gonna torch this place, Boz. Hell, they'd burn ole Boston up with us."

Boz shook his head. "Do you think those whiskey-weary sons of bitches are sober enough to have any idea what the hell they're doin', ole friend? When they're stone-cold sober the four of 'em together ain't got any more brains than a gunnysack full of tumblebugs."

"Well, you're probably right about that, amigo. Looks like they sure as hell ain't seen sober in a month of Sundays."

"Nope. They're all drunker'n Cooter Brown, cotton-mouth mean, and barnyard stupid. Even sober, ain't a single one of them idiots got sense enough to pour piss out of a boot. Surprises me some that they haven't set fire to this place 'fore now."

From behind Marshal Cobb's desk, Rufus Cosner said, "Whatever you come up with by way of a plan, if it involves going outside and facing off with Irby Teal and his bunch of cutthroats in a stand-up gunfight, have to count me out. From the time this dance started, figured I'd just hold on long as I could, then give Boston over to his brother when I got the best deal he was willin' to offer."

Boz stared at his feet and shook his head like an aged, tired dog. "You really think for a Kansas City second Irby Teal's gonna let you live, Rufus? Hell, you were dead the minute after him and his friends rode into town and he found out you, for damned sure, had his little brother locked up in here."

A look swept over Cosner's face like he'd been slapped across his open mouth with a colicky baby's loaded diaper. He tried to speak, then went to stammering. "You boys c-can't believe that," he mumbled.

"Ranger Tatum's telling you the God's truth," I offered. "Teal's kind of man has a real problem with anyone with grit 'nuff to trespass against family. You and Marshal Cobb were as good as worm meat the day you dragged this wounded piece of trash in here and slammed a cell door on him—far as that loudmouthed madcap out in the street was concerned anyhow."

Boz moved to the marshal's desk, leaned over, and snatched up Cosner's shotgun. "Locking yourself in here has already kept you breathing several days longer than you should've lived, Rufus. Hell, you're one lucky man. You could step outside with us, and I'd be willing to bet them boys couldn't kill you if we tied you to the door and gave them each a free shot."

Cosner's neck went red. Man stared at the toes of his boots. I barely heard him, when he squeaked, "Got a wife and child. Just cain't chance it, fellers. Sorry."

Boz broke the shotgun open, then examined each of its massive brass rounds. Big popper made a noisy, metallic click when he snapped it shut. My friend tilted his head to one side, as though somewhat sympathetic to Cosner's situation. "Should've thought of your family before you pinned that badge to your shirt, ole son."

Cosner moaned and looked sneaky.

"I 'uz you," Boz went on, "I'd take me a job over at the mercantile selling flour, notions, and such. Maybe tending bar, chasing cows, or rentin' rooms at the hotel. Bloody push comes to bloodier shove, my friend, appears you just ain't up for curtains of blue whistlers and blisterin' gun work."

Then my partner turned and pointed at the front door with the twin-barreled coach gun. He threw me a knowing glanced and said, "Drunk as those bastards out there are, doubt any of them could hit the jailhouse with a pistol shot, much less one of us, Lucius. So, hell, open the gate, pard. Let's see how she jumps."

"Which direction you wanna go when we get outside?" I said.

He winked and grinned. "Why don't you go ahead and step on out first, Lucius. Heel it to the right. I'll follow and go left. Figure we're close enough so's I can put lead in at least three of 'em with Deputy Cosner's big honking blaster here, first jump outta the box. So, you take who-ever's willing to do the talkin'. Figure that's gonna be ole Irby. Shouldn't be too much of a problem for me to deal with the rest."

Well, I snatched that door open so fast it almost sucked the hats off them boys out in the street. Could tell it surprised most of them, more than a bit, when I came out the entryway with a cocked pistol in each hand, followed by Boz carrying that shoulder cannon of a shotgun.

Three of the Teal bunch staggered back about half a step. But brother Irby glared at us like he wanted to rip our heads off. Man didn't move so much as a single whisker, near as I could tell. Hard-eyed and mean as hell, the man was more than ready for a fight.

"Just be goddamned," Boston Teal's oldest sibling thundered. "If it ain't famed gun hound and man killer Texas Ranger Randall Bozworth Tatum." He jerked a bullish head toward the right then added, "Keller here said he 'uz pert sure he'd seen you ride in, Boz."

A snaggle-toothed grin creaked across the unwashed face of Pogue Keller. Man straightened up as though right proud of himself. He shot a quick glance at the heavily armed dwarf on his right. The pair of them appeared to bask in that gratifying moment of unsolicited recognition like lizards on a hot rock.

Boz let out a derisive snigger. "Would say it's good to see you again, too, Irby, but I'd be lyin' like a widder woman's hooked rug if'n I did. As you're well aware, I've never cared for your more'n sorry company."

Teal either ignored Boz's remarks or was too drunk to care. A wicked sneer sliced its way across his pockmarked, dirt-encrusted face. He swung his boozy attention my direction. "And, lawsy mercy, you done brought along your up-and-comin' partner in legal slaughter, Ranger Lucius 'By God' Dodge, I see. Been hearin' a lot about you, Dodge. Rumor has it you're a real man killer."

Waited for Boz to get completely settled before I offered, "That a fact?"

The infamous outlaw rocked back on his heels. Took another long swig from his bottle. Wiped twisted lips on the arm of a bib-front shirt so dirty it got me to wondering if a bullet could penetrate the filthy garment.

Then, he let the hand holding the liquor drop to one side. The amber-colored container slipped from grit-encrusted fingertips and hit the ground standing upright. A geyser of fluid squirted out and slopped onto the leg of his grubby, woolen pants.

Irby Teal glared at me from a pair of slitted, rheumy, bloodshot, yellow-tinged eyes. The situation tensed up right quick when he let his hand hover over the walnut grip of his hip pistol. "You law-bringin' bastards've got my little brother, Boston, locked up in that shit hole of a jail. Turn him loose. Git him out here, right by-God now."

Boz said, "Can't do that, Irby, and you know it. Your brother's got murder to answer for up in Fort Worth. Gonna take him back to stand trial. Likely hang 'im shortly after that."

Teal went to shaking all over, like he might have a man-killing dose of malaria. Face got redder than I thought humanly possible. For a second, I felt certain his melon-sized head might explode.

"Be damned if that's gonna happen, Tatum," the outlaw snarled. "I'll kill every man, woman, child, and dog in this pissant burg 'fore I let you outta here with Boston in tow for a hanging."

"Well," Boz said, "given your feelin's on the matter, best go on ahead and get to work with them pistols hangin' on your hips."

'Bout then, I heard a commotion behind me. Deputy Cosner said something like, "Here's your sorry-assed brother, Teal. Start shootin'. Swear 'fore Jesus I'll blow his ugly head clean off."

I shot a quick glance to my left, and sure enough I could've reached over and touched a grim-faced, shackled, and chained Boston Teal on the shoulder. Cosner was latched onto the man's shirt collar with one hand and had a .45's muzzle pressed into one of Teal's ears. Must admit the deputy's bold-as-polished-brass move impressed the hell out of me, at the time anyway.

Now, I can't say as how I'd be able to testify for sure on the subject, given so many years have flown by since those events transpired, but I'd be willing to avow I'm almost certain that midget, China Bob Tyler, brought his amputated shotgun up and opened the ball that bloody day. Appeared to come as something of a shocking surprise to ole Irby when Boz dropped both hammers on the runtified little killer. A thunderous, washtub-sized wad of buckshot knocked the sawed-off piece of a man clean out of both his boots and sprayed a blistering curtain of lead into the other outlaws in the street as well. My God, but they did do some screeching and hollering when those buckshot pellets sliced into 'em.

As you can readily imagine, that sure as hell ripped the rag off the bush. Pistols came out all around. 'Fore a body could spit, or say howdy, Pogue Keller, Hector Manion, and Irby Teal went to grabbing at smoking shot holes in their clothing with one hand and, at the same time, spraying lead like a trio of midnight-roving tomcats staking out their territory with the other.

Racket from all those weapons going off, people yelling, screaming, hollering, and cussing, at almost the same instant, came nigh on to being ear-shatteringly thunderous. Fortunately, in spite of their lurid reputations as bad men and famed pistoleers, think I could say, with no fear of ever being contradicted, wasn't a single one of them boys could've hit a circus elephant with a Gatling gun that particular afternoon.

Blue whistlers gouged valleys in the boardwalk at my feet. Punched holes in the wall and windows behind me. And generally peppered the entire front of the jail on every side of us. Wood splinters filled the air like horseflies buzzing around a bloated corpse.

I had a right good feeling going, as I thumbed the hammers of my pistols and watched the scorching rounds I sent out hit home. Know for certain sure I put at least two in Irby Teal's sorry hide. Saw his vest jump. By then Boz had abandoned the coach gun, drawn his own sidearms, and set to ripping off shot after death-dealing shot.

Ten seconds into the noisy fracas, so much acrid-tasting,

grayish-black gunpowder swirled in the dense south Texas air it got right difficult to pick out a target. But I'd swear on a stack of Bibles I was looking right into the elder Teal brother's piss-colored eyes when I felt a burning sensation in my right side. I'm convinced to this very second he's the one who put a hole in me that day. 'Course I returned his fire without flinching, or even so much as thinking about it. Teal and his drunken friends went to ground in front of our blazing assault like wheat under an Iowa farmer's razor-sharp sickle.

When all the yelping, hollering, and thunderation finally abated, I holstered my strong-side weapon, then ran a hand into the waistband of my pants. Fingers came out covered in a sticky coating of fresh blood. Went all weak in the knees. Stumbled backward a step or two. Leaned against the jail's bullet-riddled front wall.

I glanced Boz's direction. The jailhouse door stood wide open between us. Noticed the near-headless corpse of Boston Teal was draped atop Rufus Cosner. Appeared the luckless Cosner had somehow got blasted straight to a sulfurous Hell 'bout half a second before he removed most of Boston's thick noggin with a single shot.

Boz had gone down, too. Sat with his back to the slug-peppered, cross-tie wall and worked at poking a hand-kerchief into a blood-gushing hole in his pants' leg. My partner didn't even look up when he said, "Reckon we got 'em all, Lucius?"

Ripped the bandanna from around my own neck. Shoved it against the leaker in my side. Pressed on the crude dressing and gasped for air. "You didn't even bother to glance my direction, Boz. Hell, I could be deader'n Julius Caesar for all you'd know."

A strained chuckle came from my friend's direction. "Hell, boy, figure there ain't nobody livin' right now who's gonna have skill enough, or grit enough, to kill you in a straight-up pistol fight."

"Well, you could be wrong about that, by God. Lord could've come and taken me as easy as them skunks lyin' yonder in the street. Or these two unfortunates splayed out here in the doorway for that matter. Shit, I could be just as dead as Andy Jackson right now."

My friend tightened the crude bandage around his blood-soaked leg. Then, he leaned back against the wall and let out a tired, exasperated sigh.

"How bad you hurt?" I said.

"Oh, not too awful much. Been hurt worse. Been shot in lots worse places, too."

"Well, not me. This is the first time for me, by God. Ain't never been shot before. Damnation. Hurts like burnin' perdition."

Boz struggled to his feet, then hobbled over. He pulled my hand away from the wound, then poked around in the bloody hole. "Aw, hell, boy. She ain't near as bad as you think. 'Course she's gonna take some time healin'. Gonna pain you worse'n the dickens for a spell. Might even put you in bed for a few weeks. Maybe more. Festerates could well kill you. Otherwise, figure you'll heal."

I shot a glance at his leg. "That don't look good."

He flopped down next to me and swept a pained glance up and down Rio Seco's only street. "Oh, might not do any riding for a bit, that's for certain sure. Suppose we'd best scare up a sawbones, Lucius. Wouldn't want to go and bleed out 'fore we can get these holes plugged by someone with a bit more in the way of medical experience than I've got."

Turned out as how the town's only pill pusher'd heard the commotion and came a-running. He had the pair of us cleaned up, sterilized, and stitched back together in a matter of minutes.

Bone popper couldn't do much of anything for them other boys though. First two blasts out of the box, from that big popper Boz carried, came near cutting Tyler, Manion, and Keller in half. Got to avow, though, they 'uz tough ole boys. The three of them went down blasting, in spite of being pretty much dead whilst doing it.

Once we got them on their backs, all our other shooting didn't really do much in the way of death-dealing damage. Except when it came to Irby Teal. Think me and Boz both might've put three or four each in the man. Literally shot him to pieces. Corpse leaked blood like we'd turned him into a human sieve. Could've read the *Fort Worth Ledger* through his bullet-riddled hide.

From all we could determine, Deputy Cosner had made good on his threat. He'd touched off a single round that splattered Boston Teal's pea-sized brain all over hell and yonder. Found a gory, fist-sized gob of the mess splattered across my back and shoulders. I was so preoccupied, though, I never even felt the man's skull filler when it hit me.

Me and Boz came to believe that Cosner must have figured that hiding behind Boston Teal was the safest place in town. Unfortunately the man couldn't have been more wrong. Somebody still managed to put one through his right eye, and another bored its way through the tip of his nose. Made a hell of a mess. But we did discover, later on, as how he'd lied about a wife and child. Man was simply possessed of henhouse ways.

Boz stood over Cosner's corpse, shook his head, and said, "Guess the poor boy wasn't as lucky as I figured."

And so, that bloody session of gun smoke and quick death is how me and a leg-shot Randall Bozworth Tatum came to rent a half-assed horse ranch and cattle operation out in the Devils River country, south of Sonora. We were both injured badly enough that traveling didn't seem like a good idea at the time. Figured as how we'd just lay up in the shade and set to mending. You know, rest and recuperate for a spell before we headed on back to Fort Worth. Even made arrangements to send Cap'n Culpepper a telegraph message to let him know our plans. 'Course, he wasn't at all happy with the situation but did seem to understand.

Looking back on the whole dance, our plan seemed solid enough. But, as it turned out, that's when my bad dreams started. And, not long after, that's when me'n Boz got tangled up in one of the bloodiest, most awful messes of my entire ranger career.

Thermometer I got from the Baker Brothers Funeral Home in Domino says it's 105 in the shade right now. Thank God for lemons, ice, and sugar. Sitting here in the shade with a sweat-covered glass in my hand, just thinking on that whole grisly dance of uncommon horror and how we came to meet up with a beautiful little gal named Clementine Webb. Blood-soaked tale still has the power to send shivers charging up and down my ancient spine like a herd of longhorns stampeded by pitchfork lightning. Jesus, amazing how some memories have the capacity to make my aged blood run as cold as Rocky Mountain river water.

5

"DAMN IRBY TEAL FOR A GOOD SHOT."

NOW, ME AND Boz had hoped to get far enough away from civilization to forget about doing any ranger work for a spell. But, to my dismay, we hadn't been living on the Devils River ranch much more than a few weeks when the realization thundered down on me that no hope existed of ever escaping the everyday events of my blood-soaked past.

See, when the oft avoided blackness of sleep descended, the power of dreams could, once again, bring my bygone experiences, with blood and thunder, to vivid, brutal, frightening life. Always the dreams. Nightmares to be more precise.

Looking back on it, I'm convinced that having Irby Teal plug me, in that Rio Seco dustup, was what precipitated the whole life-and-death dance that followed. Have always felt there's nothing like getting shot to put a man in touch with his own mortality. In truth, I've come to realize that I had never suffered from such a crisis of conscience before that period. Or afterward, come to think on it.

For reasons that are still unclear to me, the most compelling of the nocturnal reveries concerning my short but turbulent ranger career invariably involved the lingering, stomach-churning stench given off by slaughtered men. The acrid fragrance released by roiling clouds of spent, death-dealing gunpowder lingered in my sleep-leadened nose. The bilious odor of spilled blood hovered over my bed, along with the reek of puke, urine, and human waste. The bitter, coppery taste that swelled on the back of a man's throat and always accompanied the putrid aroma of sudden death came along for the ride as well.

Then there was the accompanying noise. The blistering roar from pistols, rifles, and shotguns when they sent the certainty of eternal damnation echoing through my quiescent brain. The entire ball of wax often seemed masked in a cacophonous, chilling cloak draped across the narrow shoulders of that insatiable, bony-fingered, skull-faced Thief of Souls.

But even worse than those skin-pimpling horrors were the agonized, screeching cries and whimpers of wounded and dying men. The nerve-grating screams of injured, wild-eyed, panicked horses. My nighttime apparitions rolled themselves into a calamitous tumult brought on by a litany of misty and confused visions of gore, thunder, and violent death, that I came to feel sure had not yet occurred but would present themselves soon.

There was no denying it, those blood-spattered nightmares seemed genuine beyond human understanding. So authentically sharp, clear, and saturated in the colors of departing mortality. Even the piercing, gut-wrenching burn of being shot felt real. The hornet-like sting of the massive, red-hot slug as it entered the fleshy part of my side caused me to groan in my half consciousness and squirm atop twisted bedding. And for way longer than necessary, I relived the events that had transpired outside Marshal Jacob Cobb's office each time my head hit the pillow and I closed my eyes.

Top of everything else, it was doubled-up summertime in Texas and hotter'n a burning mesquite stump. During the day everything with legs spent most of its time looking for any spot not deep-fried by the sun. Even the coming of darkest night brought almost nothing in the way of much-needed respite. 'Course, as I've said before, I didn't mind the heat back then.

But early on one particular morning, the unrelenting, elevated temperature snapped me awake coated in the damp sheen of an icy sweat. Seemed as though every square inch of my aching body was slick with clammy flesh. Groggy from being snatched out of my dreadful nightly tossings and turnings, I rolled onto one side.

Propped on an elbow, I hacked out a croupy cough, then wheezed as though being strangled by some evil, unseen spirit. Damn the nightmares. Ugly, confused visions possessed the uncommon power to give me a case of the waking willies. Or maybe it wasn't the dreams this particular time. Something else, possibly.

"Sweet Jesus, have mercy," I grumbled and cast a heavy-lidded gaze at the open doorway and out onto the veranda.

Fuzzy-headed from the night's short, dank siesta, I swung aching legs around and came to a stoop-shouldered, humped-over sitting position. Clawed at a spot on my throat, beneath a stubble-covered chin. It felt as though my mouth had somehow been filled with a wad of flour glue laced with a handful of straw.

My narrow, coffin-like cot—a wood-frame and leather-strapped contraption—appeared as though it had been specifically designed by hell-bred demons to torment the unsuspecting user. This medieval torture contrivance was topped by a lumpy, cotton-ticking bag stuffed with brittle corn shucks. The sack crackled and crunched with my slightest move.

"My God, but this is a right sorry mattress," I mumbled to the empty room.

Used a fist to poke at a particularly rocklike, irritating bulge near the spot that one unthinking leg usually sought out. The entire less-than-comfortable apparatus groaned, creaked, rustled, and complained as I shifted from one spot to another.

With considerably more conviction, I growled, "Damnation." Then set to rubbing my lower back. Yawned. Pawed at one sleep-matted eye with the back of a clenched fist. Picked at something wayward on my lower lip. Puckered and tried several times to spit the offending article away.

Pushing off the wobbly bed, I went to work getting completely erect. My saddle-abused spine creaked into place, one bony vertebrae at a time. Kind of like a carpenter's folding, metal-jointed ruler. Felt as if I was being stabbed with heated ice picks, when all those grating bones snapped and ground their way to the spots where each belonged. 'Course that set me to wondering what daily life would be like when I actually went and got old.

I wobbled a bit on sluggish legs. And, in the manner an ancient, solitary, battle-scarred grizzly, awakening in his hidden den, I stretched, shook all over, then snarled to warn off any wayward intruders.

Swaying in the near dark of the advancing morn, I ran shaky fingertips over the thumb-sized, near-healed weal on my right side just above the belt line. Then I slipped those same fingers around to my back and gingerly checked the spot where the bullet had come out.

"Damn Irby Teal for a good shot, anyhow," I muttered. "Guess if the evil bastard had been any better with a pistol I'd be dead, buried, and nothing but a gob of rot just like him, his brother, Boston, and their stupid friends."

Satisfied that the matching welts of angry flesh had not somehow miraculously vanished during the previous night's tussle with evasive sleep, I grunted my disapproval at the slowness of their healing and shuddered. Figured I might as well resign myself to the fecklessness of Irby

Teal's questionable aim and just try to forget about the angry-looking wound. Fat chance.

I hobbled across my sultry bedchamber. The shadow-filled room was ever so slowly, but very certainly, growing brighter with the unhurried rising of the sun.

Stopping at the nightstand, I snatched the ewer from its matching bowl. Poured lukewarm water into one hand and sucked it across dry lips, like a wary animal drinking from a tiny pond. Slapped some of the liquid onto my face and neck. Sure as hell felt good. I rattled the jug back into place, then lurched for the room's open door.

"Always darkest just before the dawn," I muttered and stared into the framed dimness of coming sunup outside.

One hand pressed against my knotted spine, I paused in the room's entryway. The broad porch of our rented, dog-run ranch house lay at my feet. I cocked an inquisitive ear and twisted my head to get better focused on the question that plagued my sleep-fogged mind.

A hundred yards away, in the trees near the river, frogs quarreled. Whip-poor-wills called back and forth to one another. Off to the north, near a barely silhouetted, rock-strewn hill, a solitary coyote yipped. Doves, surprised by something unseen, fluttered up in a flurry of racket just a few feet from the front steps and clattered their way to raucous safety. Crickets chirped and buzzed in every direction.

"Mite noisy this morning. But it's better than living up north around Fort Worth. Have to put up with the constant racket from all the damned locusts," I said to the fast-approaching light. "God Almighty, but I do hate their infernal buzzing."

Pleasant fragrance of wildflowers, carried on the approaching morning's barely detectable breezes, wafted across the grass-poor yard. The refreshing aroma tickled the edges of my flared nostrils. Distracted, I momentarily abandoned my mission and tilted an inquisitive nose up to get a better whiff of the delicate bouquet.

Lilac. But then again, maybe not. Still hadn't acquired the talent for telling one flower from the other just by the smelling. Hell of a failing for a man who spent most of his waking life out on the raw edges of civilization.

Maybe the perfume came from bluebonnets blooming somewhere nearby. Yeah, that made perfect sense. Bluebonnets. No women around this haven for us ole shot-to-a-pulp bachelors to tell me for sure.

Clad in nothing but a pair of cotton, calf-length, faded-red drawers, I grabbed the doorframe's crossbeam to steady up a bit, then leaned forward, ever so slightly. Scratched an itchy belly, then tried to pick anything by way of odd, inappropriate sounds from the soon-to-be stifling south Texas air.

I knew beyond a doubt that something out of place had snapped me from my troubled slumbers. Something peculiar. An eerie oddity that didn't belong had surely pulled me away from nightly reveries of the blood-soaked missions me and Boz had gone on.

Whatever was out there in the dark was well on the way to bringing me back to wakeful awareness. Now, I just had to ferret out whatever it was that didn't fit. The task simply required that I be patient. Pay attention. Get my fogged-up mind right.

Near half a minute passed. And then, the world went completely and totally silent, as if the hot breezes had died and all the night animals, birds, and crickets had suddenly, inexplicably vanished from the earth. Eerie as hell. Made the skin pimple and crawl up and down my achy spine in unsettling waves.

Then, there it was, sure enough. No doubt about it. None. Could barely lay an ear to the errant, distant popping. But there it was for damned sure—off in the hazy, red-tinged, gray-black distance. The distinctive, instantly recognizable sound of gunfire crackling through the early morning air. The sound vaguely echoed along the river's placid surface, climbed up the steps, invaded the house, and set my teeth on edge.

Pistols. Somebody was firing off their pistols out there. No mistaking that sound. Strange. Couldn't figure for the life of me who would be blasting away like that so early of a morning. And what in hell would they be shooting at anyway? For the most part, was still darker out yonder, in the briars and brambles, than a boxful of black kittens.

A prickling sensation of the sinister and unknowable kind crept up my pain-tinged spine again. I ran fingers through sweat-dampened hair. A widening, wavelike patch of lumpy, bristling flesh crawled up my spine and settled between pinched shoulder blades. An eye blink later, the crickets came back to life.

"Who on earth?" I said to the dimness of advancing dawn, then rubbed a chin that needed serious attention from a well-stropped razor.

6

"... MURDERED A BOATLOAD OF INNOCENT FOLKS ..."

I CAST A sharpened gaze into the reddish-gray gloom of rapidly fleeing darkness. Could hardly see the dog, but I knew ole Bear was there. Knew it as surely as I knew the sun would soon climb over the rugged hills and turn our Devils River patch of west Texas into an earthen, nigh on devilish oven.

Ever watchful, Bear rarely left the front stoop at night. Dog wasn't mine, of course. He'd come along with the house. A wayward animal might draw the brute from his guardian's perch once in a while, but not often.

The massive creature sat at attention on the creaking porch's top-most tread and gazed into the northern distance. I knew his wet, shiny nose twitched and sifted through all the air it could take in. Brute's inquisitive snout always snuffled and snorted for anything unfamiliar, out of place, or strange. His mottled, ragged, cocklebur-infested rope of a tail was surely wagging from side to side. I could hear the brushlike appendage sweeping a clean spot on the splinter-riddled, rickety step.

He twisted his battle-scarred head to one side and seemed to cut a questioning glance over a hunched shoulder at me. Thick-muscled and dangerous beyond most men's understanding, the hairy brute, conceived of indeterminate wolf and canine parentage, appeared to flash a menacing, barely visible smile.

Fight-notched, pointed, ever-shifting ears flicked from side to side, gathering the minutest of inconsistent noises. The vigilant canine easily took in the most obscure of sounds for miles around his carefully guarded domain. Anything that didn't belong in the dog's personal realm would bring an immediate, and dangerous, reaction.

I could hardly make out the hand-sized tongue as it lolled out one side of the dog's mouth and dripped slobbers. Beast cast another panting gaze up at me. He flashed a wicked set of canine teeth the size of a highwayman's trigger finger, as if to say, "You're damn right I heard all that shooting, Dodge. Wake yourself the hell up. Get a move on, man. Let's go have a look-see. Chase down the skunks making all that needless racket. Let's knock 'em over. Bite 'em in the ass. Drag 'em around in the mesquite. That'll show 'em not to roust us from our much-needed nighttime devotions."

Boz limped up out of the darkness from his crude quarters in the barn's cluttered tack room down the hill. He was all got up in nothing more than a pair of oft-patched drawers, a pistol belt, .45 Colt, run-down boots, and a knife-ventilated, palm-leaf sombrero. I'd tried to get him to sleep in the main house, but he steadfastly refused. Man preferred the ground to a real bed. Near as I was ever able to determine, my friend could sleep like a newborn babe atop a roll of rusted barbed wire and liked it that way.

A mist-like cloud of fine-powdered earth trailed behind him and fogged up around his near imperceptible feet. The gritty miasma gave him the bizarre appearance of somehow floating, wraithlike, above the dusty earth that swirled beneath those booted and spurred canoes at the ends of his legs.

He ran the flicking forefinger of one hand back and forth beneath his droopy moustache. The shaggy ornament completely obliterated his top lip and had the appearance of a living animal trying to invade a gap-toothed mouth. Ragged, wispy tip ends of the moustache dangled below his jawline and swayed in the morning breezes. That's when I realized that the pair of us had gone and got pretty damned seedy, and in right quick fashion, too.

"You hearin' all that commotion out yonder, Lucius?" Boz said, then took a seat on the edge of the rugged porch, within arm's length of the dog. He grunted, rubbed his damaged leg, then ruffled the animal's huge head. He patted the beast's furry back, then leaned against one of the crude props that offered some highly questionable support for the shaky veranda's off-kilter roof.

One shoulder lodged against my sleeping quarters' rough-cut doorframe, I gazed in the same general direction as Boz and the dog. Didn't need much in the way of heavenly illumination from a brain-frying sun to know exactly what lay out there in the receding darkness.

Swear 'fore Jesus, the entire earth appeared to spool away from the edge of the house's front veranda to the farthest reaches of the known, and unknown, world. A seemingly endless sea of hilly, reddish-brown, man-killing sand and dirt marched from our crude, leased home's front stoop to the Tinaja, Woods Hollow, and Glass Mountains, some hundred and twenty miles west and beyond.

In my personal estimation, the land, while bleak in ways hard to describe, was beautiful beyond any other place I'd ever seen. And mostly unoccupied. Few other people, if any, lived for miles around. Our nearest neighbor, as I knew of anyway, had a spread about twelve miles to the south and east, over near the Del Rio road. And that's exactly the way me and Boz had wanted it from the beginning.

"Yeah," I muttered, then fished makings from atop the chest of drawers just inside the bedroom door and set to rolling myself a smoke. "Yeah. I heard the shooting, Boz. Woke me from a right nice nap. Well, 'bout as good a one as I can hope to get these days, anyhow."

"Uh-huh. Me, too."

"Must've spent the entire time I did manage to doze a bit dreamin' 'bout some of the times we've had in the past. Good and bad." I stoked the roughly wrapped cigareet to life and took a single, lung-filling puff. Smoke cloud from the burned tobacco rolled out with my words. "Come to wakeful consciousness thinking for sure we'd just run ole Jasper Pike to ground. Hadn't so much as entertained a single thought about that murderous brigand in at least two years. He came back to me in a dream. You remember Jasper, Boz?"

An unintelligible, guttural grumble came from my friend's general direction. Unable to distinguish for certain whether the wordless response originated with the man or the dog, I flicked ash from the end of the hand-rolled with a little finger and continued with my unsolicited, meandering musings.

"Don't see how you could forget a gob of dung like Pike. Evil bastard murdered a boatload of innocent folks before we finally pulled him down. Always took a certain amount of pride in the fact that we're the ones what brought him to book."

Boz scratched a spot on his back by twisting from side to side against the porch prop. "Hell, yes, I remember Jasper," he grunted and continued his bearish exercise. "Cussed hard to forget a belly-slinkin' snake like that 'un. His kind of gutless bastard makes a Christian body wonder why God bothers to stack piles of human manure that high."

I let a crude chuckle escape despite efforts to the contrary.

"Tell you true, Lucius, older I get, amazes me as how

shit can somehow pull on boots, then get itself upright and walk around on two legs just like us regular humans."

"He was a bad one, all right, Boz. No doubt 'bout that."

"Aw, hell, bad don't come nowheres close to describing that human gob of fanged evil. As I remember the man, and I use the term *man* loosely, he drank a tubful of bad liquor, then murdered his entire family. Beat all of 'em to death with a roofin' hammer one lightnin'-spiked night."

"There you go. Even killed his kids. Was a bloody mess we found."

"If memory of the event still serves, he bolted from that god-awful scene, then went on a murderin' rip the likes of which hadn't ever been witnessed in this part of Tejas. Leastways, not since back in them days when the Co-manche used to slaughter hell and yonder out of every living thing in their path on those yearly raids of theirs down Mexico way."

"Ole Pike put a bunch of folks in the ground, and that's for damned sure."

"Uh-huh. In my humble opinion, that's a far patch of rock-strewn road worse than bad. As a consequence, by God, Jasper Pike ain't exactly the kind of bastard I'm given to forgetting about."

I thumped the still-smoldering butt of my smoke into the air and watched as the sparks arched and went to ground like a Fourth of July whizbang. "Figured you'd remember the sorry stink sprayer, Boz. Got to admit, it's most gratifying now for me to cherish the recollection of how God gave the pair of us the distinct privilege of killing the hell out of his sorry self."

Boz grimaced and rubbed his leg again. "Mostly you, as I recollect. You peppered his worthless, murderin' ass pretty good, Lucius. Put a bunch of bullets in his sorry hide. Think maybe I only drilled one good 'un in him."

"Well, I ain't so sure 'bout that."

"Uh-huh. Be that as it may, personally think I could find

somethin' better to occupy my nightly dreams, if you want to know the truth of the thing, pard. You know, women like that there hot-blooded Josephina Martinez. God as my witness, done got to where I think 'bout that gal a lot when it comes on nighttime."

"Jesus, Boz. Think you've taken to spending way too much time *thinking* about one willing woman or another."

"Well, you can *think* about whatever'n hell you want to *think* about, and I'll *think* about bow-legged gals like Josephina. Remember her? Healthy, well-fed *muchacha* from over 'round Val Verde? Now, I'll tell you, by God, don't mind one little bit dreamin' about that gal's big ole . . ."

Boz abruptly stopped in mid-thought. For a second, struck me as how he bore a striking resemblance to the dog, when he tilted his head to one side. Seemed pretty certain to me he just might cock a leg up and scratch one ear with his foot—the one attached to his undamaged leg.

"Damn, there it goes again," he said. "Sounds most like pistols to me. Maybe half a dozen of 'em. What you think 'bout it, Lucius?"

Ran the fingers of one hand through my sweat-dampened hair again, then twirled one sagging end of my moustache around a nervous finger. Right certain I appeared lost in deep thought.

Slid the same finger into my mouth, then held it out into the barely moving air. "Not so much as a light breeze out here right now, Boz. World's as still as a sack of flour sitting in an old maid's pantry. Least kind of sound can travel a long way on a morning like this. I'm guessing as much as five miles or so north along the river. Maybe more, maybe less."

"Uh-huh. Sounds about right to me."

"Seems as how the blasting just about has to be goin' on over around that pocket of ground right on the edge of Turkey Mesa. Green spot next to the river. You know the one I'm talking about."

"Yep. That's how I figured it, too. Place where Three Mile Creek seeps down to the river—when there's enough water to do anything by way of seeping that is. Passin' itinerants have always liked that particular location. Yep. All that blastin's gotta be somewhere close to that 'ere shade-givin' stand of cottonwoods and good grass, I'd wager."

"Yeah. Heard tell as how some of them old forty-niners laid over in that spot on their way to the West Coast back during the gold rush days. Can't say as I blame them much. Fine site for tired folks to take their ease. Rest up on the difficult way to wherever they might be headed. Location has pretty much everything going for it—shade, grass, water. Nice, real nice."

Those words had barely passed my lips when another round of faint popping echoed down the river, ricocheted off the surface of the glass-still water, and, without welcome, bounced onto the doorstep right at our feet. The rapid burst of gunfire tickled the edges of our pricked ears. A tingling sensation crawled up my spine like a Mexican scorpion on the prowl for something it could sting to death.

I squinted and said, "Who you reckon would be doin' that much shootin' this time of the mornin', Boz? Sun's only just now gettin' up good. Got nothin' more'n a fingernail-sized sliver of moon for real light right now. Could barely see my hand in front of my own face not more'n ten minutes ago."

I took a single step out onto the rough-and-ready veranda and cast a squint-eyed gaze along that part of the shimmering river I could see. "Be full light soon enough, I guess. Another half an hour, forty-five minutes maybe."

"Uh-huh," Boz grunted. "Still and all, ain't much of a time for folks to be out huntin'. Lest them as are doing all that shooting have a pack of dogs along to scare up some game. Doubt that."

"How so?"

"'Cause if'n they had dogs, bet ole Bear, here, would be barking and hopping around like he was on fire. Tell you what, whoever them noisy boys are, they've gotta be damned site better shots than either one of us—if they can hunt in the dark, that is."

I mumbled, "Beats all I've heard in a while." Then, with considerably more force and vigor, I added, "Well, suppose we'd best get ourselves together, arm up, and go see about it. Bothers the hell out of me that people are shooting up the property. That they woke me up. And here I am a standin' in the door, in my drawers, and don't have the least idea as to who they are or why they're doing it."

Ever the philosopher, Boz said, "As you are well aware, Lucius Dodge, I don't care for such blatantly mischievous and dangerous behavior myself. Never have condoned the thoughtless deeds of arrogant, unthinking bastards as would roust me out of a night of much-needed, rejuvenating slumber by firing off their pistols in such an unthinking and promiscuous manner."

Shook my head and grinned in spite of myself. "Jesus, Boz. I'd ask you to repeat all that, but I know you couldn't do it on a bet."

Tatum chuckled and slapped his leg without thinking, then grimaced and sucked in a quick, hissing breath.

"Well, guess maybe you'd best amble on back down to the corral and saddle us a couple of them bangtails, Boz. I'll ride Grizz—if he'll let you get close enough to catch him."

"Oh, I'll catch him all right."

"While you're doing that, I'll roust Paco out of the sack. Have him cook us up a pot of coffee thick enough to float a Colt's pistol and load us up a sack for traveling."

"He ain't gonna like gettin' woke up this early."

"Probably not. But, time we get ourselves dressed and armed he should have coffee cooked. Drink a cup before we set out."

Boz rubbed his neck. "Have him throw some of the biscuits and ham from last night into a saddlebag, too. Figure by the time we get situated, should have decent enough light to travel. Head on up to Turkey Mesa. See if we can figure out what in the blue-eyed hell's going on, and why we weren't invited to the dance."

"That'll work."

"Oh, you want me to wake Glorious, Lucius? Might need him and that big ole shotgun of his. 'Specially if we run into anything like real trouble. Besides, he knows the area a hell of a lot better than either of us."

Our friend Glorious Johnson had come down from Fort Worth on his own when he heard the news that the pair of us had got ourselves shot in Rio Seco. Man had turned out a godsend. Took on plenty of work around the place that we still had a spot of trouble doing.

"Might as well. Figure the more folks we have along for the ride the better. From the sound of all that gunfire, sure as hell seems to be a sight more than one or two of them doing the shooting—whoever they are."

Boz was on his feet before I could say anything else. He hobbled down the sloped, grassless hill toward the corral, like a man walking a ship's deck on choppy seas.

I trundled my way to the back side of the dog-run house's rough, open porch. A covered deck separated the raw, divided structure's kitchen from my sleeping quarters and personal digs. The shaded portion of the open porch also served as a makeshift dining area—weather permitting.

Bear, all happy with the excitement and movement, let out a throaty snort and wagged his thick, bur-infested tail. He shot from his preferred perch on the steps and headed down the hill behind Boz.

Second or so later I could hear my friend calling to the dog, then yelling for Glorious Johnson to hoist himself the hell out of the sack and get himself on the move. And that we had a situation to look into. That's the way Boz described all the shooting and commotion of the morning, ". . . a situation." Little could he have known just how grotesque, bloody, or god-awful that situation would prove.

7

"Somethin' Real Bad's a-Waitin' for Us . . ."

HAD TO CALL the Messican's name three times before a bleary-eyed Paco Matehuala stumbled from the shelter of the lean-to shed tacked to the kitchen's board-and-batten back wall. Never one to complain because his newly acquired gringo *jefes* kept odd hours, our sleepy-eyed, muddle-headed cook wobbled up the back steps and onto the central part of the porch. He pulled a coarse, cotton shirt over splayed hair, then, without comment or protest, staggered toward his soon-to-be-stifling kitchen.

According to my big-ticking Ingersoll pocket watch, a bit more than half an hour had flown by when Boz ambled back up from the corral. He led a pair of saddled, drooping hay burners. Bear and a yawning Glorious Johnson followed.

I snapped the turnip-sized watch's silver-washed cover closed, shoved it into my vest pocket, and watched as Paco stood on the veranda's steps and poured Tatum and Johnson a steaming cup of Arbuckles aromatic Ariosa coffee, then retreated back to his oppressive workplace.

Cup of black, tonsil-searing, up-and-at-'em juice in hand, Glorious Johnson lurched, as though still not quite awake. He groped his unsteady way around a fine bay gelding, laid a long-barreled Greener across the saddle, then, finally, focused the totality of his waking concentration on the smoldering mug.

"Damn, that's good stuff," Boz said, after his first nibble at the cup.

Johnson sipped in silence. He dipped his close-cropped, ebony head in agreement, but still said nothing and made no sound.

Fully furnished out in high-waisted pants, shotgun chaps, riding boots, spurs with Mexican rowels, and a Texas-crimped, palm-leaf sombrero the size of a wagon wheel, I hopped off the porch and jingled over to the blue roan. One-handed, I stuffed a sack of grub Paco had prepared for us into the leather bags tied behind Grizz's well-used California-style saddle.

I leaned against the ever-patient animal's muscular rump and went back to work on my own beaker of belly wash. The Messican's coffee did taste mighty good. Got to thinking as how if the day went bad Paco's stump juice might well prove the best part of our unscheduled morning.

"Tell you true, Boz," I said, after sucking down near half the contents of my cup, "this here Arbuckles sure beats the hell out of cooking parched grain, way we've often had to do during a goodly number of our other days as rangers. Beats the hell out of that stuff we used to get from down in Mexico, too. Suppose we ought to stroll on down to Del Rio soon as we have a chance. Buy ourselves another five or ten pounds of these beans. Mighty tasty."

Glorious Johnson grunted, as though still half asleep, then wordlessly went back to chewing at his still-steaming cup.

Almost to myself, since I'd got no response to my thoughtful observations, I added, "Paco says we're start-

ing to run low on the wonderful stuff. Another two weeks
or so, we'll be slap out." Pointing at Boz's mount with my
near-empty beaker, I added, "You bring that cut-down
coach gun of yours along?"

"Hell, yes, I brung it," my friend said, as he fussed over
the buckle on one leg of his chaps.

Except for a flashy, bloodred, bib-front shirt, Boz's
outfit could have easily passed for a close match of mine.
"She's loaded up with heavy-gauge buckshot and ready for
action. Put one of the Winchesters in your saddle scabbard,
Lucius. Figured between my coach gun, your big ole rifle,
Glo's Greener, and all this iron we're packing around our
waists, oughta be way more'n prepared for just about any
set of circumstances we might happen on. 'Course, if none
of that works out, and we should all get kilt deader'n hell
in a preacher's front parlor, could always use our weapon-
laden corpses for boat anchors."

A grin played across my coffee-dampened lips. "Still
referring to that amputated popper of yours as Hortence,
I suppose?"

Tatum and Johnson both flashed toothy grins at
the shared joke. Boz shook his head. "Naw. Naw. Not
anymore."

"Oh. And why not?"

"Well, got to figurin' . . ."

Glorious Johnson chuckled, then said, "Now there's a
bad sign, if'n I ever heered tell of one. Ole Boz Tatum gets
to figurin' and chickens is prone to stop laying. Both of 'em
bad signs."

Feigning mild irritation, Boz said, "As I was tryin' to
say before bein' so rudely interrupted, got to figurin' as
how a woman as wicked as Hortence Smeal don't deserve
to have a damned fine English-made shooter like this 'un
of mine named after her. Done took to callin' this here
first-rate weapon Ezmerelda, these days. After Ezmerelda
Wingfield, you see."

I let a twisted grimace creak across my face. "That one-eyed, wooden-legged witch from Fort Stockton? One who's rumored to carry an Arkansas toothpick strapped to her fake leg."

"You betcha. But you've got 'er all wrong, Lucius. Ezmerelda's a fine ole gal. Somewhat amputated like that 'ere Greener of mine. Yessir, she's a mighty fine piece of womanhood. Tougher'n a boiled boot heel I'll admit, but fine stuff nonetheless. Why, just thinkin' 'bout Ezmerelda, lack of genuine leg and all, gives me a case of the walkin' willies. Yessiree. You pack that gal into a split-front, leather ridin' skirt, and she's got a caboose on her that's so tight you could bounce buckshot pellets off'n it."

Glorious Johnson shook his head, cast rolling eyes heavenward, and mumbled, "Lord, Lord."

"Trust me now. Ole gal's one hell of a fine ride, fellers. An evenin' in her bed is close on to the same as passin' time in one of them hundred-dollar, handmade rockin' chairs from back East. Gal likes to laugh whilst she's doin' her business. Cackles like a thing possessed at times. As you are both well aware, I've always liked a laughin' woman. Yessir, surely have. 'Sides, that stumpy leg of hers sends shivers up and down my spine every time I think about it."

Glo appeared to have finally come fully awake. Never one to waste time with discussions of one-legged wayward women, he lowered his cup and said, "You gennamans done spent way too many years chasin' iniquitous white folk, bloodthirsty Injuns, and thieving Messicans. Swear to Jesus, you're the only two fellers I ever knowed what wore a Colt's hip pistol, a cross-draw gun, and a third shooter nestled agin' yore backs. And here you are, all armed up and standin' around talkin' 'bout one-legged whores whilst there's all kinds of promiscuous shootin' goin' on within hearin' distance not five miles up the river."

Boz chuckled. "Well, as usual, Glorious is absolutely

right. We do have more important fish to fry right now, I suppose. No point standin' around jawin' 'bout the dirty-legged women I keep company with on occassion. Or them as don't have a particular leg for that matter." He paused a second, then sliced a saucy grin Johnson's direction. "Did I just hear you say 'promiscuous shootin',' Glo? Now where'n hell did you happen across a two-dollar word like 'promiscuous'?"

Johnson tossed the remains of his cup aside, then gazed into the distance as though distracted. "Don't matter, Mis-tuh Tatum. Don't matter where I done heard the word. They's an evil wind blowin'. Can feel it in my bones. Evil, evil wind."

"Evil. I heard you."

"Got this here feelin', you know. A twistin' in my guts. Somethin' real bad's a-waitin' for us out there, I'd wager. Yessir, somethin' real bad."

Gritted my teeth, for I knew when Glorious "got the feelin," a reasonable body had best pay attention. Pulled one of the three hand cannons hanging from my waist. Flipped the loading gate open and checked all the rounds. Slapped the gate closed and snugged the pistol down inside a well-aged, oiled holster looped over a broad, double-row, military-issue cartridge belt. Then I made a show of single-mindedly examining all my other weapons as well.

Me and Boz both supplemented our three handguns with a bone-handled bowie knife that sported a heavy, ten-inch, razor-sharp blade. This nigh-on foot-long piece of Damascus steel hanging from my belt was honed to the point of being fully capable of lopping a man's hand off with the expenditure of a minimal amount of effort.

As Boz once said, when in one of his more philosophical moods, "Always better to have some kind of weapon and not need one than to need some kind of weapon and not have one. An extra two or three is even better still. 'Sides, I'm pert sure most of the badmen out there are a damn sight more afraid of gettin' gutted once than bein' shot multiple times with all three of these pistols I carry put together. Just ain't nothin' as gets a man's attention quicker'n havin' to hold his guts in with his own hands."

Born from much rehearsed habit and the full realization that hollow-eyed Death might well lay in stealthy wait for every unprepared man, we not only took the time to make sure each handgun was fully loaded but to carefully check them for fluid and unrestricted action. We always re-inspected all our munitions as well. Then, last but not least, we double-checked all our food and water supplies.

And so, as well-prepared as possible for what should have proven to be little more than a pleasant morning's excursion, we stepped into waiting stirrups, whistled for ole Bear, then urged our animals down the gentle slope to the trail headed north alongside Devils River—a broad dusty path that led inexorably into the hazy, unknowable, and possibly dangerous future.

We'd gone little more than a hundred yards when another cold shiver darted up my back on talon-tipped feet. I shook off the feeling of dread and tried, as best I could, to focus my total attention on the winding track ahead.

Bear, his massive head raised, sniffed the air and charged into the gathering daylight out front of our abbreviated hunting party like an angry, bush-raised, longhorn steer on the prod.

With the polished walnut stock of the long-barreled Greener propped against one thigh, Glo protected our small party's rear. In spite of the rapidly increasing heat, I heard him say as how an unexpected feeling of chill had crawled up his broad, muscular back. Made me a mite froggy, when I glanced back and watched as he twisted from side to side in his well-worn saddle. Then flicked a nervous gaze back and forth in an effort to penetrate the retreating darkness and searched each creeping shadow for the unexpected.

The man had a habit of talking to himself. So it came as

no surprise when, as though to no one in particular, I heard him mumble, "They's somethin' awful out there, Glo baby. Somethin' awful and waiting. Gots to be careful, Glo. Gots to be real careful."

Glanced over one shoulder again, about the time we got to the river. Spotted Paco still standing on the porch. He was munching on a flour taco I knew was wrapped around *huevos revueltos*, spiced with bits of fried bacon, onion, jalapenos, and sweet green peppers. Appeared to me he watched us with a tinge of growing trepidation, as we reined our animals down the slanted, grass-poor hill toward *el Rio Diablos* and began fading into the bluish-gray coming of dawn.

Pretty sure I spotted a troubled look on the peon's dark brow. Just before I lost sight of the man, he appeared to pause in mid-chew. He rubbed a hairless chin against the back of the hand holding the taco and crossed himself with his half-eaten breakfast. Then he turned and ambled back to the safety and familiarity of his waiting, oven-like *cocina*.

A quick, edgy, 180-degree glance around the viewable heavens revealed no inauspicious signs or threatening portents, as I could see. No huge, winged, cawing, black birds perched on every viewable flat surface. No shower of wart-covered toads dropped from the sky. No horned owls or other such precursors of a questionable and perhaps grisly future silently swept across the heavens. Nothing like that. Still and all, would have sworn someone had poured a bucket of slime-spiked ice water down my knotted spine.

8

"... These Poor Folks Been Shot Slap to Pieces."

THE TREK NORTH, along the easternmost bank of Devils River to Three Mile Creek, leisurely advanced along a broad, well-traveled trail of powdered silt. A route that a one-eyed man could have followed. Carved into the rugged, hilly landscape by eons of migrating animals, herded livestock, and the wooden-wheeled carts of men, the rutted path gently rose and fell before us like a spacious ribbon of meandering, chalky dust.

In the passage of less than an hour, Boz, Glorious Johnson, and me sat our tail-flicking animals atop a low, barren knoll. Boz draped a bony leg over his saddle horn and shoved a thin, rum-soaked cheroot into the corner of his mouth. Several hundred yards below, a patch of Eden-like greenery sprang from a shallow, bowl-shaped depression in the earth that bordered the two-foot-deep, slow-moving waterway coursing south for the Rio Grande.

A fiery, bubbling, coin-shaped sphere of molten-iron perched on the eastern horizon—a burning ball atop a vast, brown table. Cast by the rising sun, eerie, slithering shadows squirmed and wriggled through the lush stand of trees. With silent stealth, they darted amongst the weeds, crawling like snakes as the hot sunlight crept across the warming earth.

Off a bit to my left, Bear rested on hairy haunches atop a flattened, slablike piece of rock. The animal's lips curled away from its teeth in an atavistic sneer. With brush-notched ears at attention, like an extended set of funeral home fans mounted on its gigantic head, a subdued growl rumbled deep inside his thick canine chest. Every ropelike muscle trembled with strained anticipation, but he would not move from his chosen spot until told to do so.

I extracted a surplus cavalry officer's spyglass from a weathered and age-battered case that dangled from the end of a leather thong tied to my saddle horn. I snapped the telescope out to its maximum, five-segment length and scanned the copse of verdant, whispering cottonwoods at the bottom of the hill. Swept the entire area, back and forth—three times. Examined every tree, bush, rock, and blade of swaying grass. Meticulously inspected those view-able portions of a canvas-covered wagon nigh on hidden by all the tree trunks and greenery.

"Quieter than the bottom of a fresh-dug grave at midnight down there," Boz muttered between teeth clenched around his twiglike, unlit cheroot.

"Can't make much out," I said, left eye still pressed against the leading lens of the foot-long telescope. "Appears as though there's some kind of wagon pulled up under that thickest stand of cottonwoods down yonder."

"Thought somethin' didn't look right," Boz mumbled.

"Yeah. Spot nearest the creek where it drops off the mesa into the river. Looks like a cross between an old-fashioned prairie schooner and a trail-drive chuck wagon. Has a water barrel mounted on the side facing us."

Boz chewed on the cheroot. "Hear tell as how some town folk are buyin' them old chuck wagons just so's

they can gad about the countryside these days. Convertin'
'em over just for travelin' around. Campin' out and such.
Leastways, that's what I've heard. Don't that just beat all
you ever heard? Town folk campin' out just for the fun
of it?"

"Umm, well, maybe it is a converted chuck wagon.
No chuck box left on the back though. Grass growing all
around the site looks like it's probably close to belly deep
on the horses. Pretty well trampled down in some spots,
though. From up here, it's kind of like looking through
a series of weed-choked windows. Only allows a body a
small piece of the scene at a time."

"People? You see any people, Mistuh Dodge?" Glorious
said.

"Not a soul, Glo. Leastways none that's upright and
moving around. Do spy a couple of lumps, or mounds, on
the ground near the wagon's back wheels. Sad to say, but
they look an awful lot like bodies to me. All those weeds
render any solid observations, from this far away, little
more than an educated guess though."

Boz pushed his hand-creased sombrero to the back of
a sweaty head, pulled a blue-and-white bandanna, and
mopped at a dripping brow. "Damn. Cool of the mornin'
sure 'nuff didn't last long."

Me and Glo grunted our agreement. Bear breathed a
snarling sound around a dripping tongue, like some monstrous wild animal.

"You know, that's mighty suspicious lookin', even from
up here, you ask me, Lucius," Boz said. "Oughta be able to
see somebody movin' around. It's more'n a bit worrisome,
by God. Mighty worrisome. Earlier, we heard a right smart
amount of shooting coming from this spot. Crop of dead
folks won't surprise me much. You see anything else as
might look like bodies?"

Several seconds of oppressive silence followed. Then
Grizz impatiently pawed at the ground with one iron-shod

front foot. The bit and reins rattled when he shook his equine head and softly whinnied.

I lowered my glass, shoved it back into the protective sheath, and let the whole package dangle from the leather thong. "Not real sure, Boz. Just can't make out much from this far away, 'cause of all the brush and such. Driver pulled that wagon up so far beneath those trees a body would have to really be looking for the thing to even know it was down there."

Boz grunted, "Uhmmm," but added nothing more.

"Seems most like he was trying to hide it from anyone who might happen to pass by. No fire as I can detect. Not even a ghostly wisp of smoke. Doesn't appear that whoever might be left alive down there even bothered to put one together." Another brief bit of wordless silence passed between us before I added, "Or maybe they just never got the chance."

"Gonna make damned fine targets if we go ridin' in there sittin' up tall on these hammerheaded bangtails," Boz offered. "Figure we'd best dismount, fan out a bit. Walk in. Maybe do a little of the ole Comanche tiptoe," he said and stuffed the damp bandanna back into his pocket, then snugged his battered hat down.

I swung off Grizz. Pulled the heavy, octagon-barreled Winchester hunting rifle from its boot in a single practiced move. Levered a hot round into the big shooter's chamber, as Boz and Glo stepped off their animals and loosed their own long guns.

"Gimme a few minutes to get over to the camp's far side, Glo," Boz said, then shoved the spit-soaked cheroot into his vest pocket. He breeched the coach gun and rechecked each massive brass-cased round. The weapon made a loud, metallic, thunking click when he snapped it shut.

With the blaster draped across one arm, Boz cast a steely, squint-eyed gaze from one side of the stand of trees to the other. "Once I'm set up, Glo, I'll give a yelp. Then you can move in on this side. Lucius can take the middle. Three of us close in on the camp at the same time, from different directions, should spread the fire from any hidden, back-shootin' varmint as might be lying in wait."

"Ya, suh, Mistuh Tatum. I'll be right 'hind yuh."

Silently nodding my agreement of the suggested strategy, I threw Boz a quick smile, then winked. "Sounds like a good enough plan to me. Guess we aren't getting any younger just standing around, twiddling our thumbs. Let's head on out and get 'er done."

I watched as my friends wordlessly turned and moved off through the waist-deep dry grass.

My compadres in position, I cast a quick, unblinking glance toward Heaven. Said, "Lord, let's try not to let anyone get hurt today. Want all my folks sitting down to one of Paco's suppers at the same time later this afternoon when we say grace over our food. Okay?" Then I snapped my fingers and motioned Bear into action.

The dog snorted out an enthusiastic growl and hit the ground running. Rifle at the ready, I hunched over and slipped into the already parted weeds, silently trailing behind the happy beast.

A stricken look carved deep lines of pain and concern into Glorious Johnson's already creased face. He squatted at the edge of a semicircle of flattened grass and trampled earth near the remains of a pair of oozing corpses.

Nearby, Bear flopped on his hairy belly and let out a series of low guttural yowls.

Appearing as though lost in confused thought, Johnson gazed at the bullet-riddled bodies, then sadly shook his head. The recently departed lay on their backs and gazed with unmoving, sightless eyes, at cotton boll clouds pinned onto a crystalline, turquoise sky.

Caught in a hailstorm of blue whistlers, the dead couple had fallen near the back of the refurbished Studebaker. The entire side of the vehicle's wooden freight box facing the river was riddled with fresh, splinter-decorated bullet holes. A team of fine-looking mules lay dead in the traces.

In the manner of a gory carpet, a clotted mat of blood and viscera, as thick as half a family Bible, covered the well-trampled earth for several feet around the bodies of the man, woman, and their animals. Here and there, like flakes of blood-flecked snow, bits of brain matter and splintered bone from the couple's shattered skulls decorated the thin exposed areas of crushed grass and packed dirt.

Shotgun at the death-dealing ready, Boz circled the wagon.

I stood near the dog and swept a piercing gaze from one side of the campsite to the other. Hissed, "Can you make any kind of sense from all this, Glo?"

Johnson pushed a sweat-stained, gray flop hat to the back of his head, then scratched a spot over one ear in puzzlement. "As you see, Mistuh Dodge, these poor folks been shot slap to pieces. Done bled slap out right where they fell. Just like them poor defenseless mules."

I shook my head in disgust. "Damned sorry business all right. Damned sorry."

"Looks to me like whoever done fer 'em wanted to make certain sure they didn't get up once they 'uz down. Both these poor folk been drilled through the head bone several times—least twice, maybe more. This here pitiful feller's skull's splattered all over hell and yonder." He paused, then as an afterthought added, "Woman's, too. Top of all that, they's bullet holes in the dirt all around 'em. 'Pears near half a dozen men stood over these unfortunates and just blasted the by-God bejabbers out of 'em."

"What about them as done the deed?"

"Gone, Mistuh Dodge. Leastways, near as I can tell. Ain't been gone long, but them as done this sorry deed come and left in a mighty big hurry. Five, six, maybe seven of 'em. Made such a mess right here around the wagon it's hard to tell exactly."

"Anything else?"

"Well, can say for sure as how the killers rode their animals right up from the river. Got down, walked up here, caught these folks unawares. Shot 'em dead, then lit a shuck away from their crimes. Didn't waste a single second from the looks of it."

"Uh-huh."

A visage of sadness and regret flashed across Glo's strained, ebon face. "Most like them raids we done made when me'n Mr. Boz 'uz rangerin' and trackin' them Messican killers down in Coahuila out on the Rio Salado. 'Member as how we used to storm right into their camps, whilst they 'uz sleepin', pistols a-blazin'. Kilt 'em all. Learned the method from the Comanche, back when I used to go out and slaughter them folks, too."

I watched as Boz drew to a halt near the wagon's tailgate and shot a troubled glance at the ground beneath the back axle. A separate, substantial pool of near-black, gooey, congealed blood had accumulated atop the grass near the wagon's back entry. Blood that obviously didn't belong to either the man or woman. Thumb-sized droplets dribbled from cracks in the Studebaker's wooden bed and splattered atop the still widening pool.

He eased up to the tail flap and pushed the canvas aside with the barrel of his shotgun. Stood for several seconds, staring into the vehicle's dark, musty interior until his eyes adjusted enough to take in the horror that lay waiting in the vehicle's rank darkness.

Of a sudden, my friend made a smothered retching sound. "Sweet merciful mother of Jesus," he said and stumbled backward as though slapped across the cheek by an invisible hand.

"What is it?" I called out, then rushed to my ashen-faced amigo's side. "What's in there, Boz?"

Grabbed the heavy canvas cover and flipped it aside. Took a second for my own light-dilated eyes to adjust to the central gloom. The wagon's horrific contents brought on a stunned feeling not unlike being struck in the chest with a closed fist the size and weight of a blacksmith's favorite anvil.

Despite a level of self-control most men would never know, or even aspire to, my eyes flashed wide in awestruck horror. I yelped, "Damnation," and took a step backward to stand shoulder to shoulder with Boz.

Swear all the air tried to rush from my compressed lungs at the same instant. Felt as though my heart and brain had locked themselves into a struggle to disconnect for several seconds. Intellectually, I could acknowledge the ghastly truth of what lay inside that benighted vehicle. But oh, my friends, a heart made tender by an inability to understand such butchery refused to concede that the hellish, unspeakably evil scene was real.

Felled into a hideous, twisted pile, not unlike seedlings caught in a cyclone, the deformed, broken bodies of three bullet-blasted children lay one atop the other amidst piles of dolls in a misshapen, bird's-nest-like mass. Given the quick, stomach-churning examination I allowed myself of the grisly, macabre scene, there were two boys and a girl.

Blasted nigh to shreds by a hot curtain of concentrated lead, whatever features of youthful beauty that might have existed a few hours prior to our arrival had been effectively obliterated. I kept thinking as how, perhaps, the stack of bodies was just three young girls. Nigh impossible to tell, really. But continued examination revealed the error of my hurried, horrified, initial observations.

When confronted by the surprise and unspeakable terror of certain death, the youngsters appeared to have covered their eyes with tiny hands, as though in denial of the reality facing them. Their childish faces had vanished, for the most part. Legs and arms lay splayed and twisted in monstrous, unnatural ways. Atop thin, childish chests their hands lay shattered beyond any practical use, even if they had managed to, somehow, survive the fiery onslaught. The blasting was so intense it appeared as though hell-sent imps had painted the entire interior of the grisly vehicle with gallons upon gallons of human blood. Not a single inch of available space had been spared the gory coating that seeped through the wagon's floor and onto the ground below.

Grim-faced, I jerked the flap back into place, took two stumbling steps, then grasped the wagon's wooden tailgate to steady myself. I coughed, toed at the dirt, and coughed again. Snatched my hat off and slapped a trembling leg with it. Then I rubbed a flushed, dripping face against the sleeve of my shirt.

Jammed the hat back on before I was able to say, "Swear 'fore Jesus, Boz, figured as how, between the three of us, we'd seen just about everything godless men could do over the combined years we've shared as Rangers. But, with sweet Jesus as my witness, it's been a damned long time since any of us has had to look on a scene as appalling as this one."

Boz swung a misty-eyed gaze toward the tops of the swaying, murmuring cottonwoods overhead then turned teeth-gritting attention onto the toes of his boots. He picked at a frayed spot on his vest. "My, oh, my, Lucius, but ain't that the Lord's truth. Truly hoped I'd seen the last of such as this. Makes my heart hurt just to think on it."

Then, within a matter of fleeting seconds, it suddenly felt as if an iron bar had been inserted into my spine. I straightened and turned. Shook a finger at Glorious Johnson.

Like an angry animal, I growled, "Get after 'em, Glo. Take Bear. Set the dog on these monsters' trail. Find 'em. Find which direction the bastards who did this came from and where they're headed. Only a few places men who'd commit such an atrocity can go from a spot as remote as this."

Glorious Johnson nodded and, as though distracted,

mumbled, "Sho 'nuff, Mistuh Dodge. I'll find 'em. You know I will."

I continued thinking aloud to myself. "Figure the men responsible for this sorry deed are gonna need a stiff drink and damned quick. Bet all I've got, and all I'll ever have, they're headed for the nearest cantina."

Boz toed at the ground beneath his feet. "I agree, Lucius. Men as would murder a woman and three little kids are gonna need a tubful of strong liquor to wash memories of this massacre away. Once you've got a bead on these sons a bitches, Glo, get back here quick as you can. Don't let 'em see you. And whatever you do, don't try and take 'em alone."

I gazed into Glo's strained face. The man appeared to have aged a thousand years in a matter of seconds. He slowly rose to his feet and stared into my hardened visage. He, Boz, and me had ridden together on dozens of other raids and searches. Both men had seen that same grim look on my face before. Hard-eyed, jaw clenched, back teeth grinding against one another.

Better than just about anyone living, Glorious Johnson understood what the look meant. As clear as staring into a traveling gypsy's crystal ball, he could see the blood-soaked future of the killers in my flint-eyed gaze.

Men who had never heard of Rangers Lucius Dodge, Randall Bozworth Tatum, or Glorious Johnson would pay dearly for the death and destruction they had wrought on the banks of Three Mile Creek. They were dead men on horses and didn't have the slightest clue that their departure from the ranks of the living had already been written into the golden pages of the Angel of Death's eternal book.

Those men's damnable names, and ten times damnable deeds, were already inscribed in flowing script by the blood-dipped finger tip of a dangerous man most people didn't even know. I could tell what my friend was thinking. For the slaughter of this unknown family, Lucius Dodge's

ruthless, relentless, unstoppable judgment was now focused on them like a narrow pointed shaft of August sunlight falling through the cottonwoods beside Three Mile
Creek. Mounted on a blue-gray horse, bony-fingered death
was headed their direction—and his judgment was coming
damned quick.

Solemn with respect for what he detected on my stony
countenance, Johnson grimly nodded. "Yes, suh, Mistuh
Dodge, Mistuh Boz. Don't you be worrin' none. Me'n ole
Bear, we be findin' 'em fellas as done this horrible thang.
Fast as a vengeful God'll let us," he said.

Johnson made a clucking sound, snapped his fingers at
the dog, then turned and vanished into the thick patch of
weeds with the snuffling animal hot on his heels. As he
strode away, I barely heard it when he muttered, to no one
in particular, "Thankee Lord God for not makin' me help
burry them poor childern. Not sure I coulda took part in
such a gruesome task."

I watched Glo disappear into the curtain of tall grass
between the blood-soaked green spot and where we'd left
our animals. Then I propped my rifle against the wagon's
back wheel, unbuckled my pistol belt, and draped it over
the sideboards.

Set to rolling up my sleeves. "Best see if we can locate
a shovel, Boz. Two would be even better. Need to get ourselves busy digging graves. Might as well go on ahead and
get these poor folks underground 'fore they get too ripe on
us. Time's a-wastin'."

Boz stared into the heavens, as though silently hoping
for some sort of divine intervention. Perhaps a miracle the
likes of which he'd never witnessed in his long life. When
none came, he turned to me and said, "Where you suppose God was when this happened, Lucius." A single tear
streamed down his leathery, stubble-covered cheek. He
wiped the droplet away on the sleeve of his shirt. I'd never
witnessed such an open display of emotion from my best

friend before. Never. His momentary loss of control had a profound and powerful effect on me.

Couldn't do much of anything but say, "Don't have a single idea, Boz. Just don't know." I hemmed and hawed around some, then clumsily added, "Appears pretty certain he wasn't anywheres around these parts. Must've had more pressing business elsewhere."

Boz toed at the dirt again and shook his head in sad resignation.

I tried to smooth the situation over a bit in the only way I knew how. "Figure the best thing we can do for these poor folks is get them in the ground quick as possible. See to it they're covered up where nothing can get at 'em. Don't you think?"

Boz rubbed a reddened eye with a scruffy knuckle and tried not to look at me when he croaked, "Yeah, I know, Lucius. You're right as rain. Hot as it is, and as hot as it's gonna get 'fore dark finally comes, these poor people gonna be getting mighty rank," Almost as an afterthought, he coughed, stared at Heaven again, then added, "Gonna be all swole up 'fore a body can spit. Putrefied quicker than double-geared lightning."

Squint-eyed, I nodded. No point debating the brutal truth of the situation. I turned my back to the wagon and its contents and stared at the river.

Remember thinking, sweet Jesus give me strength in this time of unparalleled horror and uncommon butchery.

9

"Snapping and Biting Like a Rabid Dog."

BOZ AND ME stood barefoot in the lazy, fetid trickle of Devils River. Pants legs rolled up to bone-white knees, both of us sloshed water over forearms soaked all the way to the elbows with dried gore. Burial of the five bullet-shattered bodies had proven more difficult and taken longer than either of us had anticipated.

Rather than attempting to dig individual holes in the sunbaked, near impenetrable earth, we'd been forced to scratch out a single, shallow grave barely large enough to accommodate the entire massacred clan. The excavation took two hours of backbreaking, debilitating labor. We spelled each other in that grueling effort, using the only shovel to be found amidst the blood-soaked wreckage left behind by merciless killers.

Worst part of the nightmarish enterprise was carrying, or dragging, the still-seeping corpses of the children and their parents for placement inside the crude riverbank tomb. During the grisly interment, it took the total of our concentrated, gulping effort to keep Paco Matehuala's early morning coffee and breakfast tacos from coming back up in a rush of bitter, pukey, stomach-churning bile.

The gruesome task proved especially problematic during that period when we worked to cover the pathetic bodies of the dead kids with several blood-encrusted, rigid, scab-like blankets retrieved from the wagon. When finally satisfied with our best possible efforts, we threw dirt over the sad corpses like reluctant family members forced into a surprising and deplorable undertaking. Finished off the soul-wrenching job with a layer of all the rocks we could retrieve within fifty feet of the rude burying. Then we decorated the grave with as many blooming cactus plants as I could wrench from the clutches of a reluctant, covetous earth.

Sweat drenched and soaked in gore, Boz had squatted at the foot of the completed tomb. Crestfallen, my friend scratched in the loose dirt with a cottonwood twig and wiped leaky eyes on a filthy shirt-sleeve. He shook his shaggy head and muttered, "They murdered the children. And just a bit earlier this mornin' we 'uz rememberin' ole Jasper Pike and how he'd done as much for his own pitiful family."

"I know, Boz." What else could I say?

"Musta been some kinda omen, Lucius. Swear it's enough to make a body wanna puke up his socks. My, oh, my. What's this ole world a-comin' to?"

He repeated himself over and over, as though his brain had locked on this single notion. His thoughts appeared focused like a fifty-ton Baldwin locomotive headed in a preordained direction that had no way of diverting itself from the narrow track.

Once finished with our fractional Devils River wash, I pulled dust-covered boots onto still-wet feet. Stamped into them, then set to toweling off with my shirt. Slid the damp garment over a sopping, drippy head and turned to find Boz staring at me with all the baggy-eyed gravity and tremulous intensity of an abandoned, starving bloodhound.

"You are gonna read over these folks, ain't you, Lucius? Maybe say some good words for 'em?"

I tucked a sodden shirttail inside the waist of my pants, then pulled up my blue-and-yellow-striped suspenders. Slipped into my vest before I said, "Didn't think to bring a Bible along, Boz. Must admit, had not the slightest inkling we'd find one dead body when we set out this morning, much less five of them. And the kids, sweet merciful Jesus, the kids. Just wrings a body's heart so hard makes you want to commence blubbering and never stop. Can't imagine the kind of men as could commit such an act. Just can't imagine."

Tatum kicked in the dirt with the heel of his boot and jerked a disconsolate thumb toward the mounded, rock-strewn, blossom-littered burial site. "Well, puttin' them cactus flowers on their final restin' place was a fine, thoughtful gesture. Must admit, rough as it is, the gravesite does look right nice. Glad you thought to add the flowers."

I nodded.

"Still and all, feel as how these pitiful folks deserve to have their pathways to Heaven greased, just the least bit, with some high-soundin' words, Lucius. Even if we don't happen to have a Bible along with us. 'Specially them three buttons, you know. Hell, I trust your memory. Willin' to bet these folks would appreciate whatever you can do for 'em by way of talkin' with God. Figure anything you'd care to offer up's better'n nothing at all."

I cast a corner-of-the-eye glance at the graves. Let my chin rest on the damp upper part of my shirt for some seconds, then swept my hat up from the sandy riverbank. I nodded and, followed by the closest friend I had in the world, we ambled back to a spot near the foot of the mass grave.

With broad-brimmed hats lodged in a spot of honor over our hearts, I cleared an emotion-parched throat. After a bit of pinch-browed hesitation and thought, I began—slowly, reverently. As reverently as I knew how.

"Our most gracious heavenly Father," I said, "neither Boz nor I knew these traveling unfortunates. Pretty good chance we may not ever know who they were. Sure enough didn't find much in the wagon to identify any of them. But that don't matter. Can't begin to imagine what they did to deserve such an unspeakable departure from this earthly life. Especially the children. Whole dance is sad beyond our meager ability to understand. But, as a poet of some note once wrote many years ago, 'To every man upon this earth death cometh soon or late.' Sad but true, what that feller said applies to innocent kids as well."

I hesitated for a second, gulped, then scratched at an unwilling throat. Kind of lost my train of thought there for a right uncomfortable stretch. Twirled my sweat-stained Stetson around in both hands, by the brim, while I searched for the right words.

I coughed a time or two then added, "That stealthy ole Thief of Souls has most certainly passed our way today. Sent this poor man and his innocent family beyond any earthly aid we might have rendered. Genuinely regret as how our arrival on the scene didn't occur early enough to prevent such a terrible outcome, Lord. Sincerely pray the entire family was delivered into the safety and comfort of Your divine care and affection. Now, my friend and I come to You in humble supplication and ask that You gather their sad spirits to Your righteous bosom and see to their heavenly comfort for the rest of eternity. We appeal for that eventuality in the name of the only Son You sent to cleanse us all of our earthly sins and pave our way into Your presence. Amen."

Still felt right uncomfortable. I shifted, back and forth, then stuffed my hat on a soggy head. Turned Tatum's direction, seeking something of a complimentary reaction from my longtime compadre by way of acknowledgment for my prayerful efforts. The expected nod and grin of approval he usually provided proved nowhere in evidence.

Openmouthed, unspeaking, and flush-faced, Boz pointed a shaky finger toward the knife-edged ridge of sloped, lifeless dirt some sixty or so yards away. The shallow bowl's steep rim almost completely encircled that riverbank hollow of lush greenery, violent death, and freshly departed souls where we stood and gazed up slack-jawed.

Staring down on us from the forty-foot-high crest of crumbling earth stood a girl—fifteen, maybe sixteen years old. Hell, what little I knew of young girls at the time, she could've been a lot older or a lot younger.

Gal swayed like a creekside weeping willow in the hot breezes that hissed over the sun-scorched earth beneath her feet. Wisps of shoulder-length, straw-colored hair fluttered across a pretty, grime-smeared face. Her flowered cotton dress flapped around equally filth-encrusted legs.

Under my breath, I mumbled, "Lord above, Boz. Looks as if she's trying to chew a thumbnail all the way up to her elbow. Snapping and biting like a rabid dog. Spitting out the bits."

His flabbergasted gaze locked on the ghostly, ethereal apparition, Tatum shook as though in the throes of malaria and muttered, "Sweet merciful Jesus, how's this possible?"

Air rushed from between clenched teeth when I hissed, "Looks most like the child's been living underground. Killers had to have missed her. She escaped. Found a hidey-hole somewhere close, I'd be willing to wager." Pretty sure I might've sounded as if I was questioning my own reasoning.

Boz moved to take a step in the specter's direction only to witness the girl turn and vanish from view. By unspoken agreement, we heeled it for a steep, slanted wash nearby. The craggy, earthen cut was the only ascending access within close proximity that led to the crest of the dirt bluff.

I managed to scramble to the sheer bank's disintegrat-

ing summit a few steps ahead of Boz. A quick survey of the
rough, table-like expanse of Turkey Mesa, as it spread away
from the river, revealed that the child had scampered near
a hundred yards, stopped, then stared back at us again.

Boz huffed and puffed his way to a spot beside me.
Wheezing from the unexpected exertion, he sucked air
like a winded racehorse. He waved and, between gasping
breaths, called out, "You come on back now, girl. Won't
harm you. We're here to help." He got no response.

I shrugged, then said, "We'd best go round her up,
Boz."

Soon as we started her direction again, the urchin bolted
like a frightened deer. For half an hour the fleeing child
scuttled over the rock-strewn, rattlesnake-, cactus-, and
scorpion-littered landscape with us clumsily clambering
along behind. The chase finally brought us to the entrance
of an ugly, deep, funnel-like gash in the earth's hoary hide.
An abbreviated, canyon-like wound that our prey had no
chance of escaping.

At the bottom of the narrow ravine, the cornered waif
wedged her back against the fissure's farthest and high-
est wall. Arms flung wide against her earthen prison, she
crawfished from side to side in agitated terror. Let out a piteous howl, like some kind of wounded, terrified animal.

Eyes the size of ten-dollar gold pieces and panic-
deepened to a shade of blue near those of a pharmacist's
cobalt-colored drug bottles, she glared up at Boz and me
from the floor of her dusty refuge. The angry, defiant, and
sullen look etched into her panicky visage appeared fully
capable of wringing tears from a Civil War veteran's glass
eye.

Of a sudden, the girl seemed to mine the depths of some
unseen inner strength and assumed the stance of an ancient, witchy crone. She made strange, incomprehensible
sounds and gestures at us. Things that didn't sound of this
earth came from her mouth. Then, in a voice sheathed in

ice and death, she growled, "Come down here, and I'll kill both you sons a bitches."

My God, but her surprising, raspy warning sent icy shivers up and down my sweaty spine.

10

"MY DADDY DIDN'T RAISE
ANY COWARDS ..."

I MOTIONED FOR my out-of-breath partner to stay put. Then, one careful, hesitant step at a time, I advanced on the agitated child. Held my hands out, palms upturned in supplication. And, in the manner one might use when speaking to a frightened animal, said, "No need to be scared, girl. Not gonna hurt you. Swear, we're not gonna hurt you."

The troubled youngster flashed a bug-eyed, brittle gaze at me that was filled with needle-pointed daggers. A tormented groan reverberated in her narrow, heaving, child's chest. From somewhere amidst the folds and pleats of her tattered, print dress, she produced a glistening, heavy-bladed butcher's knife. The wooden-gripped weapon's curved, razor-sharp edge gleamed in the advancing sunlight that sloshed into the narrow pit from above.

Cracked, chapped lips peeled away from the trembling gal's teeth in a snarling scowl. As though speaking from the bottom of an empty rain barrel, she growled, "Don't you come any closer, mister. Not another step. Get near enough, swear I'll cut your heart out, if I get the chance. I swear before sainted Jesus, I will. I'll do it. I will. I will kill you graveyard dead."

In spite of all efforts to the contrary, I couldn't help but smile. Drew to a rocking halt, leaned back on my heels, and cocked my head to one side. "Now, now, no need for that, miss," I said. "Can promise you, Boz Tatum yonder and me are friends. Could well be the best friends you've got right at this unfortunate juncture. Rest assured we have no intention of doing you any harm."

For a single, bullet-fast instant, unanswerable questions appeared to flit around behind her confused, darting, trapped-animal's gaze. One cheek twitched when she snapped back, "You expect me to believe that load of horse manure, mister? After you and your gang rode up from the river in the early morning dark and. . . ." A racking sob shook her from head to foot before she gasped, "And murdered my parents."

Hands in the classic gesture of surrender, I said, "No one here had anything to do with your family's terrible passing, miss. Before God, I swear it. Me and Boz live not far down the river. We run a little bit of a horse-raising operation, for the immediate time being anyways. All the shooting woke us before the sun got up good. Came on quick as we could. Deeply regret as how we didn't make the trip as fast as we probably should've. Just had no idea of the urgency."

Face covered in a layer of sweat, muddied with the powdery red dust of west Texas, she gritted her teeth so hard it sounded like a squirrel breaking walnuts. She sliced the knife back and forth through the sultry air. A single, enormous tear formed in the corner of one eye. The salty pearl bled onto her twitchy cheek and carved a tiny gully through the dirt down to the edge of a grime-caked jaw. Jewel-like droplet hung there for a second, then fell onto her heaving breast.

"How do I know you're telling me the truth?" she yelped.

"I got away during all the confusion. Went back when I thought you and your men had finally ridden away."

Shook my head. "Wasn't me or Boz," I said. "Can't say it enough. We had nothing to do with what happened earlier this morning."

"Well, say what you will, I saw what evil men did to my parents. Oh, God, all that shooting scared me so . . ." A racking sob sawed its way through the girl's body. She rubbed bitter tears on the upper part of a dirty arm. "So much noise and confusion. I ran. Couldn't stay. Ran until I found this spot to hide myself in."

"You don't have to run, or hide, anymore, child," I said. "We're not here to hurt you."

Her face twisted into a mask of deeper fear and pain. "I'm still not sure what happened to my little brothers. Don't know exactly what has become of them." Then as though speaking to someone not there, she mumbled, "I suppose it's likely they died in just as dreadful a manner as my poor mother and father."

Not much I could've added to her brutal assessment. So I just kept silent and waited.

Then, of a sudden, she crow-hopped sidewise, stumbled, but regained her footing. She waved the knife at me again. The haggard look of stark terror and puzzlement on her pretty face intensified as she said, "For all I know, you could just be spinning a windy whizzer, mister. Just so I'll give up my only weapon. Only thing I've got to protect myself. Perhaps my only salvation."

In a voice tinged with sadness and understanding, Boz called out from his spot at the mouth of the ravine, "Oh, no, child. The man's tellin' the truth. My friend Lucius Dodge don't lie. Honestly, we come here to help."

The panicked girl's nervous eyeballing flicked from one of us to the other. Then, she growled like a kicked dog.

"Broke our hearts when we found your ill-fated kin," Boz continued. "'Specially them poor buttons. Took us the most part of the mornin' to make sure they was all properly cared for. Even put God on notice as how their immortal souls 'uz comin' his direction. Now, why don't you lay that big ole gut cutter aside, come on back to the ranch with us?"

I took a hesitant step or two toward the tormented child's defensive position. Drew to a halt just a few feet away from her. Offered an open-palmed hand and then said, "Believe me, you're safe now, darlin'. Truly, there's no need for the knife. Why don't you go on ahead and give it to me?"

The wary waif's darting, sapphire gaze sizzled as it flitted from one of our faces to the other. "I'm not your darlin', mister. I don't even know you. Either of you," she sneered. "My daddy didn't raise any cowards, fools, or shirkers. So, I think I'll just keep the knife, 'less you'd like to go on ahead and try to take it away from me."

Another short-lived smile flickered across my parted lips. I took half a step backward. Hands raised in submission, I feigned shock and fear. "Well, no, miss. Don't think I'd want to attempt disarming a determined young woman like you," I said. Then, I tapped the side of my head with one finger. Thought of something I should have known to ask at the very outset. Said, "My friend, Boz, there, has already told you my name. Got any problem with telling me yours, miss? Do have a name, don't you, child?"

As if I had somehow reached across six feet of open space and slapped her, the straw-haired youngster's head snapped backward and bumped against the dirt wall at her back. Appeared to me that the thought of sharing her name with strangers—strangers who might have had a hand in murdering her luckless family—had not occurred to the feisty youngster.

"Uh, well, uh. Why don't you go on ahead and tell me yours again?" she demanded.

In as soothing a voice as I had ever heard my rough-and-ready partner use, Boz came nigh on to whispering when he eased up a step or so behind me and said, "We can do that, missy. If it'll make you more comfortable, we can sure 'nuff do 'er. Like I done said before, this here's Lucius Dodge. Man's famed near and far as a fearless enforcer of the law and protector of women and the downtrodden. My name's Boz Tatum. Me'n Lucius been friends for almost as many years as you've been alive. Now, how 'bout you? What's your handle? Your name, that is."

"Boz is only trying to reassure you, child," I added. "Wouldn't want you, or one of us, to get hurt, now would we? Especially after everything that's already transpired this sad and fateful morning."

Then, as though suddenly overcome by a power outside herself, the hesitant youngster appeared possessed of a steely calm that surprised both of us. She made a little show of sliding the heavy-bladed butcher's knife behind a thin leather strap tied around her narrow waist. Then, she held both skinny arms and empty hands out for us to examine.

"I've put the knife away" she said. "No knife. See?"

Boz and I both nodded.

Then, as if she had only just that moment managed to remember something long forgotten, she said, "Clementine. My name's Clementine."

"Well, now, that's a right pretty name," I said. "Yes indeed, that's right pretty."

"Don't treat me like I'm stupid or helpless," the girl snapped. "I've matriculated at Miss Hildegard Tyler's School for Young Ladies in New Orleans. Studied reading, writing, mathematics, history, philosophy, and debate. I'm smarter than most grown men, by a long shot."

Couldn't help but smile at her feistiness. Said, "Why, yes, ma'am. Believe you likely are."

"On top of that, my father taught me to ride like a Comanche Indian and shoot like Hickok by the time I'd turned six. The both of you should hit your knees tonight and thank a loving God I couldn't get my hands on a rifle, shotgun, or pistol. Both of you'd be as dead as a pair of rotten fence posts by now."

Boz rubbed a spot on his chest as though feeling for an invisible bullet hole, then sucked in a heavy, ragged breath.

I wagged my head from side to side, like Bear did when he was tired. Made a patting motion at the teary-eyed girl, then said, "Calm yourself, child. Please. There's no need to get excited again."

"And I do not like being called *child*. Don't mind *miss*, or *missy*, but don't care much for this *child* business," the girl grouched. "My name's Webb. Clementine Webb. Fifteen years old, soon to be sixteen. Know there are some who don't acknowledge my age 'cause I look younger, but I'll have you know I am not a child." She threw her thin shoulders back. "I'll go along with you and your friend, Mr. Dodge. But I'll keep the knife," she said and fingered the blade's wooden handle.

I pitched a questioning glance at Boz.

He shrugged then nodded, as if to say, "What the hell? Was me I wouldn't give up the knife, either."

"Well, all right, Clementine. That's fine with us. You keep the knife," I said and motioned for her to follow. "You can tag along behind, if that'll make you more comfortable with the situation. Keep as much distance between you and us as makes you happy. We have horses waiting down by the river. Food and water, too. You can ride behind me, or my friend here, when we head out for the ranch. Let you choose which when we get back to our campfire. Does all of that work for you?"

A short-lived wave of irrepressible panic appeared to dart across Clementine Webb's youthful, painfully clinched face. Just as quickly, she regained control of her emotions again, then made little shooing motions at us and said, "Yes. Yes. That's fine with me. You two go on ahead.

Lead the way. I'll follow." She gripped the wooden handle of her only weapon, wiped a dripping nose on the back of her free hand, then added, "Try anything funny, either one of you, and I swear I'll cut you up. Filet the pair of you like pond-raised sunfish."

We did an about-face, trudged out of the gulley, and headed for the river. From the corner of his grinning mouth Boz muttered, "Do believe she woulda made good on them threats, Dodge. Just mighta gone and turned you from a rooster into a hen, if'n you'da got close enough. Spunky little thang, ain't she? Have to admire that."

"Spunky ain't the half of it, Boz. Given what she's witnessed this morning, got to figure the little gal's tough enough to hunt mountain lions with a willow switch," I whispered back. Shook my head, then added, "'Course, she's going to need every bit of spunk, nerve, grit, and backbone available when the full weight of what's happened finally hits her. Yep, every single bit of it."

11

"...AND KILL THEM, ONE AND ALL."

LITTLE MORE THAN an hour later, Clementine Webb stood near the foot of her family's crude burial place. She clasped a cup of Boz's campfire Arbuckles in one trembling hand and absentmindedly held the half-eaten remnants of one of Paco's meat-stuffed tacos in the other.

I eased up beside the Webb girl and quickly noted that, while she made no sound, a river of salty tears flowed from her swollen eyes. Muscles around her lips involuntarily trembled and twitched. For all her previous displays of nervy, self-possessed grit, the scruffy teenager appeared as though teetering on the knife-edged precipice of emotional collapse.

Then, to my stunned surprise, our newfound ward cast the half-filled cup of coffee and unfinished taco aside and dropped to her knees atop the crude grave in a quivering, sobbing heap. "I want to see my little brothers again," she screeched, then clawed at that pile of rocks and fresh-turned earth like a wild animal. "I didn't get to see them when I came back before. Sweet Jesus, I need to see them one last time."

For several painful seconds I stood rooted to the ground. Shocked and dumbfounded by the abrupt, poignant, and powerful turn of events. Then, as gently as I could manage, I lifted the struggling girl off the grave, held her at arm's length, and said, "There's no seeing any of them again, Clem. They're all gone. In your heart you know it's true. We told you as much on the way back here. Understand as how it won't be easy, but you've got to turn this all loose. Give the whole horrible mess over to God. Put these tragic events on his shoulders. Let him handle them. Trust me, it's the best way."

The Webb girl wrung her hands together, then ran shaky fingers through her hair. Sounded nigh on unearthly, eerie, when she cried out, "Oh, God. I can't see 'em again. I can't see 'em again. Not ever. Not ever."

"No, darlin'. Not ever," I said.

"But my brothers. My poor, innocent, little brothers."

"I know, Clem. I know."

I placed a reassuring arm around the weeping orphan's narrow shoulders. She leaned her full, delicate weight against me. Grabbed the front of my vest with both hands and buried her face in the safety of my waiting chest. A strange, strangled, sobbing rumbled up from somewhere deep inside the grief-stricken child. Pain, the likes of which I'd not seen or felt in years, flowed between us and shook me to the soles of my run-down, stacked-heeled riding boots.

I stroked the beautiful Clementine's heaving shoulders as she sobbed and said, "I know it's difficult for you, darlin'. Simply isn't anything harder than dealing with the sense-less death brought on by sheer wickedness. But you've got to buck up."

The girl's racking sobs grew louder. Her grasp on the lapels of my vest grew more pronounced. I thought, for a moment, she just might twist the garment to shreds.

In the manner of a concerned parent, I drew her closer and caressed one shoulder. Said, "Seen more than any man's share of senseless brutality during my life, child. Been forced, by time and circumstance, to bury some of my own family in years past. Several of them perished at the hands of an evil skunk named Slayton Bone in a sorry act of violence some years back. That particular brand of vicious, gun smoke–laced, unexpected death just isn't ever easy to take. 'S what makes me certain the passage of your parents and brothers is especially difficult for one of your tender years. But you must trust me when I tell you that the shock will pass, and eventually the pain will lessen. Won't go away, but there'll come a time when this tragedy will move to the back burners of your wounded memory."

Clementine coughed and smeared a runny nose across the front of my vest from pocket to pocket. Her childlike action left a snotty, tear-stained, snail-like trail.

I placed one hand on the sobbing girl's cheek. "Don't you worry, young lady. My friends and I will find the men responsible for this shameful deed. We'll search them out, discover why they would be party to such a shocking endeavor, and make certain they never commit a heinous act such as this again."

Clementine tilted a tear-streaked face up and stared into my tense, pinched countenance. She jerked at the vest with a talon-like grip. From behind bloodshot, rheumy eyes, and with tears pooled in the corners of a quavering mouth, she said, "Is that a promise? Do you swear it, Ranger Lucius Dodge?"

Tried not to let any hesitation creep into my voice when I placed a hand on each of Clementine's skinny shoulders and said, "Absolutely. As God is my witness. The animals responsible for what occurred here, on the banks of Devils River this sad morning, will pay for what they did. And, by God, they'll pay dear."

Eyes closed, the Webb girl tossed her head from side to

side, as though trying desperately to clear a confused mind and wounded soul of a spider's web of unwanted thoughts, horrific images, and the pain lying at her bare feet. She latched onto my forearm with an iron-fingered grip that belied her youth and childish, rail-thin scrawniness.

In spite of the protection of the sleeve of my heavy, bib-front shirt, Clementine Webb's dagger-sharp fingernails gouged through the material and into the skin beneath. I stared down into the girl's emotion-etched face. Could physically feel her boring gaze, as it augured into my very soul.

She popped up on tiptoe and pulled my hatless head down to her level. In a croaky, emotion-choked voice that sounded like cold spit on a red-hot stove lid, she whispered into one ear, "Will you swear it? Will you swear before God and me, Mr. Dodge? Swear that you'll ride down the men who brutally murdered my family. Swear to me that you'll run the scum to ground like rabid dogs . . . and kill them, one and all."

"Well, I . . ."

"Swear it," she hissed.

"Already promised, Clem. We'll do what we . . ."

She jerked on my arm so hard I came nigh on to losing my footing. She twisted the sleeve of my faded shirt into a blood-blocking knot with her bony, child's fingers and glowered up at me like a thing crazed, demented. Then she threw her head back and moaned as though her soul was being tortured.

I drew myself up with the implacable Clementine Webb still attached to my arm. Stared down into twin pools of hard-edged vengeance. "We're working on catching the folks what done this foul act as we now speak, darlin'. Have a man out looking for them at this very instant. But there's some things I need to know . . ."

Didn't get a chance to finish my thought. The sound of horse's hooves slopping their way across the shallows of

Devils River brought everyone's attention around to the west.

Clementine released my arm, then grabbed on to my pistol belt and moved slightly behind me. From beneath my protective arm, she flashed a gaze filled with death-dealing lightning bolts at the new arrival.

I rubbed my elbow, then pointed. "In fact, that's my man coming now, Clem. Hairy beast lopin' out front's Bear." The girl's grip tightened. I patted her hand and added, "No need to worry yourself. Ole Bear wouldn't hurt a flea." Then, to an unhearing world in general, I said, "Not 'less Glo first told him he could, anyways. Then it's Katy bar the door."

12

"...Blew the Whole Top of the Man's Head Off..."

GLORIOUS JOHNSON ROOSTED atop a broken, leafless cottonwood limb Boz dragged to a convenient spot near our sputtering campfire. Wisps of gray-black smoke swirled above the heap of sticks and logs in an angry, spiral-shaped, cyclonic cloud.

Elbows propped on bony knees, flop hat pushed away from a sweat-and-dirt-stained face, Johnson sipped at his battered, tin coffee cup. Said, "Yah, suh. I'm certain, Mistuh Dodge. Ain't no doubt in my mind a'tall. Them murderin' skunks what done fo' these poor folks is headed south and east."

"Del Rio?"

"Yah, suh. 'Pears they'll eventual end up in Del Rio fo' certain sure." Glo glanced at the cowering girl who peeked from beneath my arm and added, "Sorry, miss, don't mean no disrespect fo' yore poor departed family members or nuthin' by mentionin' murderin' skunks and such. Sad to say, but that's just the way things has turned out, you know?"

I patted the girl on the shoulder. "Her name's Clementine, Glo. Clementine Webb," I said.

Glo touched the brim of his hat, nodded, and tried to smile. "'S my pleasure, missy. Sorry we has to meet under such tryin' circumstances."

Clementine, who still kept to the safety and protection of a spot slightly behind and to one side of me, gave a dull nod of the head, but offered nothing else by way of reply. The largest part of her attention, at that moment, appeared focused on the dog. Bear sat at her feet and wagged his knotted tail like a happy puppy as he nuzzled and licked at her hand. The creature appeared totally entranced by the girl.

Surprised by the animal's somewhat less-than-usual response, I allowed myself a wide grin, gave the girl's shoulder another tap, and said, "Seems you've made a new friend, Clem. Not many folks as can say that."

Glo tossed away the last few drops of the up-and-at-'em juice left in his cup, then said, "Them boys gonna end up in Del Rio, or Ciudad Acuna, sooner or later. But right now, 'pears to me as how they's headed nigh on straight for Arturo Mendoza's Cantina over in Carta Blanca. Should hit the Sonora-Del Rio road there, then hoof it south, once they's finished gettin' red-eyed, rubber-kneed, and whiskey weary."

With nervous fingers, Boz tapped the brass tops of bullets in the loops of his pistol belt. "Makes sense to me, Lucius," he said. "Mendoza's trail-side whiskey and tequila locker in Carta Blanca is the closest place for 'em to tie on a good drunk 'tween here and Del Rio. Maybe grab a bite to eat as well."

I scratched my chin and frowned but said nothing.

"Bet all them fellers as had a hand in sendin' Miss Clementine's family to eternal rest," Boz continued, "are a-lookin' to drown some of the bloody horror of what they went and done in a river of bad tonsil paint. Ain't a man of good conscience who could face his God after such a monstrous act. Figure they're likely goin' straight to horned Satan just as fast as bad whiskey and good horseflesh can carry 'em to 'im."

Glo grunted, nodded his agreement, then said, "Everthang you just said could well be true, Mistuh Tatum. But you know them fellers ain't in no special, horse-killin' hurry to get theyselves to Mendoza's, or anywhere else for that matter. They's ridin' along all slow and cocky, real arrogant-like. Done set me to thinkin' as how they figures ain't nobody knows, or cares, as how they done went and kilt off the most part of an entire family."

"Taking their time, are they?" I growled between clenched teeth.

"Yah, suh. They 'uz draggin' around so slow I almost rode right up on 'em, no longer'n I 'uz gone this mornin'. Trailed 'em till they weren't no doubt in my mind where them fellers was headed. Way I got it figured, if'n they keep up the pace they 'uz makin' when I turned back, likely be bellyin' up to the bar at Arturo's jus' about now. Be good'n knee-walkin' drunk in another hour or so. Passed out or pukin' up they sorry guts whence it comes on dark."

I picked at my teeth with a splinter of wood, stopped a second, and said, "How many of 'em, Glo?"

"They's five, Mistah Dodge. Whole party stopped a time or two so as to rest they animals. Offered me a chance to get up close enough to give 'em a pert good lookin' over through my long glass. Mighty rough bunch if'n I ever seed one. Could well be the roughest we ever done went out after, you ask me. Even worse'n some of them Messican bandits we chased down into Chihuahua some years back."

"Get any five gun-totin' men in Texas together and they're usually a rough bunch, Glo. All together the three of us have chased enough bad ones over the years that, of all people, you should know that," I said.

"Yah, suh. I knows that. My mama sho' 'nuff didn't

raise no fools. Knows 'bout badmen. But I think maybe the gennuman leadin' this crew's 'bout as bad as it's gonna git. It's somebody we already knows."

Boz slapped the butt of his hip pistol, frowned, and growled, "The hell you say, Glo. Who'n the red-eyed name of Satan would any of us *know* that's capable of the brutal, senseless massacre of a man, woman, and three of their innocent kids?"

Johnson cut Boz a slicing, peculiar look, then said, "'S Pitt Murdock, Mistuh Boz. Gives me the willies to say it, but the man leadin' this buncha killers is none other'n Pitt Murdock."

The name snaked around our sputtering campfire as if God had stepped down from His heavenly throne and cracked a lightning tipped bullwhip in our midst. Me and Boz danced from foot to foot and shot knowing looks, back and forth, at each other.

Clementine Webb immediately detected the moniker's impact on her newfound guardians. With the tail-wagging Bear glued to her side, she stepped away from my protection and glanced from troubled face to troubled face. Her puzzled gaze finally landed on Boz.

Girl came near whispering when she said, "Who's Pitt Murdock? Do all of you know the man?"

Boz's squint-eyed gaze darted to the inquisitive girl, then flicked over to Glorious Johnson, then me, then back to Glo. He sounded incredulous when he said, "Pitt Murdock? You're absolutely sure 'bout that, Glo? Ain't no doubt in your mind that the man you seen was that stink-sprayin' polecat Pitt Murdock?"

Glorious Johnson nodded. "Man that ugly, course I'm sure. Ain't the worst of it neither, Mistuh Boz. Not by a long shot. Pert sure one a them other'ns, ridin' along with Murdock, is Tanner Atwood."

Boz kicked at the end of a smoldering tree limb that jutted several feet beyond the dying fire, then said, "Sweet

Jesus riding a golden armadillo." He wagged his head from side to side like a winded horse. "For true now, there's not a single doubt in your mind, Glo? Two of the men responsible for leaving all the bodies we found here are Pitt Murdock and Tanner Atwood?"

"Yah, suh, Mistuh Boz. I knows them men. Familiar enough wid the both of 'em to know who they wuz soon as I seen 'em pop up in my spyglass. Been face-to-face with that Atwood more'n once. Still have a crystal clear memory of how Murdock got that nasty scar on his butt-ugly face. Swear 'fore Jesus, the man ain't changed much since last I seen him. He's still uglier'n a sack full of bullfrogs' assholes. Sorry, for the languauge, Miss Clementine. Jus' the man's a bad 'un, you know."

I shrugged, stroked the yellowed-ivory grips of the pistol lying across my belly. I said, "To this day, still avow as how I whacked Murdock hard enough to kill him. Laid the whole side of his head open when I clubbed the bastard. Man's face opened up from his hatband to his chin. But Lord a mercy, that murderous slug's head was harder than a frozen turtle shell. Thought sure I'd gone and broke the barrel on a spanking new Colt Peacemaker. Gun never did shoot worth spit after that particular incident. Finally had to give up on it."

"Uh-huh. Yah, suh. Well, there you go. That's it. Jus' the way I remember it happenin'. Pitt Murdock. That be the man, right enough."

Boz swayed back and forth like a two-hundred-year-old live oak in a cyclone. He said, "Sweet Jesus, Lucius, that's goin' on five, maybe six year ago, ain't it? Was the time we caught up with Pitt and that bunch of killers he used to ride with from over in Fort Stockton. They 'uz runnin' from the murder of that luckless clerk he shot in the head when they tried to rob the Buckhorn Bank and Trust up in San Angelo."

"Yes," I said. "Lot of water's passed under the bridge.

Give or take a few months, your memory of the events sounds about right."

"Never forget the clerk," Boz said. "That bastard Murdock blew the whole top of the man's head off with a single blast from a shotgun. He did the sorry deed right in the middle of a bank filled to overflowing with end-of-the-month customers. Just because the poor teller didn't move fast enough to suit 'em ole boys that was a robbin' 'im."

"Terrible killing," I agreed.

Boz dug at his ear with one finger, then stared at the digit's tip as though he expected to find something sparkling and precious. "Poor dead feller's name was Chidester, as I remember. Yeah, Hiram Chidester."

"Lef' four or five chil'ren and a grievin' wife," Glorious Johnson muttered. "That 'un were a right sad case, right sad."

Boz sucked at his teeth, spit, then said, "Damn right. And that smarter'n hell Austin lawyer got him off with twenty-five years to life for the deed. He's supposed to still be servin' hard time over in the Huntsville State Penitentiary, ain't he, Lucius? Choppin' cotton, splitin' wood, breakin' rocks, pickin' peas. What the hell's an evil, man-killing bastard like Pitt Murdock doin' runnin' loose way out here in this neck of the woods? And a keepin' company with scum like Tanner Atwood, to boot?"

"Swear fo' Jesus, Mistuh Boz, I done thought as how the man 'uz dead and in the ground," Glo offered. "Pert sure I heard more'n a few folks tellin' tales as how one of them other convicts tried to cut Murdock's head off with a knife he'd done fashioned out of a sharpened soup spoon. Dem folks claimed as how Murdock died a horrible death. Made me right grateful to hear such."

"Yeah, I heard that story, too," Boz said.

Glo's head bobbed up and down. "Gotta tell ya, come as quite a shock when a man what's s'posed to be dead went and popped up in my long glass the way he done—ignert, ugly head still sittin' on his worthless shoulders and all. Uh-huh, tell you fo' true, I done went to breathin' hard. Came right near passin' out, most like the fat woman what tried to run a foot race on the Fourth of July."

Chewed at my bottom lip and stared off into the emptiness of the western distance. After near a minute of silent thought, pretty sure it sounded as if I'd stepped out of my body and become possessed when I said, "Guess we'd best get after them fellers, quick as we can, boys. When men like Murdock and Atwood go to work killing people, they're not the type that's inclined to stop till most of a guiltless world's ankle deep in blood and bullet-riddled bodies."

"But, but, wait now, Mistuh Dodge. Ain't had a chance to tell you everthang. No, suh. No, suh. See, that ain't the whole of it."

Well, that sure enough snapped my head up. Must have looked like a man who'd been slapped with an open palm. Flush-faced I said, "What? What the hell else is there, Glo? What more could there be?"

"Well, cain't be sayin' fo' absolute certain on this here part, but I be thinkin' them other three travelin' with Murdock's them Pickett boys."

I couldn't help but let a groan slip out. "Roscoe, Priest, and Cullen?"

"Yah, suh. Dem's the ones, all right."

In the manner of a still-smoking cannon being realigned for its next shot, Boz's head swiveled around on its stalklike neck. His narrow-eyed, squinty gaze fell directly onto Clementine Webb. He sounded like a man amazed, when he said, "Who on earth are you, girl? Why would a pack of murderous animals such as them Glo just named want to kill off your entire family?"

Clementine Webb ducked back beneath my sheltering arm. She latched onto to the bullet-laden pistol belt around my waist with one hand and held tight. Peeked up at me with wide, watery eyes.

Tail still wagging, Bear followed, flopped down at the girl's feet, and stared up at her. He pawed at her leg and groaned in an obvious effort at regaining her attention.

I pulled Clementine around by one arm, then gently held the girl in place with a hand on each shoulder and said, "Perhaps the better question just might be, who on earth was your father, girl?"

13

"I'LL NOT HAVE YOU RIDE OFF AND LEAVE ME."

CLEMENTINE WEBB DREW into herself. The girl seemed to shrink and tried to pull away from me. She shook her head as if dumbfounded by an unfathomable question. Her trembling lips parted several times. She tried to speak, but nothing came out. On the third or fourth attempt the clearly agitated girl finally sputtered, "Wha-wha-what do you mean?"

"Who was your father, Clem?" I repeated. "What was his name?"

"Webb, of course. Just like mine. What else would it be?"

"No, his given name. What was his given name?"

"Nathan. Nathan. Nathan Hawthorne Webb."

I bent closer. My gaze narrowed. "From Austin? Your father, the man Boz and I buried just a few hours ago, was none other than Nathan H. Webb of Austin?"

The girl humped up at me a bit when she said, "Yes. Yes, Nathan Webb was my father."

Boz pushed his hat onto one side of a sweat-drenched

head. He scratched at a spot above his ear. A look of puzzled consternation and confusion crept onto his craggy, weather-beaten face. "Nathan Webb? We don't know anybody named Nathan Webb, or Nathan H. Webb, or whatever'n hell she just said. Do we, Lucius?"

Let my hands fall away from Clementine's shoulders. Suddenly felt tired, stumbled back a step, then straightened up and said, "We might, Boz. Yes, indeed. We just might. Leastways, I now have a pretty good idea who the man once was before we found him this morning."

"Who? Who do we be knowin' name a Nathan Webb, Mistuh Dodge? I doan be rememberin' no one like that," Glo said.

"Minor Texas politician. One of the lesser lights in the great Lone Star State's political heavens. Senator, as I recall. You boys rarely bother to read those newspapers friends of mine have sent me from Austin. Otherwise you might've seen the name," I said. "If a stretched-to-the-limits memory still serves, this child's father was the elected representative of the good folks down around Uvalde. That right, Clem?"

"Yes. My father is . . ." She stumbled for a second, appeared confused, then quickly regained her shaky composure and continued, ". . . Was, he was, a Texas state senator. We live—or did live—in Uvalde during those times when Papa doesn't—didn't—have to be in Austin on the business of the people. We have a house at Number Twenty-three Pecos Boulevard."

Boz moved closer to me and the girl. "What were y'all doin' way and the heck over here on the backside of nowhere Texas, so far away from home, child?"

"Camping."

Pretty sure Boz had already deduced as much himself, but he still sounded mildly incredulous when he shook his head, frowned, and grumped, "Camping?"

Finally, given something she could grab hold of to occupy her scattered mind, Clementine Webb appeared to grow stronger, more tenacious and controlled with our pointed questioning. A distinct, huffy resoluteness tinged her voice when she replied, "Yes. *Camping.* A week or so ago Papa rushed home early from his office. Said he'd decided to take us all camping. Said he needed a few days away from the cares and worries of civilization and the burdens of political responsibility. Said what we all needed was a family trip. There was nothing wrong with that."

It sounded like an echo when Boz mumbled, "A family trip?"

Clementine's voice became icier. "Exactly as I said, Mr. Tatum. So, he and my mother packed a few necessities into the wagon. The whole event seemed a bit hurried, now that I come to think on it. At any rate, we struck out the next morning and, three days later, arrived here by the river. My mother deemed it a lovely, inviting spot."

"No doubt 'bout that, missy," Glo mumbled.

Boz shook his head. "A lovely, inviting spot," he muttered.

"Not sure why, but I got the impression she and my father might have visited this particular spot before. In any case, we've been camped right here ever since." Clementine's voice faded as she scratched the dog's fly-notched ears and added, "And we were having a right wonderful time—a right wonderful time. Until this morning."

I stepped away from the dewy-eyed, flush-cheeked child, turned and gazed up at thick, roiling, puffy-white clouds, threw one arm across my chest and rested the other atop it. Striking a thoughtful pose, I tapped my chin with one finger.

To no one in particular, but loud enough for Boz to hear, I said, "Then, out of the clear blue, some of the worst men in all of Hell and the great state of Texas showed up and killed everyone. Entire family. All of them but this one child. Why? Why would men like Murdock, Atwood, and

the Pickett brothers follow the upstanding family of an in-
nocuous Uvalde politician all the way down here to our
front doorstep, commit such an odious act, then beat a hot
path for Del Rio? Now, there's a puzzler. A real, blood-
soaked puzzler."

I came out of my self-imposed cave of deep thought
when Boz made an all-inclusive sweeping motion with one
arm and said, "Well, by God, don't matter one whit to me
why murderin' skunks like Murdock, Atwood, and them
sorrier'n hell Pickett boys showed up here on the banks
of Devils River. Only thing as matters to me is what they
went and done, Lucius. And what they done was murder
five people, mostly children, on land we're responsible for.
Far as I'm concerned, we need to be hot on their trail right
damned quick and put this sorry deed to right. Hang the
men who had a hand in this mess, or kill 'em all. Quicker
the better, by God."

Glo stood, snatched up his long-barreled Greener, and
laid it in the crook of one arm. "You know me, Mistuh
Dodge. I'll ride five hundred miles outta my way to avoid
any kinda gunfight. But in this instance, Mistuh Boz is
right. Men as would kill innocent women and chil'ren
need sendin' to the good Lord for His heavenly judgment.
Figure if we hit the trail, right quick-like, probably catch
Murdock and that bunch with 'im whilst they's still eatin'
and drinkin' and womanizin' at Mendoza's. Then, we can
send 'em on their way so's Jesus can usher them on to Hell,
where they can shake hands with the Devil hisself."

I shot a resolute gaze back and forth from one grim face
to the other. "What about Clementine?" I said.

Boz waved the question away as he said, "Guess we
probably need to take her on back to the ranch. Leave her
with Paco. Figure he can take care of 'er till we can get
back."

Glorious Johnson shook his head. "No. Cain't do that,
Mistuh Boz. Gonna use up a buncha valuable time makin'

a trip all the way back down to the ranch. Then we be havin' to come back out here 'fore we actually gets started after them sorry killers."

Boz slapped the oiled, walnut grips of the glistening pistol strapped high on his hip. "Well, we damn sure cain't let this here little-bitty girl ride along with us, Glo."

It surprised the heck out of all three of us when Clementine Webb snapped, "Don't you dare talk about me like I'm not here." Looking angry enough to bite the head off a ball-peen hammer, another round of tears piled up in the girl's eyes and, one at a time, streamed down reddened cheeks. "I'll not have you ride off and leave me. No, by jiminy, that's not about to happen."

"Well, what *would* you have us do, little missy?" Boz said.

An uncomfortable silence fell over the scene. Got so quiet the whispery rustle of cottonwood leaves on the near-undetectable west Texas breezes became readily apparent. An attentive listener could have easily perceived the sound of water in Devils River as it trickled past and headed south for the Rio Grande.

Me, Boz, and Glo locked our gazes on Clementine Webb and waited. For some seconds the girl appeared incapable of bringing her wounded gaze off the ground. Bear sat up, nuzzled her hand, and leaned against the girl's leg when she scratched his ragged ears. The three of us couldn't do much but fidget and paw at the ground with the toes of our boots.

Finally, Clem cut a nervous glance at her family's piteous gravesite. Stooped and a bit defeated-looking, of a sudden she came erect. She snapped her shoulders back in the manner of a young soldier recently called to action by the sound of trumpets, drums, and the possibility of quick death.

The gal wiped leaky eyes on the back of her arm, pointed at the grave, then said, "You're not leaving me behind, and there's the reason why. I'll be going along with you to find the men who did this."

Be willing to bet that less than half a heartbeat had passed when I snapped, "Now wait a minute, Clem. I . . ."

So quick I could hardly fathom how it happened, Clementine Webb was standing on the toes of my boots, her trembling finger almost pressed against the end of my nose. "You can't leave me here, and I won't let you take me to your ranch so Paco, whoever in the wide, wide world that is, can take care of me. If there's one thing I don't need right now, it's a Mexican caretaker."

"We only have three horses, Clem," Boz offered.

"I'll ride behind Mr. Dodge," she snapped without taking her eyes off me. "What little I weigh, it'll do until we get to Carta Blanca. I can buy a horse there."

"Look, don't mean to sound cruel or insensitive, Clem," I said, "but where would you get the money for a horse? Boz and me went over the wagon pretty close, child. Didn't find anything of real value. Nothing but blood-soaked clothes, bedding, and maybe enough food for about another week out here in the wild places. Figure if there was any money at all Murdock and his bunch probably took it."

The feisty girl turned on her heel and marched to the bullet-splintered wagon. She appeared to give no thought to the action when she began jerking at the length of rope that lashed the water barrel to the wagon bed. The leaky, dripping vessel sat atop a small platform between the front and rear wheels.

With forearms resting on the grips of the brace of pistols strapped high on his hips, Boz shook his head and called out, "What're you doing, child?"

'Course she ignored him. Continued to wrestle with the rope until it was completely loosened. Then she climbed onto the wagon's back wheel and, holding on to one of the wooden bows that normally kept the canvas top in place, kicked the barrel until it tipped over and dropped onto the ground.

The wooden container landed with a resounding splat and burst open. Splintered staves and water flew in all directions. Clem hopped down, scratched around in the wreckage, and fished out a wallet-shaped package. She strolled back over and offered it to me.

"What's this, Clem?" I said.

"Open it. See for yourself."

With some understandable hesitation, I took the parcel. The bundle was tightly wrapped in oilcloth, like a primitive, waterproof birthday present. I pulled my bowie, sliced through a thin strip of rawhide tied around the whole she-bang, and clawed the wrapper away to find a leather wallet inside. As I fingered at the contents, my eyes most surely grew wider.

"Good God, Clem," I said. "There's probably five thousand dollars in here, maybe ten."

Hands clasped behind her back, the Webb girl stared at the ground. She shuffled her feet, shrugged, and said, "Really didn't have any idea how much was there, Ranger Dodge. By accident, I caught Papa hiding it before we left home. He made me swear not to tell anyone. Said the money was for emergencies. Have to admit, never expected an emergency like this one, but here it is. Appears to me I could easily afford to buy a horse."

I shook the sheaf of bills in Clementine Webb's face and said, "This don't change a thing, girl. You can't go with us. Such an endeavor is just too dangerous. Don't you understand?"

Something in her eyes had definitely changed when she raised her head and focused in on me again. A hard, calculating glare pegged me to the ground. Then, fisted hands on her narrow hips, she snarled, "Then I'll pay you to find the men who murdered my family. A thousand dollars each. But only if you take me along on the hunt. You run Murdock, Atwood, and the Pickett brothers to ground and kill them all, like you promised earlier, and I'll pay you each a thousand dollars in good Yankee cash."

Clementine Webb's astonishing proposal fell on me and my friends like a thunderclap. Glorious Johnson stood with his eyes closed and appeared as though counting on his fingers. Boz Tatum's mouth hung open like the unlashed boot on the back of a Concord coach. My loot-heavy hand dangled in the air as if suspended from a string.

Eyes wide in surprised childlike wonder, Boz muttered, "Jesus, Lucius. A thousand dollars? Each? That there's a buncha money. We'd work our fingers to the bone chasin' badmen for Cap'n Culpepper for such an amount. Hell's iron bells, that's more money than all three of us together'd see in a year. Maybe two."

Glorious Johnson's eyes popped open. "Heard you right, didn't I? You'd give us each a thousand dollars, miss? Each?"

Clementine quickly seized on her advantage. Perked up, grinned, and said, "Give you an additional thousand to split three ways if you can find out why those men did what they did. You know I can do it. You're looking right at the proof of my ability to pay up."

I let my cash-heavy hand drop to my side. "We can't do this, fellers."

"Oh, yes, we can," Boz snorted. "Oh, hell yes, we can. Leastways, I sure as hell can."

Glo appeared to stiffen. "Look here. I ain't never had that much money in hand at one time in my whole life, Mistuh Dodge. How come we cain't take it? Do what this here chile wants and get paid. We's gonna go after them mens anyway. Gonna hang 'em, or kill 'em, if'n we catch 'em. Ain't no doubt about that. For once, we might as well get paid well for our troubles."

For the first time that day, Clementine Webb flashed a toothy, satisfied grin. "Then is it settled? Do we have a deal, gentlemen?"

I slapped my leg with the stack of bills. "Well, now wait just a minute. I never said any such thing."

Glo propped his shotgun on one shoulder. "We done always took a vote when things got difficult in times past, Mistuh Dodge. Think we'd best take one now."

Boz looked pleased that someone had come up with a viable method for solving the problem. He grinned like an opossum in a plum tree when he said, "There you go. A vote, by God. We'll take a vote. That's the ticket. Democracy in action. Right out here on Devils River. I vote yes. We should take Miss Clementine Webb up on her offer of one thousand dollars each for killin' Pitt Murdock and his gang of sorry-assed cutthroats. Who's with me?"

14

"... COULD GET LUCKY. KILL THE WHOLE BUNCH OF US ..."

A BRITTLE SUN, the color of liquid gold, dangled low in a heat-blasted, late afternoon sky. Fiery orb appeared as if pasted there by an angry God. I drew my froth-covered mount to a halt on the western bank of the Dry Devils River. Stood in the stirrups and stretched the knotted muscles of my aching back.

Clementine Webb slid from the animal's muscular rump and set to slapping at her sweat-drenched, dust-covered clothing. Boz and Glo pulled up alongside us. Bear stuck to the girl like a happy, tail-wagging puppy.

Bone tired, us man hunters stepped down and held the reins as our animals drank from the barely moving, ankle-deep tributary of the larger, deeper Devils River. On the far side of the sluggish stream, less than a hundred yards to the east, wiggly, squirming waves of midday heat rose from the baked buildings and tired landscape of the near-nonexistent village of Carta Blanca.

"Place ain't never been much of a town," Boz said and

fished a nickel cheroot from his inside vest pocket, then stoked it to life.

Using my hat, I whacked at the layer of coarse, irritating grime that covered me from head to foot. Stood in the cloud of powdery, swirling grit I'd generated and said, "Looks like it's even less of a town now than it was the last time we were over this way."

"World's kinda passed on by, Dodge. Done heard rumors as how Dusty Biggerstaff's Nueces Billiards Parlor went and burned slap to the ground several months ago," Boz offered. "Came close to breakin' my heart when I heard tell as how the fire just ripped the guts right outta what little was left of this place."

I leaned against Grizz's side. "Yeah, I heard that one, too, Boz."

"Damned shame," he continued. "Ole Dusty had the only decent snooker table within a hundred miles of these parts. Plus, his hangout was, for damned sure, the spot a man could depend on to have a mug of cold beer and a friendly game of nine ball goin' anytime you 'uz travelin' 'tween Sonora and Del Rio. Yep, done spent many a pleasant, idle hour with a pool cue in my hand in that joint. And now she's gone. Nothin' but a heap of stinkin' ashes left."

I knelt in the wet sand, dipped my hat in the lethargic stream, then slapped the waterlogged chunk of handwoven, Mexican palm leaf back on my sweaty head. The soothing liquid ran down my neck and onto my broiling shoulders as I rose. Hands on hips, above the grips of my pistols, I glared across a glass-smooth waterway that looked almost as though it had frozen in spite of the blistering heat.

For as far as a man could see, in either direction, a single dirt trace ran along the easternmost bank of the river, from north to south. Carta Blanca's narrow, central thoroughfare split off the wagon-rutted Del Rio road and snaked its meandering way through the forlorn village.

Half a dozen aged, shabby, run-down businesses lay scattered about on either side of the town's gloomy Main Street. All the crude buildings a body could lay an eye on stood at odd, incongruent angles to one another, as though the berg had been platted, drawn up, and then carelessly erected by a troop of drunken, giggling children.

Behind the few remaining shops and stores, low, adobe houses roofed with layers of limbs and twigs, stained in washed-out shades of pink, blue, or yellow, cropped up amongst stunted live oak and mesquite trees like blocky, out-of-place wildflowers. Built into the base of a squatty, rock-strewn hillock, Mendoza's Cantina proved the exception to that rule. Locals all knew that Mendoza lived in rooms behind the bar that he'd tacked on to the back of his watering hole.

As I swabbed at my dripping neck with a frayed bandanna, I said, "Well, boys, if Dusty's place has sure enough burned, doesn't leave a passing man much to do in Carta Blanca but drink. From here, thank God, appears Big Jim Boston's corral and smithy operation is still cranking along over yonder to the south."

"Yeah," Boz said, "can see smoke wafting off the forge."

"Looks like Miss Martha Hooch's rooming house is still standing, too," I continued. "Only two-story building in this part of the country. Guess a body could still purchase a decent meal there, long as he's willing to pay dear for it. And it seems as though Eldritch Smoot's pissant-sized mercantile outfit, next to Big Jim's, is still operational."

Glo squinted, shaded his eyes with a dripping hand, shook his head, and said, "Done heard tell as how mos' dem houses and buildings yonder's emptier'n last year's rattlesnake nests, Mistuh Dodge. Might remember when my friend Moses Blackstock stopped in at the ranch for a visit month or so ago. Mose said there warn't 'nuff people left in Carta Blanca for a decent card game."

Slipped my long glass out and socked it up against one eye. "Can't see but two horses out front of Mendoza's. Big bay mare and a piebald gelding."

"Them hosses belongs to two of the Pickett boys," Glo offered. "Priest and Cullen as I remembers. Leastways, them's the ones what was ridin' hosses like them you've described when I snuck up on 'em earlier this mornin'."

"Roscoe on either animal?" Boz said.

"Naw. That 'un they calls Roscoe was mounted astride a big ole hoss what was blacker'n a sack full of witches' cats on a moonless night. Hoss gave me the creepin' willies jus' lookin' at it. Swear as how Satan, his very own self, musta rode that animal straight up out of the smolderin' pit. Kep' thinkin' maybe the beast was actually gonna breathe real fire whilst I 'uz lookin' at it through my own long glass."

The scope made an angry series of metallic clicks when I slapped the big end with an open palm. "Would be the two worst of them Pitt boys we've caught up with, wouldn't it?"

Boz let out a derisive chuckle. "Sweet Jesus, Lucius, all three of the Pickett boys is in serious cahoots with horned Satan. Their reservations for a room in a festerin' hell were made the day they got born. Whole family's lower'n a snake's belt buckle. Even the women. Hell, that sister of theirs, Winona, is just about tougher'n the snout on a wild sow."

From behind us, Clementine scratched Bear's ragged ears and called out, "Are the three of you bold gentlemen just gonna stand here by the river and talk all day? Might as well throw some blankets on the ground and have a picnic. Skip rocks on the water. Play hopscotch. Or maybe you gents can pull your pocket knives and play mumblety-peg."

I cast a sidelong glance over my shoulder. Didn't take much for a body to recognize that a stern hardness had replaced the girl's earlier displays of fear, emotional loss, and hesitant indecision.

"You seem a might anxious for more bloodshed, Clem," I said.

The Webb girl flipped her shock of straw-colored hair to one side and kicked at a fist-sized rock with one foot. "Yes. You could say that, Mr. Dodge," she snapped. "I've contemplated what would happen when we caught up with these killers. Pondered the problem all the way from the site of my family's sorry grave. I've come to the conclusion that the men responsible for my present situation owe me their blood—every drop of it. And you've already sworn to deliver their blood to me. So, let's get this hoedown started."

I swung my gaze back to the grubby collection of buildings across the river, slapped a glove-covered palm with my reins, then said, "All right, here's how I think it'd be best to handle this dance. We'll circle around to the south. Ease up on the backside of Big Jim's stable. Spend a few minutes talking the situation over with Jim. Then we can decide on how to approach the problem from there. Everyone okay with that idea?"

Boz and Glo both nodded and grunted their approval at the same time.

Clementine strode up beside the horse. "Let's be on our way then. Quicker those men are in the ground, the better I'll like it."

I climbed back aboard, then helped the girl up to her spot behind me. Once she'd settled in, I touched Grizz's side with one rowel and urged him into the shallow stream.

Unnoticed, our small posse slipped along the riverbank around Carta Blanca to the south. In a matter of minutes, we arrived at the back entrance of Big Jim Boston's dilapidated corral and smithy concern. The busy, musical sound of metal ringing against metal sang through the sultry air.

Boston's weathered, board-and-batten livery barn sported a comic, drunken lean toward the east. Boz sat his animal in the building's wide-open back entrance. He flicked a grinning gaze from one side of the structure to the other. During a lull in the noisy shoeing, he called out, "'Bout one good gust of wind outta the west and Big Jim's gonna be wearing this place around his ears like a wooden hat."

From the stable's dark interior, a low, earth-thumping voice rumbled out, "I heard that, Tatum. If'n you don't particular like my place of commerce, for one reason or 'tother, then you can, by God, take your trade sommmers else. Hear tell as how folks have several fair to middlin' blacksmiths in Del Rio. Don't like the way any of their places look, might have to head on over Uvalde way. 'Course, the best man there's my brother, Jake."

As our party dismounted, a totally bald, shiny-pated, bullet-headed man the size of a freight wagon stepped from the barn's murky shadows. Adorned with a stained leather apron, the giant sported a moustache the size of a draft horse's hind leg. Covered in a layer of soot, grease, and grimy grunge, he wiped ham-sized hands on a ragged chunk of nasty burlap, then flipped the rag onto an equally grubby shoulder.

I moved forward, flashed my friendliest grin, grabbed one his enormous smithy's hands and shook it. "Good to see you again, Jim," I said.

Eyes the color of coal flicked a narrow, inquisitive gaze from me, to Boz, and to Glo, then finally landed on Clementine Webb. The big man's glance lingered on the girl as he said, "Been a spell, boys. You fellers ain't had much business over this way lately. Ever since y'all went and set up house out yonder on Devils River, don't think any of you've been by more'n once or twice. Not like the old days when ya'll used to come breezin' through these parts two or three times a year chasin' Injuns, rustlers, crooked gamblers, footpads, and killers."

"Been livin' the unhurried, leisurely life of gentlemen horse ranchers, Jim," I said. "Spend most of our time these days sitting on the front porch whittling and spitting. Trying to rest our various hurts and bullet holes."

Fisted mitts on muscular hips, Big Jim Boston glared at us from beneath a knitted brow. "What're you ranger boys doing over this way this mornin' then? Sure as hell ain't much goin' on in this dried-up, dyin' berg." The massive smithy's black-eyed gaze zeroed in on Clementine Webb again, then knifed back to me.

I hooked both thumbs over my pistol belt. "Got two, maybe three men drinkin' over at Mendoza's, Jim?"

Boston waved a filthy hand at the slab of darkness at his back. "Workin' on one of 'ems big ole black mount right now. Threw a shoe. Animal's borderin' on the most uncooperative, spiteful beast I've ever took in hand."

"Three of them waiting for you to finish up?" I said.

"Sounds right to me. Was five of 'em earlier, I believe. Maybe six. Not exactly sure. Caught a glimpse of 'em ridin' by when they first came into town. Rough lookin' bunch, Dodge. That bunch is rougher'n the calluses on a barfly's elbows. Got myself back inside. Just hopin' they'd do their drinkin', leave me alone, then head on out."

"Appears that didn't happen," Boz offered.

"Naw. Think maybe two or three of 'em stopped about long enough to throw down a single shot of Mendoza's least lethal cactus juice, then they hit the road headed for Del Rio. Leastways, that's what I figured on anyhow. Made me mighty happy to see them as headed out to leave. Wish the other three had gone with 'em."

"How long ago?" I said.

Boston rubbed a stubble covered chin with the back of one immense fist. "Oh, be guessin' at it, but I'd say they've been gone two hours or so, maybe a bit more. Seems as though them three what stayed in town set down to some serious drinkin'. Know they ran all of the regulars off pretty quick. Then, one of 'em paid Mendoza's helper to bring this black devil over here for me to work on. Peon's sittin' out front waitin' for me to finish so's he can return this monster to its owner soon's I'm done."

Rubbed the back of an aching, sunburned neck, then said, "Could you call the man back here so I can talk to him?"

Boston swiveled at the waist and yelled, "Gustavo. Gustavo Morales. *Adelante*, amigo."

Barefoot and stooped, a white-haired Mexican, sombrero held against his wizened chest like a shield, shuffled up to a spot near Boston and stopped. "*Sí*, senor. I am here. Is the demon *caballo* ready?"

Boston grinned, shook his sweaty pate, waved my direction, then said, "This gentleman's a Texas Ranger. Wants to ask you some questions."

Gustavo Morales's black eyes widened. Lines of worry creased the old man's forehead when he said, "*Sí. Es no problema.*"

Pushed the still-dripping hat to the back of my head with one finger. "No need to be afraid, Senor Morales. Simply want you to tell me where the men who sent you here are sitting in Mendoza's Cantina. As I remember there's only room enough for four tables inside the joint. So, are they up by the front door, in the middle of the room, or in back near the bar?"

Morales's darting glance flicked from face to face until it reached the angelic visage of Clementine Webb. Of a sudden, the ancient peon stopped twisting his hat and appeared to relax a bit. As if unable to comprehend the reasons for her presence, he continued to stare at the girl as he said, "Near the bar, senor. *Muy borracho*. How you say, very drunk. *Muy ofensivo*. Dangerous hombres, senor. Mendoza is very afraid. He did not say it, but I could tell."

Boz slapped his good leg with his reins and said, "Be foolish to go in there after 'em, Dodge. Mendoza's joint is way too cramped for a six-man gunfight. A one-eyed, three-fingered jasper who couldn't hit a washtub with a shotgun could get lucky. Kill the whole bunch of us in such confined circumstances."

"Ain't dat duh truth," Glo chimed in.

Big Jim Boston ran a hand beneath his leather apron and scratched a tub-sized belly. He said, "Sure you boys have a good reason to be talkin' 'bout gunfights, killin', getting' killed, and such. Mind tellin' me why you're after these men?"

I knifed a sidelong glance at Clementine Webb, then said, "Tracked them all the way here from over on Devils River not far from the ranch, Jim. They helped murder this child's entire family in a stand of cottonwoods where Three Mile Creek dribbles into the river."

"Jee-zus. Sorry to hear that," Boston muttered.

"Yeah, well, we'd like to get one of them alive. But I'd be willing to bet they'll go down shooting. Sons a bitches will fight rather than let us take them in for the most brutal killings any of us have come across in years. Those fellers have an absolutely certain date with a bullet or a piece of short hemp and a long drop."

Boston stared at Clementine with renewed interest. "Right sorry to hear about your loss, young lady," he said.

Clementine pulled the dog closer and silently stared at the ground as though she didn't care for the topic of discussion.

"Gonna have to call 'em out onto Mendoza's porch, or maybe into the street, if we can figure a way to get 'em to come that far," I said.

I turned on my heel, strode to my animal, and slipped the Winchester from its scabbard. As though I'd somehow mysteriously lit a hidden fuse, Boz and Glo hotfooted it to their own animals. They quickly armed themselves with their big-barreled blasters, too. In a flurry of activity, the three of us retrieved additional ammunition. Once again, we went through the process of making certain our weapons were ready and in working order. When finally satisfied with the condition of their hardware, Boz and Glo looked to me for instructions.

"Okay, here's how it'll go down," I said. "We'll spread out. Since we know from past experience that Mendoza's doesn't have a back exit, we'll approach the front in a three-pronged assault. I'll go at the front door head on. Boz, you move up to the veranda on my right. Glo, you take the left. Want you boys to get around behind 'em by moving to the corners of the cantina's front façade where they can't see you. Then stay out of sight until I need you."

Boz and Glo nodded.

"Once we're set, I'll call 'em out. Maybe the Pickett boys are drunk enough by now to think I'm alone. If they get to figuring the three of them can take me without much effort, be willing to bet they'll come out onto the porch. Once they're all outside we'll have 'em in a crossfire. Right where we want 'em."

"Then what?" Boz said.

"Well, if I need you boys to move out where they can see you, I'll call for you to step on out and show yourselves. Should it prove necessary for you to have to make the move, get well situated as quickly as possible. Given where you're gonna be standing, gotta stay sharp. Sure as the devil don't want you shooting across the porch with those shoulder cannons of yours and accidentally hitting one another."

Big Jim Boston danced from foot to foot like a trained bear in a traveling circus. He nervously rubbed both hands up and down on the sides of his leather apron. "Well, none of this sounds good. What 'er you intendin' to do here, Dodge?"

The rifle made a loud mechanical racking noise when I levered a shell into the Winchester's receiver and left the hammer back.

The harsh, metallic click of the rifle's lever slapping against the stock's grip jerked Clementine Webb's head up. An eerie unearthliness crept into the girl's voice when she hissed, "He intends to kill them all. Don't you, Ranger Dodge?"

I refused to look at the girl. Boz and Glo in tow, I strode past Big Jim and headed through the wide-open barn's back door and, from there, toward the front entrance. "We'll see," I said.

Then, over one shoulder, I called out, "You stay here, Clem. Keep the dog with you. Don't let him get to wandering around till the shooting's over. Anyone bothers you, just snap your fingers and tell Bear to go get 'em."

15

"... USE YER PERFORATED HIDE
FOR A FLOUR SIFTER..."

LINED UP NEAR elbow to elbow, we drew to a halt outside Boston's front entrance near a decrepit rail fence that surrounded the livery's horse-poor corral. East of the empty enclosure stood the ramshackle grocery and mercantile business of Eldritch Smoot. Men's and women's ready-made clothing, draped over wooden hangers, nearly covered the boardwalk outside Smoot's street-facing windows.

Beneath the fading shirts and dresses were a number of rickety tables beset with mounds of tarnished pots, pans, galvanized washtubs, and discolored bolts of cloth. The floorboards of the store's raised veranda were littered, here and there, with piles of ancient, dust covered, army-surplus McClellan saddles. Above the shabby concern's open door, a weather-scarred sign invited shoppers inside by boasting the availability of guns, boots and shoes, dry goods and clothing, hats and caps.

Boz, me, and Glo cast darting glances toward Smoot's. We eyeballed each nook and cranny of Carta Blanca's main thoroughfare, then carefully gave Mendoza's one more final going-over.

We viewed the rough cantina at something of an angle that made it somewhat problematic for us to see the entire front façade all at one time. Off to our left, the slap-dash, westernmost side of the saloon ran away from us and toward the low hill the joint's back wall abutted.

The place appeared to have grown up in bits and pieces, like a patch of unwanted ragweed. Half the establishment's front façade, on the most distant side of the entrance, was constructed of crumbling, adobe bricks. The remainder of the shanty-like affair seemed to have been built from discarded scraps of wind-aged lumber taken from the remains of other long-gone houses, businesses, and saloons.

The most easily viewable exterior side of the structure was nothing more than a jumbled series of weathered, paint-blistered, wooden doors nailed one edge atop the other like shake shingles. A sloped roof covered a rickety front porch constructed of rough-cut, never-planed boards laid directly atop the parched, dusty ground. A number of shaggy, white-faced curs lazed around in the ever-shrinking rectangle of moving shade provided by the veranda's overhang.

Scattered here and there, empty whiskey barrels of various sizes stood beneath the scruffy porch like a milling group of tipsy loafers seeking a spot of shelter from the sun. The largest of the metal-bound casks sat atop its own separate elevated platform. The container supported one end of a V-shaped, wooden gutter. The wishfully crude setup was for catching whatever sparse rainwater might someday drip from the roof's front edge and rotting corners.

A pair of six-over-six glass-paned windows, located on either side of the front entrance, provided the only possibility for occupants to see outside. Above the chaotic porch's pitched roof, a near-indecipherable sign informed the prospective imbiber that he was about to enter MENDOZA'S CANTINA DE CARTA BLANCA.

A wispy dust devil swept along the street all the way up from the river. The miniature cyclone paused between Boston's livery and the saloon, then blew itself out as it twisted east and disappeared over the low hills that placed the dying west Texas village in a bowl-like earthen cavity.

I nodded, and my partners heeled it for their assigned spots at either end of Mendoza's rude porch. "Careful, boys," I softly hissed at their backs, "Don't let your attention stray. Wait for my call. Try not to shoot me or each other."

I stood in the swirling dust and waited until both my friends were properly stationed and had signaled their readiness. Then I strolled to a spot twenty or thirty feet distant from the liquor locker's front entrance.

Mendoza's only obvious method of egress and exit stood wide-open. It sported but one half of a weather-beaten batwing door that dangled from a single, bent, spring-loaded brass hinge.

After a quick glance at each of my partners, I held the Winchester's stock against one hip, touched the trigger with my thumb, and fired off a single shot. The weapon's thunderous report echoed off the surrounding hills. It ricocheted around a bit, then escaped west, back across the river, like a frightened animal fleeing from larger predators.

One-handed, I levered a fresh round in, then laid the gun across my left arm. Cupped my right hand to my mouth and yelled out, "This is Texas Ranger Lucius Dodge. You Pickett boys best come on out right now. We've got things to talk about."

Didn't take long to get the easily predictable results. No more than ten seconds had passed when inquisitive faces oozed up out of the interior darkness of the blasted entryway, then bobbled around behind the busted batwing like carnival balloons tethered to a string.

The decrepit café door squawked open, pushed to one side by a disembodied arm.

I recognized the first of the murderous Pickett bunch to slither out onto the porch as Priest. Tall, lank, and gaunt, the scowling killer dressed himself in the garb typical of most working cowboys—sombrero, faded cotton shirt, brightly colored neck scarf, high-waisted pants, shotgun chaps, riding boots, and massive, silver-plated Mexican spurs. His elaborate pair of horse rakers sported rowels the size of a grown man's palm. He drunkenly crabbed-walked to one side of the porch.

Behind him came Roscoe, then Cullen. Although separated by one to three years, the men could have easily been mistaken for a set of stubble-chinned, grim-faced, rheumy-eyed triplets. As the dodgy, dangerous trio spread from one end of the veranda to the other, all the skinny dogs, hairless tails tucked between their legs, cautiously rose and slunk out of harm's reach.

Priest edged his way to my left. He reached the farthest porch pillar and leaned a bony shoulder against it. The gunny had picked a spot not five feet from where Glo hid with his back pressed against one of the wooden doors that made up the cantina's strangest wall.

The squint-eyed thug propped a booted foot atop one of the empty barrels. He hoisted an open, half-filled bottle to twisted, snarling lips. A goodly amount of the nose paint missed its target and ran from the corners of his mouth and down his neck.

He wiped his ragged chin across the sleeve of a bib-front shirt that appeared to have once been bright yellow. The lethal skunk cast a nervous, tight glance at his elder brother Roscoe, who had stepped off the watering hole's rough porch and now stood in the street less than twenty feet from me.

Hat pulled low over mean, beady eyes, a smoldering hand-rolled ciga-reet dangling from the corner of a cruel mouth, Cullen Pickett leaned against the most distant prop on the opposite end of the porch from brother Priest. The man was totally unaware that Boz Tatum stood behind him, a buckshot-charged coach gun leveled at his murderous guts.

Roscoe, oldest and widely proclaimed by those who knew the family as the most dangerous of the slavering pack of human animals, rocked in the stifling afternoon breezes. He pushed the leading edge of his broad-brimmed, palm-leaf sombrero away from sun-tortured eyes.

"Just be goddamned. Truly is you, ain't it, Dodge," he said. "Heard you'd been outta circulation for a spell now. Hell, at first, we all thought you 'uz dead. Fact is, figure as how damned near everyone in this part of Texas thought you 'uz dead. Know we all hoped so leastways."

Wind-dried lips curled off my teeth in a tight grin. "Sure do hate to disappoint a man like you, Roscoe. But you've gone and thrown your saddle on the wrong horse. I'm still very much alive, as you can readily see."

The leader of the Pickett bunch let out a honking, derisive grunt, glanced at each of his lesser brothers, chuckled, then said, "Truth is I'm gladder'n hell you're still with us, Dodge. Cause that's gonna give me a chance to polish up my reputation by killin' the hell out of you myself."

Then, the stupid bastard made quite a production of rolling up his right shirtsleeve. He cut a quick glance down at the bone-gripped pistol pressed against his left hip and said, "See this here silver-plated, scroll-engraved, Colt layin' 'cross my belly, Ranger Lucius 'By God' Dodge? Well, I'm gonna snatch 'er out shortly and blast the hell outta you, you irritatin', badge-totin' son of a bitch. Gonna use yer perforated hide for a flour sifter when I'm done."

I snorted back at him, then said, "That a fact?"

"Damned right. Natural fact. Been hearin' all kinda stories and tall tales 'bout you and that Winchester of yours for several years now. How fast and deadly you were with it and all. Never believed any a them silly-assed fables my-self. Ain't no man alive can crank one a them long guns fast as I can draw and fire. Jus' been bidin' my time, waitin' for a chance like this to come my way."

"Looking to put more notches on your gun, Roscoe?" I offered.

"Never pass up a chance to rub out law bringers like you, Dodge. And, bless my britches, if you don't stroll right up here askin' fer me to come on out here and give me the pleasure of killin' yuh."

I let his more-than-stupid comment pass without replying.

Several seconds of silence flew by, then he said, "You know, when me and the brothers looked out the door just now, Dodge, swear I couldn't believe my good fortune. Thought to myself, well, son of a bitch, this must be your lucky day, Roscoe. Truth is, you can't even begin to imagine how much I'm gonna enjoy puttin' four or five smokin' holes in your law-bringin' ass."

Squiggly shadows had got unnaturally long when I swung the Winchester around with one hand. Leveled the muzzle up on the man's chest as I steadied the weapon by grasping the forearm. "Best throw all your pistols in the dirt right now, boys. Give yourselves up, so I can take you to Del Rio for trial and suitable hanging. Any of you go and do anything stupid and all three of you'll end up under ground just like those poor folks you murdered out on Devils River earlier this morning."

Priest Pickett's foot slipped off the barrel top. The heavily booted appendage hit the plank porch with a resounding thump and the amber-colored liquor bottle slid from the man's already questionable grip. The container bounced on the crude pile of wobbly boards beneath his feet, sprayed alcohol from the jug's open top and peppered one leg all the way from the mule-ear pulls of the gunman's stovepipe boot to his waist. A wild-eyed look swept over the gunny's acne-ravaged, pockmarked face.

"Hellfire and damnation, Roscoe. Did you hear what that son of a bitch just said?" Priest yelped.

Brother Roscoe's arrogant demeanor changed in less than half the time it would take to blow out a kerosene lamp. His head cocked to one side, hand hovering over his cross-draw weapon, the leader of the Pickett boys glared at me from one bloodshot eye. "Shut your drunken, stupid mouth, Priest," he snapped. Then to me, he growled, "What the hell 'er you talkin' 'bout, Dodge? We don't know nuthin' 'bout no killings over on Devils River."

I shot him another slight grin. "You're a lying stack of walking horse dung, Roscoe. We tracked you boys all the way from the scene of the killings right to the spots where you're standing this very instant. Now, I'm a reasonable man. Be more'n happy to entertain the possibility of taking you to Fort Worth for suitable trial and hanging, long as you give up your weapons, right by-God now, then let us slap you in shackles and chains." Under my breath, I whispered to no one in particular, "You'll never do it, though, will you, you son of a bitch? Now, jerk that smoke wagon and give me a reason to send you straight to Satan."

Roscoe Pickett's feral eyes flicked from side to side as though trying to look through me. A twitching hand still hovered over his pistol's bone grip. He took a half step back toward the cantina's porch. The entire trio sucked away from me and moved ever so slightly in the direction of the tavern's entrance like a small, nervous, human wave.

"You jus' said 'we' and 'us.' Where's them others, Dodge?" Roscoe snarled. "Got some more men with you? Where are they?"

"It's enough you know that my posse's here and can come if I need them. Now pitch all your pistols, knives, hideout guns, and such out here in the street. Then step away from Arturo's front door and get your faces down in the dirt where they belong."

Roscoe's lips twisted into an angry, tense sneer. "Damned if we will. Ain't givin' up my gun to no man. Gonna have to use that long-barreled shooter a yern, Dodge."

"Me, neither," Priest growled. "Keepin' my pistol fer damned sure."

I could easily see the belligerence of the coming fight grow in their intoxicated eyes before any of them had even made the slightest move toward their weapons. Then, from nowhere, the mute Cullen Pickett's hand suddenly dropped to the ivory grips of the Smith & Wesson Russian model shooter snugged high and crosswise against his left hip.

A horror-stricken Roscoe tried to wave his unthinking brother off, but before either man could clear leather, the Winchester thundered, bucked, and slapped a massive blue whistler into the bony, centermost part of the elder Pickett's chest. Sixty grains of spent black powder delivered a 395-grain chunk of pure lead into Roscoe's breastbone, and from thence out his back and into the wall behind him. A fist-sized wad of the man's blood and splintered bits of rib bone followed the bullet. The club-like blow knocked the stunned killer backward onto the porch amidst a cloud of swirling wood fragments.

The barrel of Cullen's cocked weapon had almost topped his gun leather's front lip when the second ear-splitting blast from my rifle punched a hole in the man's forehead just above his left eye. The red-hot bullet plowed a furrow through half his addled brain, ricocheted around inside the man's skull. The massive slug knocked his palm-leaf hat off when it exited through the top of his head, then carved a blood-spattered hole in the roof above. In spite of being dead where he stood, Cullen's handgun went off. The blast ripped the entire face out of his holster. The wayward shot kicked up a flying cloud of dirt a few paces into the windblown street. Woman-killing scum went down like all the bones had been jerked out of his body at the same time.

The only man on the porch who'd not uttered a single word during the entire confrontation went to the ground like a load of brick dropped from the roof of a San Antone whorehouse. I knew without bothering to check that Cullen Pickett was deader than Wild Bill was when his head hit the poker table in Deadwood's NO. 10 Saloon.

In his whiskey-sodden haste to get outside and pick a fight with a man who appeared to be alone, Priest Pickett had completely forgotten to flip the hammer thong away from his weapon. The sound of my two shots still hung in the air as he panicked and jerked on the uncooperative shooter once, twice, three times.

On the third try, the crazy-eyed varmint's sweaty fingers slipped from the oiled walnut grips with such force he came nigh on to slapping himself right in the face. Terrified, flusterated, and unnerved, he grabbed at the weapon again and fired a burning shot down his own right leg that chewed a massive hole in the plank porch at his feet. Then, the confused child murderer screeched like a wounded animal, turned on his heel, and went to running like he'd lost his mind. Darted past Glorious Johnson's hiding spot around the corner.

Standing amidst a roiling cloud of spent black-powder smoke, I levered a third shell into the rifle's receiver and called out, "He's yours, Glo."

With the stock of the Greener pressed to his shoulder, Glo stepped away from his hiding place like a man on a leisurely stroll to Sunday school and yelled, "You can go on and stop runnin' now, Mr. Pickett."

Guess Priest made two more steps before a cannon-like wad of tightly grouped buckshot blasted him between the shoulder blades. A gob of lead lifted the fleeing killer out of his boots like a rag doll and dumped him onto his face. A handful of witnesses, who had viewed the action from inside the paltry group of functioning business in Carta Blanca, would later tell anyone who'd listen that it was as if someone had run up beside ole Priest and hit him in the back with a long-handled shovel. The murderous wretch landed in the dirt deader than a brass doorknob on an outhouse. Didn't even flop.

16

"DAMNATION, GIRL..."

I SHOVED THREE fresh rounds into the Winchester's loading gate and watched as a dying Roscoe Pickett dragged himself to Mendoza's nearest porch pillar and propped one shoulder against it.

Rifle held out with one hand to cover the wounded outlaw, I strolled over to a position a few feet from him and squatted down to where the fading man could see me. Coach gun at the ready, Boz sidled up from his spot behind the now-dead Cullen's original position.

"Well you sure as hell kilt the bejabbers out of these two, Lucius. Didn't leave much for me," Boz mumbled.

Blood poured from the corner of Roscoe's twitching mouth and oozed from between the fingers clutching the hole in an already drenched chest. "Damn," he gurgled. "That was fast. Cain't b-b-believe it. S-shot me s-so quick. Son of a bitch. You done w-w-went and shot me through and th-through. Shit. Hurts like hell on a b-b-burnin' stick. Prol-ley done went and kilt me deader'n a rotten stump. God Am-mighty. K-Kilt my brothers, too. D-d-damn you, Dodge."

"Yes," I said and nodded. "Yes indeed. Your sorry brothers are both very dead. And you're headed to Hell with 'em."

The outlaw groaned, rolled his head from side to side, then gasped, "W-w-well, soon's I'm gone, you can roll me over, p-p-pull my britches down, bend over, and k-k-kiss my ass, Dodge."

Rustling movement caused me to twist on the balls of my feet and glance over one shoulder. A step or so away from the bloody carnage of dying and dead men, I spotted Clementine Webb, with one hand rested on the panting Bear's thick neck. From somewhere the girl had acquired a spanking-new Mexican palm-leaf hat.

"Ask him where the others went," she said through gritted teeth.

I swung my concentrated attention back to Roscoe. "We already know where they're going, Clem. Big Jim said he saw them heading out for Del Rio, remember?"

Her voice sounded like broken icicles falling from a frozen roof in Kansas when she snarled, "Where, exactly, Ranger Dodge? Those that kept running must've been in a hurry to meet somebody, somewhere, don't you think? Who were they in such a hurry to see? Where did they intend to meet? How long do we have before they get completely away?"

I flicked a glance at the dying sun, then stared at the ground between my feet for a second and said, "Well, you heard the lady, Pickett. Who're Murdock and Atwood so hot to meet up with in Del Rio that they would leave you boys here and go on ahead without you?"

A gurgling stream of pinkish-red froth bubbled from between the claw-like fingers clutching at Pickett's chest. An uglier, darker river dribbled out onto his chin. "Ain't—ain't—ain't tellin'. Ain't tellin' you bastards a goddamned thang. Sure, s-s-sure's hell ain't got nothin', nothin' to say to no runty, s-s-smart-assed split-tail of a girl."

I felt the crackle of Clementine's sleeve as it grazed my elbow. It sounded like fresh-fired bullets sizzling past my ear when she hissed, "Well, then, you're completely useless to me or anyone else, aren't you?"

From the corner of one eye, I saw the little pistol flash up in the girl's hand and immediately recognized the weapon as a New Line .32-caliber pocket pistol.

For reasons I could not have explained to God, or anyone else, afterward, the fact that Clementine Webb had the barrel of a loaded weapon pressed to the end of the dying Roscoe Pickett's nose just didn't register with me for about half a second. When it finally dawned on me what was about to occur, I made an awkward, squatting lunge at the miniature shooter just as it went off. Burning powder singed my fingers when they wrapped around the weapon's tiny cylinder.

The little gal's well-aimed bullet hit the gravely wounded Roscoe right in the mouth. A searing chunk of peanut-sized lead knocked all his front teeth out, carved a tunnel through the soft tissue at the back of his throat, and blasted its way through a spot in his neck just below the skull bone. The bullet shoved most of his shattered teeth out the newly acquired port in his head and splattered the entire hair-covered mess onto the wooden porch prop he leaned against.

I ripped the smoking pistol from Clementine's grasp, then rolled into the dust on my bony rump. Clumsily, I hopped up with all the red-faced embarrassment and alacrity of a suitor who's just fallen down a series of steps right in front of a woman he was trying his best to impress.

"Damnation, girl," I yelped, then flicked a glance at Roscoe Pickett's shattered teeth, blasted skull, and sagging corpse. I shook my head in total disbelief, then locked Clementine in a narrow, steely gaze and added, "You've grown a mighty thick layer of hard bark around your heart since this morning, darlin'."

The girl's ferocious, crazed, turquoise gaze flashed from Pickett to me and back again. It sounded damn near unearthly when she snarled, "I thought about what these men did all the way from Devils River to here, Ranger Dodge. He deserved to die. Moreover, he deserved to die by my hand. Truth is, they all deserved to die by my hand." She ran trembling fingers through her hair, as though clearing away any arguments against her conduct, then added, "It's biblical, by God. In the Scripture. An eye for an eye. A tooth for a tooth. Blood for blood."

I cast a bewildered glance toward heaven. Felt as though she'd somehow confused me into silence. After several seconds, I glanced at the tiny pistol in my hand and snapped, "I told you I'd take care of this. Gave you my word."

"True," the girl snapped back. "Just thought you could use a little help bringing this particular part of the dance to a suitable conclusion."

I wasn't thinking when I went to offer the pissant-sized .32 back to her. She tried to snatch it from me as I asked her, "Where in the blue-eyed hell did you get this anyway?"

There was no hesitation when the stone-faced girl snapped, "Bought it over at that falling-down mercantile store next to Big Jim's. Same place I got my hat." She made an insistent *gimme* motion. "And I want it back. I paid good money for that gun, and I want it. Might need it again when I catch up with the other two."

With considerable reluctance, I extended the weapon and said, "Think it best that you get on back over to Big Jim's and wait for us. We'll take care of these boys and get after them other two quick as we can. Probably best to go after 'em tomorrow morning. Not a good idea to be on the Del Rio road at night. Even for men like us. Just never know what might happen."

"Then where'll we stay?"

"Big Jim's livery with the horses."

The girl shook her head, turned on her heel, and stomped away. Me, Boz, and Glo stood amongst the carnage and watched as Bear gave a slobbery yelp and loped happily off behind her.

After near a minute of silence Boz said, "How 'bout we go inside and have a drink? Hell, maybe two or three. Don't know you boys feelin's on the subject, but I could sure as hell use one right now. Given what we just seen and did and all."

With a loud metallic click, Glo broke the Greener open and extracted the brass jackets of the spent shells. He dropped the empties into his coat pocket and fished out a fresh pair of hot loads. He shoved the new shells in place, snapped the weapon closed, leisurely checked to make sure the hammers were down, then said, "Sounds like a good idea, Mistuh Boz. Back of my throat feels like a barbed wire bird's nest."

I stepped over Roscoe Pickett's corpse, stomped onto the plank porch, and headed for the cantina's door. Stopped a step from the rude threshold, turned, and gazed back at the bloody wreckage my friends and I'd wrought.

I let a flinty gaze flick over to the skull-shattered corpse of Cullen Pickett. The dead man had come to rest lying nigh on directly in the cantina's entryway. After several seconds my gaze moved to the now-toothless carcass of Roscoe, gape-mouthed and held upright in an ungainly, twisted position against the porch prop. Then for several seconds, I glared over at the lifeless body of their brother, Priest, cut nearly in twain by a double-barreled load of Glo's expertly delivered buckshot.

"Yeah," I grunted, then laid the rifle across my arm again. "Sure enough. Think we could all use a drink 'bout now. Fact, more'n one sounds like a good idea to me."

I suppose we stayed longer at Mendoza's than we should have. 'Course, it took some time to negotiate the hows and whys of Arturo Mendoza's disposal of the Pickett boys. The old bandit finally agreed when we told him he could keep everything they'd arrived with—including their horses, guns, other trappings, and such.

We were sitting at a table by the front door, working on our second tumbler of tequila, when a small band of Messicans showed up out of nowhere and went to carrying the corpses away. Took a spell, but when they finished you couldn't see a spot of blood on Mendoza's porch. It was darker than a barrel of black cats when we dropped money on the table and headed for Big Jim's. Time we got back to the stable it must have been around ten o'clock. I dropped into my bedroll and slept like a felled tree.

I woke up next morning to find Glo standing over me. Do believe he looked more distressed than I'd seen him in quite a spell. Said, "'At 'ere li'l gal done gone, Mistuh Dodge. Figure she could already be in Del Rio by now."

Swear 'fore Jesus, if God himself had reached down from Heaven's front gate and slapped the bejabbers out of me, don't think I would've been any more surprised. But, hell, it was becoming more and more clear to me that Clementine Webb was chock full of such mind-boggling astonishments.

I covered my eyes with one hand, thought it over for about a second, then said, "Go on and get after her. Me'n Boz will be comin' along quick as we can. Probably catch up 'fore you can get to Del Rio."

Glo hit the door running. Minute later he was nothing more than a fading memory and a lingering cloud of dust.

Getting myself in gear and moving took some doing that morning. Felt like somebody stood over me the night before and beat me with a single tree. Boz appeared to have the same problem. When I finally did scramble up and set to the task, I must have said "Damnation," twenty-five times or more while I saddled my animal. Just about had the job finished when Big Jim Boston strolled up and leaned against the stall rails. I glanced over at him and said, "You knew Clementine had struck out, didn't you, Jim?"

The mountainous smithy had his hands shoved behind the bib on his scarred and soot-covered leather apron. He gifted me with a sheepish nod, then said, "Gal paid me to keep quiet till you boys woke up this mornin', Lucius. Easiest money I've made in more'n a year."

"She paid you?"

"Hell, yeah. Dropped a pair of ten-dollar gold pieces in my hand like they weren't no more'n a couple a grains a sand. You got any idea how long it takes me to make twenty dollars around a windblown dump like Carta Blanca these days?"

"Not a clue," I said and jerked my saddle's cinch strap into place. "Sure it's right tough though."

One skillet-sized paw came from behind Big Jim's apron. He waved at the world outside in a kind of meaningless, general, all-encompassing gesture. "Damned right, it's tough. Takes a couple a weeks to make that much money these days, by Godfrey. Whole town's a-dryin' up like rotten fruit layin' on the ground around a dyin' tree. Couple more years won't be nothin' left but blowin' dust and tumbleweeds 'round here."

"Yeah, well, everybody's got problems, Jim. You shouldn't have let her go it alone. Gal don't have no business roving the countryside around these parts unaccompanied."

"Come on, Lucius, gotta cut me some slack here. What that little gal gave me to keep shut, plus what I made on the horse and saddle I sold her is more money than I've seen at one time in three, maybe four months. Hard to pass on a deal like that when you have a family to feed. 'Sides, she strikes me as the type who can damn well take care of herself."

Snatched up the reins and backed Grizz out of the stall. Led him toward the door with Boston hobbling along beside me. "Unfortunately that's the same mistake a lot of women make these days. But this one's not a woman yet. Only a girl, Jim," I said. "And a mighty young one at that."

"Maybe so, Lucius. But, I'll tell you true, sure as hell wouldn't wanna be either of them ole boys she's a chasin'. I mean, shit, she kilt the hell outta Roscoe Pickett 'thout so much as blinkin' one a them cold blue eyes a hern. Gal looks at me, my blood runs cold."

"How would you know 'bout her doin' for ole Roscoe? You weren't there when it happened."

"Tatum tole me 'bout it. Said it was the damnedest thang he'd ever witnessed. And I seen what was left of Roscoe afterward, when you boys was drinkin' it off."

Hand-rolled dangling from his lips, Boz leaned against his horse and waited for me near a water trough just outside the barn's double-wide door. He nodded and said, "'Fore he left, told Glo to keep an eye peeled for anythin' unusual. Said we'd catch up with 'im quick as we could."

"Told him the same thing myself," I said.

Big Jim shook his head and stared at his feet. Said, "Well, good luck with catchin' up with her, boys."

Boz pulled the smoke from between cracked lips, spit a sprig of tobacco at his feet, then said, "What the hell's that supposed to mean, Jim?"

The big-bellied Boston grinned. "Sold that gal a paint pony that you fellers would have trouble runnin' down on the best day any of you ever had. Big ole horses of yours are all loaded down with men twice that little gal's size and lots of iron. Wouldn't even be a race. Bet them gold pieces she gave me she's already in Del Rio by now."

I gazed over my saddle at the smithy and said, "Well, you'd best offer up a prayer that we do exactly that, Jim. Any harm comes her way, I just might come back here and take it out of your lardy ass."

As I threw a leg over Grizz's back, Boston patted the beast's enormous rump and said, "Ain't gonna worry much 'bout that, Lucius. Figure you'll see the light of reason 'fore then. 'Sides, it'd take you, Tatum, Johnson, and two hard-rock miners armed with sharpened picks to get anything out of an ass the size of mine." He grinned then gave Grizz's rump a resounding smack.

Me and Boz headed out of Carta Blanca like red-eyed, fork-tailed demons were dogging our trail. Along the way, I offered up a silent prayer that we got to Clem before she found Murdock and Atwood. I had the uneasy feeling in my heart that either man would likely kill the girl graveyard dead and not so much as bat an eye, if'n her true identity should be discovered, that is. Could hardly bear the thought of another slaughtered child's funeral in my near future. Whole business weighed mighty heavy on my heart.

17

"...Walked Up to Miss Clementine and Took Her Pistol..."

THE ROAD TO Del Rio plummeted south from Carta Blanca in the manner of a carpenter's snapped chalk line—flat as a tabletop and straight as a planed board. A harsh countryside of colorful wildflowers, stunted greenery, dry washes, and reddish brown, rock-strewn earth fell away on either side of the rugged trace like the last remnants of a hellish world blasted by Satan's own fiery vengeance. A world inhabited with every form of biting, stinging, fanged, and clawed form of instant death a body could imagine.

My heart got to beating like a hand-pumped San Antone fire wagon the more I thought about the deadly consequences of what might well occur should the headstrong Clementine Webb err but a few steps off that rough path. Nothing I could've conjured up, in my wildest imaginings, however, came anywhere close to preparing me for the strange, twisted reality of what lay waiting as we drew to a clod-slinging halt near a Mexican peon's stick-sided, hay-roofed *jacal*, just a few steps off the road, about four miles from downtown Del Rio.

A pen of bleating goats off to one side of the makeshift dwelling raised almighty hell as we stepped off our animals. A troop of scrawny chickens squawked, flapped, and scattered in every direction and added to the general hubbub of racket caused by our thunderous arrival.

A buck-nekkid child of about three or four stood in the hut's open doorway and sucked his thumb. A disembodied female arm snaked from the interior dark and drew him away as we approached the place on foot.

His ever-present shotgun draped over one arm, Glo rose from a shaded bench beneath the pitiful shack's stingy overhang. He strode out to meet us, handed me a fresh-filled canteen, and said, "Ain't gonna believe what I gots to tell you, Mistuh Dodge."

I took a swig of the refreshing liquid, then handed it off to Boz. Wiping my damp lips on the sleeve of my shirt, I said, "Well, gonna hope over hope it's good news."

Glo shook his head. He narrowed his gaze and peered off to the south, as though distracted. "Naw, sur. Cain't say as how it is. Don't appear good at all. Not to me. Leastways on the surface of it."

Boz dragged his hat off and upended the canteen over his sweaty mop of hair. He wagged his soaked, dripping noggin back and forth like a wet dog. Managed to sling huge, soaking drops of the water all over himself, me, and pretty much everything else within ten feet.

He offered the canteen back to Glo, then slicked his hair down with one hand and said, "Well, go on ahead, Glo. Tell us. Might as well have it all. Cain't be that bad. Can it?"

Glo stared at his feet again. The canteen still dangling from the strap in his hand, he glanced up, then pointed toward the road behind us. "Pert sure I found Murdock and Atwood's trail. Neither one of 'em made any effort to cover up. Miss Clem, her tracks are right on top a what those bad men left." He stopped and for several seconds didn't say anything more but let the container of water fall to the ground next to one foot.

"Well," I said and impatiently motioned for him to go on.

Our old friend glanced up and nodded toward the spot he'd pointed out before. "Whole trail got right messy over yonder by that big rock, 'tother side of the road."

"Whaddaya mean by got pretty messy?" Boz said.

"Well, near as I could figurate, Mistuh Boz, when they got here, sometime late yesterday afternoon, Murdock and Atwood met up with two other riders over yonderways. 'Pears them others came straight outta Del Rio, joined up with them two murderin' skunks I 'uz trailin', then they all rode on back into town together."

"But you're just figuratin' on that one, right?" Boz said. "Actual events might not have transpired quite that way a'tall."

"Well, naw, suh, Mistuh Boz. Actually happened exactly that way," Glo said and hooked a thumb toward the *jacal.* "See, the feller what lives here, name of Benito Suarez, tells as how he seen them fellers a-sittin' they hosses and talkin' for several minutes 'fore they struck out for town."

"What about the girl? What about her?" I said.

Glo shook his head. A pained look scrunched his tense, ebon brow into a series of darker, tighter lines. "Well, I followed her and the rest of 'em on into town, see. She trailed up right behind 'em others."

"Little gal went into Del Rio behind Murdock, Atwood, and a pair of unknowns? That what you're tellin' us?" Boz said.

"Yah, suh. Course, gotta remember, she come on quite a few hours later. But sho' 'nuff, that's what I'm sayin' all right. Think I come close to catchin' her 'bout the time she reined up out front of a joint on Del Rio's Main Street named the Broke Mill Saloon."

"Came close?" Boz said.

"Couldna been behind her more'n a minute or two. Oddest of circumstances though, don't you know. Seems as how Murdock, Atwood, and them other two was standin' outside under the Broke Mill's awning when she rode up. Gal musta stopped when she seen somethin', or somebody, familiar. Confronted them boys like she's gonna kill 'em all right on the spot. I watched a goodly bit of the noisy business from the doorway of a big ole grocery store and dry-goods outfit, 'tother side of the street."

"Confronted? Confronted?" Boz blustered. "How'n the hell would Clem know who to confront? Girl wouldn't have known Murdock and Atwood from a pair of red-eyed cows."

"Didn't say her attention was aimed at either of them boys. Right doubtful she recognized either one of them skunks," Glo said and eyed each of us as though heavily burdened by some kind of mystery-laced secret.

I rubbed my jaw with the knuckles of one hand and said, "You mean to say Clementine challenged one of the two men we haven't identified yet?"

A reluctant nod of the head, and Glo added, "Yah, suh, that's the story for sure. Swear 'fore Jesus, Mistuh Dodge, gal acted like she done knowed one of them men. Most like she mighta knowed him all her life. Thought it was right strange-like and mysterious myself."

Boz spanked one leg with his hat. "Now wait a second. This ain't makin' no kind of reasonable sense. Let's back up some. Go at it from the beginning. Start with a place where I can get a real handle on this, Glo."

Glo ran a hand up to the side of his head, scratched a spot over one ear, and looked puzzled. He said, "Well, like I done said, I followed the trail on into town. Spotted Miss Clementine outside the Broke Mill. Slipped up on that store's covered porch to see what was happenin'."

"Store's covered porch," I mumbled.

"Yah, suh. Did kinda surprise me some when I seen

Miss Webb a-standin' there in the street. She had that little pistol of hers out, you know. Appeared she 'uz a yellin' at them four men what was just a standin' on the boardwalk out front of the saloon."

"Confronted them right out in the street?" Boz mumbled.

"Yah, suh. Well, kinda. Started out like that but didn't last, you know?"

"No, we don't, Glo. Go on, clarify this thing for us," I said.

He took a deep breath and ran a finger back and forth under his nose as though something was tickling his upper lip. He coughed, then backed up again. "See, I got there right behind the girl. Seen her jump off that pony Big Jim done sold her. Bear, he right in the middle of it all, growlin' and snappin'. She went and pulled her pistol. Goes to yellin' at one of the fellers on the porch."

"You hear any of the conversation?" I said.

"No, suh. Couldn't, for certain sure, make out what was being said. Too far away. But, lawdy, Mistuh Dodge, that 'ere little gal was some kinda fierce upset with one a them fellers in particular. Sounded most like she called him ever kinda name she could lay her tongue on."

"You didn't recognize the man Clem singled out?" I said.

"Naw, suh. Never seen that particular man before."

"So, standing outside the Broke Mill Saloon there was Atwood, Murdock, a feller you didn't know that the Webb girl was yellin' at, and one other gent. You recognize the other gent, the forth one, by any chance?" Boz said, while swiping at the drenched, inside band of his hat with a faded bandanna.

Glo stared at the ground and kicked at the brittle, dusty earth with the toe of one worn boot. "Yah, suh. Sorry to say, but I knowed 'im alright. I done seen 'im before. Took a spell of studyin', but I knowed 'im for sure."

A second or so of silence followed before I said, "Well, you gonna tell us, or do we rub the bumps on your head and hope it just comes to us through our fingertips?"

Glo almost looked embarrassed when he hissed, "Hateful to say, but I'm pert sure it were Eagle Cutner, Mistuh Dodge. Didn't recognize him at first. Like I said, too far away. Got a better look a minute or so after the dance started. Man turned my way, pushed his hat back. That's when I recognized him. Was Cutner alright."

Boz's hat slipped from his fingers and plopped upright onto the peon's manure-covered yard. He stared at Glo, as if the man had slapped him across the face with a paper bag full of rotten cow guts that had a hole in the bottom of it. Came nigh on to whispering when he said, "Shit almighty. For sure? Eagle 'Mad Dog' Cutner?"

"You're absolutely certain, Glo?" I said. "Ain't no doubt the man you saw Clem jawin' at was traveling with Mad Dog Cutner, Pitt Murdock, and Tanner Atwood?"

"Yah, suh. 'S right as rain. Scared the pure bejabberous hellfire outta me, Mistuh Dodge. Figured on bringin' that little gal back this way with me, leastways till I seen Cutner. Always heard as how that man's a good one not to mess with. Bet I've heard a hundred people tell as how he's meaner'n ten acres of snakes and will kill you dead as Hell in a Baptist preacher's front vestibule. Most folks say he's killed more people than a body can read about in the first three books of the Bible. Worse, he's had his evil ways wid more women than any dozen other men'll ever know in a lifetime."

I could see the puzzled pain in Boz's eyes when he said, "Do you believe this, Dodge? Three of the worst killers in Texas and they're all here, together, at the same time. Two of 'em just recently left the company of them stinkin' Pickett brothers for the company of a murderer and brutal rapist of the first water like Eagle 'Mad Dog' Cutner. And somehow, they're all related to the massacred family of a little-known state senator name of Webb. All them poor folks killed on property we're responsible for."

I felt like my brain flip-flopped inside my skull. Rubbed one temple with a fingertip. "I thought sure as how ole Mad Dog was locked safely away in prison over in Huntsville. Seems I heard tell as how he finally got caught in the very act of committing heinous acts on a lady from down Reynosa way."

"Me, too," Boz mumbled.

Right certain I looked most like the man who'd been slapped sillier than a bag full of tumblebugs when I said, "Anything else you can tell us, Glo? Anything else you might recall but didn't mention."

"Naw, suh. 'Cept that feller I didn't recognize, he stepped off the saloon's board porch, walked up to Miss Clementine and took her pistol away like he was dealin' with his very own child. Like he was her father, or somethin'. And that's when Pitt Murdock went and shot the dog. Kilt poor ole Bear like he warn't nothing more'n a passin' nuisance."

Boz snatched his hat off the ground and whacked it against his leg again. A roiling cloud of powdery dust puffed up around him. Gritted his teeth and snarled, "Damnation. You mean to tell me the son of a bitch shot Bear?"

"Yah, sur, Mistuh Boz. Kilt that poor unarmed animal deader'n Santa Anna. Little gal went to screeching like a gut-shot panther. That there feller I didn't know grabbed her by the wrist and set to draggin' her off sommeres. But I ain't sure to this very minute exactly where they went. Just seemed to vanish of a sudden, like a couple a puffs of driftin' smoke carried away by an invisible wind."

Felt like I was eating an entire beehive when I snapped, "Murdock went and killed Bear, did he? Well, he'll pay for that, by God. I'll see to it if it's the last thing I ever do. Dog never hurt a soul—lest he was told he could."

Boz looked like a man whose fevered brain was about

to explode when he growled, "You sure you didn't see anything else we need to know about?"

Glo stared at his feet again. "Naw, suh. Didn't stick around after I seen that feller take Miss Clementine's pistol away and Murdock went and kilt Bear. Figured there weren't nothin' a man alone, like me, could go a doin' with gents like Murdock, Atwood, and Mad Dog Cutner hangin' around. Decided as how I'd best be gettin' on back this way fast as I could 'fore somethin' happened to me. Hoofed it back so's I could let you fellers know what's a waitin' for us just down the road a piece."

There was more than a bit of shuffling and dirt kicking after that. Finally, Boz pawed at the grip of his belly gun and said, "Well, how you wanna handle this poisonous mess, Dodge? Go along with anything you can bring to mind."

I shook my head, then said, "Not sure, and that's a pure fact, Boz. Hatful of unknowns in this twisted spider's nest. Sure don't want to do anything to jeopardize Clem's young life, if we can keep from it. However we go at this manure pie, though, don't sound like it's gonna be any kind of party, does it?"

Boz squinted and pushed at his hip pistol's shiny, well-used grip with the heel of his gun hand. He scratched a whiskered chin, then said, "Well, here's how I see it, Lucius. We might as well just go on ahead and grab the bull by the tail. Face on up to a really bad situation. Don't you think?"

"Yeah, suppose you're right," I offered. "If nothing else, we should still have the advantage of surprise on our side. No way any of those boys can have the slightest inkling we're fogging up behind them, unless Clem lets that particular cat out of the bag before we can get to her."

Boz unlimbered the cross-draw hand cannon snugged against his bony left hip. He flipped the loading gate open, then rolled the cylinder down his arm, and eyeballed the primers of each round. "Might as well start at the Broke Mill," he said. "I could sneak around back while you and Glo hit 'em from the front. That way we can brace whoever might still be hanging around from both directions. Confronted by enough guns, maybe they'll think twice 'bout getting all froggy and jumping into a fight."

"Sounds like a good 'nuff plan to me," I said. "Would like to talk to at least one of them skunks 'fore we have to kill the whole damned pack though."

"Well, you know that might prove hard to do, Lucius. Especially if the girl's still somewhere nearby and they can get at her," Boz said and re-holstered his weapon.

"What about local law?" I said.

"Ain't enough to worry ourselves over," Glo said. "Del Rio's got a town marshal, but way I done heard it, he don't do much but shovel all the horse manure outta the streets, keep the pigs run off and sech. Locks up a drunk railroader now and again. Railroad takes care of most of its own problems. Have their own troop of lawmen for dealin' with railroad problems."

"Hell with local law then," Boz said. "We're Texas Rangers, by God. Go wherever'n the hell we need to and do whatever we have to do when the occasion presents itself. Personally think we should stick to the plan. March right in, brace any of them bad boys as we can find. If that don't work, we can always adjust our methods to whatever the situation requires."

So, that's how we decided to play it. Got ourselves mounted and headed straight for the Broke Mill Saloon. Tied our animals outside a grocery and mercantile across Del Rio's main thoroughfare named Rocha's.

Wagon traffic passing up and down the street didn't pan out near as problematic as I'd figured it might. Glo allowed as how most of the railroad's numerous track crews were probably somewhere out west of town and wouldn't return until a good bit after dark. Sounded reasonable to me.

Boz pulled his cut-down shotgun. He hoofed it for the alley between the Broke Mill and a leather-working outfit, where it appeared the owner mostly dealt in custom-made saddles.

According to my big-ticking Ingersoll pocket watch, Glo and me gave Boz five minutes to get situated. Then we sauntered across the near-deserted thoroughfare to a spot on the boardwalk out front of the watering hole's fancy, bloodred batwing doors.

Being as how Pitt Murdock would for sure recognize my face first jump out of the box, I had Glo peek inside and give me a description of the layout. He stared over the door for near a minute before he nodded to the left and held up two fingers. "'S Murdock and Atwood," he hissed.

Seemed some of our prey had gone missing. Didn't matter one whit to me. I pulled at Glo's sleeve and said, "Either of 'em goes for his weapon before we can brace 'em, don't you dare hesitate. Send 'em straight to Jesus."

We pushed our way inside. Unlimbered my belly gun as I stepped across the joint's rugged threshold. I was immediately enveloped by a dark curtain of interior coolness. Cocked the weapon and held it next to my leg as we quickly sidestepped to the right. Heard the heavy hammers come back on Glo's long-barreled Greener.

We eased our way over to the middle of the narrow, oblong room and took up spots about midway of a marble-topped, hand-carved, mahogany bar. Other than that astonishingly out-of-place liquor serving counter, wasn't much that could be called fancy about the Broke Mill Saloon in the remotest stretch of the word's definition.

The joint sported a dozen or so crude tables along the wall on our left. Spittoons the size of a Messican's favorite sombrero were jammed under virtually every table and a thick layer of fresh sawdust covered the rough-cut board floor. Customers were scattered here and there, but not that many.

A snooker table, in serious need of a new covering of felt, filled the open bit of floor space at the far end of the bar. A couple of beer-swigging cowboys smoked hand-rolled ciga-reets and bumped balls back and forth. I spotted Boz standing near a potbellied stove in the corner opposite the dilapidated billiards table.

I can't even begin to say how happy it made me when I spotted those two skunks huddled together like a couple of old biddies perched on the last railing in a henhouse. They were sitting at a table near the back of the room. Had their heads together and were engrossed in such deep, whispering discussions that neither of them appeared aware of me and Glo—leastwise, not at first.

A number of the regular tipplers sure enough took notice of our arrival, though. Right difficult not to detect a pair of heavily armed, hard-looking men who appear on the prowl for a fight. Several of the red-faced drunks eyeballed us like we carried some form of horrible disease that needed to be avoided at all costs. We had barely got situated when a good many of those boys threw down the remnants of their drinks and scurried for the door like cockroaches running from the light.

Guess me and Glo stood there next to the bar for nigh on fifteen seconds, letting everything sort itself out, before Pitt Murdock glanced over the rim of his dripping whiskey glass and spotted us. I flashed a friendly grin his direction and nodded like we were long-lost family that hadn't seen each other in a spell.

I thought sure the man would have a brain-killing, eye-popper of a stroke. The beaker of panther sweat he held between trembling fingers hung on his bottom lip as if he'd suddenly become petrified. The ropelike scar I'd put across his ugly countenance, with a pistol barrel, glowed pink and suddenly got pinker, then damn near turned bloodred.

Color flooded up in the man's neck and tinted his ears. Another second or so of glaring at me, and he threw the entire shot of hooch down in one swallow. He slammed the glass onto the tabletop with a resounding thud, then reached over and touched Tanner Atwood on the arm. He cut a rheumy, bloodshot gaze back our direction and nodded.

Atwood twisted in his wobbly, creaking seat, then let one hand fall beneath the table. He glared at me like he wanted to twist my head off and take a dump down the hole left in my neck. Then he whispered something to Murdock from the corner of a sneering, twisted mouth. The pair of them got to looking right wormy, but calmed a bit when Murdock glanced over his shoulder and spotted Boz standing in the corner behind them with his shotgun pointed their direction.

I nudged Glo with my elbow and whispered, "Well, let's stroll on over and say howdy."

Tension in the room shot through the roof as we moved to a spot less than ten feet from that pair of murderous swine. Couple of the remaining local boozehounds finally realized something dangerous was definitely afoot. Could see it on their pinched faces as they hastily threw back what remained of their most recent beaker of scamper juice and headed for the safer climes of anyplace except where gunfire might be about to ensue. Hollow-eyed Death himself had very definitely strolled into the Broke Mill. Anyone who could get out of Ole Bony Finger's way was, for damned sure, heeling it for the perceived safety afforded them somewhere out along Del Rio's central thoroughfare.

18

"DO YOUR WORST."

PITT MURDOCK BROUGHT both hands up to the tabletop, pushed his chair back onto two legs, and said, "You're just about the last man on this earth I expected to see today, Dodge. Swear to Jesus you are."

Cocked pistol still held behind my leg, I grinned and said, "Sorry to put a crimp in your drinkin', Pitt."

Murdock twisted his stringy-haired head to one side like a mangy dog about to lift a foot and scratch a flea-riddled ear. He said, "See, Dodge, I done heard tell as how you'd went and got kilt all to hell and gone over in Rio Seco. 'Course I offered up prayers of thanks soon's that more'n welcome news hit my baby-pink, shell-like ears."

Showed him as many teeth as I could manage, when I smiled again. "Well, Pitt, all I can say 'bout that is that the numerous ugly rumors of my unfortunate, bloody, and unplanned-for demise have been greatly exaggerated."

"As my friend Atwood, here, and I can well see," he grumbled. "Damn near breaks our hearts—as I'm sure you can well imagine. See, I hate your law-bringin' ass for the way you went and treated me in the past."

I glared at the idiot and snapped, "Be totally truthful, I couldn't care damned less how you feel, Murdock— heartfelt or otherwise. Come here today to take you into custody for murder."

He flashed me an insincere, shocked grin. "What murder? Doan know nothin' 'bout no murder."

"That's bullshit. You know exactly what murder I'm talking about. Tracked you boys directly here from the scene of the slaughter. Already took care of the Pickett boys. They're all deader than a six-card poker hand. My friends and I killed the bejabbers out of 'em yesterday."

Murdock shot Tanner Atwood a look that could've peeled paint off a barn door.

"You cain't prove none a that," Atwood mumbled and glared at me like a cornered weasel.

"Don't have to prove anything," I said. "Figure as how we're just gonna kill the hell outta both you skunks soon as we find out what we came for. 'Course I might be prone toward a bit of leniency if you get to telling me what I want to know, and right damned quick."

Murdock squirmed in his seat. "And just what is it you think we can tell you about anything, lawdog?"

From his vantage point in the back corner near the door, Boz called out, "Enough of this bullshit. Where's the girl, Pitt? Give 'er up and maybe we won't kill the pair of you today. Just maybe we'll let you start runnin' again and live a little bit longer. Then run you down later and kill you like the rabid coyotes you are."

Atwood threw a snarling glance over his shoulder at Boz, then swung back around my direction. "What girl?" he said, as if he were something akin to an innocent babe.

"We don't know nothin' 'bout no girl," Murdock grumped. Then he spat a fist-sized gob of tobacco juice into the glop-covered spittoon on the floor next to his chair leg.

"Well, now, Pitt, my man, that's exactly the wrong answer to Ranger Tatum's rather pointed question," I offered.
"Gonna have to come up with something better than that.
A lot better, as a matter of pure fact. Otherwise I just might
have a problem keeping ole Boz from cutting loose with
that big-bore scattergun of his and splattering you two barn
weasels all over hell and yonder."

Murdock slid both hands off the table and raised them
to his chest. Palms out, he looked like a man attempting to
hold off an attacker. "Now, I can most certainly see that
you boys mean business, Dodge. Don't want any of you to
go and jump the gun here and do something the pair of us
might end up regrettin' a minute or so later."

"The hell with 'em, by God," Atwood growled under
his breath.

I said, "Should you manage to live more'n another
minute, Pitt, way I recall it, think both you ole boys are
supposed to be locked up in an iron-barred cell over in
Huntsville. Figure, even if we don't kill you, we're gonna
have to take the pair of you into custody at the very least.
Have some of our law enforcement friends look into why
you're not in some stinkin' cell where you belong. Very
likely have to send you back to prison soon as we can. Lock
you up so you can go back to pickin' peas and choppin'
cotton for the state for a few more years. You bastards are
a menace to society."

Atwood twisted in his chair as if his pants were about to
burst into flame. He said, "Ain't nobody sendin' me back to
Huntsville, Dodge. And that's for damned certain. I done
had all of that hellhole I'm willing to take in this lifetime,
by God."

"Where's the girl?" I said.

Crazed eyes twirling in their rheumy sockets, Murdock
slapped the tabletop with a calloused palm and snapped,
"We don't know nothin' 'bout no girl, Dodge, and that's
the truth of it."

"Guess you don't know anything 'bout killing my dog right outside the door of this place earlier today, do you? Or rubbin' out most of an entire family name of Webb yesterday mornin'," I said.

If I had walked over, snatched his hat off, then pissed on his head, don't think Pitt Murdock or Tanner Atwood, either one, would've been any more surprised and shocked. Both men set to fidgeting and looking sneaky.

Murdock cut a shifty-eyed, worried glance at Atwood, then said, "Well, now, wait a second, Dodge. Maybe we can work something out here. You done gone and mentioned it twice, but I swear we don't know nothing 'bout no family gettin' rudely slaughtered. But seems like I might remember somethin' 'bout a girl showin' up here earlier today. Yeah, maybe I do."

"Best keep that rain barrel of a mouth of yours shut 'bout that particular subject, Pitt, or anything else this lawbringin' bastard mentions," Atwood snapped. "Just shut the hell up and right by-God now. Talkin' to this son of a bitch can get you killed, and right quicklike too."

"Being as how we've already sent three men to the grave of recent. And being as how I'm feelin' almost generous, you tell me where the girl is, Pitt, and I might consider letting the two of you get up and walk right out of here. Guess I could even let you have a day's worth of head start, maybe two, before we come find you and then kill you," I said.

A look of relief washed over Murdock's face. "Ain't kiddin' now, are you? We can just walk on away from here?"

"That's what I said. Have my word on it. Let you boys walk right on out. Have forty-eight hours' head start. Hell, you could probably be in Nuevo Laredo by then. Sipping tequila and sporting a Mexican senorita on each arm."

"Well, I . . ."

Murdock didn't get to finish his thought. In a barely audible tone, Atwood hissed, "Shut the hell up. Damn your stupid ass. This bunch *might* not kill us. But, by God, you go and open your mouth and I can pretty much gar-n-tee Cutner'll show up, and he for damn sure will. That crazy bastard'll chase us to Hell's front doorstep to rub us out. So shut your gob."

With both hands resting atop the table once again, a look of considerable distress chewed its way onto Pitt Murdock's scarred, greasy countenance. "Look, Dodge, here's the thing. Maybe the girl I'm thinkin' 'bout ain't the one you're lookin' for."

"Then again maybe she is, you stupid son of a bitch," Boz yelled from his corner.

Murdock's weasely gaze darted from Glo, to me, to Boz, and back again. Then he said, "Blond, blue eyes, maybe sixteen . . ."

Then, I swear 'fore Jesus, the entire top of that poker table exploded with a thunderous, ear-splitting report. Shards of glass from a shattered whiskey bottle, wood fragments from the tabletop, and chunks of green felt filled the air like an angry swarm of multicolored bees.

About half a heartbeat later, I came to the stunned realization that Tanner Atwood had fired a single pistol shot that caught Pitt Murdock beneath the chin. A .45-caliber slug bored through all the bony passages of ole Pitt's sizable skull and exited through the top of his surprised noggin.

The thuggish bastard's hat flew off, followed by a shower of brain matter that splattered the wall behind him. He twitched, wiggled a bit, then came to rest sitting upright in his chair. A budding, flowerlike gusher of blood spouted from the hole in his head. Unmoving, he stared at the ceiling with frozen eyes, while a ropy stream of gore coated everything within arm's length.

I had my weapon up like double-geared lightning. A nigh on deafening blast from the two-and-a-half-pound Colt delivered a chunk of lead that hit Tanner Atwood in the upper right side of his chest. Monstrous, slow-moving pellet knocked him out of the chair in the manner of some enormous, invisible hand that had reached down from Heaven's front doorstep and slapped the unmerciful hell out of him. Wasn't exactly a killer shot. Needed his sorry ass alive. My slug caught the worthless bastard in just the right place to jar his weapon loose and paralyze him to the point where he couldn't do much of anything after being shot. Except maybe roll around on the floor and moan like a dying wolf.

I waved Boz and Glo off quick as I could. A thick cloud of spent gun smoke from the two pistol shots still swirled around the table. Didn't want either of them cutting loose with those big ole shotguns of theirs and accidentally blowing Atwood to blood-soaked smithereens before we had a chance to talk with him.

I hustled over to the squirming, groaning killer and pulled him into a sitting position by the collar of his shirt and vest. Slapped the hell out of him in an effort to bring his rubbery, swirling eyes out of the top of his head and back into focus.

Then I got right up in his face and yelled, "You've done for your trail mate, Atwood. He ain't gonna be talkin' to no one but God from now on. My unanswered question falls to you. Where's the girl, damn you? You men helped murder her whole family. She's the only one left alive, you worthless son of a bitch. Now give it up. Where is she?"

He grunted and made a series of guttural sounds like a dog being drowned. Then, between frothy, blood-soaked gurgles, he said, "Hell with you, Dodge. Hell w-w-with all of you."

I couldn't believe the cold-eyed boldness of the evil snake's response. Pretty sure an uncontrolled look of frustration and consternation creaked itself across my brow. Tell the truth I felt totally stymied. Then, as it sometimes happens, fate stepped up and took a hand in Tanner Atwood's dwindling time amongst the living.

19

"... WEBB GAVE HER TO EAGLE CUTNER."

BOZ STROLLED OVER. He glanced down at the wounded outlaw as if he'd found a dung beetle swimming on its back atop his bacon-and-egg breakfast. He flashed a crooked grimace of a grin at Atwood, then placed a foot on the wounded man's heaving chest and pushed him onto his back again. He ground the stacked heel of his boot into the fresh bullet wound the way a man would squash some kind of poisonous spider. That mean-mouthed, bold-as-brass outlaw squealed like a baby piglet, then whimpered in the manner of an injured child.

"Man asked you a question, you dyin' son of a bitch," Boz growled. "Best come up with an answer for Ranger Dodge, and be quick about it, or you'll sure as hell wish you had. Get me to working on you, mister, and you'll wish you'd stayed the hell away from the Devils River country like it was infested with the black plague."

From behind a mask of torment and pain, Atwood pawed at the bullet wound and said, "S-S-Screw you, Tatum. I ain't got nothin' to say to either of you badge-totin' turds."

Boz turned his head slightly sidewise, then snarled, "'Fore you leave this world, you skunk-ugly son of a bitch, and meet up with a forgiving Jesus for judgment, I'm gonna make you wish you'd never seen my face. I'm right on the ragged edge of becoming the worst element of your most horrible nightmare."

Atwood huffed and puffed and groaned again. Bloody slobbers dribbled from both corners of his mouth. He said, "Hell with you, Tatum. You law-bringin' b-b-bastards ain't gettin' nothin' outta me today. A-A-And you can take that to the nearest Cattleman's Bank. Put it on deposit and draw interest, by God. I done kilt P-P-Pitt to keep him from tellin'. D-D-Die 'fore I'll tell you another goddamned thing."

Boz shook his head as though amazed by Atwood's brazen comeback. He held his big popper out for me to take. Then he hauled ole Tanner up off the floor by his shirtfront. Didn't like the look I saw on my friend's face one little bit. I detected something crazed and dangerous there I'd only seen a few times before. I knew beyond any doubt that something worse than awful might be afoot when he got that look on him. A wildness had crept into the man's eyes that would've given a rabid grizzly pause. Ole Boz didn't lose control often, but when he did, Katy bar the door.

Glo and I stood aside and watched as Boz dragged the blood-gushing, screeching brigand across fifteen feet of rough-cut pine flooring and then jerked him on top of the saloon's snooker table. Atwood took on all the aspects of a dead man laid out in a green-felt coffin. He appeared ready for burying when Boz let him loose and then turned toward the half-filled rack of cue sticks hanging on the back wall.

The cowboys who'd been shooting snooker when we arrived scampered from behind the bar. Spurs a-jingling, chaps a-flapping, they hit the saloon's batwings in a dead run. They came near removing those café doors from their squeaky hinges when they rammed their way through them so hard. I could hear that pair of exited brush poppers yelling back and forth to each other as they hoofed it down the street and away from any real or perceived danger.

The hairless, sweaty-scalped bartender eased his way from a hidey-hole beneath his liquor selling counter as well. He waved a damp bar towel at us and yelped, "Now, see here. This is a damned nice establishment. Nicest in town, by God. We ain't never had anything occur to match this in the Broke Mill before."

I said, "Might want to follow your customers on outta here, mister. Not sure you want to be a witness to what's about to happen."

"You fellers got no right behaving in such a manner, by God," the drink wrangler said. "Killin' folks in cold blood and such. Think you should leave this establishment right this minute. Right this very minute, by God."

"Naw, suh, we didn't kill nobody," Glo said. "Man on the pool table, he the one what kilt that feller sittin' yonder in the chair. Naw, suh, we ain't kilt nobody—yet."

Boz snatched a cue stick from the half-filled rack and carefully checked the blue-chalked, leather-padded tip of the polished length of hickory as though about to start a fresh game. Then he whirled around but didn't even glance at the mouthy drink slinger when he growled, "You don't want to see somethin' awful, mister, you'd best beat a hot path away from here like Ranger Dodge suggested. Don't let them swingin' doors hit you in your fat ass on the way out."

The barkeep started backing his way toward the street but couldn't keep his wagon wheel of a mouth shut. He shook that rag at us one more time before he hit the boardwalk and said, "I'm goin' for the town marshal. Gonna put a stop this promiscuous behavior, right by-God now. You fellers best be gone when the marshal gets here. Yessiree, bob sir. He's a dangerous man. Kill all three of you at the drop of a hat."

Pool stick that Boz grasped in both hands sounded like another pistol shot when he cracked it over one knee. He held up the two freshly rendered pieces as though looking for something special. Compared both halves like a jeweler working on an antique watch. Laid the narrowest and sharpest of the pair on the table next to the side cushion. One handed, he waved the big end over Atwood's nose.

"You're gonna answer Ranger Lucius 'By God' Dodge's questions, Tanner, or I'm gonna beat the hell out of you," Boz said and grinned. "You don't get to jabberin' like a trained parrot, swear 'fore a benevolent Jesus, you're gonna wish your mama'd never given birth to your sorry ass by the time I get finished."

Atwood rolled his wobbly head Boz's direction. He let out an overly confident snicker. I've always felt the man's conduct was ill considered at best, but I thought him downright crazy when he hissed between bloody teeth, "Do your worst, Tatum."

Chest shot, bleeding like hell, well on his way to a certain death, no doubt in my mind the man couldn't have been thinking straight. This misguided challenge was all the encouragement Randall Bozworth Tatum needed.

Those poorly chosen words had barely died on Atwood's lips when my friend brought his homemade club up two-handed and whacked that mouthy outlaw a crushing blow across the bridge of his nose. Gristle and bone made a cracking noise like a rotten cottonwood limb breaking. Damn near made me want to puke my spurs up. People out in the street must've heard it. And if not that, then they heard the piercing, surprised screech that escaped the man's twisted lips before he passed slap out and lay on that table in the manner of a dead man for near a minute.

A gusher of blood squirted from the middle of Atwood's face and bedecked the wall behind the snooker table like red paint delivered from a fire hose. Boz stepped aside to avoid getting doused. Then he examined the bulbous end of the heavy stick and said, "Well, don't appear as how his nose damaged my club much. Big, ugly honker of his barely put a dent in it." Then he turned to Glo and said, "Bring me a bucket of beer."

Glo looked puzzled. He swayed from foot to foot and toed at the boards under his feet. "Bucket of beer, Mistuh Boz?"

Tatum propped his club against the wall and said, "Yeah, Glo. A bucket of beer. A bucket of beer. Gonna take me a much-needed drink, then use what's left to revive this bastard."

I could tell our old compadre didn't care for the direction things had taken. Not sure I did, either, but I knew there was no stopping Boz once he'd started down such a path. Any attempt to bring a halt to his efforts could put a man's life at risk.

Shaking his head the whole time, Glo shuffled over the beer tap behind the bar. With a metallic click, he laid his heavy shotgun on the drink serving station's polished marble top. He dragged out a tin bucket from somewhere and proceeded to fill it.

"This ain't good, Mr. Boz," Glo said when he handed the froth-covered pail of liquid over to Tatum.

Boz turned the metal container of cold liquor up and took a long swallow. Wiped suds from his drooping moustaches with one arm, then walked over and poured a glass or two into Tanner Atwood's crushed, gore-spattered face. The pitiless child killer coughed, choked a bit, then revived enough to cough and spit out a fist-sized glob of bloody drool and broken teeth onto his own chest.

Atwood's eyes swam in their sockets when he tried to sit up. He said, "G-G-God A-A-Almighty, T-Tatum. N-N-Never figured you for anythin' like this. You done busted my nose. Musta knocked out nigh on half my forkin' teeth, you vicious son of a bitch."

Beneath an arched eyebrow, Boz snarled, "You helped

murder the most part of an entire family, you scum-sucking bastard. Decent, God fearin' people, no doubt. You know where the only one of those folks left living is. Best get to coughin' up her location and right by-God now. Or, I swear 'fore Jesus, Tanner, you're gonna wish yourself dead a thousand times over 'fore the sun goes down today. Get started and it can take me hours to finish up a project like this."

I couldn't believe my eyes or ears. Tanner Atwood actually spit a raspy, blood-soaked chuckle into Tatum's face. He said, "S-S-Screw you and the horse you rode in on, you badge-totin' son of a b-b-bitch." Then he hacked again and spit blood onto my friend's bib-front shirt. Sweet merciful Jesus, but that single act proved a horrendous error in judgment.

Slower than an Arkansas hound dog in August, Boz leaned over and placed the half-full beer bucket on the floor next to one of the snooker table's thick, wooden legs. Then, quick as blue-tinted, pitchfork lightning, he grabbed up his makeshift cue-stick club and went to whacking on Atwood's shins.

My God, but I've never heard such a load of screaming from a single man in all my entire life, before or since. It sounded like Tatum was beating on a metal barrel filled with baby kittens. Made the hair on the back of my neck stand up and sent prickly, crawling chicken flesh running up and down between my sweaty, scrunched shoulder blades like waves on a storm-blasted beach.

Think Boz might've missed his target once or twice and cracked the murderous sack of hammered manure's kneecaps a time or three. Looking back on that unmerciful beating, I'd guess he must've hit that poor, hard-headed brigand ten or fifteen stunning licks before he started slowing down. Appeared to me as how he just suddenly got tired. Decided to give that stick of his a rest.

Once the yelping and screeching died down a bit, Glo

moved up next to me and said, "Mistuh Boz, you gotta stop this. Jus' gotta stop this. Ain't no call for such behavior. We ain't the kind what does such things. We don't be about torturing people. Even low-life, ass-lickin' dogs like this 'un."

The crazed wildness in Tatum's eyes had grown more pronounced. Frightening thing to witness, you ask me. He leaned against the edge of the snooker table as though winded and said, "If you can't handle what it's necessary for us to do, Glo, go outside and wait on the boardwalk till I'm finished. This child-murderin' slug's gonna talk if it takes me till next week to make it happen."

Glo gazed at the bloody mess that had, only a few minutes before, been a bold, self-assured, and confident Tanner Atwood. Great day in the morning, but that killer appeared to be floating in a growing pool of blood. That snooker table resembled the felt-covered floor of a barn where someone had slaughtered a sizable pig.

"Please, Mr. Boz. Let it go," Glo said. "My solemn promise, I'll track down them as took Miss Clementine. You know I can do it. No matter what it takes. I'll start sniffin' out their trail soon's you want. Get on the track right now, might even have 'em in our sights 'fore night can fall. Help you kill 'em."

Boz waved one hand at the battered, groaning, quivering glob of wickedness on the table. He stabbed a finger into Atwood's heaving chest. Then he glared at Glo and said, "This evil bastard knows something he's not telling us. Something that could easily get us all killed graveyard dead. Or maybe get Clementine Webb killed. Or both. Or worse, maybe she's already dead. Top of all that, this tight-lipped weasel helped murder a man, his wife, and three kids in the most brutal fashion I've seen since the days when you and me used to chase them murderin' Comanche all over Hell and Mexico. You forgot that already? Forgot what you saw in that little spot of green out on the river a few miles from the ranch?"

I could tell Glo was getting more agitated with each passing second. "Ain't forgot nothin', by God," he snapped. "I 'uz there when we found them chil'rens, and you know it, Mistuh Boz. It's just that torturin' this poor, damned soul ain't proper. Just ain't the right thing for men like us to be a-doin'."

Think Boz could've bit the shoes off a draft horse when he growled, "Poor soul, my big hairy ass. Tanner Atwood's about as far from a *poor soul* as a livin' body can get. Hell, he just killed one of his own *friends* right in front of our faces. Blew the top of ole Murdock's head clean off to keep the man from talking to us. Did the sorry deed with no more feeling than a body who'd just crushed a louse between his thumb and forefinger."

Glo stared at his feet. "Seen the sorry deed my very own myself, Mistuh Boz. Damn well know as how I 'uz right here when it happened. Seen it," he mumbled.

Boz snatched the pail of beer up and took another long, sloppy swig. He wiped his lips, pulled at the corner of his droopy moustache, and said, "Whatever it takes to save Clementine Webb is as right as rain, far as I'm concerned. Comes a time when good men have to step up and do whatever they have to do in an all out effort to save innocent lives. Right now we have it in our power to save the only remaining member of the entire Webb family. I won't let that chance escape me without finding out exactly what we need to know, Glo."

Glo said, "Be the first to admit as how we done terrible things when we 'uz killin' Comanches back in the bad times, Mistuh Boz. But that were then, this is now, and this is different."

"Not as far as I'm concerned. This is a bad time, too," Boz said and shook a finger in Atwood's direction. "And if I have to drag this son of a bitch down the street by the heels to the nearest butcher's shop and feed him through a hand-crank meat grinder one bloody chunk at a time, then that's what I'm gonna do." He paused, pointed at the batwings and added, "I'll turn his sorry ass into chili meat without a second thought. You can't deal with it, or don't want to deal with it, you need to wait outside 'cause this dance is about to get a helluva lot worse."

A look of pained, muted panic rushed over Glo's face. "What you gonna do now?" he said.

Boz snatched the pointed end of the stick from beneath the pool table's cushioned railing. He held the jagged piece of polished wood up in Atwood's face. Bent over next to the gunny's ear, he hissed, "I'm gonna shove this into the bullet hole Lucius put in his chest, then I'm gonna lean on it till I push it all the way through him and the tip hits the slate under his back."

Atwood sucked in a ragged, terrified gasp. He twisted back and forth like a snake trying to get out of a hot frying pan. Took in a number of terrified, bloody, gurgling, wheezy breaths. "All right," he spat. "All right, for the love of God, I'll tell you whatever you want. Just don't go stabbin' me with the broke end of that stick."

Boz suddenly looked tired to the bone. He tossed the broken piece of hickory onto the floor at his feet. The two-and-a-half-foot-long splinter of wood bounced and made a loud clacking sound, then rolled to a spot against the wall.

My friend snatched his hat off. He wiped thumb-sized beads of salty sweat away from his forehead with the sleeve of his shirt, then tiredly said, "Question's still the same, Atwood. Hasn't changed since first asked. Where's the girl?"

I had to move closer to Atwood's blood-soaked resting place to hear him. In truth, the man appeared but a step or two from his own demise and could barely speak. He said, "God's truth, Tatum, I-I-I don't k-k-know—exactly. Swear I don't. Just know Webb gave her to Eagle Cutner. Told Eagle he could do with her as he pleased."

Atwood's surprising remark shot right past me and Boz.

But Glo heard him well enough. He strode to the table like he just might pick Tatum's stick up off the floor and go back to whacking on Atwood's shins himself. He glared at the outlaw and growled, "You said, '*Webb* gave her to Eagle Cutner.' Ain't that right, mister? Didn't I just hear you say, '*Webb* gave her to Eagle Cutner'?"

"Damned if he didn't," Boz mumbled and scratched a stubble-covered chin. "Heard it myself."

Frothy, pink slobbers dribbled from the corners of Atwood's grinning mouth. He coughed. A gobbet of blood the size of a hen egg squirted out onto his chest. A wet, bloody, almost unearthly chuckle rattled out from somewhere deep inside the dying outlaw. "That's right. 'S exactly what I said. Got you boys doin' a-right smart a-thinkin' now, d-d-don't I?"

20

"WHERE WOULD CUTNER TAKE THE GIRL?"

"PROP ME UP," Tanner Atwood wheezed. "Gotta get me off my back, boys. Can't seem to suck down enough air a-layin' here like this."

Glo grabbed several of the cushions off some of the cane-backed chairs provided for the Broke Mill's snooker lovers. We helped the groaning, back-shooting lowlife into a sitting position and jammed the well-worn pads under his head, neck, and shoulders.

Once we'd got him somewhat comfortable, Boz offered the battered man another run at his tin bucket of beer. Atwood refused. Said, "Could sure 'nuff use some water though, Tatum. Mighty dry right now. Feels like I ain't had a good, long, refreshin' drink of water in years."

While we waited, Glo rummaged around behind the bar and came up with a heavy-bottomed mug filled to the lip with cold, clear water. He helped get some down Atwood's gullet, then, under his breath, I heard him say, "Best get to talkin', Mistuh Atwood. Not sure we can stop Mistuh Boz again, if'n he takes it into his head to go a beatin' on you some more."

"I'll try," Atwood said, then gasped for air. "Gar-n-tee I'll sure 'nuff try."

Glo nodded, then added, "Well, I'll gar-n-tee, if you don't have somethin' important to offer him, little girl's screamin' voice you're gonna hear beggin' for mercy is gonna be yours."

Atwood gulped down near half that mug of liquid before he stopped. 'Course that set the thumb-sized hole in his chest to pumping blood out at a considerably faster pace. He set to clutching at the wound and let out a series of pitiful, near heartrending moans.

All that yelping and moaning got me to thinking as to how the evil skunk might be right on the edge of passing on over to the other side. But to everyone's surprise he perked back up a bit. Appeared the man was holding on with his last fingernail. Guess he didn't want Satan to get a grip on his immortal soul for at least a few more minutes.

Surprised the bejabbers out of me, when, out of nowhere, Boz's hand snaked out. He delivered a rattling, openhanded, five-fingered rap across Atwood's unprotected cheek. Then he grabbed the man by the chin and said, "Don't you dare go and die on us. Swear if you die now, I'll drag you out into the middle of Del Rio's central thoroughfare and set your sorry ass ablaze."

Bubbling, foamy slobber dribbled down Atwood's chin. A look of panicked despair creaked across the outlaw's face when he said, "You wouldn't do that. Tell me you wouldn't do that, Tatum." Then he cast a horrified glance my direction and yelped, "You wouldn't let him do that, would you, Dodge? Would you?"

Appeared to me a serious case of loco was camped behind Boz's eyes when he said, "Don't matter what Dodge thinks. 'Cause I'll damn sure light you up if you don't get to talkin'. You don't give me something substantial, you're gonna burn like a cord of last winter's firewood. Get you flamin' up good while you're still here so the Devil won't have to waste so much effort when you land on his front porch."

In a halfhearted attempt to reassure him, I patted the terrified man on the shoulder and said, "Get on with it. Sure 'nuff wouldn't want to watch you burn."

"Who's this Webb feller? One you said gave Miss Clementine to Mad Dog Cutner," Glo said.

Atwood groaned. Talon-like fingers squeezed the seeping chest wound. Sounded as though he was being strangled when he said, "He's the girl's uncle. There, you happy now?"

"Uncle?" The word popped out of all three of our mouths at the same time.

A self-satisfied, mischievous, almost childlike grin danced across the wounded brigand's quivering, blood-encrusted lips. "Yeah. Crazy, ain't it. The Honorable Nathan Hawthorn Webb's baby brother. Charles Axel Webb. All us ole boys from Huntsville who've been travelin' with the man of recent call 'im Ax."

As if he'd been slapped, Boz recoiled and took half a step backward. "God save us. Ax Webb. Webb for cryin' out loud. We shoulda known. Shit. I just didn't make the connection. Did you, Lucius?"

"No," I said. "Don't figure I ever would've, either. Just so far beyond the pale as to be nigh on impossible to fathom."

"Why?" Glo said. "Why this man behind killin' his own kin? Turns my stomach just thinkin' on such a heinous crime."

Though racked by waves of easily observable pain, Atwood let out a croupy, staccato laugh. Then he wiped another frothy pile of spittle from his twitching lips. He welded me to the floor with a cold-eyed stare and said, "Might remember as how ole Ax got sent to p-p-prison 'bout five years back for a number of daytime bank robberies he staged all over south Tejas. P-P-Prosecutors tried to nail him with a couple a killing's that took place durin' them particular raids as well. Didn't work. S-S-Still and all, jury sent him up the river for a hundred and f-f-fifty years."

I nodded.

Atwood sucked in a wet, ragged breath, then wheezed, "Whilst rottin' in jail, Ax's younger brother managed to git his smart-alecky self elected to the Texas state senate. Ax felt as how Nathan shoulda done everything he c-c-could to get his elder siblin' outta that hellhole. Didn't happen. Hell, Nathan wouldn't even come for a visit. So, Ax got hisself out."

"He escaped," Boz near whispered.

"Yeah. Brought a bunch of us ole boys with him when he got loose. Hell, we was just sittin' 'round waitin' on the Devil to come take us to perdition. Ax Webb saved us. S-S-Said he had plans for his brother Nathan." Atwood paused. Appeared to give considerable thought to what he was about to say next. "S-S-Sure as hell didn't think the man's plans would involve me b-b-bitin' the last bullet in this stinkin' Del Rio saloon."

Atwood's eyes snapped closed. He gritted his yellow-stained, blood-covered teeth so hard it sounded like squirrels chewing into black walnuts. Grasping fingers clawed at the hole in his chest and twisted a tight knot into the front of his gore-soaked shirt.

"Don't you go and die on us yet," Boz yelped, then grabbed the man by the shoulders and shook him like a rag doll. "Die on me now, by God, and I'll add ten more holes to the one Lucius put in your sorry hide. Then I'll set you on fire."

A big, stupid grin spread over Atwood's pain-racked face as his eyes gradually crept open again. "Thought I 'uz a goner there for a second, T-T-Tatum," he said. "'Pears as how you did, too."

Boz pushed away. He backed off a step and pointed an

accusatory finger in Atwood's face. He said, "Get on with your story, you belly-slinkin' snake. Go passin' out on us again and, by Godfrey, I'll have another go at you with my stick."

A strange, creepy, mocking chuckle emanated from Atwood's hollow-sounding chest. "Huh-a huh-a huh-huh-huh. Time you get through doing ever-thang to me you've threatened, T-T-Tatum, you'll be so wore out you won't even be able to walk. H-H-Have to crawl on your hands and knees all the w-w-way back to your horse."

"Don't worry 'bout me, dry-gulcher. Just keep on talkin'," Boz snapped.

"Well, like I 'uz a s-s-sayin' 'fore tryin' to d-d-die on you, we got shed of Huntsville. Managed to kill a guard or two in the process, though. Course 'at got every lawdog in south Texas a-chasin' us. Had to sneak, hide, and lay low for n-n-nigh on a m-m-month. Finally got ourselves armed up by b-b-breakin' into a hardware emporium up in Kerrville. Then we all headed for Uvalde. Figured we'd help Ax k-k-kill his sorry-assed brother there."

"But somehow the brother figured out you boys were coming," I said. "Man loaded up his family and skipped town."

"Yeah. Did the jackrabbit thang on us. Went to runnin'," Atwood said, then groaned and wiped big beads of sweat off his forehead with the sleeve of his shirt. "So, we set to c-chasin' 'im. Was easy, really. Man warn't much at hidin' his trail."

Boz slapped the grip of his belly gun. "And you bastards caught up with him out on the Devils River not far from land we've been leasing, didn't you?"

Atwood let out a pitiful, raspy, blood-soaked whimper, then offered up a halfhearted nod. "Yeah. G-God help us. We shot that wagon, and them folks standing outside it, all to pieces."

"What 'bout them chil'ren?" Glo said and toed at a spot

on the rough board floor. "You know you'd gone and kilt all them chil'ren?"

The words had barely fallen from Glo's lips when the Broke Mill's batwing doors creaked open. A badge-wearing, red-faced, fat-gutted slug carrying a long-barreled shotgun eased to a point where he stood half in and half out of the doorway.

The saloon's wide-eyed drink wrangler, who'd earlier threatened us with a man-killing town marshal, peeked over one side of the saloon's battered, scroll-topped café doors and made wild pointing motions our direction. He said something to the lawman, who from all appearances might've eaten his own brother, that none of us could plainly hear.

Mr. Fat Gut cocked his head to one side. He listened intently to the yammering bartender for a second or so like an overfed cat mystified by the intricacies of higher mathematics. Finally, he turned away from the near hysteric bartender and said, "What the hell's a-goin' on here? What kinda mischief are you men about?"

Appearing irritated right down to the leather-poor soles of his run-down, well-worn boots, Boz cast a quick, squint-eyed, sneering glare toward the door. He yelled, "We're rangers, you squirrel-brained idiot. This is official ranger business. Best head on back to your office, Marshal. We don't need any of your help. Leave this matter to us. We'll take care of it."

The noisy discussion at the door picked up again and got louder. Appeared Marshal Fat Gut wasn't having any luck dissuading the Broke Mill's angry drink pusher when it came to the slick-pated barkeep's heated complaining.

I lost interest in the pair of yammering morons in less than a barely felt heartbeat. My briefly diverted attention swung back to Atwood just in time to hear him gasp, "Didn't know t-t-them kids was in that wagon till after we'd b-blasted it to bits. Made me s-s-sick when I lit a lantern, looked inside, and seen them pitiful little bodies. Knew right then we 'uz on the short list for a ticket straight to a fiery Hell soon's somebody else come along and found all them dead folks. Just our k-k-kind a luck it'd be three man killers like you b-b-boys."

The blistering argument between the Broke Mill's bug-eyed bartender and Del Rio's visibly reluctant town marshal kept getting louder. The blubbery lawman tried his best to move back out onto the boardwalk but the drink peddler wasn't having any of it. Right quick-like, angry swearing was coming from their direction and painted the air near the door a deep purple.

"Where would Cutner take the girl?" I asked.

Tanner Atwood squirmed in the growing pool of blood beneath his already saturated back. "J-Jus' head on out t-toward Uvalde. Ole Mad Dog keeps a rough c-cabin near the base of Turkey Mountain. Cain't miss the place. Stands out like a sore thumb. 'S sittin' right next to the only road goin' up to the t-top of that overgrown haystack."

Boz pulled a ready-made ciga-reet from his shirt pocket, fired the smoke, then thumped the smoking match onto the floor. He picked the coffin nail from between his lips, and, with an air of suddenly discovered concern, placed it be-tween Atwood's. The gasping man took a single drag on the smoldering tube of rolled tobacco, then motioned for Boz to take it back.

My partner recovered the ciga-reet, then said, "You fig-ure there's anyone else sittin' up there on Turkey Mountain with him, Tanner?"

The rapidly fading outlaw puffed out an abbreviated lung of smoke, coughed, then said, "Have n-no way of knowin' that, T-Tatum. No one else there w-when we first picked him up after our escape from the pen. D-Do know this though. You don't get up there damned quick, Cutner's the kind of feller what'll use that little gal up like a man d-drivin' nails in a fence post to hang b-barbed wire on."

Then, as God is my witness, like a drowning swimmer, Atwood suddenly sucked in one long, ragged breath. Man's entire body jerked as if a massive, unseen hand grabbed him by the buckle on his pistol belt and pulled up. He bowed up on blood-soaked shoulders and went as rigid as a length of steel railing. His eyelids fluttered in the manner of a broken window shade. Then, he made a series of odd grunting noises. He collapsed as Death stepped up, wrapped bony fingers around blood-filled lungs and heart, and squeezed all the man's remaining life out.

After near a minute, when the to-be-expected noises of dying finally stopped coming from the corpse, Glo said, "Think this 'un's done gone on to judgment, Mistuh Boz."

Boz nodded and said, "Yeah. Think he's done went and shook hands with eternity, Glo. Satan oughta have his worthless hide in hand by now. Should be roastin' and toastin' over Hell's cook fires right quick-like."

Pretty soon after that, we left the bodies where they fell and hoofed it for the street and our animals. The local marshal trailed up behind us soon's we hit the dusty, windblown street.

"Name's Isaac Goolsby, fellers. Marshal Isaac Goolsby," he called out as he waddled along. "Reckon you fellers could slow down a second and talk some."

We all nodded but kept on foggin' it.

Goolsby huffed and puffed like a hundred-year-old locomotive as he tried in vain to keep up. "Cain't just go and walk away from this kinda thang so easy, boys. Need some help from you so's I can explain these killin's should anyone come a-pokin' around these parts askin' questions."

Three of us stopped beside our animals long enough to make sure everything was still in order for the run we were about to make to Turkey Mountain. Goolsby sidled up to a spot about ten feet away like he was afraid to get too close. Shotgun laid across one arm, he set to yelling out his endless stream of questions.

"What y'all 'spect me to do? Cain't jus' let you boys go and ride off 'thout explain' this mess. Ain't I got two bodies over yonder in the Broke Mill? Hell, that's two more'n we had all the rest of this year. What the hell am I s'posed to do with 'em ole boys?"

I pulled a square of paper and a stubby piece of pencil from my vest pocket, wrote Cap'n Culpepper's name on it, then mine, then Boz's. Strode over and handed it to the excitable gent.

"Got any problems, just send a letter to our captain care of general delivery in Fort Worth," I said. "Got expenses, let him know. He'll take care of 'em. We'd like to talk this whole mess over with you some more, Marshal Goolsby, but we've got the life of a young woman hanging in the balance. Don't have time, at the moment, to discuss it with you."

Boz threw a leg over his animal's back, wheeled the beast around and gazed down at Del Rio's obviously flusterated lawman. "'S enough you know that those two jokers in the Broke Mill were part of a murderous group of escaped killers that brutally murdered a Texas state senator and most of his family out on Devils River. Girl we're lookin' for is the only member of that same clan as is still living. We don't hurry, might not be able to save her."

Got myself mounted, twirled my animal around beside Boz, and said, "Just do like I told you, Marshal. Cap'n Culpepper'll take care of any problems or questions you might have."

I turned in the saddle to make sure Glo was primed and ready. He pulled at the brim of his sweat-stained, floppy, gray hat and nodded. "Let's turn 'em loose and let 'em buck, Mistuh Dodge." He slapped his mount's muscular rump with the animal's reins, then kicked past Boz and me like a bolt of hair-covered lightning.

As we thundered out of town, Boz glanced over a shoulder at me and yelled, "You think we can get to Cutner 'fore he can kill the girl, Lucius?"

"Don't know, Boz," I yelled back. "But if we don't, swear on my sainted mother's memory, I'll storm the darkest recesses of Hades and bite Satan's horns off to find Eagle Cutner and Ax Webb. And I'll kill 'em both graveyard dead."

Glo assumed all the aspects of a man on a God-sent mission. Took me'n Boz nigh on an hour to catch up with him. By then he'd almost made it to the Sycamore River.

21

"...A Bad One Named Eagle 'Mad Dog' Cutner."

GLO SLOWED A mite. He was walking his mount when I pulled up beside him on the Uvalde stage road. He twisted in the saddle and said, "Have an old friend what has a small horse-raisin' operation few miles 'tother side of the Sycamore, Mistuh Dodge. Anyone 'round these parts knows how to find Eagle Cutner's place up on Turkey Mountain, it's Honus Lavender."

Boz eased up next to me and patted his winded animal's neck. "I remember Honus. He's fought the Co-manche, Messican bandits, and badmen of every sort imaginable down here on the border for more'n fifty years. Hell, the man used to be famous. But, tell the truth, Glo, I thought he was dead. Been rumors of his demise for near a decade, maybe more. Hell, man must be goin' on a hunnert years old if he's still alive."

Appearing pleased to be away from the carnage we'd left strewn all over the Broke Mill Saloon, Glo let a toothy grin play across his ebon face. He gazed east and said, "Man's sho' 'nuff still alive, Mistuh Boz. And he ain't no hunnert years old. 'Course he could be on up there knockin' real hard on seventy, I suppose. Ain't seen him in a few years myself, but I'd bet he ain't changed much."

We turned off the rutted, dust-choked roadway about five miles past the Sycamore and headed in a northeasterly direction from there. Guess we hadn't gone much more than another mile or three when we came on a sweet-running creek that dribbled into the river a few miles off to the west. We let our animals stand in the shallow stream and drink for a minute or so.

On the far side of the ankle-deep waterway, beneath a thick canopy of seventy-foot-tall cottonwood trees, we spotted a rough board-and-batten cabin. The rustic dwelling's only obvious nod toward anything like refinement was a deep, covered porch that ran the entire length of the front façade. A number of comfortable-looking rockers laden with thick pillows sprouted like overgrown plants from one end of the shady, inviting veranda to the other.

Black feller the size of a Concord coach stepped onto the porch as we waded our mounts across the creek and headed up into his leaf-sheltered front yard. Steel-colored hair poked from beneath a hand-ventilated, palm-leaf hat. Muscles as thick as the hawser for a ship's anchor bulged beneath a faded bib-front shirt. He carried a cut-down, double-barreled coach gun in the crook of one arm and eyeballed the three of us with considerable suspicion. Nothing in his appearance, or demeanor, indicated a man of advanced years.

"'S close enough," he called out when were still a good thirty or forty feet away. "You men can just stop right where you are. Get to statin' your business from there."

Boz crooked a finger at Glo and urged him forward with a jerk of the head. Glo heeled his mount and moved two or three steps out ahead of us.

The man on the porch brought the shotgun around, leveled it up, and cocked both barrels.

Glo reined the horse to a stop and raised his hands. Calm as a frog under a cabbage leaf, he said, "Careful with that big popper, Honus. Wouldn't want you to accidently kill any of us."

"Get on with it. Who the hell are you?" Lavender growled.

"Don't you be recognizin' me, Hounus? It's Glo. Your friend, Glorious Johnson."

Took several seconds, but a tight grin began its gradual spread across Honus Lavender's broad, friendly face. "Glorious Johnson. Just do tell. That's for sure 'nuff you, old man?"

Glo let his hands drop, flipped the reins over his horse's neck, and rocked forward and back in the saddle. "Sho 'nuff. Who else you think be coming up on you bold as men like us. Hell, our mamas didn't raise no idiots. Ain't a soul within a hundred miles of here don't know as how you'd be takin' your life in your own hands if you do anything to threaten a man as dangerous as Honus Lavender."

Lavender let the hammers down on the big-barreled weapon and propped it against the frame of his rugged front door. "Just be damn. Never thought to see you again, old man." Then he made a come-on-up motion. Waved us to the hitch rail at one end of his house and said, "Tie all them beasts of yours over yonder by the water trough. Let 'em drink. Then step on down. Come up here in the shade. 'S a sight cooler on the porch."

A chuckle came from deep inside Glo's chest. As he climbed off his horse, he said, "Who you callin' old man, you old coot. Be lookin' like you was around when the Dead Sea was just a little sick."

Fisted hands the size of Carolina hams on his hips, Honus Lavender watched us clamber off our animals and grinned. Scratched his cheek and said, "Well, tell you what, Mistuh Glorious Johnson, looks to me like you be jus' about ready for a warm corner and a checkerboard yo'self. Bet you ain't had nothin' tougher to chew on than

oatmeal gruel in a good ten years. Prolly cain't do nothin'
with a beefsteak but gum it."

Then, a toothy grin plastered on his face, Lavender
hopped off his welcoming porch and the two men embraced
like long-lost brothers. I couldn't help but notice that, for a
man his size and age, Honus Lavender still moved with all
the ease and panther-like grace of a man fully half his age.

After several seconds of shoulder slapping and manly
grunting, Glo backed away and said, "Might remember
Ranger Boz Tatum and Ranger Lucius Dodge."

My hand disappeared into Lavender's like a small
child's would into that of a giant. Then he gave the hand
back, grabbed Boz, and almost shook my friend's arm off.

"Ah, me'n Mistuh Boz we done fought them Comanche devils more'n once. This here man done saved my life
down on the Rio Sabinas some years back, Glo. Comanches was about to turn me into a gelding."

Boz smiled. "Good to see you again, Honus. Was
afeared you didn't recognize me there for a spell."

Lavender kept pumping Boz's extended hand, then
slapped my friend on the shoulder. He threw his massive
head back and laughed. "Didn't. Was just before tryin' to
figure out how I 'uz gonna manage to kill all three a you
boys. But, when Mistuh Johnson spoke up, recognized him
soon's he opened his mouth. Then the mystery of who you
other fellers were fell right into place."

We stepped onto Lavender's homey-looking front porch.
I removed my sweat-dripping hat and fanned my face with
it. "Well, I for one am sure glad you didn't open up on us
with that big popper of yours. Would've sure 'nuff resulted
in a bloody mess."

He slipped past me and headed inside the house. Over
one shoulder he said, "You men take a seat. Any seat you
like. Get some cold, clear spring water from my pump inside here. Help us all cool off a bit."

Few minutes later, perspiring glassware in hand, we'd

all gathered our lumpy-cushioned rockers up around a small table a few feet from Lavender's front door.

Honus took a sip from his dripping beaker, leaned back, then said, "Kinda rare event for folks to be a-comin' out here in the smack-dab middle of Nowhere, Tejas. Bettin' you fellers didn't make a special trip to Hell's front doorstep just for a friendly visit and stroll down memory lane."

Glo sat his half-empty tumbler on the little table. "We chasin' a bad one named Eagle 'Mad Dog' Cutner. Need to find the man quick as we can."

Honus Lavender's brows scrunched together over coalblack eyes. "Well, ain't that a wonderment? Saw that evil rattler late yestiddy. Rode right up over there where you boys let your horses drink."

Some trepidation in my voice, when I said, "Alone?"

"Naw. Had someone with 'im. Looked to be a young girl. Real young as I recall. Sure 'nuff surprised me some, too. He's been comin' and goin' for a spell now. Never had any female companionship before. Leastways none as I knew about."

Boz sat up and moved closer to the table. "'S exactly why we're here, Honus. We've come for the girl."

"And to kill Eagle Cutner as well, if he gets in the way," I said. Then I added, "And maybe even if he don't."

Glo's voice dropped to the conspiratorial level. He touched his friend on the arm and said, "One of his cohorts in crime done tole us as how he's got some kinda cabin up yonder on Turkey Mountain. You know 'bout that? Tell us anything that might be helpful."

Lavender eyed each of us in turn. "Sure. Always pays to know who your neighbors are. Cutner's the only man living anywheres close to me. 'Course I stay away from him. Man's known to be dangerous. Kill a body easy as most folks would swat a pesky fly and not even bat a guilty eye a doin' it. Truth is we've never even so much as spoke during his whole time up there."

"Can you take us to his cabin?" Boz said.

With a slow nod of the head, Lavender said, "Suppose I could do that. Sure. He ain't that hard to find, if'n you know where to look. Showed up 'round these parts some-time back. Figure he mighta been on the run at the time, but he ain't bothered me any. And I sure as hell weren't about to bother him."

"Given what you know about the area, how hard you reckon it'd be for us to take 'im?" Glo said.

Lavender shook his head. A look of mild puzzlement and concern flashed across his deeply creased face. "Well, gents," he said, "sho' ain't gonna be as easy as shootin' fish in a rain barrel."

Boz leaned closer into the converstion. "How so?" he said.

Lavender squirmed deeper into the cushions of his seat, then said, "That house he's livin' in up yonder ways got built outta native stone lotta years ago by an old pio-neer feller name of Felthus Duvall. Man had to fight off them murderin' Comanches ever year during the Killin' Moon whole time he lived up there. House is wedged into the side of a solid piece of rock right at the foot of the mountain."

"Sturdy soundin'," I said.

"Suppose you could say that, Mistuh Dodge. Only parts of the place you can see, from any vantage point you can pick, are the front and either end. No windows, just gun slits here and there. Roof's covered in two feet of dirt. Couldn't set that place on fire with a Napoleon cannon."

"Jay-sus H. Himself on a crutch," Boz mumbled.

The corners of Lavender's eyes crinkled and a slight smile played across his lips. "Been up there and explored that house more'n once over the years 'fore Cutner showed up. Thought to move in the place myself, but I liked this location a lot better. So, I built my place to take advantage of the water, trees, shade and all. During one of my early raids up that way, discovered as how the house does have one glaring weakness."

I bored in on Lavender and said, "And what might that weakness be, Mr. Lavender?"

Looking pleased with himself, he said, "Unless Cutner's a right smart handier'n I figure, the old place ain't seen a carpenter's hammer in years."

Guess we all looked a mite puzzled.

Glo said, "So? What's that got to do with anything?"

Lavender slapped one knee and chuckled. "Front door's all of six inches thick, ole friend. Heavier'n a frozen long-horn. But she's hangin' on leather hinges been there since the day that place got built. I'm a thinkin' if a feller put a shoulder to that slab of wood just right, it'd come down easy as a hot knife through butter."

The three of us nodded and grunted our agreement, then leaned away from Honus Lavender's assessment of the cabin's construction for a few seconds of mulling our future prospects. Guess we'd been thinking the thing over for almost a minute, when Boz said, "Question is, should the need arise, can we get close enough to ole man Duvall's bank vault of a door to knock it loose?"

Behind a nod of the head, Lavender said, "Yep. That be the big conundrum, don't it, Mistuh Tatum? Suppose it all depends on how quick and determinded Cutner'll be to keep us away from the place. If'n the man's fast enough, can keep up the right amount of covering fire, and move from gun port to gun port right fast-like, he'll be harder'n a double-buried Alabama tick to root out."

Boz eyeballed the sky and then gazed west. "Still got plenty of daylight left. How long'll it take us to get to this place?"

"No more'n an hour," Lavender said, as he came to his feet. "Just give me a few minutes to saddle up, gents, and I'll take you right on up there to it."

22

"... THIS SPOT GIVES ME A CASE OF THE CREEPIN' WILLIES."

HALF AN HOUR later, according to my Ingersoll, we sat our froth-covered animals beneath the only tree I'd seen since leaving Honus Lavender's pleasantly shaded cabin next to the creek. The stunted but green and amazingly leafy, live oak had achieved just enough height to offer the most desirable kind of shelter from a anvil-melting south Texas sun. The bloodred sphere pounded on our dripping heads with a crushing heat that could only be likened to the thudding rumble of springtime thunder.

Over baked shoulders, the boiling globe hovered about two fingers above the parched horizon. On their wiggly way to heaven, heat thermals squiggled upward from the desiccated terrain in the manner of earthworms being fried alive in an iron skillet.

A bead of salty-tasting sweat trickled into my eye like a tiny river, coursed down a dusty cheek, then dove into the corner of my mouth. I wiped the droplet away with one finger and flicked it into the dense air, as I peered through my five-segment, calvary-surplus telescope. Tried, with little in the way of satisfying success, to make sense of the uninviting scene laid out before us.

A good two hundred yards distant, at the lowest point of a saw-shaped, gently descending cup of sloped sand and scattered bolders, sat ole Felthus Duvall's abandoned house. Fortresslike, the mortar-and-stone dwelling jutted from beneath a thick shelf of jagged rock like an ugly wart on the earth's reddish-brown rump. The entirety of the viewable earth between us and that man-made cave appeared totally barren of life. Not a single blade of grass, clump of weeds, flower, or bush grew within a hundred feet of the bleak, sinister-looking dwelling.

With surprising abruptness, the stunted breeze that had followed us to that spot like an old dog looking for a handout seemed to die. It sucked away, as though frightened by something unseen. Something larger, more dangerous, more deadly. It left us surrounded by an unearthly stillness—a troubling, nerve-jangling quiet. To this very instant, I can close my eyes and easily reacall a feeling of eerie uncertainty and apprehension about the entire, peculiar setting.

I rocked back in my saddle, as if involuntarily trying to move away from what I could not see, or know. And in spite of the day's brutal, body-sapping heat, an unwelcome, sweat-drenched chill crept up my horse-weary spine. A baffling, creeping kind of eerie gloom wrapped clammy fingers around a backbone that ached. Got the uneasy feeling some invisible, iron-fingered fist had delivered an unexpected crusher of a blow to the spot directly between my shoulder blades. Remember as how I grimaced. Then, I twisted sidewise, as though some stealthy back shooter was about to dry-gulch me from the open maw of a dark alley on a moonless night.

"Don't know 'bout you fellers, but this spot gives me a case of the creepin' willies. Just can't imagine, for a single second, why anybody'd want to build a place to live way the hell and gone out here."

Boz nodded and added, "Think you're right, Lucius. Cain't see a damned thing to recommend this particular spot. Looks exactly the way I've come to imagine what the surface of the moon must resemble. Or some place in hell, or maybe the ass end of the whole world. Only a damn sight harsher."

"'S why I lives down by the water," Honus Lavender mumbled and toyed with the hammers on his shotgun. "Done been a complete mystery to me why ole Duvall built this place way out here. Spot sure's the dickens got nothin' to recommend it, far as I've ever been able to tell anyhow."

Boz, Glo, and I grunted our mutual concurrence with Lavender's assessment.

"As many times as I've been up to this spot," Honus continued, "still don't like bein' here. 'Course when you're tryin' to keep the Comanche from killin' you and your family, in the most horrid fashion imaginable, like ole Duvall was, guess you'd do whatever necessary to make certain that didn't happen."

"Impossible to know another man's heart or mind," Glo offered.

"Don't matter none 'bout the heart or mind, Mistuh Johnson," Honus said. "They's ghosts livin' in that place. Worst kinda ghosts. Evil spirits and sech."

Boz forced a crooked grin and shook his leonine head as though more than a bit amused by talk of ghosts, spirits, and such. He used his long glass as a pointer. "There's a corral at the east end of the house, Lucius. Pair of horses pinned up back there right now. Both of 'em look to be un-saddled. Horrifyin' thought, but I'd bet the girl's still down there."

Tapped my own scope against one chap-covered leg and said, "Wonder how ole man Duvall managed to get water to this place?"

"No need to worry none on that problem," Honus Lavender quickly offered. "They's a well inside the house. Appears Duvall even imported a custom-made hand pump from back East once he got 'er dug. Not sure how far down the man had to go 'fore he struck plenty of liquid. Musta been pert deep though, and a hellacious job for a single feller with nothin' but a shovel to accomplish such a task. Anyway, them folks as are still inside, if they's the ones you're lookin' to find, have access to water, and plenty of it."

Those words had barely fallen from Honus Lavender's lips, when a high, thin, piercing wail rolled up that sandy slope and boxed all of us across our ears like an open palm. While muted by stone walls and distance, the sound of the girl's pitiable scream sent prickly chill bumps charging up and down my spine.

"Well, that for damn sure rips the rag off the bush," Boz said, then snatched his coach gun from its bindings and hopped off his animal.

The rest of us quickly followed Boz's lead, hit our feet, and grabbed for the heaviest weapons we carried.

Before things got out of hand I said, "Wait, now. Gotta go at this with some thought be—" Another round of stomach-churning screams stopped me cold. I paused 'til the screams died away and I could get my breath back. Figure I was talking about a mile a minute when I finally said, "Honus, you're familiar with the interior of the house. Want you to draw us up a quick sketch of the floor plan. You can do it right here in the dirt."

"No need to draw nothin', Mistuh Dodge," Lavender said. "'S all just one big room. Long as the front façade and maybe ten, twelve feet deep."

"No interior walls?" Boz said.

Lavender gave his head a vigorous shake. "None as I recall, Mistuh Tatum. One long, easy-to-defend room. That's it."

"How 'bout furniture? Any furniture left?" I said.

A puzzled look played across Lavender's deeply creased face. After some seconds of head-scratching thought, he said, "Just some old busted, broke-down stuff. Not much really. Only complete piece as I ever seen was the remnants of an iron bedstead."

"Where?" Boz demanded.

"What you mean, Mistuh Boz?"

A hurried urgency spiked in Boz's voice when he snapped, "Where in the room? Front corner? Back corner? Which end of the room when we go through the door?"

Lavender gazed into Boz's eyes as if staring at a man who'd lost his mind. "What you mean, when we go through the door? If'n we go and step one foot too close to that place, and Mad Dog Cutner just happens to take a gander outside, he'll cut us down pocket high faster'n God can get here and stop the killin'."

A loud metallic click snatched everyone's attention my direction when I broke open my shotgun and eyed the primed and ready loads. Another barely discernable, trilling screech clawed at my ears as I snapped the weapon shut, then thumbed the hammers back.

"Ain't got no choice in this particular matter, Mr. Lavender," I said. "Once we've left this spot, we'll head for the front door quick as we can hoof it."

"Then what?" Lavender said as though stunned and amazed.

Big popper propped on one shoulder, Boz said, "Then, me and Lucius'll each blast hell outta one side of the door with both barrels of these shoulder cannons of ours. That'll blow us a pathway inside. Once we get inside, we'll kill the hell out of Cutner and save the girl. That about it, Lucius?"

I flashed him a tight grin then said, "Sounds right to me."

Lavender shook his head and took several steps backward. "Done all the killin' as I ever intend to do, gents. Already in too deep with God over my past killin's as it is. Jus' cain't go bein' a party to this 'un."

A look of surprised confusion on his face, Glo said, "What you mean, Honus? That man inside there is the worst we've ever encountered. Ain't no arguin' the point. And he has a defensless young girl in there with 'im. We gotta go on down there and get 'er out. Whatever it takes."

Lavender took another step backward, then moved to his animal's side. He jumped into a stirrup and quickly threw a leg over the beast's broad back. The horse shook its head, rattled the metallic pieces of the California headstall and curb bit against one another.

"Got you mens up here like I said I would. But ain't gonna be party to no more killings, 'less it's done to save my own life. Y'all go on and do what you has to do. I completely understand. Trust me, I do. Just count me out of it."

Then, God as my witness, he wheeled that big ole gray of his around and kicked for home. Seconds later, Honus Lavender didn't amount to any more than fleeting memories and a cloud of swirling dust headed for safer climes.

Glo stared at his feet as though dumbfounded. "Hadn't seen it myself, wouldn't of believed it, Mistuh Dodge. Never knew the man to have a craven bone in his body. 'Fore now anyway."

Boz turned and gazed down at Duvall's stone dwelling. And, in that strange, philosophical way he often assumed, said, "Well, ain't nothin' cowardly 'bout the man, Glo. Of late, must admit I've come to understand his position completely. Like a lot of others I've known, 'pears as how, at some point, Honus Lavender has simply reached that point where killin' another man is as foreign to his way of thinking as payin' to watch a troup of armadillos play banjos and square dance."

"Doesn't matter whether he's with us or not," I said, "the

job's still the same. Ain't nothin' more 'n a day's worth of gun work fellers."

And with that, and a quick nod of agreement to one another, we struck out. Heeled it for Duvall's derelict stronghold like a trio of men on a deadly mission. Clementine Webb's piteous screeching rang in our ears every step of the way.

23

"Screw You Law-Bringin' Bastards . . ."

I CANNOT IMAGINE what kept us from being discovered as we hoofed our way down that treeless, barren hillside. We sure as hell didn't attempt anything in the way of concealing our approach. No point. Nothing to hide behind. Perhaps the worst part of the deadly stroll was that Clementine Webb's noisy, tortuous treatment became louder, more real, and more difficult to stomach the closer we got to our objective.

Suppose we couldn't have been more than ten feet from the rock-bound chamber of horror's sturdy-looking front entrance when we came to a huffing, puffing stop. I turned to Glo. Locked him in a narrow-eyed glare and said, "Boz and I'll take the door down, then go inside. Want you to wait out here. If ole Mad Dog makes it past us alive, don't you dare hesitate, Glo. Drop both hammers on his sorry, woman-stealin', murderin' ass. You assume he's already shot hell out of the two of us and most probably sent the girl to Jesus as well. Kill 'im graveyard dead."

Boz let out a derisive snort, then added, "Damn right,

Glo. That son of a bitch manages to eleminate the both of us, once you've put 'im down, drag his corpse out into the middle of nowhere and let the coyotes have him."

Glo pawed at the sandy ground with one booted foot. "My, oh, my, Mistuh Dodge. Sho' do hope ain't nothin' like that's in the cards today. Sho' don't want this dance to end in such a terrible tragedy. Cain't begin to imagine what I'd do if'n y'all men went and got kilt."

"You'll do what's necessary," Boz said. "Same as we would do. Same as always."

Raised my weapon and aimed for the hinged side of the door. "You ready to start this ride, Boz?"

"Screwed down and sittin' deep in the saddle, Lucius." He brought his weapon up on the opposite side of the rugged entryway, then said, "Turn 'er loose and let 'er buck. Let's see which way she jumps."

Thunderous report from four barrels of heavy-gauge buckshot rendered the weather-shriveled door, the frame, and goodly parts of the stone and mortar wall on either side of it to nothing more than a cyclone of flying splinters and roiling dust. An ear-thumping roar from our blasting still hung in the air, when we cast those big poppers aside. Filled our hands with cocked pistols and stormed through the run-down building's newly fashioned front opening like a pair of mad men running toward the worst of a moonless midnight's bad dreams.

I darted for the right corner. Boz hoofed it to the left. I'm fairly certain no more than two or three seconds passed once we crossed over that shattered threshold before I could truly see anything of life-saving importance.

Appeared as how Cutner might have moved what remained of the bed Honus Lavender described for us. The rickety piece of junk sat in the middle of the unkept, nigh-on-empty room. The sagging metal frame and springs were but a few feet from the door we'd just reduced to a fog-like mist of black-powder gun smoke and toothpick sized kindling. Covered by our pistols, Cutner had dragged Clementine to the back wall near one side of an enormous fireplace. The massive hearth appeared fully capable of accommodating entire trees.

The pair of them were as naked as glory-be-to-God jaybirds. Near as I could tell, in the half-light of inner darkness and still swirling clouds of grit, Clementine Webb had either totally lost consciousness or already walked amongst the dead.

The girl's appearance bordered on the hideous. Finger-shaped smears of crusted blood painted her beautiful, child's face in a hellish, demonic mask. They decorated her boyish body in weird, fiendish, wavelike curlicues, and peculiar patterns in the manner of painted-on lightning bolts.

The totality of the bloodcurdling scene sent me to the edge of retching like a man coming off a month-long drunk. Realization of what that animal might have done to her made me mad enough to bite a chunk out of the head of a double-bit ax.

That bastard, Eagle Cutner, had one stringy-muscled arm clamped around the skinny girl's neck. She dangled in front of the bug-eyed killer like a kid's corn-shuck doll held up by nothing more than raw strength, propelled by fear. The murderous despoiler's free hand gripped a short-barreled Smith & Wesson .44, the muzzle tightly pressed against Clem's temple.

Sounded like a kicked dog when Cutner yelped, "Who'n the bloody hell 'er you sons a bitches? And what'n the blue-eyed hell you want from me, for the love of sweet Jaysus?"

An ominous, peculiar, creeping silence ran around the room on cat's paws. Several seconds of striking stillness passed before Boz near whispered, "We're the angels of death—your worst nightmares come to life, outlaw."

"Horseshit," Cutner snorted. "Angels of death, my ass."

"We're the men placed on this earth to protect little

children and especially defenseless girls. A benevolent God has sent us to erase your sorry, woman-defiling self from the face of the earth," Boz added. "You don't drop that pistol, I can guarantee you'll end this day a-beggin' for death to come for you like a blind, one-armed, no-legged Civil War vet shaking a tin cup."

All I could see was the top of Cutner's head and a pair of darting eyes when he let out another derisive grunt. He spoke into Clem's shoulder when he growled, "The hell you say. If you bastards think Mad Dog Cutner's afeared of a pair of blatherin', smart-mouthed jackasses, who just happen to be wavin' pistols around, well, the two of you've got a couple more thinks a-comin', by God."

"We're Texas Rangers, you ignorant wretch," I called out. "We came for the girl. You don't give her over, then I'll go a bit further than my partner. Warrant as how your time amongst the living is just about up."

Then, in an effort to get a better eye on the situation, I slowly sidestepped a shade to my right.

Surprised me a mite when Cutner twisted his head the opposite direction. With a stubble-covered cheek pressed against the girl's back, he spit on the wall, then snarled, "Texas Rangers, my cankered ass. Doan give a single hoot in hell or a paper sack fulla dog shit who you sons a bitches *think* you are. Or how bad you *think* you are. Can tell you one thing for by-God sure, though. I'm as bad as both of you put together and this here little gal's a-stayin' with me. If'n you two walkin' assholes do anything foolish, I'll sure 'nuff kill the hell out of her."

I could detect the icy hint of imminent death's approach in his voice when Boz said, "You harm the girl any more than you already have, Cutner, and I'll see you die in a way that'll make you wish your sorely put-upon mama'd never dropped you on an unsuspecting world."

Eagle "Mad Dog" Cutner glared at Boz like he wanted to pull the man's head off, then spit into the open wound.

"Tell you true, mister, you push this hoedown the wrong direction," Cutner barked, "and I'll blow this little gal's head clean off just for the fun of it. Then I'll kill both you shit-eatin' dogs to boot. Figure I ain't got nothin' to lose here."

Tried to sound mollifying when I said, "Don't go and do anything stupid, Eagle."

Boz let an odd, near-lunatic-sounding giggle slip out. Then, from beneath a viciously curled lip, he said, "Aw, hell, Lucius, poor ole Mad Dog just can't help himself. Dim-witted fool was born stupider'n an entire family of opossums. Grew up dumber'n a snubbin' post. And he's gonna die a blankethead, if he don't give us Clem and mighty damned quick."

I got another fleeting glance of Cutner's wide open eyes. As though surprised down to the soles of his bare, bloody feet, he said, "Lucius. Lucius. You're Lucius 'By God' Dodge?"

"That's me," I said.

"And that 'un yonder's Boz Tatum?"

Soon as the breathy question slipped his lips, I knew we'd finally got his undivided attention.

Boz flashed a toothy grin, then said, "That's us in the flesh, you worthless piece of trail dung."

A sound of reckless unease tinged Cutner's voice when he snapped back, "I've heard of you—both of you. But it don't matter none. Hell, don't matter a single whit. 'Cause I already owe you bastards for the fist-sized wad of wood splinters stickin' outta my damaged, bony ass right now. Shit, these things hurt like burnin' perdition. Prolly won't be able to sit a horse for a month. Gonna make you pay for puttin' all these sticker's in me 'fore the day's out, by God."

I flipped the barrel of my pistol at Boz. He nodded, and we both took a pair of bold-as-brass steps Cutner's direction. The thug scrunched as far down behind Clementine's slender, limp body as he could. He moved his arm from around her fragile, teenager's neck, then used it to quickly encircle her boyish chest. The cowardly skunk raised her up like a human shield, then peeked over one of her skinny shoulders.

"Best stop right where you are, boys," he sang out and seemed to push his pistol's muzzle against the girl's skull with added force. "Make another move my direction and this here li'l gal's gonna be huggin' Jesus, the rest of the heavenly host, and swappin' spit with real, honest-to-God angels."

"Give us the girl, and maybe we'll let you live a little longer," I said.

With his forehead pressed aginst Clem's spine, Cutner spoke into the girl's back when he hissed, "She's mine, by God. Girl's mine. She was give to me. Ain't give'n 'er up. Gonna do as I please with this here little bit of split tail, till I get tired of it, then I'll probably kill 'er and go on to the next 'un. And ain't nothin' either of you can do about it."

Cutner didn't have to prod Boz any farther. He holstered his weak-side pistol and turned sidewise, like a New Orleans duelist. He brought the freed hand up to support the polished walnut butt of the pistol in his right. Went as rigid as one of those bronze statues they keep in them museums back East.

Sounded like a crosscut saw ripping through oak boards when he snarled, "I'm ready when you are, Lucius. You call it and we'll bring this shindig to an end."

"You've got 'im, Boz?" I said.

"You bet. I've got 'im dead to rights. Now have Eagle 'Mad Dog' Cutner's head bone sitting atop my front sight as we speak. No job a'tall to empty his pea-sized brain out onto the floor. So, you just give me the word, I'll let 'er rip. Blow all the rusted-up filler in his malignant thinker box from here to kingdom come."

Now, Boz and I'd confronted similar situations any

number of times in the past. We pretty much knew what to
expect from a skunk like ole Mad Dog. And Cutner didn't
disappoint. Did exactly what both of us figured he would.
Silly idiot scrunched farther down behind Clementine—as
far as he could—then raised the girl up a bit higher to protect his worthless, empty noggin.

Unfortunately, for him at least, he'd gone and made a
serious error in judgment. Went and exposed his dangling
manhood in the process of trying to conceal himself behind the girl's limp, blood-smeared torso.

I knew without even having to think about it, Boz Tatum
had already spotted the same thing I had. I sliced a quick,
corner-of-the-eye glance my partner's direction. Could tell
by the faint grin etched across his thin, chapped lips that
he'd already picked his target and was happier than a fat armadillo chewing on a big ole nest of yellow jacket larvae.

Couldn't help but grin myself when I said, "You've got
one more chance here, you back-shootin' bastard. Gonna
say it one more time. Let us have the girl. Give her over
right this very second or suffer the consequences. And
trust me when I tell you, Cutner, you ain't gonna like the
consequences of holding on to her."

I couldn't see any of his face at all when Cutner went to
cackling like something crazed. Idiot still thought he had
the upper hand. Between gasps for air, he huffed, "Screw
you law-bringin' bastards and the horses you rode up on."

I turned to my compadre. Said, "He's all yours, Boz. Do
whatever it takes."

I saw the muzzle of my running buddy's pistol drop
about two inches. Then, an instant later, a thumping, ear-
shattering explosion lit the murky room like a Fourth of
July whizbang at midnight. A thumb-sized, 255-grain
chunk of forty-five caliber lead turned Eagle 'Mad Dog'
Cutner's family jewels into nothing more than a cloud of
bloody, mist-like memories.

Amidst an instant, wavelike cloud of dust, raised by

the pistol's head-ringing blast, Cutner let out a single, ear-shattering shriek. Honest to sweet Mary, screech he let out sounded like a stagecoach ran over a mountain lion right in front of me. No doubt about it, Boz's well-placed shot did the trick, and then some.

Cutner turned his pistol loose like it was a fresh-forged horseshoe. The still-cocked weapon skittered across the packed-dirt floor and ricocheted off the stone wall. He dropped Clem, then grabbed at his blood-gushing crotch with both hands. Went down on both knees then rolled onto one side. Hit his unprotected shoulder like a felled tree. Set to whooping, hollering, and thrashing around in the dirt as if Boz's shot had cut his head off.

I holstered my pistols, jumped across the ten or so feet that separated us, and snatched Clem away, while Boz snatched Cutner's pistol up off the floor. He shoved the short-barreled blaster behind his own cartridge belt. A beaming grin painted across his face, he stood over a freshly neutered Eagle "Mad Dog" Cutner and watched as the man rolled around on the floor, slinging blood every which direction.

Quick as I could, I carried Clem to the ramshackle piece of a bed. Laid her out atop a blanket that was horrifyingly smeared in what I figured had to be her own blood.

I covered the girl up best I could manage, with anything I could lay a hand on. Pressed two fingers against her gore-caked neck in an effort to find something akin to a pulse. Bent over and listened for breathing, then put an ear against her chest. I could barely hear her heartbeat 'cause of all the yelling and hollering Cutner was doing.

"She's still with us," I said more to myself than to anyone in particular. "Think if we can get her awake, cleaned up, and moving around, she just might make it. Gotta get on it fast as we can, though."

Boz eased up beside me. He jammed a fresh shell into the empty chamber of his pistol. Slapped the loading gate closed, then shoved the gun into his hip holster. Thumbs hooked over a hand-tooled Mexican cartridge belt, he rocked back on his heels and frowned. "Hard thing to think, but given the way the poor child looks, be nothin' short of a miracle if she lives another ten minutes, you ask me, Lucius."

From outside, I heard Glo call out, "How is it in there with you, Mistuh Boz? Mistuh Dodge? You gennemens okay? Y'all still be alive and kickin'?"

I turned and yelled, "We're fine and dandy, Glo. Still breathin'. Still kickin'. Need you to run back to the horses. Get the blanket tied behind my saddle. Also all our canteens and my saddlebags. Bring everything inside here quick as you can."

Hadn't quite finished my instructions, when I spotted him standing in the blasted doorway. Thought for a second or so the man would break down weeping when he said, "Sweet merciful Jesus, Mistuh Dodge. What'd that animal go and do to the poor chile? Top of everthang else she's done suffered, what'd he go and do?"

I stood beside the shaky piece of a bed and gazed down into Clementine Webb's scabrous, splotched face. Took the whole of my self-control to keep from breaking down like the girl's very own father. "Sweet Jesus, don't know for sure, Glo. Doubt we'll ever know all of it for certain. Whatever he did, we need to get her warm and cleaned off right quick-like. Want her outta here and shaped up as best we can manage 'fore she manages to regain some semblance of consciousness—if she ever does."

"Goin' for the blankets, water, and sech right now, Mistuh Dodge. Back fast as these ole legs and the good Lord'll let me."

Glo's words were still hanging in the air when I heard Eagle Cutner moan. He sounded most like a man being tortured by a band of Satan's red-eyed imps.

I stomped my way across the room and tried my dead

level best to put my booted foot completely up his no-account backside. Guess I must've kicked the unmitigated hell out of him four or five times. Would've probably kicked him slap to death, but then Boz slid up from behind, grabbed me around the shoulders, and dragged me back a few steps.

Arms still locked around me in a viselike grip, mouth right next to my ear, Boz hissed, "He's still alive, Lucius. Son of a bitch is still alive. Doubt he'll die from losing them there gonads of his'n. And we don't wanna kill 'im completely dead just yet."

Still mad enough to eat raw bees, I grunted and tried to wrench myself from his grip.

"Think, now, ole friend," he hissed into my ear. "Wanna get at the head of this beast, we've still gotta find out where that stink sprayer Ax Webb went. Keep on kickin' ole Eagle and he just might give up the ghost."

Can't remember a time when I've let my emotions get hold of me to the point where I seemed to lose all reason like I did that day. But, my glorious God, appeared as how Eagle Cutner had gone and done deplorable things to Clementine Webb, and I wasn't in anything like a forgiving mood. Felt like my head might explode if I couldn't stomp a bloody ditch in his sorry hide, then stomp it dry.

Boz didn't turn me loose until I'd relaxed a mite. Got to admit, it took an almighty heap of self-control to keep from finishing the job I'd started. I clomped a path all the way around that big ole room a time or two. Kicked at every piece of broken-down furniture handy. Was trying like the dickens to shake off the urge to go back over and put the boot to Eagle Cutner till I'd stomped him slap to death. Pretty sure, at the time, the simple act of killin' the bee-Jesus out of him would've made me feel one hell of a bunch better about the whole situation.

After about two or three minutes of fuming like a forest fire on the verge of bursting loose and flarin' up like Hell's lowest circle, I finally calmed down enough to go over and squat down beside the castrated son of a bitch.

He was still rolling around in his own filth. Man had both blood-soaked hands clamped between his legs and had descended to the point of whimpering like a hurt dog. Was enough to make me want to puke up my balbriggans, socks, boots, and silver-mounted spurs. Sweet Jesus, he was pathetic.

Arms crossed over his chest, Boz slouched against one end of the rotting fireplace mantel and watched. After a few seconds of contemplation, he set to rolling himself a ciga-reet.

As I recall it, Boz'd already started on his smoke by the time I grabbed the sniveling stack of walking scum at my feet and snatched him onto his nekkid back. Knees hiked up against his heaving chest, Cutner fingered at the still-bleeding ribbon of flesh between his legs, whimpered and mewled. Just typical. Cowardly bastard's real self had popped out with the loss of his manhood. And he couldn't hide it any longer.

24

"Go On and Kill Me."

NOW, I HAVE to confess, I might've gone and slapped the blue-eyed hell out of Eagle Cutner a time or two, maybe three, that fateful afternoon. As I now recollect the events of that day, my open palm across his cheeks did tend to make loud cracking sounds. Pretty sure I left a goodly share of red welts that looked like my fingers on his surprised countenance.

Once I'd finally got his undivided attention, I grabbed the sorry bastard by the throat and said, "You've gotta clear your mind, Eagle. Whatever there is left of it. Gotta perk up. Pay attention. You'n me, and ole Boz Tatum here have unfinished business to discuss."

Cutner groaned, then made the kind of pitiable sounds that would normally have had the power to pull tears out a glass eye, but not that day. From behind his own set of piss-yellow orbs, he whimpered, "Ain't g-got nothin' to say to either of you star-carryin' b-bastards. Skunk ugly a-assholes done turned me into a geldin'. One pistol shot.

Damnation. One shot. Cain't b-believe it. Went from bein' a rooster to a hen in a s-single heartbeat."

"Best shot I've made in years," Boz said, then let out a self-satisfied chuckle.

"Ain't nothin' no more—not even a m-man. W-Why didn't you just go on ahead and put one in my skull bone, like you said you's gonna do? Just get it over with and k-kill me. Go on and kill me. Kill me now. I'm ready to go. Ready to meet Jesus."

Boz took a lung-filling drag off his hand-rolled, picked a sprig of tobacco off his bottom lip. He glared at the offending morsel, then said, "Well, we can still do that, but I don't think Jesus would wanna talk to a walkin' pile of murderous, hammered manure like you, Eagle."

Cutner groaned and rolled back and forth in the dirt like a fresh slab of country bacon frying in a hot skillet.

I said, "'Course, unless you bleed out while you're rollin' around down there in the mud, the blood, and what used to be your tiny hoo-hahs, you'll most likely live through this little setback. So, why don't you just buck up, you mangy pile of chicken shit? Rancher castrates a bull, animal don't even act like he feels it."

Cutner twisted back onto one side. He moaned again. "Well, by God, I ain't no bull. An' I fer sure felt this 'un."

Then, good Lord as my witness, the quivering skin sack puked all over hell and yonder. Let loose with a real gusher. Something that looked like half a gallon of bunkhouse chili. Then he rolled onto his back again, coughed, and geysered the awful stuff a good three feet in the air. Nasty-smelling crap rained down all over him. Covered his chest, face, and damn near everything else. I had to jump out of the way to keep from getting hit myself. My God, having to witness such behavior's enough to put a man off his feed for a solid week.

"Aw-w goddamn," Cutner snarled. "A little setb-back, huh, Dodge? That's what you've decided to call this horrible thang you bastards have gone and done to me? Shit a-runnin'. Had my pistol, I'd give you two a real setb-back."

The smoldering quirley dangling from the corner of his mouth, Boz grinned and said, "Well, you could be deader'n Crockett and Travis right now, by God. If Lucius had given me the word, 'bout two seconds earlier, what little there is of your more-than-worthles brain would be decorating that wall yonder instead of your tiny set of *huevos*."

Behind me, I heard Glo at the door. "I's back, Mistuh Dodge. Got all them thangs as you wanted me to bring."

Didn't take my narrowed gaze off our bleeding, puking prisoner. "You go on ahead and see if you can get Clem cleaned up some, Glo. Boz and I are still a bit occupied with Mr. Cutner."

Could tell from Glo's voice my instructions distressed him some. "But, Mistuh Boz, maybe it'd be best if'n you . . ."

Still squatting beside Cutner, I twisted around so Glo could see my face. "It's okay. You go ahead and clean her face, neck, arms, and legs, as best you can. Check over all those spots for cuts, bullet wounds, and such. Me'n Boz'll do whatever else we can when we're finished here."

With a dumbfounded look on his face, Glo nodded. "Yes, suh. Do what I can. But you know I . . ."

"Telling you it's all right. Trust me. No need to worry yourself. Go on ahead and clean up what you can get at. We'll be over to help you with her shortly."

"Yes, suh. I'm a-goin', I'm a-goin'," he said and shuffled his way toward the bed as though it might contain a horror story beyond his ability to grasp.

I turned back to Cutner and put a serious eyeballing on him. "Here's the deal, Eagle, you tell me where Axel Webb is, and I won't kill you. Swear it on my dear ole sainted grandma."

Sounded as though he might be weakening, when Cutner mewled, "Aw, hell, if'n you don't d-do fer me, Ax sure 'nuff will when he finds out as how I done went and betrayed him. Pair of you fellers might want me to wake up shovelin' coal in the Devil's f-favorite furnace, but I know for sure Ax would send me there and not even bat an eye."

"Well, trust me when I tell you that I'm not gonna kill you today. And I won't let Boz kill you, either. Or Glorious Johnson, yonder. You cough up the information I need, and we'll leave you a pistol with one pristine, brain-ready bullet in it. Then we'll hit the trail runnin' and let you figure out how best to write the end of your own sorry story. Ax Webb don't need to have any hand in that."

"Awww, sweet, merciful Jaysus," Cutner moaned. "Why've I always been so put-upon? Go to my grave not bein' able to understand why I've had to deal with meddlin', badge-totin' assholes like you three bastards all my natural l-life, Dodge. Sweet glorious God, save me from lawmen."

"Sweet dancin' Christ," Boz mumbled. "Ain't nothin' about your life's been natural, Eagle. Been rapin' and killin' folks all over Texas, Oklahoma, Arizona, and New Mexico for years. 'Bout time the law caught up with you and put a stop to all the mayhem you're responsible for."

"Besides, Ax Webb is responsible for the deaths of a boatload of people out on the Devils River," I said. "You're gonna tell us where he went. One way or the other."

Cutner crawfished to the stone house's back wall. He left a trail of blood in the dirt as he elbowed his way to a sitting position. Groaned like a dying calf, then said, "Don't know nothing 'bout no killin's out on Devils River. Didn't have nothin' to do with any killin's done there."

'Course, he was right about that. Said, "We know you weren't there when Senator Webb and his family were murdered. Otherwise you'd already be dead."

"Wish I wuz already dead, by God," Cutner said, then stared at a bloody hand as though it didn't belong on the end of his own arm. "What you sons a bitches done to me's worse'n gettin' kilt."

"Keep jerkin' us around, and you're gonna be dead and right soon. Can assure that eventuality quicker'n double-geared lightnin'," Boz snorted. "Send you to Satan myself. Keep on talkin' and not sayin' anything useful and I can guarantee it won't take much for me to grant your wish and put a bullet in your brain pan, then ride on out of here."

The message of real, impending death must've finally bored its way into Cutner's worthless brain. The man damn near shouted when he said, "Uvalde. Webb said as how he 'uz goin' back to Uvalde."

"What in the blue-eyed hell would he wanna go and do that for?" Boz snapped.

Cutner groaned again. Sounded right pitiful when he whined, "Gimme some kinda rag so's I can wipe away some of this blood, Dodge. Swear I'll tell you boys whatever you wanna know. Just help me out some, fellers. Please."

I turned and hooked a thumb at Glo. He nodded, ripped a square of rag off whatever he'd been using on Clem. I strolled to Cutner's side and dropped it over the man's oozing crotch.

"Thank God," the outlaw wheezed. "'Pears as how I've just 'bout finally stopped bleedin', but this'll sure 'nuff help."

He mopped at his damaged goods for almost a minute before Boz got tired of waiting. "That's enough. Get to talking, you scurvy dog. We've wasted all the time we're going to on you."

Cutner rolled his head from side to side. Looked to me like he might puke again. But he surprised me. Suddenly, inexplicably, the man got control of himself. In a stronger voice he said, "Ax went back to his brother's house. Said he was pretty sure the man had a safe full of money there. Said he musta just missed it the first time he searched the place."

Boz nodded and mumbled to himself, "Makes sense to me."

Cutner swatted at flies buzzing around his crotch. "Ole Ax is obsessed," he said. "Wanted that brother of his dead. Wanted all the man's money. And by God he's intent on having both of 'em."

"Safe fulla money, huh?" Boz said.

"Yeah. Swear that's all I know, fellers. Swear it." He cried and whimpered some more before adding, "Don't know nothin' else. If you're gonna kill me, might as well get at it right now. Gonna leave me here to bleed out, best head east and burn leather for Uvalde. Bet everything I ever had, that's where Ax Webb is right this minute."

I turned to Boz. "If Axel didn't find whatever it is he's looking for the first time he searched the place, it'll likely take him a spell this time for sure. Bet he'll still be digging around inside the senator's house a week from now. Means he'll likely have to tear the place down to the foundation 'fore he finds anything."

"Guess there's no real hurry then, is there," Boz said.

"Not for you and Glo," I said.

Boz strolled over so he could stand next to me. He turned his back on Cutner and went to whispering. "What the hell's that mean, Lucius?"

"I want you and Glo to take the girl back to the ranch. See to it she's cared for. Figure the ordeal should be a lot easier on her if she's back there. I'll deal with her sorrier'n hell uncle."

Boz twisted his neck back and forth. I could hear the bones grind and pop against each other. "We've been through somethin' of a shit storm with this 'un, Lucius. I figured on seein' it right up to the gruesome end—whatever that might turn out to be. Cain't say as how I'm all that happy with your plan."

I placed a hand on my friend's shoulder. "You've gotta get Clementine out of here and back to the ranch, Boz.

Doubt Glo can do the job alone. Might turn out a full-time nursin' task 'fore she's able to get up and get around again. Not sure any of us should take on such a chore single-handed. Figured as how you wouldn't mind goin' on back with him. Girl's life might depend on it. 'Tween the two of you, I have no doubt Clem'll be seen to with all proper diligence."

"And Ax Webb? What're you gonna do about him, Lucius?"

"Don't you worry bout that skunk, ole friend. I'll take care of Axel Webb myself."

About then, I heard Glo say, "Mistuh Dodge. Mistuh Dodge. Gots to get over here. Little girl done woke up."

With Boz hot on my heels, I hoofed it to a spot beside the filthy bed. I took Clem's tiny hand in mine. The beaten girl's eyes were so swollen, I bent as close as I could in the hope she might be able to see me. Near to whispering when I said, "Clem. Can you hear me, Clem? It's Ranger Dodge. Come on, darlin', say something for me."

A single, crystalline tear rolled from the corner of one blackened eye and streamed down the side of her bruised, encrusted cheek like a miniature salty creek. Her voice sounded like a rat-tailed file going through petrified oak when she said, "Ranger Dodge?"

Tell you true, friends, at that unexpected moment, my heart soared. Never figured to get such a response from anyone as badly beaten as she appeared. "Yes, child. It's Ranger Dodge. I'm right here with Boz and Glo. We came for you, darlin'. Came as fast as we could. You're gonna be okay. We'll see to it."

She twisted atop the sorry pile of raggedy, blood-spattered bedding. "Sorry I ran away. S-should've waited. But I was so angry. So angry. Made a terrible, terrible mistake. All my fault. Hope you can forgive me."

I bent over and placed as tender a kiss as I could manage on her blood-smeared brow—perhaps the only undamaged spot on her entire body. Leaned back and whispered, "Oh, none of this is your fault, darlin', none of it. Whole of this tragedy falls on the head of a single man, and I'm gonna make it right. Just like I swore to you I would out by Devils River. Gonna make it right."

Not sure the terribly damaged child heard anything I said after I planted that kiss on her forehead. When I'd wiped away a tear of my own and checked once more, she looked to have lost consciousness again.

I placed her limp hand on the bed. "Glo, I want you to carry Clem outside. Take her up on the hill where we left the horses. Got one more thing I've gotta do. Then we can all be on our way."

Glo nodded. He lifted Clem from the bed as if she didn't weigh any more than a bag of feathers. Boz and I watched as they disappeared through the door.

I glanced over at Boz. He forced a tight, crooked smile, then said, "Misjudged you, Dodge. Sounds to me like you've got somethin' special in mind for the phantom-like Mr. Webb."

Came near whispering again when I said, "Yes. Something special. Something very special." I bumped him on the arm with my fist and added, "Gimme ole Mad Dog's pistol."

On my way to the sorry pile of human flesh propped against the back wall, I shucked all the shells from his big Smith & Wesson. I squatted in front of the man and made a show of shoving one bullet back into the empty revolver. Snapped the piece closed, then said, "Should kill you for what you did to her, Cutner."

Eyes clenched shut, brows pinched in pain over his hawk-like beak of a nose, Eagle "Mad Dog" Cutner slobbered on himself. I thought the man would break down crying when he sniveled, "Prolly. Yeah, you prolly should, Dodge. Wouldn't blame you if'n you did. Know I'd k-kill you, given half a chance. 'Sides, never fooled myself. Always figured my life would come to some such sorry end."

I got to my feet and pitched the pistol onto the floor. The heavy weapon made a loud thumping noise when it landed at Cutner's feet. "One shell in the gun. If'n I was you, I'd use it wisely. But you know, I'm figurin' you for gutless, Cutner. Yeah, figure you'll just slink off and vanish into nothing."

Ole Mad Dog groaned like he might die just any second. He twisted his head to one side, as if he didn't want to look at me, or hear what I had to say. But his behavior didn't stop me.

"But should you decide to get off your worthless behind and go on with the rest of whatever remains of your sorry life, know this. You commit so much as one crime that comes back to my ears—spit on a sidewalk, get drunk and rowdy, kick a wayward dog, say so much as howdy to the wrong woman, whatever—we'll drop everything we're doing to come find you. And when we do, I swear on my mother's grave, I'll hitch your arms and legs to horses, whip 'em up and let 'em pull you apart. String your guts on barbed wire fences all over south Texas."

And with that, I motioned for Boz to follow me. We hit the door and headed for the hill where Glo had laid Clem out in the dwindling afternoon shade. He'd already started work on a pole drag, so she'd be as comfortable as possible for the trip back to our Devils River lease.

Had just thrown a leg over my mount when I heard the shot—muffled, barely discernable up where we were. I gazed toward heaven and said, "Thank you, Lord. Already spilled enough blood over this business as it is."

Boz slapped me on the leg. "Yeah, but you've got one more to go. Sure you'll recognize Axel Webb, Lucius?"

I pulled my bandanna and set to wiping the sweat out of my hat. "Well, we buried his brother. Been my experience that brothers do have a tendency to look a lot alike. So, figure I shouldn't have any trouble in that particular area."

He extended his hand and shook mine. "You be careful, Lucius. Webb's already proven himself an extremely dangerous man. Responsible for more killin's in a shorter time than anybody we've brought to book in years. Be more'n willin' to bet the ranch, he ain't gonna like bein' run to ground for this mess."

I grinned back and said, "Yeah, think you've hit that nail right on the head, Boz. But, hey, he doesn't know me, either. Or that death's coming along for the ride."

And with that, I turned my blue roan, Grizz, in a tight circle, put the spur to his flanks, and kicked for Uvalde.

25

"... DON'T KNOW NOTHIN', AIN'T SEEN NOTHIN'..."

DAMN NEAR RODE Grizz slap into the ground on that trip. The promise I'd made Clementine Webb, at the foot of her entire family's pitiful grave, rang in my heart like Sunday morning church bells with every step that animal took.

Got to Uvalde in what had to have been record time. It was already good and dark when I reined up out front of a noisy, busy-looking watering hole that had a barely discernable, rough billboard hanging over the batwing doors. Faded, bloodred letters, painted atop the sign's rapidly vanishing yellow background, identified the joint as Mi Tio's Cantina.

Didn't know all that much about the town, other than the fact that I could find my way around easy enough in the daylight. Had conducted a bit of business there a time or two before, but not enough to be completely comfortable wandering the streets at night.

I remembered as how Clementine had mentioned the exact address of her home, when we'd talked out on the banks of Devils River, but the specifics had pretty much escaped my memory. Figured there was no point fumbling about in the dark in what would likely prove a futile effort to find Senator Webb's place somewhere on Pecos Boulevard.

So, I tied up to the nearest hitch rack and strolled over to Mi Tio's entryway. Took the time to peer over the batwings for a spell just to get the lay of the land. Didn't spot anything wayward. Pushed through a set of café doors that complained like a flock of squawking ducks. Felt as though every head in the place turned to get a good look at the stranger who'd just crossed the bustling joint's rude threshold.

The cow-country oasis was jammed wall to wall with people—vaqueros, businessmen, gamblers, loose women, railroaders, cowboys, pimps, cardsharps, and cattlemen. They were packed into that roadside establishment elbow to elbow and, in places, damn near nose to nose. I fought a crooked path through the crowd and bulled out a reasonable good spot to stand at the bar. Jumpin' Jehoshaphat, Mi Tio's had folks crammed all around me like a fat woman's tightest pair of stockings.

A muscular bartender, who could've easily been mistaken for a carnival worker that made his living driving stakes and erecting tents, cast a decidedly unconcerned glance my direction. He was working as though his life depended on swabbing out the bottom of a shot glass with a damp towel when he said, "You want something to drink, mister, or'd you just come in to stand at the bar and take up space?"

I motioned him closer, leaned over, and said, "Be most grateful if you'd pour me a shot of whatever you got in the way of decent Tennessee sippin' whiskey, friend."

The moustachioed bruiser slopped the drink into a freshly cleaned glass, then shoved it my direction. "Ranger, ain't you? Sure as hell have the look," he said.

"Yeah. Texas Ranger Lucius Dodge."

"That right? Well, sorry, but I ain't ever heard of you. 'Course that don't mean much 'cause I just got to this part of Texas a few weeks ago. Not sure what you want, but whatever it is, I cain't help you."

I twirled the glass around in a circle of the spilled liquid atop the bar. "Well, be that as it may, I could sure enough use a tiny bit of information with my drink. That is if you could bring yourself to help me out."

I threw the whiskey down 'bout the same time the drink slinger said, "Already told you. Ain't in the information business, Ranger Dodge. Don't do nothin' but sell whatever people want to drink. Other'n herdin' liquor bottles and cleanin' glassware, I don't know nothin', ain't seen nothin', and don't wanna know nothin' or see anythin'. Kinda stuff you might want to know could easily get a man kilt deader'n a rotten fence post around these parts."

I forced a tight smile and tried my level best to keep on looking and sounding friendly, rather than reaching over the crowded countertop and snatching his nose off. "Look, all I need is for someone to point me toward Senator Nathan Webb's house. Get me goin' the right direction, figure I can find it on my own."

Bartender's face twisted into a mask of obvious displeasure. "Don't have a single clue. Like I said before, ain't been in Uvalde that long myself. Couldn't find Senator Webb's house for you with a weepin' willow divinin' rod and a week to do it."

Bearded man beside me, who looked like a Mexican version of Father Christmas, turned my direction. He flashed a liquor-fueled, cherry-cheeked grin. He drained a doubled-up glass of tequila, thumped the empty beaker onto the bar, and ran his sleeve-covered arm across wet lips. "I know thees place you speak of, senor."

"Ah. That a fact? It's nearby, I hope."

"Oh, yass, senor. Ees very close."

"Senator Webb's hacienda? You're certain about that?"

"*Sí*, senor. I know it well. *La casa de las muñecas.*"

"*Muñecas? Muñecas?*"

"*Sí*, senor. How you say it? Ah, house of dolls."

"House of dolls?"

"Yass. The senator, his casa filled with children ever since he arrive here. They collect many dolls over the years. All kind. Hang them from the walls, trees, bushes. In the courtyard. Very beautiful."

"Beautiful?"

"Oh, *sí*. Until they suddenly leave, that is. Now, there are many peoples who say the hacienda she ees haunted. Many peoples think that Senator Webb and hees family all *muerto*. Dead. They see strange lights there at night. Strange mens come and go."

I couldn't believe how, with no hard evidence, the man had hit on the exact way of things. Stared into the quarter of an inch of whiskey left in my glass and said, "Can you take me there right now?"

"*Absoluteamente*, senor. Ees no problema. Be most happy to guide you there myself, senor. Have to walk right past the senator's deserted casa on the way to my own home."

He grabbed me just above the elbow. The man might have looked like a fat gob, but he had an iron-fingered grip. If I put my mind to that particular event, pretty sure I could still feel his fingers wrapped around my arm to this day.

The friendly tippler damn near dragged me through the dense crowd and back onto the street. Once outside, he made a flamboyant, one-armed sweeping motion off to our left. "Come. Mount your trusty *caballo*, amigo," he said, then let out a belly-shaking laugh. "Jesus de Sangre weel gladly lead the way. Ees but a short distance from thees place of drunkenness and carnal pleasures, I assure you. Eees not far at all."

I had to hustle over and hop on Grizz's back quick as I could. My newfound friend might well have been the size of a Concord coach, and obviously close on to being knee-walking drunk, but he proved light on his feet as well. He almost disappeared into the dark before I could get myself mounted.

Jesus de Sangre staggered some as I followed and talked to himself with almost every stumbling, booze-belabored step. Even talked with people who weren't there, or within shouting distance, near as I could tell.

He led me down a number of smelly, garbage-littered alleyways. Unseeable dogs prowling through the trash yapped and snarled at our passing. In several places we had to pick our way around crude houses, or *jacales*, made of little more than a series of sticks jammed into the hard ground. Most appeared to be filled with laughing children and busy women. After a spell, I came to feel as though we were doing little more than traveling in a big circle. Then, of a sudden, we hit a spacious, tree-lined boulevard of impressive haciendas, each surrounded by its own ten-to twelve-foot-high stucco-covered adobe wall.

A cold, gray, death's head moon, that provided little in the way of illumination, hung in the inky, cloud-laced sky off to the east. Lack of good light made it nigh on impossible for me to tell exactly where we were gonna finally end up.

Suppose we'd fumbled along in the dark for close to half an hour. Of a sudden, my escort rocked to a wobbling stop. He slapped his ample belly and laughed, raised a stubby finger and pointed out a barely discernable wooden gate lit by a flickering lamp that gave off little more light than a candle.

The rough entryway hung from iron hinges mounted into a stone wall plastered over with a coat of pink stucco that glowed in the glittering darkness. Eerily, dozens of blank-faced dolls dangled from pieces of twine all around the entrance, or were tacked directly onto the door's pitted, splinter-laced surface.

My thick-gutted guide said, "'S heere, senor. Thees ees Seenator Webb's *grande* hacienda. *La hacienda de las muñecas.* Jesus was *correcto*, no? That bartender at the cantina, he lie like a yellow dog. He knows where ees Seenator Webb's hacienda. Everyone knows."

Ole Jesus didn't say another word or wait for anything by way of a reply. He simply flashed a toothy grin, tipped a sombrero the size of a wagon wheel, threw a one-handed wave over his shoulder, and stumbled off into the all-enveloping darkness. Suppose he couldn't have gone more than a dozen steps when I heard dogs yapping again. Big dogs. Kind of animals a feller wouldn't want chasing him. Then, there was a round of hot-sounding Spanish that I took to be rather pointed curses.

I stepped off Grizz and tried the gate. The heavy entry-way swung open on well-oiled hinges with absolutely no resistance. I could easily see, from my new vantage point, that several rooms in the house were still lit. Bushes outside the casa's windows, and the trees scattered around the courtyard, dripped with all maner of dolls that looked like some kind of odd fruit. A big ole live oak, in one corner of the courtyard, sported dozens of those tiny figures. Eerie sight sent a cold wave of chicken flesh up my spine.

Kerosene lamps, or perhaps candles, bathed each of the visible, interior spaces with a dancing, yellowish-orange, near unearthly glow. Someone moved from room to room, then stopped.

I pulled one of a pair of hand-braided lariats from a thong on my saddle. All rolled up, that piece of leather felt like a length of coiled steel. Strolled over to the nearest puddle of light bleeding through a set of glass-paned double doors on the ground floor. Took up a spot just on the edges of the shimmering glow, so as not to be seen. A dull, watery radiance oozed from a large, central room behind the glass doors and spread across the sheltered, tile-covered veranda highlighted by a fountain that made a pleasant trickling sound.

Inside the house, directly across the room from where I hid in the darkness, a man stood in a chair and worked at balancing himself. He had his back to me as he ran both hands along the edges of the wooden frame that surrounded an enormous, colorful painting of a bullfighter. The picture dangled from a thick piece of wire draped over a nail driven into the wall above the fireplace mantel. With as much stealth as I could manage, I slipped across the terrace's open space and tried one of the horizontal, metal door handles and found it locked.

I thought the situation over for a racing ten seconds or so. Suppose I could've kicked the door to pieces. Wasn't much there but milk-colored glass held together by some flimsy-looking wooden framing. But I figured as how shattered glass and yelling people might bring a crowd. Gunshots could easily prove even worse. I did not care for the possible results brought on by either eventuality.

Made a hasty decision and headed for the hacienda's front entry. Gave the door about half a dozen hard-fisted raps. I held my lariat against one leg and turned a bit sidewise and away from the spot where I figured the light would fall on me.

It took a spell, but the door suddenly popped open. Gent I'd seen standing on the chair carried a kerosene lamp in one hand. He peeked around the opening he allowed for several seconds, then stepped out so I could see him. Up close, he bore an astonishing resemblance to the slightly older Nathan Webb's bullet-riddled corpse. He peered at me across the threshold, as if he wanted to slap me nekkid.

A wicked sneer curled his upper lip when he growled, "Who'n the hell're you and whatta you want this time of night, mister?"

I whipped off my hat and bowed slightly. Stuffed the hat

back on, then flashed my badge. Tried to sound humble and apologetic at the same time when I said, "Lucius Dodge, Texas Ranger. Sorry to be a bother, sir, but are you Senator Webb?"

26

"...WE'VE SEEN MORE'N OUR SHARE OF BLOOD..."

AXEL WEBB TURNED at the waist and cast a nervous glance over his shoulder, as if he thought someone might be trying to sneak up behind him. He glared at me again, shook his head, and looked even more irritated, but also a bit puzzled. His confusion appeared to have abated a bit, when he said, "No. Sorry, but Senator Webb can't be contacted at the moment. He, well, he's out of town on business. Yeah, out of the state actually. In Denver, I believe."

"Might I inquire as to when you expect him back, sir?" I said.

"Not absolutely certain. But there's every chance he won't return for several weeks—most likely. In my estimation, the senator could be gone as long as a month. Perhaps more."

I tried my best to feign the aspect of a man utterly surprised and deeply disappointed. Toed at the foot-square, rust-colored Mexican tiles beneath my feet. "Damn. That is a shame," I said. "Real shame. My superiors felt certain we could find him here." Patted the front of my jacket. "I have important communications for the senator. Rode all the way from Austin. Didn't even stop along the way."

A more than inquisitive look crept onto Axel Webb's softly lit face. "Well, I'm his brother. Closest and only kin he has that's still living. You can tell me anything you wanted to tell him. Shouldn't be a problem. I'll make sure he gets any message you might choose to leave."

I cast a series of suspicious glances around the empty courtyard behind me, then turned back to the brazen killer. He took a half step back when I leaned into the doorway and whispered, "Well, don't want to be a bother, but I think it would probably be best if I came inside, sir. Wouldn't want anyone to accidently pass by in the street and hear what I've got to say. 'S a matter of fairly significant state business, you see. Great deal of money at stake. If the information I carry should get out, could result in dire consequences, dire. Sure you'll understand."

"It's that important, huh? Money, you say?"

"Indeed, sir. Indeed, yes. Communications I carry on my person come directly from the capitol. Office of the governor, you see. My instructions were that I should hand these documents over to Senator Webb himself. But, if he's not here, I suppose it'd be all right if I left this particular bit of news with you, sir. Seein' as how you're his brother and all."

I could still feel a degree of resistance and lack of enthusiasm when Ax Webb testily placed the lamp on a table just inside the door, stepped to one side, and waved me over the hacienda's rugged threshold. 'Course, I gallantly removed my hat and motioned for him to lead the way.

We'd just crossed into the room off the patio, where I'd first spotted him, when I whacked the brigand across the back of his head with that heavy length of twisted leather. The lariat made a slight hissing sound just before it caught him below, and behind, his right ear. The son of a bitch struck the floor like a man who'd got hit in the head with the butt end of a .10 gauge coach gun. Thought sure I'd knocked him into the black oblivion of the next week.

Must admit I was some surprised when the hardheaded bastard bounced up off that tile floor like a kid's rubber ball. He came to unsteady legs and turned on me with all the ferocity of a caged tiger. Didn't do him any good though. I used the lariat to give him another resounding wallop across the face that knocked him sidewise.

The stink-spraying skunk stumbled and tripped over a low, wooden table sitting in the middle of the room. He rendered that piece of furniture to splinters when he went through it and landed on the floor again. There was a loud, watery, smacking sound when his thick skull ricocheted off the floor. In a matter of a second or two, he was rolling back and forth in a puddle of blood and groaning like a man dying.

I didn't wait that time but grabbed him by the collar of his shirt. Got him to his feet again. Brought the rope up from a spot about level with my spurs and laid it across his jaw. Force of the blow put him back on his knees. He swayed like a creek-side willow in a stiff, south Texas wind.

I tossed the length of braided leather aside and took a good, balanced stance. Delivered an iron-fisted haymaker that bounced off his eye socket. My other fist caught him in the temple. Soon's he was down again, I set to kicking the hell out of him. Kicked that child-killing son of a bitch all over the room. Kicked and stomped on him till I got downright tired. He bled like a stuck hog. The sorry cuss moaned and groaned as if he was about to pass on for final judgment as I maneuvered him into a chair and lashed him down good.

I rummaged through a cabinet near the door, once I got him situated the way I wanted. Found an unlabeled bottle of what I figured had to be some kind of rye and poured myself a full tumbler. Pulled me up a second chair a few feet in front of the insensible wretch, flopped into it, and waited for him to find his way back to consciousness.

Took ole Ax almost half an hour to come around from the hellacious stomping I'd put on his sorry ass. Blood dribbled from a broken nose and a number of nasty-looking facial lesions when willful perception finally grabbed hold of him again.

Spitting red when he dragged his head up enough to see me, he said, "Who'n the hell are you?"

"Exactly who I said when I came through the door."

"Texas Ranger? You're a Texas Ranger?"

"Yes."

"Got a name, ranger man?"

"Told you before, Lucius Dodge."

"Ah, ah. Now that I think on it, seems I've heard of you."

"Good chance you have."

"Whatta you want with me, Dodge?"

"Oh, come now, Ax. Just really put your mind to it for a few seconds. Bet you can come up with something. Surely you still have the mental capacity to ferret out the hint of an idea on the subject hidden somewhere in that muddled, criminal brain of yours."

He torqued his head around, raised one shoulder, and tried to rub his split, bleeding lips on his shirt. He eyeballed me again and said, "No. No. Can't think of a single thing. Nothing. No reason for you, or any like you, to come in here and beat on me like this."

I took a sip of my drink, then placed the glass on the floor beside the chair. From behind steepled fingers, I said, "Me'n my friend Boz Tatum buried your brother and most of his entire family out on Devils River the other day. Sorriest spectacle either of us have ever had to deal with."

Of a sudden Webb stopped struggling. A look of focused fear spread over his bruised, lacerated, sweat-dripping face.

"And me'n Boz, doin' the kind of work we do, well, we've seen more'n our share of blood, by God. Tracked the men who did those sorry murders down and killed them one and all. In the process found out that you're the man behind all that needless butchery."

His wide-eyed gaze darted around the room. Then, for some seconds he stared into the ash-laden fireplace. When he finally brought his fractured attention back to me, he said, "Suppose there ain't no denyin' it then, is there?"

"Nope. None a'tall."

"You killed Murdock, Atwood, and the Pickett boys?"

"That we did."

"Those were some damned tough men, mister. Kinda fellers you could bounce cannonballs off of. All right if'n I don't believe a word of what you said concernin' them, lawdog?"

"Sent Mad Dog Cutner to hell as well."

Don't think Axel Webb would've been any more surprised if I'd pissed in his hat, then tried to make him drink it. He made a kind of halfhearted, non-believer's hissing sound, then said, "You killed Eagle Cutner?"

I couldn't help but smile when I said, "Yep. Well, let me amend that a bit. I gave the man a simple choice. But I'm pretty sure he picked the right path."

Webb coughed and spit a mouthful of blood onto the floor. He bit his already lacerated lip, then said, "What the hell does that mean?"

"Simple. I handed him a gun with one bullet in it. Pretty sure he's shoveling coal in Hell this very minute. Swappin' lies with Satan's imps. Wonderin' why he let a man like you lead him into his own death."

"Eagle Cutner killed himself? That's bullshit. I don't believe a damned word of it. You're a lyin' son of a bitch."

Locked him in a cold-eyed glare and said, "You gave your sixteen-year-old niece to that crazy bastard, Webb. We took her back and, given some fairly limited choices,

Eagle 'Mad Dog' Cutner decided to end his own life. Personally, I think he made the right decision. Had I set Boz Tatum loose on the man, you would've heard him begging for mercy across nearly fifty miles of some of the roughest terrain in the whole of Texas."

Webb sagged in his seat. Sounding defeated, he stared at the floor between his feet and mumbled, "Bullshit."

I leaned back and pulled a hand-rolled ciga-reet from my vest pocket, fired it to glowing life, then pitched the smoldering lucifer onto the paper-and-dirt-littered floor. Calm as a horse trough in a drought when I blew a tub-sized smoke ring then said, "No, Ax, all those men you got to commit the equivalent of biblical murder are gone, along with your brother and most of his family. Now death has come for you, ole son. And you've been lookin' right into his face, since the second you opened the front door."

That's when he started trying to bargain with me. "Look here, now, I never meant for Nathan's wife or kids to have the smallest part in any of this. Only bad feelin's I harbored were reserved for my brother. Didn't know his family'd been rubbed out until Murdock and Atwood dropped the news on me over in Del Rio. You cain't hold me responsible for what those idiots, and them half-witted Pickett boys, went and done."

Figure it had to have sounded like cold spit hitting a red-hot stove lid, when I growled, "Oh, but that's where you're dead wrong, Ax. I don't give a bagful of rotten horse dung why you had those evil sons of bitches chase your brother down and kill him, but his wife and children are another matter. Don't care what you might've done in the past that put you in prison down at Huntsville in the first place. Can't raise the least bit of sympathy that your brother didn't bother to get you turned out. But I can tell you this. Tonight is your last night amongst the living. Before the next hour passes, you'll be with your friends, and I'll be on my way back to Devils River to take care of your badly damaged niece."

Webb shot a hot-eyed, trapped-rat glance up at me. "Just what'n the blue-eyed hell you gonna do, Dodge?"

A second or so of charged silence hung in the air between us before I near whispered, "I'm gonna drag you outta here and hang you from a limb of that tree out in the courtyard of this house. The live oak with all those kid's dolls dangling from it. Figure you'll just resemble something akin to a bit bigger doll to most folks passing by in the street. 'Specially after you've shriveled up in the sun like a sack of beef jerky for about three or four weeks."

"No. You don't mean that. You can't possibly mean that. Can't go and string a man up without so much as a by-your-leave."

"Oh, but I meant every word. Never joke about hanging a man. Any man. No matter how low, sorry, or worthless he might be."

"Now, wait just a damned minute. You're sworn to uphold the law, you son of a bitch. You're a ranger for the love of God. I-I'm entitled to a fair trial. Fair trial by a jury of my peers. I've got rights, by God. Rights. That's the law. 'S in the Constitution. 'S in the Constitution, you son of a bitch."

"Now where in the wide, wide world would any judge find a jury of your peers? You're the man responsible for the brutal murders of your own brother, his wife, and three of their innocent children. Members of your own family for the love of God. Kind of murders branded on your soul tend to negate any constitutional rights, or privileges, as far as I'm concerned anyway."

"Ain't right. Just ain't right. Can't just go and hang a man without a trial."

"Wouldn't go bettin' the ranch on that one if I was you."

Webb threw his head back and bounced the chair up and down several times while he made strange and indecipherable noises. "Yep, far as I can see, you're guilty of all those sorry killings as surely as if you'd pulled the trigger yourself. Might not have been out on Devils River in person, when the bloody act occurred, but, far as I'm concerned, you're as guilty as branded Cain."

"Sweet Jesus, ain't right."

"And that's not to mention the associated, kind of ricochet deaths, of those rank-assed bastards who escaped from prison with you and who you somehow persuaded to do the dirty deed."

Webb jerked at his bonds and howled like a caged wolf. "Lemme go, you bastard. Lemme go. You cain't do this. Cain't just go and hang a man 'thout seein' to the legalities."

I leaned toward the man, blew smoke his direction, then added, "Almost as bad as all that, you handed your brother's only living child over to an animal like Eagle Cutner. Lord God, man, what in the hell were you thinkin'? From what I saw of her, I'm not sure the girl will ever recover from whatever it was that snake did to her. Do you really, for a single moment, think that I'm gonna walk away from here and let you live after *all* that."

For a moment Axel Webb stared at me as though he'd found some new form of poisonous scorpion crawling on his pants' leg. Then, the man's eyes got as big as dinner plates when he hissed, "Y-You really intend on setting me to kicking and pissing myself, don't you?"

"Absolutely. Little more'n twenty paces from where we're sittin' right this moment."

"No appeal."

"None."

"No mercy in your heart?"

Almost laughed when I said, "Not a single shred. Lost it all when I found Mad Dog Cutner and saw the consequences of what he'd done to your beautiful niece, Clementine."

Webb went to struggling against the rope again. He bucked up in the chair and bounced it across the floor. Seat's wooden feet skittered and squawked against the tiles. The thing almost toppled over a time or two. Panicked wretch was near out of breath when he huffed and puffed, "Goddammit, you can't do this. Can't just string a man up like a side of beef. Can't just hang me like a common criminal."

In spite of myself I grinned. "Oh, but I can. 'Cause, you see, Ax, that's all you are—a run-of-the-mill, common murderer. And once you're knockin' on Hell's front gate, I'll sleep like a baby tomorrow, tonight, and for the rest of my natural life. You see, I'll know beyond any doubt that I've rid the world, and Texas, of a lethal, boot-wearin' pestilence."

Then, with no further ado, I stood and started around behind him. A look of stunned horror flashed across the heartless bastard's face. All the color in his bulging countenance drained into his shirt collar. His head swiveled around on its bony stalk as he tried to follow my movements.

"Wait. Wait. Wait," he squealed. "I've got money, Dodge. Lots of money. Hidden money. I'll give all of it to you. Every red cent. You can retire, live like a south Texas cattle baron till the day you die."

I grabbed the back of the chair and leaned it onto the two rear-most legs. The heavy, wooden seat made angry, piggish, squealing sounds against the stone floor as I dragged it out onto the hacienda's shadowy patio, and then to the live oak that spread out over one corner of the terrace like a living umbrella. As I remember it, Axel Webb howled like a tortured wolf till I got him situated under the limb I'd chosen.

Icy shafts of cold, silvery moonlight knifed through that tree's rustling leaves overhead. The ghostly glow flickered across Webb's upturned, panic-stricken face. He continued to struggle against his bonds as he eyeballed me and said,

"Please. Please. Don't do this, Dodge. I'll admit I made a mistake. Made a terrible mistake."

"Well, that's putting it lightly."

"Oh, God. Oh, God. Please. Listen. Please, listen to me. I know I shouldn't have done what I done. Regret the whole mess. Honest. Honest to God. I-I've had a religious epiphany. Swear it. God's done come into my heart and made me realize what terrible things I've done. Have mercy, man. Have mercy."

"A religious epiphany?"

"Yeah. Oh, yes. You've gotta believe me, Dodge. You turn me loose, and I'll walk the straight and narrow for as long as I live. You'll never hear the name Axel Webb and criminal activity of any sort mentioned in the same breath again. Swear it on my dear ole mother's sweet brow."

"Swear it on your mother?"

"Oh, yes. Sweet merciful Jesus, yes. Just cut me loose. Let me out of this chair. I'll live the rest of my life like a saint. Swear I will."

I'd heard all I wanted to hear. And what I'd heard was enough to make a man sick. Stuffed my bandanna into his mouth and left him sitting there stewing in his own juices. Retrieved Grizz and led the animal into the courtyard. The big gelding's iron-shod feet made loud clopping sounds against the patio's stone floor.

Then I threw my second lariat over the tree limb. I draped it around Webb's neck and pulled the noose up tight. Man's head was about to explode. His eyes had gone wild. He bucked and snorted in the chair. Yelled, screamed, and whined into the bandanna, but it was a complete waste of effort.

I patted him on the shoulder and said, "Sure you have plenty you'd like to say right about now. Tell the righteous truth, I don't care to hear any of it. Sure God doesn't want to hear it, either. So, only thing I want, at this particular moment, is to watch you die."

I moved to Grizz's side and urged the big animal back a step or two. Webb's squealing grunts became louder, more pronounced, more panicked. Kept the horse moving backward. Got the chair four or five feet off the ground before I stopped and patted the animal on the neck. Ole Ax struggled with all the might he possessed. The terrified son of a bitch even ripped one thick, wooden arm completely off that chair. For about thirty seconds, I thought he was on the verge of getting himself loose. But a decided lack of air soon robbed him of his remaining strength.

Still and all, it did surprise me some at how long it took that murdering skunk to give up the ghost. Have to admit, the man damn sure loved his life and put up one hell of a fight before death finally came and wrenched it away from his grasp. Guess he must have grunted and thrashed around in that heavy chair for every bit of five minutes. Maybe longer. In the final analysis, though, he didn't do himself any good. You squeeze off a man's ability to breathe and sooner or later, he's gonna die. And that's all there is to it.

When the wicked slaughterer finally stopped flopping, I led Grizz around the tree several times, just to tighten the rope's hold and make sure the load wouldn't slip and end up on the ground. Lashed everything off good, so the dead man dangled amongst all those dolls, just like I'd promised he would. Tell the gospel truth, it was a freakish scene I left in that place. Damned freakish. Right eerie. Kind of sight that had the power to make even the boldest man shudder. Knew when folks finally found him, the stories and legends would start coming fast and furious. But I didn't care.

I climbed on Grizz and gave Webb one last look. True to form, his neck was a good bit longer than when I started his last dance with horned Satan. Have to admit something about the sight suddenly sent an icy chill down my spine and made my blood run cold.

I kicked for Devils River. Didn't bother to look back after I got past the hacienda's front gate. Not once. Tell you for true my friends, a boatload of years have passed since that fateful night, and I've not lost a single second's sleep over what I did. Truth is, given the exact same set of bloody circumstances and the opportunity, I'd do it all over again the exact same way quicker than a hummingbird's heart can beat.

27

"I'VE COME FOR MY NIECE."

THE DAYS CAME, and the days went. Me and Boz and Glo looked after Clementine as best we could for almost two months. We stayed out on the Devils River place a good bit past the time we'd promised Cap'n Culpepper we'd be back in Fort Worth. And while the girl's physical recovery took place over the short matter of a few weeks, I'm not to this very instant sure she ever really came back to us.

During most of that gloomy, silent period, the stone-faced child took up space in a chair out on the front porch and impassively stared at the river. 'Bout the only time she appeared to perk up occurred every evening when flocks of doves made their way to the water to quench their thirst and bathe. Clouds of the birds swirled and darted over the willows and created an endless, eddy-like, ever-shifting painting against the backdrop of a blazing, color-saturated sunset. Would bet all the money I'll ever have, Clem didn't speak a dozen words during that entire time. Seemed to the three of us as though Eagle "Mad Dog" Cutner had damaged her spirt beyond any living human's poor ability to repair it. He'd robbed her of all the spunk, enthusiasm, and drive we'd so admired when she first came into our lives.

'Course someone managed to discover Axel Webb's worm-riddled corpse just a few days after I strung his sorry ass up. And while I did mangage to keep under wraps most of our direct involvement in the various events surrounding all those murderous doin's—especially the part about how ole Ax ended up dangling from a tree limb in his dead brother's front yard—a goodly bit of the Webb family's tragic tale of mindless slaughter and madness did manage to spool out like an unwinding ball of twine and go public.

The tragic clan's saga of jealously, anger, and fratricide eventually hit the front page of damn near every newspaper from the Red River to the Rio Grande. Hell, the heartrending tale was just the kind of thing people still love to read about and spend time gloating over.

Before you could spit we found ourselves knee-deep in a troop of investigating rangers who worked out of Austin, self-righteous committee members of the Texas senate and house, and nigh on every stripe of morbid, inquisitive jackass a body could imagine in his most fevered nightmares.

I was about at the end of my string with those idiots, and had loudly threatened bodily harm to several of the intrusive skunks, when a most singular event occurred. Me and Boz were sitting on our rickety front stoop late one afternoon, locked in heated discussion over the prospects for Clementine's future, when a fine-looking spring wagon rolled up. Painted a bright yellow, with red wheels, the conveyance was pulled by a matched pair of shiny-coated mules.

A right handsome woman, sportin' a brace of bone-gripped Colts, occupied the driver's seat. She removed her broad-brimmed, sweat-stained, palm-leaf sombrero and dropped it on the seat beside her. Ran the fingers of one hand through wheat-colored hair that had begun to go gray on her.

Striking blue eyes twinkled when she offered us a friendly, tooth-filled smile and said, "Which one of you boys is Marshal Lucius Dodge?"

I propped myself against the higher step at my back, waved one hand, and said, "That'd be me, ma'am."

The lady nodded, tied the wagon's reins to the brake lever, then climbed down. She sagged against the front wheel, set to jerking at her leather gloves, then flicked a dangling lock of sweat-dripping hair out of one eye.

"'Pears you've had a long trip, ma'am?" I said.

"Yes. Yes, indeed. Has been a right long haul. You boys ain't the easiest folks in Texas to find, bein' as how you're way'n the hell and gone out here in the middle of nowhere."

"What can we do for you, ma'am?" Boz said.

She pushed away from the wagon and came several steps closer. She stopped and, with fists clenched on her hips, said, "Name's Linda McKinley, Marshal Dodge. You can call me Annie, if'n you like. Have a livestock and wagon selling operation up near Tyler way. I've come for my niece."

Well, that got us on our feet, hats in hand, pretty quick. While surprised right down to the soles of my boots, I must admit I was, at the same time, greatly relieved. I glanced over at Boz and could see he shared my feelings.

We invited our visitor up on the porch. Something we'd not done with any of the other invaders who'd recently made our lives a shade more difficult. I offered her a chair. One with the best pillow on it. And dragged up ladder-backed seats of our own.

When everyone got settled, I said, "Can I offer you a dipper of cold water, ma'am? Or perhaps a cup of Arbuckles? Maybe something to eat? Our man Paco sets a fine table."

"No, thank you, Marshal Dodge," she replied. "Just like to rest my weary bones a bit." She bent over at the waist, rubbed her lower back, then scrunched down into the seat's thick cushion. "'S right comfortable. Bet you boys fight over this chair every afternoon 'bout dark, don't you?"

"Not so much recently," Boz offered, "Clem tends to like that spot, so we're more'n happy to let her have it."

The McKinley woman nodded. "I see," she said. "And how is Clem?"

Arms laid across my knees, I said, "God's truth, we're not sure. Just not sure. Perhaps she'll do better with you. Us ole bachelors have come to think that, while we've walked on eggshells during this entire ordeal, maybe we're just not at all suited for the task of seeing to certain parts of a young lady's healing. Woman's touch might be just what she needs, Mrs. McKinley."

She flashed another brilliant, friendly smile. "That's Ms. McKinley, Marshal Dodge. Annie to you boys. Mule kicked my husband in the head several years ago. Didn't kill him right off. Man took almost a month to turn loose and let go of his life. But in the end, he died. So, with his death and my sister's violent passing, I'm alone now, and I'd like my niece nearby."

"She's asleep right now, Ms. McKinley. Girl sleeps an inordinate amount these days. 'Course we can't blame her much, given her circumstances of recent."

The McKinley woman sagely rubbed her chin with the back of one hand. Then, as if she'd thought the question over for quite a spell, she said, "You boys willing to tell me the whole story? No bull. Entire ugly weasel, teeth, hair, and all?"

And so we did. Took nigh on two hours to sort through the whole account and answer all her questions as best we could. We offered to take her out to the spot where we'd buried her sister, but she shook her head, then said, "No.

No. I have no desire to see where Elizabeth's buried. Just knowing you men did the best you could for her is enough. In fact, it's more than enough."

We had just finished up with our story when Clem slipped through the front door and came up short when she spotted our visitor. I'd never seen anything like what happened next. The girl fell onto her aunt's lap, and the pair of them wept as though the world had surely come to an abrupt and painful end. It was so emotional on that porch, Boz and I got to feeling like intruders and crept away. We waited down by the corral with Glo, till all the crying and such finally stopped.

Ms. McKinley proved beyond any doubt that she was all business. The lady only stayed with us one day. She packed Clem's meager belongings into that wagon of hers and, the following morning, was primed and ready for the trip back to Tyler. We tried to get her to say over a bit longer, at least another day or two. She refused. And to tell the righteous truth, appeared to me Clem was ready to leave as well. Can't say as how I blamed her any.

Girl still didn't say much of anything, last morning I laid eyes on her. Even right up to the moment for all the good-byes and such. She demurely shook hands with Boz and Glo. But when she got to me, the teary-eyed child pulled me down to her level, hugged my neck, pressed her lips to my ear and whispered, "Thank you for keeping your word, Marshal Dodge. I won't ever forget what you did for me." And just like that, she climbed onto the seat of her aunt's wagon, turned her gaze north, and they were gone.

There was nothing holding us to the Devils River country after that. So, we headed on back to Fort Worth less than a week later. Cap'n Culpepper sure enough laid into us when when he got a chance to rake his spurs across our tender rumps. But, hell, for all the spitting and sputtering, he finally threw up his hands and admitted that crime and criminals were running roughshod over nine-tenths of Texas. Said he hated like blue-eyed hell to admit it, but he needed our singular expertise to do all we could to stem the bloody tide.

Guess I didn't hear anything of Clem for about two years. Then a letter Ms. McKinley wrote caught up with me while I was down in Huntsville to witness an execution. Her short missive mentioned as how Clem had met a young man and that they planned to get married. Must say, I was right pleased.

Number of years passed before I got any word on the girl again. Nothing but an envelope that contained the front page of the *Tyler Tribune*. Return address said as how it had come to me from Ms. McKinley. Dead center of the page, the twenty-four-point headline read, "Local Woman Killed by Oncoming Train." No doubt about it, that was the worst ten minutes I've ever spent reading anything. Seems a lady named Clementine Webb Stubbs, formerly of Tyler, had stepped into the path of the Texas and Pacific Flyer somewhere out on the outskirts of Longview on the darkest night of the year.

High-balling engineer testified as how he tried to stop the train soon's he spotted the woman in his headlight but just couldn't manage the feat. Said she opened her arms, appeared to wave good-bye, and welcomed death like it was an old friend returning home from a long trip. Said she smiled at him right up to the end. She left behind a grieving husband and two small children.

Given that I knew a bit of Clem's earlier history, I suppose I shouldn't have been surprised, or so grief stricken, by her sad passing. And I know it probably ain't the manly thing to admit, but I broke down and wept like a baby before I could finish reading the full description of her tragic demise.

All that happened almost fifty years ago. But, you know, sometimes now, all these years later, when I'm sitting on the back porch of my little spread out here on the Sulphur River, if the sun gets just right on the western horizon, and the doves come to the river to drink, my heart goes back to that sad girl and all the blood that flooded over her at such a tender age.

The blood, unimaginable abuse at the hands of Eagle Cutner, and youthful disappointment are the only things I can imagine that would bring her to walk into the engine of a fast-moving freight, smile on her face, to meet her own end. My sweet God Almighty, but what else could account for such an action?

I sometimes suppose misplaced love could prompt such a dreadful event to occur. But you know, I'll go to my own grave believing that Eagle Cutner might well have jerked all the love the girl ever had right out of her body with whatever'n hell it was he did to her. Guess I'll never know for certain sure. Any chance of understanding the mystery died on a lonely set of Texas and Pacific train tracks, in the middle of the night, so long ago that I might well be the only person left alive who even remembers.

Oh well, think I'll pour myself a doubled-up beaker of panther sweat, then hit the sack. Cooley Churchpew sold me some special under-the-counter single-malt whiskey from Ireland the other day. Said as how the bottle crossed the Atlantic in the cargo hold of a ship. Being as how a man can easily drive himself to the brink with the kind of thoughts I've been having, maybe the whiskey'll stem the tide of recurrent Clementine memories that have so completely occupied my mind of recent.

Just hope like hell the girl don't show up in any of my sometimes chaotic dreams tonight. Then again, maybe if she was to make an appearance I could ask her why she'd chosen to go to the Maker the way she did. Then again, maybe I wouldn't. Maybe I'd just hold her close, and as a final reminder, I'd whisper into her ear, "It's all right now, darlin'. Everything's gonna be just fine. You can go on and live your life. Live it to the fullest. All those who did you harm, they're gone. No longer amongst the living. I killed them, just the way you wanted. But more important, I sent them to judgment exactly the way they deserved—one and all."

Don't miss the best Westerns from Berkley

LYLE BRANDT
PETER BRANDVOLD
JACK BALLAS
J. LEE BUTTS
JORY SHERMAN
DUSTY RICHARDS